Cracking the Secret Code of the Universe

In

The Black Book of Cardinal Benedict

By

Marie Schwarzer

Whoever Lives and Believes in Me Shall Never Die

There has always been evil on Earth. Even Pure Evil. But Never ever an evil as vicious and Blood thirsty as Monk Salvatore one of XII Spider Monks. Each a trusted member of the Omega Templar Secret Society, living inside the Vatican, and sworn to protect the life of the Pope and the many secrets that have been guarded for many thousands of years. The Omega Spider Monks are never allowed to leave Vatican City except in a coffin after their death.

One day Cardinal Benedict also a Spider Monk and a good man whispers quietly to the Pope about a vast inheritance belonging to Monk Salvatore and a sealed Letter written by God's hand given to his Son Jesus along with a Holy Key. Elements, which together will unlock and crack the Secret Code of the Entire Universe. Jesus never read the letter because he was crucified.

Enraged! Spider Monk Salvatore having learned of his inheritance and the existence of the three elements needed to unlock and crack the code of the universe.....The Holy Book, the Holy Key and the Letter written by God's hand.
Monk Salvatore planned and executed a daring escape from the Vatican to search for, find and combine the three elements enabling him to exact a horrific revenge on the Entire World!

Only Cardinal Benedict can stop Monk Salvatore before he unleashes pure Hell on Earth.

We Never Knew Our Destiny Was Already Engraved in the Holy Stones by God Himself

Prologue

Rome, Italy, July, 1955

After a short summer shower, a rainbow beamed in the distance and a cool breeze swept the fields filling the air with the aroma of new growth.

'*Just a few more to go,*' six year-old Marcillie thought to himself as he ran through the field of fresh wildflowers, picking handfuls and holding onto them tightly.

These particular flowers only grew along the small creek that wound its way by the edge of his family's property. In the distance, he spotted a cluster of his mother's favorite dark purple flowers growing next to a fence post. He hurried over and picked them admiring their exquisite beauty.

"Marcillie, it's time for supper!" His mother's voice called out from across the field. Marcillie finished gathering the last few flowers and ran toward the house.

The smell of fresh stew and homemade bread wafted through the open window, the aromatic smell making young Marcillie's mouth water as he stamped his feet at the front door.

"Go wash up for supper," his mother said, calling to him from the kitchen.

"Yes Mother," he said as he carefully laid the flowers he picked for his mother down on the floor, he loosened the laces of his boots and slipped them off of his feet, placing them next to his fathers' house slippers then headed into the kitchen.

"I love you mom," he exclaimed with a big

smile on his face as he held the flowers out to his mother.

"I love you too Marcillie, now go wash up." She said taking the flowers from him and placing them in a vase. Marcillie gives his mother a hug then runs up the stairs to wash up.

"Wash behind your ears Marcillie," his father calls out from his bedroom as Marcillie rushes by.

"When you are finished come in here I have something that I want to show you."

"Yes Papa," Marcillie replied poking his head into his fathers' bedroom.

His father a thin studious man with glasses perched at the tip of a long thin nose sat reading through a stack of papers, he reaches for a journal and scribbles down a few notes, Marcillie hurries to the bathroom and washes, making sure to clean behind his ears. He dried his hands and walked down the short hall that leads to his parents' room stopping to knock before he enters.

"Come in Marcillie, and have a seat right here next to me," his father calls out. The boy sat down next to his father and looked at the papers wrapped in a deteriorated leather cover that sat on his father's desk. His father opened the leather binding, pulls out a particular page with a drawing on it.

"What is that father?" Marcillie asked.

"I'm not sure son. I received it after one of my lectures on antiquities at the University today."

"Who gave it to you?" Marcillie asked with wonder.

"Italian Monk, he said he knew of my research and he had something he wanted me to decipher for

2

him. I've looked at these drawings since I received them. The implications these papers suggest are incredible. Can you read this?" his father asked pointing to a line of writing on a piece of old looking parchment.

"The revelation of truth written by the hand of God with his own blood," Marcillie sounded out proudly.

"Very good son, now look at the drawing what does it show?" Marcillie tilted his head down, looked closely at the drawing of a man and a woman, the man was handing the woman a scroll, his other arm was out stretched pointing to a cross on a distant hill, there appeared to be blood dripping from his out stretched finger tip. In the lower right corner of the drawing there was a stylized capitalized Greek letter Sigma-Σ.

"It is a picture of a man giving a lady something he is pointing to a cross."

"Very good Marcillie, what else do you see?"

"In the right hand corner there is a Letter Σ with foreign letters surrounding it." His father smiled at him reached into a drawer in the desk and removed a beautiful leather pouch. He opened the pouch and removed a golden medallion. "It looks kind of like this does it? Look at the back of the medallion," he said. Engraved in the back of the medallion is the letter Σ.

"Just like in the picture father," Marcillie said as he looked at the medallion his eyes shining in wonder.

"Is it really gold?"

"Yes it is son," his father replied, "It is the symbol used by those that seek the truth above all else, having no preconceived notions that are not

3

grounded in absolute truth." Marcillie looked up at his father asking,

"Does the medallion help people that are seeking truth to find it?" His father looked down at him proudly.

"In a way yes, it is but one key that is needed to unlock the codes hidden within these ancient texts. There is one more key necessary to fully understand what is written."

"Where is it at Father?" Marcillie asked. His father laughed softly,

"I wish I knew son, I wish I knew." He looks down at Marcillie and strokes his hair. "Marcillie, I know you're young but I want you to know that this medallion is yours it has been in our family a long time. If anything happens to me, you must continue the search for the truth. Promise me Marcillie." Marcillie looks up at his father and sees how serious his father is.

"I promise Father." He stood up and handed the medallion to his father. His Father took the medallion and carefully put it away. He looked down at Marcillie.

"Now let's go eat," he says smiling.

Outside night had fallen, a man from the Vatican Secret Police stands quietly just outside the house watching the family eat their dinner. I wonder if they know this is their last meal, the man thought to himself, as he casually fingered the pistol in his waistband and checked the knife that he carried, it was time.

"Who wants dessert?" Marcillie's mother said as she rose from the table gathering up the now

4

empty plates. "Me," Marcillie said.

"I would love some darling," Marcillie's Father replied putting his arm around his wife's waist pulling her close to him. She smiled and bent over to give him a kiss.

"I'll bring it right out." She walks into the kitchen and takes a blueberry pie out of the oven. The sound of a muffled knock at the door startled her causing her to jump and almost drop the pie.

"I'll see who it is." Marcillie's father stands and heads toward the door he pauses as he passes Marcillie.

"Go into my bedroom and get the leather bundle with all the papers and the medallion I showed you. Take it to your room, open your window, and run as far as you can if you hear anything strange, okay."

"Dad you're scaring me," Marcillie said in a soft voice.

"Don't be scared just do what I am telling you, son."

After gathering the bundle and medallion, Marcillie stands near the open window in his room. He hears the door open and his father voice ask,

"Can I help you?"

"Are you Victor Benedict?" an unfamiliar voice asked.

"Yes I am. Who is asking?"

"I am here to retrieve the leather bundle that you were given today," the strange voice said.

"What bundle?" his father asked without knowing that he was followed after the lecture at the university.

"Wrong answer," the sound of a gunshot

followed by his mothers' screams. One more shot and then silence.

Marcillie stood frightened, the sound of footsteps on the staircase motivates him and he grabs the bundle, climbs out of his window, and runs hard disappearing into the night. It would be the longest run of his entire life.

Chapter I. Discovery
Rome, Italy

Deep beneath the Vatican in the well guarded Secret Theological Library, Cardinal Benedict sits alone working at a table covered with ancient scrolls, books, and maps. He is completely absorbed in his work. His job as head researcher of ancient works for the Vatican the past twenty years has kept him very busy. He has always done his job well and is respected among his peers.

One afternoon while sitting in the library looking over a scroll, Cardinal Clemens walks in and places in front of Cardinal Benedict a bundle of ancient scrolls wrapped in deteriorated leather.

"We would like you to decipher the contents," Cardinal Clemens said sternly. Cardinal Benedict carefully opens the bundle and suddenly something triggers the memory of him running from his house when he was a boy. Running long and hard holding onto a leather bundle just like this one. He stares for a moment. Cardinal Clemens looks curiously at him,

"Benedict is everything alright?" Cardinal

Benedict snaps out of his memory and looks up at Cardinal Clemens.

"Everything's fine. I will let you know what I uncover," Benedict responds politely. He reads the ancient scrolls sitting before him taunting him, challenging him to decipher its soulful meaning. He must gently, seduce it out of the scroll. He whispers,

"Talk to me." He imagines the scroll whispering back, telling him he must work for it, there must be understanding. For what is locked inside of it is truth.

Cardinal Benedict leans back in his chair and takes a deep breath. Truth, its meaning is different for everyone. Truth for the masses has become vacant, empty, hidden and painful. He knows some truths, truths about the Catholic Church, about humanity, about protecting lies, lies now called truth. He leans back over the scroll and stares deeply, intently, with purpose. He gently strokes the edge of the scroll, his fingertips noticing slight variations in the parchments texture. He pauses for a moment and gently strokes it again. He looks beyond his fingertips his old eyes fail to see exactly what his fingers know. He grabs the magnifying glass sitting to his left never taking his fingertips away from the anomaly in the parchment for fear of losing it. He places it over his fingertips and slowly moves the magnifying glass in place.

As his eyes begin to focus, he notices the binding is slightly thicker in one area. He turns it over and looks on the opposite side where it appears to be normal. He flips it back over and counts the raised threads. He turns it over and counts each of the other seams finding anomalies in all of them. He stops for a moment.

This isn't the way this particular parchment was made in its era. He decides to try working with numerical values. He scribbles quickly on his notepad as his heart begins pounding so hard it becomes audible in his ears. As he counts, he writes down the numerical value of the anomaly in each of the seams. Back to mathematics he thinks, the beautiful universal language, the true key to understanding.

Looking at his notebook he writes down the letters that correspond to the numbers that he's deciphered.

Judas the Beloved the Key to the Book of Blood. Intrigued, he thinks about this, *The Book of Blood* must have been what the **Lost Memoirs of Christ** had originally been called, the very book now missing from the Vatican's archives. He double checks the works before him and verifies his translation stunned by his discovery. He looks at the pad of paper he's been writing on and holds his breath as he reads it a second time, there it was, one more piece to the puzzle, perhaps the most crucial piece.

Suddenly paranoid, he looks around to see if he is being watched and sees nothing but the security cameras, these tiny mechanical sentries that oversee the whole library. He stares at his notes, his mind whirling with the implications of his newly discovered information and what to do with it.

Just one more piece is missing, the ancient manuscript that contained the **Lost Memoirs of Christ**. Its disappearance from the library a few weeks ago coincided with the disappearance of three Monks. Monk Salvatore being one of them. His suspicion of Monk Salvatore and not the other two was justified in his mind because of what he knows about this particular Monk.

Monk Salvatore belonged to an elite group of monks known as the **Omega Templar Secret Society**, the first in rank as well as the closest society to the heart of the Vatican with the highest degree of initiation. The **Omega (Ω) Templars** shares their guarded secrets only among themselves passing them down from generation to generation. They are well protected by the Vatican Police and live by the strictest of codes. They are never allowed to leave Vatican City. They report directly to the Pope on all contentious matters. They seldom speak to anyone and around their necks they wear a stone medallion containing a poisonous microchip which they must ingest upon capture by their enemies.

Benedict contemplates that one so close to the heart of the city and so well trained would disappear without evidence of a struggle, could mean only one thing in his mind, Monk Salvatore was alive and he had the book. He gathered up his things and headed to his quarters he needed to think, he had to find the Monk if he hoped to ever find the book.

Cardinal Benedict paces back and forth in his room. In his mind he replays over and over all of the conspiratorial whispers that he's heard since the Monk's disappearance. His fellow Cardinals and Monks all speculating on what could have happened to Salvatore and to the book.

Since the disappearance, security had been doubled in Vatican City, after all, it wasn't just any book; it was the **Lost Memoirs of Jesus** a book so controversial that the Vatican continually denies its very existence. The betrayal felt over the loss of the precious book deepened the wound and created quite a scandal the past few weeks. The burning question on everyone's lips was, "Where did these three Monks disappear to?"

Cardinal Benedict stops pacing and sits down at his desk fearing his heart is beating too loudly, afraid that someone will know what he has discovered. He takes a long look around. This has been his second home for many years and he has accomplished so much for the Vatican. He is a trusted member of the Secret Society known as the **Sigma Templars,** which is the second in rank in the Vatican City. He wonders what his brothers will think of him when he leaves. He wonders what whispers will be told of him what dark thoughts will be in the minds of his long time friends.

'I must leave Vatican City and find Monk Salvatore,' he thinks to himself. 'I must find the missing book and complete my discovery.'

Frustrated, beads of sweat find his brow as he realizes it is impossible to walk out of Vatican City unnoticed. Anyone who leaves on foot must go through two heavily guarded gates. The secret police now screen everyone coming in and going out.

Every member of the Secret Society has an engraved letter on his chest and left hand; the **XII Templars** have a letter Omega, Ω, and the **Sigma Templars**, have a letter Σ. It would catch the attention of any security service in the Vatican City they would be looking for it now that the monk was missing.

'I wonder how Monk Salvatore got out.' he thought to himself, 'I will have to plan this perfectly.'

Cardinal Benedict thought about how he could travel to a small town near the Baltic Sea where Monk Salvatore was born, he would take a sabbatical requesting to go on another fact finding mission. He would then travel to Salvatore's hometown and search for him there.

He sits at the desk in his room and writes, signs, and seals his sabbatical request to his superiors. The only thing left to do was to steal the *Gospel of Judas* and the scrolls that contained the information linking the Gospel with the missing memoirs. "That's going to be a challenge," he mumbles as he prepares for bed, he washes his hands and face insuring to wash behind his ears. Lying on his bed he thinks of his mission as he drifts off to a troubled night's sleep.

The next morning he begins preparing for his departure. He eats a small breakfast and heads to the library. The thought of his mission causes a wave of nervousness to come over him making his knees feel weak.

Once inside the library he continues about his daily routine to insure that he doesn't raise suspicion. As he works he places the needed scrolls, maps, and ancient manuscripts from the Vatican Library in the pockets under his frock making sure to be mindful of the security cameras. He keeps himself busy in the library until six o'clock and then heads off to eat supper like always. To everyone else he appeared to be going about the same routine but tonight he was a thief. Those who work in the library know him. He's passed the same exit every day for twenty years but his heart is pounding fiercely in his chest. He prays

11

silently,

"Dear God, please know that I am doing what I must with the best intentions. I only seek the truth, your truth so that I might share it with the world. Please grant me safe passage and let me walk in your grace." He looks at the security guards and hopes his prayer will be answered and they won't suspect anything is amiss.

As he passes the first exit, he waves his left hand with the letter Sigma, Σ, engraved in the middle. He reminisces on how long he's had the letter Σ on his palm. He remembers the monks who came to the orphanage, took him away, and brought him into the Vatican City Catholic School. He remembers his studies, taking his oath, and the branding of his palm. He quickly snaps out of his past as he approaches the second exit. He keeps his stoic appearance as he walks past the security room looking inside to see what guard was on duty tonight. 'Yes, maybe a break,' he thinks. Lukas, a dedicated young monk so humble and eager to do his job, that his respect for the Cardinals keeps him from speaking to them.

He passes the second exit and walks out into *Saint Peter's* square. He glances at *Saint Peter's* Basilica and then over at the Security Guards standing at their posts, he shudders for a moment and continues walking. He pauses for a second thinking about the twenty years of ritual he's practiced and now he ponders freedom. He inhales a deep breath as though he had forgotten what aromatic scent freedom had.

'Just a little bit longer.' he thinks to himself. 'You're not out of the woods yet.'

The walk across Saint Peter's square seems to be the longest walk of his life; with each step he can feel the hands of the Security Guards grabbing him and dragging him off to the holding cells to await interrogation.

As he approaches the exit, he spots the taxi parked in the waiting area near the front gate. He raises his hand in hopes that the driver will notice him and not leave. Luck is his mistress tonight as the taxi driver raises his hand in reply. He walks up to the Swiss Guard and stops. The guard looks at him back.

Cardinal Benedict feels his face going flush. He thinks, 'Maybe he knows. I'm doomed and my plan is doomed too, and I will spend the rest of my life in prison.' he thinks to himself. He opens the faces of his palms toward the guard about to ask for forgiveness. The guard looks at his palms and says simply,

"Nice to meet you, Cardinal."
The Cardinal surprised at the Guard's behavior keeps walking. He makes his way to the taxi. He plays the action with all the guards over and over again in his head. 'How did that happen? I'm a free man again.' he thinks to himself. He remembers his motion just before the Guard looks at his open palm. The letter Sigma, Σ, saved him, the symbol that has confined him to the ways of the Vatican for so many years just set him free.

Engrossed in his thoughts, he hears the taxi driver yell at him.

"Sir, where are we going?" Cardinal Benedict snaps out of his introspective mood.

"Rome Intercontinental Airport Leonardo Da Vinci," he replies. The taxi driver speeds off. He turns up the music on his radio and begins singing obnoxiously loud and out of tune. Cardinal Benedict's thoughts move forward to his plan. Once at the airport, he will purchase a ticket to fly to the small town of Kalin located near the Baltic Sea.

Suddenly, the Cardinals mind rushes back, present time gives way to the past. He is six years-old and being led down a hall in the Vatican City Catholic School by an austere monk. The Monk gruffly opens a door and pushes young Marcillie through it. Marcillie looks around the sterile classroom frightened. All the young boys sit silently staring blankly at him. The Monk teacher slaps his ruler on the desk, "eyes front," he grunts out.

The Monk Pontius points out to the only empty chair in the room and the Monk that led him here pushes him toward it.

"Go sit and be good," he tells Marcillie.

Marcillie looks up at him and squints as he sees there is no love for him in this man's face. He looks around and sees there is no love for him in this room. He pushes a foot forward and then the other. Slowly with trepidation, trembling to his very core, he makes his way to the empty chair and gently sits down. He hangs his head low, wondering if his parents would approve of this cold and frightening place. Head still hanging, he carefully looks from side to side.

He notices that the young boy sitting on his left looks just as afraid as he does. He feels sadness for this boy and wonders if he's sad as well. He musters up the courage to lift his head, turns to the boy and whispers, "Hello." The young boy is startled by the greeting. He turns to Marcillie and whispers back, "Hi." Marcillie asks, "What's your name?"

"Venicio Salvatore," the boy responds back.

"I'm Marcillie Benedict."

Their gentle greeting is interrupted by a loud slap on the desk.

"No talking, pay attention," the teacher Monk barks out. The boys straighten up and keep their eyes forward.

Chapter 2. Monk Salvatore's Bloody Beginning
Vatican City, Rome

In the middle of a warm afternoon sitting by a small stream pondering his next move, Monk Salvatore watched the water hurry over the rocks, giving them a cool bath then rushing off to bathe the next ones. His thoughts shifted. 'If life were always this simple, the world would be grand,' the thought flittered in and out of his mind quickly. He looked at the stream then glanced at the shoes on his feet. He untied one shoe lace then the other. He pulled both his shoes and his socks off. He warily stuck one foot in the water, shivering as the water rushed over his toes, a new feeling for him.

"How odd to be so old and not have had such small enjoyments in my life," he said out loud.

The sound of his own voice surprised him. He realized he was talking to himself and looked nervously around to see if anyone heard him. Being a Monk, practicing the strict discipline day after day throughout so many years he realized had made him bitter about his life.

"I should have had more fun," he said aloud again. A deep pain filled his heart. He looked up into the sky and shouted with all of his might,

"Why me? Couldn't you have picked someone else and let me live?"

This time he didn't look around, he hoped someone would hear him. Not just someone, he wants God to hear him and he wants God to answer him back. He wants an explanation of his parents' murder, of his being taken to that awful Catholic School and of being put into the **XII Omega Templar Society.**

"My youth is gone, I've never loved a woman, had any children, or had any real friends since I was a boy," he spoke tenderly pushing back the lump building in his throat.

"I want it back; please give it back to me." A lonely tear gathered in the corner of his eye. As it threatened to fall, he quickly wiped his eye as though the weight of this one tear would drag out many more. This is not what he was taught to be. He was taught by the strictest order on the planet. Be strong, be diligent, guard the secrets, do not speak to anyone except the Pope, and last but not least, his life was only worth something to the Vatican. But sincerely inside he hated everyone and especially the Pope as a cause of his misery.

He knew the burning pain in his heart grew more over the past few weeks than in all of the time he's spent at the Vatican. The wooden box, his inheritance, the only thing left from his parents was

16

about to be returned to him very soon. He was stunned by that news without knowing how the box came to the Vatican in the first place. 'Who gave those monks or anyone else the permission to release the box without his consent?' He questioned inside his mind. 'How they found me, and why now the box is so important,' he thought. 'There must be some kind of conspiracy, and the Pope is involved in it. Why is it happening?'

No one in the Vatican was able to open the box so two Monks showed up at his door. They presented him a letter with the seal of the Pope. The letter's content was to Monk Salvatore giving him permission to speak to the two Monks. They explained to Monk Salvatore that they brought it to him to see if he could remember how to open the box. When Salvatore saw the box, he was overtaken by long lost memories of his childhood. He held his stoic look in front of the Monks who presented him with the box and insisted he did not know anything about it. The Monks asked him several times, explaining to him that it belonged to his family and how they were all now dead.

"You are the only remaining member, so someone must have told you how to open this box," one of the Monks replied.

"I don't, I've never seen it before," Salvatore assured them. The Monks continued to ask for what seemed an eternity while Salvatore stood there expressionless.

"We must take it back to the Pope. He will assign a special team to open your box."

The Monks took the box and walked out of his room, shutting the door behind them. Salvatore briskly walked to his door, put his ear to it, held his breath, and focused on the sounds in the hallway. His trained ears methodically separate the footsteps from the sound of the voices and hone in only on the voices. He listens as the Monks talk about the box and how it must contain the key. They turn the corner and are out of range. 'What key are they referring to?' Salvatore wondered.

He walked away from the door, paced back and forth in his room. He remembered everything, his mother, his father, his life with them up until they were killed and that box, his box. He remembered how his father sat him down and told him that it was his inheritance, his little treasure and the content needed to be kept a secret and passed down to his children and to tell his children to pass it on to their children. His father told him the box must be guarded and never given to anyone outside of their family.

Salvatore stopped pacing. He knew what he had to do. He must see the Pope before the Monks arrived there, he thought. He sneaked through the open window, climbed the walls and finally reached the Pope's windows. He knew exactly where he was and what time he was to be in his room. He entered the room quietly and hid behind heavy velvet purple curtains. The Pope walked in and sat in a soft armchair to relax. Salvatore peered out from behind the curtains and saw the Pope was sitting with his back to him. 'How easy,' he thought. Salvatore walked up to him and paused for a second. As he was about to put his hands around the Pope's neck, the door opened and the two Monks walked in with the wooden box. 'I'm too late,' he thought.

They spotted Salvatore and were a bit surprised. Salvatore was stunned and quickly escaped out the window. Now he knew exactly what he must do next. He must liquidate the witnesses and fast. He climbed back to his room, lay on the bed and devised a new plan. He knew where the Monks rooms were. He would get the box back from them, and honor his father's wishes.

A few minutes past midnight, Salvatore stood up against the building of the Monks rooms. His gaze followed the height of the building upward. One Monk was two stories up, the other was three. Salvatore found his first handhold, then his second and pulled himself up. He scaled the wall as gracefully and as quickly as a spider. He was trained as a Spider Monk and didn't require any equipment to complete his task. Throughout his years, he's continued his training as did all of the Spider Monks. Never knowing when or where they would be called.

He reached the second floor window, gently pushed it open, peered inside, and entered the room. The Monk lay asleep in his bed, snoring loudly. Salvatore looked around the room for the wooden box. It wasn't there. It didn't matter; he had to dispose of this Monk nonetheless. He knew already too much about Salvatore's action. Salvatore stood over the Monk staring at him for a few moments. Should he make it quick and painless or should he disable his vocal chords and make him suffer. Salvatore thought about this, about the actions he was ready to take and about the man lying before him.

"Mercy," the Monk cried.

Salvatore struck the Monk, a deadly blow to his

temple. The Monk's body convulsed, his breath spewed out of him, and then his body went limp. Salvatore lifted him up, threw him over his shoulder, peered his head out of the window, climbed out, and back down the wall. The dead Monk's weight pulled at his aging shoulder. Salvatore ignored the pain as he was trained to do and continued his descent. When he was standing on the ground again, he looked around making sure no one was in sight.

Stealthily, he made his way over to the crematorium they have on the premises. He hid silently high above in the perfectly landscaped trees. He draped the body over a large sturdy branch. Salvatore knew the guard on duty always walked to each end of the building and scanned the premises once every hour. He waited patiently for the guard to make his round.

A ringing tone erupted from the guard. The guard reached into his pants pocket and pulled out his mobile phone. He pressed a button and placed it back into his pocket. Once the guard started his walk, Salvatore looked at his watch and marked the time. He has sixty minutes to get the other Monk.

Salvatore leapt out of the tree and without a sound, hit the ground, rolled, and stood up as though performing a graceful dance. He made his way back to the Monks building and scaled the wall. He climbed to the third floor and as he reached the window, he quietly pushed it open and climbed in.

The Monk was sitting on his bed waiting for him with the wooden box sitting beside him. Salvatore stood tall and with purpose.

"I knew you were lying," the Monk spoke softly.

20

"Did you?" Salvatore responded the tone of his voice cold and still.

"I won't beg you for my life," the Monk said sternly.

"I wouldn't expect you to," Salvatore said as his gaze drifted to the box. The Monk noticed and said,

"You can't have it, what's inside isn't for you, it's for the church."

"It belongs to my family not the church," Salvatore responded.

"I will kill you," the Monk replied as he leapt off of the bed and straight for Salvatore. Salvatore dodged him as he swung at the Monks head. The Monk barely avoided the blow as it grazed his skull. His head hurt and he could feel the warm blood rush to the wound as the hematoma formed instantly. The Monk recoiled and took his stance guarding the wooden box still sitting innocently on his bed. He watched as Salvatore jumped into the air and threw a deadly kick at him. He moved to the side and noticed that as the kick didn't connect to its target, Salvatore pulled back as though not wanting to waste the forceful motion.

The Monk took the offense and threw a punch and then a kick, neither one connecting as Salvatore moved away effortlessly. Salvatore simultaneously extended two fingers and lunged into the Monk connecting them with his neck. The Monk lurched forward in pain paralyzed from the neck down. He felt his body falling to the floor; fear overtook him as Salvatore caught him and grabbed his head in both hands. A quick and forceful thrust and twist of his neck sent him into blackness.

Salvatore held the Monk so his body wouldn't hit the floor. He looked into his vacant eyes and passed his hand over his face closing them ever so gently. Salvatore threw his body over his shoulder, grabbed the wooden box, tucked it securely into his belt, and exited the room through the window. He reached the tree where he had left the other body. He looked up and saw it was still hanging from the branch. He placed the second body on the ground and climbed the tree. He lowered the first body onto the ground and again lowered himself. He made his way across the yard to the guard and struck him. The guard fell to the ground and Salvatore pulled him out of sight and gently left him sitting up against the wall. Salvatore knew the pressure point he struck would ensure the guard stayed unconscious for a few hours. When he awoke, he wouldn't feel any pain and would believe he just dozed off.

Salvatore took the guards key off of him and then picked up the first body. He entered the crematorium and set the body down near the oven. He left it there to retrieve the second body. He entered the room with the second body and turned on the oven, sending it into its warm up cycle.

He grabs one of the cardboard boxes and places it on the rolling table. He places both bodies into the cardboard box; he rolls the box into the cremation chamber, and turns the oven all the way up. He watches through the glass door as flames spew out of every nozzle burning their contents.

Salvatore turns and takes a seat on a chair. He pulls the wooden box out of his belt and looks at it. He softly strokes the box. 'It is old and beautiful,' he thinks to himself. He works his memory to find the key to open the box. He recalls his Mother sitting at the edge of his bed and singing him to sleep, fishing with his Father, family dinners, and his last Christmas with his parents. He wasn't at the orphanage long enough to have Christmas there and no one ever visited him on Christmas once he was at the Monks school. He snaps out of his lonely recollection and focuses back on the box. Examining it closely, a spark ignites in his mind. "*The Book of Jesus*, Father mentioned the *Book of Jesus*."

The ringing bell on the oven snaps him out of his daze, he stands and walks over to it and opens the door. He pulls out the bottom panel and gathers the two Monks remnants. He puts them into the processor and turns it on. As the processor grinds the remnants to ash, he tidies up so no one will know he was there. The processor finishes and he pours the powder out into a container and seals it tightly. He meticulously cleans the processor. He looks at his watch, it's a little after five a.m. the sun will be up soon as will everyone else. He hurries out of the door and gingerly passes the guard who is groggily waking up. He makes it back to his room and closes the door behind him. He walks over to his closet and places the wooden box inside; he will find a better hiding place for it after he finishes his next task. He walks into his bathroom, opens the container, pours all of its contents into the commode, and flushes it.

"Thank you for returning my box," he says with the same cold, emotionless tone he spoke to them with when he met them.

Chapter 3. From a Child's Lips

It was early Saturday morning and Cardinal Benedict landed safely in Kalin. He caught a taxi from the airport into town. The taxi driver pulled in front of a small chapel its doors open and welcoming. Cardinal Benedict paid the driver, stepped out onto the curb and walked into the chapel. He found the priest who held his sermons there. He politely introduced himself.

"Hello, I am Cardinal Benedict and I've just arrived here from the Vatican. I'm on Sabbatical and would like to know if you have an empty room."

"Hello Father, welcome. I'm sorry I didn't know you were coming. We don't have any rooms at the moment. Perhaps if you give me a few days, I can make arrangements for you," the Priest said nervously.

"Its fine, don't worry yourself. Do you know of any rooms for rent close by?" Benedict asked.

"Yes Father, there are always rooms for rent in town," the Priest responded.

"Then I shall head into town," Benedict told him."

"Thank you again and have a good day," Cardinal Benedict said and walked out.

"You as well Father," the Priest called out.
It was a beautiful day and Cardinal Benedict walked around town watching the locals and looking for a room. Suddenly a young girl's voice called out from behind him, "Monk Salvatore, Monk Salvatore!" He

turned around just as the young girl reached him. He looked down and a pretty little girl stopped dead in her tracks. The look of surprise on her face spoke volumes to Cardinal Benedict.

"I'm sorry sir, I thought you were someone else," she sounded embarrassed.

"Who did you think I was," he asked.

"I thought you were Monk Salvatore," she said innocently.

"You know Monk Salvatore?" he asked attempting not to sound overly anxious and scare her.

"Of course sir, he was staying at my house," she sang. Cardinal Benedict was overjoyed, luck was once again with him and he was going to make the most of it.

"Are you related to Monk Salvatore?" The Cardinal asked her quizzically.

"No sir, he was renting a room at my house," she sang again. What a sweet girl, she seems to be fond of Monk Salvatore, he thought.

"You have such a pretty voice," Benedict said with a smile.

"Thank you, I sing in my school," she said proudly.

"Would you mind taking me to your house, I would like to speak to your parents?" he asked.

"Of course not, follow me," she said as she turned around and began walking. As they walked to her house, Cardinal Benedict noticed that they were passing the chapel that he was in earlier and then they turned down a street that he hadn't gone down. 'How fortuitous to have this young girl think I was Monk Salvatore, I may not have visited this road.' He thought to himself.

A little more than a block past the chapel, she turned to a quaint looking two-story, old house surrounded by cherry trees and a beautiful rose garden. 'How peaceful,' the thought passed easily through his mind. A sign in the window read; **'Room for Rent.'** He followed Charlotte up the walkway to the house and knocked on the door. A young, pretty woman answered the door.

"Hello, Charlotte you're home early." Her voice was sweet and calming.

"Hello, she confused me with a friend of mine, Monk Salvatore. She said he stayed here and I thought I would come by and see if he happened to tell you where he was going?" he said.

"No he didn't. He left one day without a word and hasn't returned." Her voice was so sweet now he understood where Charlotte inherited it.

"I saw the sign in your window as we walked up, do you still have a room for rent?" the Cardinal asked politely.

"Yes Father, come in and I will show it to you," she said. The Cardinal followed her. She led him up the stairs as Charlotte trailed behind the two of them. She opened the door to the room, she and Benedict walked in while Charlotte stood in the doorway. As Benedict looked around, he noticed the only furniture in the room was a bed, a small dresser, a small round table and a chair. It was decorated plainly except for the blankets that had a floral pattern.

"If you rent the room, it includes breakfast and dinner," she said.

"I like it, I'll take it," the Cardinal replied.

"I will tell the children not to bother you," she stated with a hint of concern. "Children?" he questioned.

"Yes, I also have a son; they are very well behaved and shouldn't bother you."

"I don't mind at all," Cardinal Benedict responded.

"Good, when will you be moving in," she asked politely.

"Right now if that's alright with you," Benedict said happily.

"Well then, I'll let you unpack," she said as she left the room grabbing Charlotte by the hand.

Cardinal Benedict's frock was heavy and he unpacked his belongings. He carefully placed the hidden scrolls, manuscripts, and books inside the closet in an empty attaché.

Later that night at the dinner table, they all sat introducing themselves and talking. Charlotte's father, Henry, a short, round man with a very tidy mustache was an ambitious, small town architect. He ate heartily as he complained about how the town was too small for him to be successful. He also spoke of his heart condition and of his heroic activities during his time in the military.

Charlotte's Mother, Alice, was an underpaid high-school math teacher. Alice explained that teaching at the private school was a way to get Charlotte and Peter into the school. She continues to tell him that taking on boarders has helped their situation as her children's education is very important to her. Reflecting on the past two weeks, Cardinal Benedict smokes a Cuban cigar as he gazes out of the window watching the rain descend onto the golden yellow and red leaves. He has been happy here, the family breakfasts and dinners have brought him comfort and the children have delighted him with their tales of their daily school activities. He thinks about Monk Salvatore and how he hasn't found one clue about him since he's been in Kalin. No one has seen him and despite telling Charlotte he would return, he hasn't. As he focuses on the drops of rain sliding down his window, he hears a faint voice coming from downstairs. He recognizes it as Charlotte's voice. Hoping Charlotte might remember a tiny detail that would help him in his search. He extinguishes his cigar and makes his way downstairs.

Sitting in the modestly decorated living room, Charlotte taps her foot on the floor as she looks down at the book in her lap.

"What are you reading, Charlotte?" he asked with wonder.

"Actually, I can't read this book but I like looking at the colorful pictures so I pretend I know what it says. I also like the smooth pages, they smell like sweet cherries and spiced fruits," Charlotte said in her pretty voice as she smiled at him.

"Why can't you read it?" he asked curiously.

"I don't know the language," she replied.

"Well I speak several languages. Maybe, I can help you! Let's have a look," he said. She looked at him, smiled, and trustingly handed him the book. As his eyes scanned the pages they widened with shock. He recognized the old Hebrew known as Masoretic text, partly Hebrew and partly Aramaic, the language used only by the highest priests over two thousand

28

years ago.

"Charlotte, where did you get this book?" he asked stupefied.

"Monk Salvatore gave it to me just before he left. He told me that he'd be back for it," she said.

"I want you to think carefully my child; did Monk Salvatore tell you where he was going?"

"No father, just that he was going to meet his friends in town that afternoon but he never came back," Charlotte replied.

"Did he give you anything else besides this book?"

"No sir," she replied as she shook her head.

"May I borrow the book? I will translate it and then I will read it to you," he said with excitement.

"Yes father," she said. He took the book up to his room and methodically began translating it. The codes this particular book held weren't studied anymore and only a few people in the world knew how to decipher it. Luckily his obsession with ancient codes led him to its study and mastery. This code was used by Jesus and taught to his disciples. As he translated the book and the words appeared before him, he thought he was dreaming.

'Could it be real,' he thought.

'Am I really looking at **The Lost Memoirs of Jesus**,' he gasped? Excited, he continued to translate; not missing a single word discovering it was only Part I. 'This can't be all, where is Part II?' he thought. He got up from his chair and headed downstairs to find Charlotte. Charlotte was still sitting on the couch now doing calculations of her math homework.

"Charlotte, are you sure that he only gave you the one book?" he interrupted. "Yes, I'm sure," she replied with a smile.

"Maybe he took the second part with him or it is still hidden in the Vatican," he said concerned.

"I don't know father. We could search your room," she replied.

"I already did," he concluded and thought to himself he must find the second book. After translating it, he knew Book I was unfinished so the answers he was looking for must be in Book II.

"You seem upset Father," she said.

"Not at you, this book is priceless. It is almost two thousand years old. It reveals the ancient truth about God's secret world and holds secrets about the universe. The Vatican's Secret Police are looking for it. They are against sharing the knowledge with people," in his excitement and frustration, he didn't realize he had been speaking his thoughts.

"Why did Monk Salvatore have it?" she asked sadly.

"I don't know," he sighed.

"What shall we do?" Charlotte exclaimed.

"I'll take care of it. I would like to show you something, can you please call Peter and follow me," the Cardinal said. Charlotte ran to the front door, opened and called out to Peter who was playing in the front yard.

"Peter come here, hurry up!"

"What do you want?" Peter responded.

"Come to the Cardinal's room, hurry!" she said.

Charlotte and Peter walked into Cardinal Benedict's room and saw him sitting at the small

30

table. He had his attaché opened and there were books, maps, and ancient scrolls sitting on the table in front of him.

"Sit down children; I want to show you some things I borrowed from the Vatican Secret Library. You must promise me you will keep this a secret," the Cardinal said.

"Yes, Father," Charlotte and Peter said simultaneously.

"I don't have many friends in town but I trust you and I would be very grateful if you could help me. These items in front of me are priceless. I'm sure that once my brothers in Vatican City discovered I was gone as well as these artifacts, they would know that I took them and turn their backs on me. I must confess that my desire to possess these pieces and discover the truth was stronger than my unconditional love to my brothers in Vatican City. I hope God will forgive me my sins. I need to show this evidence to the world," the Cardinal said. He continued solemnly,

"Life is so uncertain, you never know if today is your last day alive."

Charlotte shivered as he spoke these words. He proceeded, "Listen to me very carefully and try to remember the things I tell you today so that years from now, you'll tell my story to others. I want you to study this **Black Book**. It belongs to me, I have written in it all the information you will need; the translation of these ancient scrolls, books and the interpretation of a two thousand year old map that is supposed to lead to a *hidden Holy treasure*."

"A real treasure," Peter excitedly interrupted.

"I don't know what kind of treasure yet Peter or

31

where it is," Benedict answered. He continued,

"I must continue my studies I feel I'm getting closer. I must finish decoding it first and then we will know exactly what we are looking for. I have to find the second part of the Holy Book. I feel as if I am running out of time and I don't have enough evidence yet."

"What can we do Father?" Peter asked.

"If something happens to me, when you grow up, you must publish this *Black Book* so the world will know the truth," Benedict said as seriously as Charlotte's eyes widened.

"Children do you have a secret hiding place?" Charlotte sprang up.

"I do and nobody knows about it but me."

"I would like you to hide these things for me so that only you and I will know where they are and no one else can find them," he said.

"I can show you that place right now," she whispered in his ear.

"Wait a minute my child, let me tell you something first," he added, smiled and then began. Peter and Charlotte sat eagerly awaiting his story.

"I must show you some important pictures I've taken over the last twenty years. Look at them and let me know what you think? On the back of each picture I wrote where and when it was taken. I traveled excessively with my two best friends Chris and John from country to country searching those old churches and taking hundreds of pictures of the written messages on their walls. Thousands of years ago, when the first Christians built those old churches all over Europe, Asia, Africa, and Egypt, they wrote the

32

code on the walls, in Latin, Hebrew, or Greek. They didn't tell anyone how to decipher the messages and the people who did set out to translate them gave up too quickly. I'll need your help with this. You must learn what order these pictures go in and learn to read and decipher the code. I've completed almost seventy percent of the decoding. I don't know how many years it would take to finish this job but it's worth it. The knowledge we could gain from this is infinite. I will help you where I can. We must find the **key to unlock the door to the secrets of the universe.** The knowledge buried under the stones for millions of years is ready to be unlocked. Otherwise it can't breathe any longer."

"Father Benedict, this is getting really very interesting. These pictures are a real treasure. You can feel centuries of history buried inside the ancient walls of the monasteries. I'd like to live in one of them one day. I hope, we can help you Father," Peter said with excitement.

"I'm sure you will! It makes me happy to see that I've ignited a spark of energy inside of you. This is only the beginning," Benedict said with a burst of enthusiasm. Benedict took a long deep breath. Not wanting to burden these young children but knowing deep inside they might carry on his works prompted him to continue.

"There is more. Over the years my job with the Vatican has given me the privilege to meet some very interesting people and it has provided me with an opportunity to experience things that few people in history have been able to experience. Two such interesting individuals became my dear friends and confidants, their names are Chris and John. Christian or Chris as he likes to go by, is a physicist, his specialty is in the field of Quantum Mechanics. He built his first quantum computer. I met him at a lecture he was giving at Oxford University; it was titled, 'Physics and the **Quantum Paradox**.' John and I met at Cambridge University where he is tenured. He is a Professor of ancient history and considered an expert regarding early Christianity and its roots. The three of us would as often as possible get together and discuss topics of similar interests. We became the best of friends, always talking late into the night about Physics or Theology.

On one such occasion, I asked them to join me as my consultants on a trip to Egypt, home to some of the earliest known Christian Monasteries. We excitedly made plans each of us behaving like young boys off on a grand adventure. Within a few weeks we were in Egypt. Indeed I felt like Indiana Jones riding around on camels and climbing through ancient ruins. Let me tell you, it was quite an adventure.

Our first destination was the St. Catherine Monastery, built during the 5th century located at the foot of Mount Sinai near the Red Sea. The monastery was one of a kind adorned with priceless mosaics, frescos, icons, oil paintings, and reliquaries. Many of the objects in the monastery had distinctive insignias carved or written on them. Chris recorded it all with a video camera that he brought along carefully describing the things he was filming. He would later use software he created to generate a 3-D *holographic* display that we could use to revisit any piece of art in detail. While there, we were able to view one of the largest collections of illuminated manuscripts in the world, second only to the Vatican. The collection consisted of more than four thousand five hundred volumes in Coptic, Greek, Hebrew and various other ancient languages.

We stayed there for a few days recording our finds. I found a few very rare manuscripts and asked Chris to record the pages for me. My attention was drawn to the one manuscript in particular. On the first page was a very detailed picture of Christ, he was holding a black book engraved with the letter **Q.** Inside of the letter Q was the letter **D**. Could the D stand for Deo which means God or did it mean something else and if so what did the Q mean? I found myself repeatedly drawn to this illustration, something in the way he held the book. It looked like he wanted to tell me something, something important. I stared for hours at his lips and felt as they were whispering to me, revealing me the hidden secrets.

Our next stop was in Upper Egypt, at the Monastery of St. Simeone located in the city of Aswan. We saw more beautiful wall paintings with Coptic and Arabic texts written on them. Once again I saw the picture of Christ holding the same book.

I wondered was it a coincidence? Or perhaps there was something more, some hidden meaning that I could not quite seem to grasp. We traveled to many other sights and in each one we would discover a slightly different version of the painting some times in a manuscript or in a fresco and other times in a mosaic.

We came to what would be the most amazing part of our journey, we traveled to the east bank of the

Nile, to a place called Church of the Holy Virgin, there are many legends told by the local monks of miracles taking place at the church. We decided to spend a few days at the monastery, to see if we could record anything supernatural taking place.

The next morning as we were looking around inside the old church, we found a passage hidden in between two rooms that butted against each other. It was covered by a large flowing drape. We would not have noticed the passage but for a strong gust of wind that blew through the monastery. The passage led us to a short staircase and into a large cave. The interior of the dwelling was simple but expertly hewn directly out of the stone. On the left a large bench carved straight from the same stone jutted out of the wall. In the center of the cave sat a large table surrounded by benches also carved from rock. On the right hand wall was a nook carved directly into the rock of the cave. The nook extended about three feet into the stone wall and was three feet tall by six feet wide. On its surface a deep depression had been cut. John suggested that it was probably used to store water. Toward the back of the dwelling lay a stone sarcophagus with no distinguishable markings. On the wall above the sarcophagus hung a single icon. It was of the Virgin Mary holding the baby Jesus. In the backdrop stood the twelve Apostles, each holding a book in their left hand. The cave had an extraordinary ambiance so we decided to place a few of Chris' cameras inside. We left and went to get the cameras and hurried back to set them up. As I mentioned to you previously, Chris is an expert in quantum physics, before our trip to Egypt he was working on a rather revolutionary concept. A computer that was correctly able to predict the random nature of quantum particles, in essence a 'quantum computer.'

It was his belief that through his computer, he would not only be able to capture an image and be able to reproduce it in true 3-D, but that he would be able to capture energy patterns as well. It is also called paranormal activity. Thus he brought his computer to Egypt with him to complete a field test. As we finished setting up the equipment, Chris' excitement grew. "I have a good feeling about tonight!" he exclaimed as he made the final adjustments on his computer. "If something happens we will capture it."

We sat on the stone bench reminiscing our past, and joking about the possibility of meeting 'ghosts.' We had been waiting for hours and were all getting tired.

"I'm going to get some sleep," I said, "Wake me if anything unusual happens."

I walked over to the empty sarcophagus; lay down inside and closed my eyes. I tried to sleep but sleep evaded me. So I just lay there, staring into empty space listening to Chris and John telling their stories. Shortly before midnight Chris got a strange reading on his equipment.

"Wake up guys I think I have something," Chris said excitedly. I hurried over to the computer and peered at the screen.

"I will turn on the holographic imaging display," Chris said as he pressed a key on his computer causing a small holographic version of the cave to appear.

The painting above the nook started to glow, faintly at first and then gradually it became brighter. The light continued to intensify, bathing the room; the painting now looked like a shimmering pool.

From out of the light two forms appeared, it was like watching a shadow in reverse. The forms began to take on a more recognizable shape as they moved further away from the painting. They walked toward the stone table seemingly oblivious to our presence.

My friends and I stood there transfixed by what we were seeing. Chris was the first to break the silence, "I think this is Mary and the little boy Jesus," John replied. "Maybe this is the miracle that the local monks talk about." I was completely blown away by what I was seeing. It was real, I could not only hear their voices, but I could smell them. They spoke in Hebrew but the dialect is no longer used and sounded strange to me. I could make out bits and pieces of their conversation; Mary was telling the boy Jesus that she would like a drink of water. Jesus smiled at his mother and walked over to the nook where the empty water hole was. He reached in and picked up a handful of the dry, silky, white sand. He held the sand above the depression and spoke in an ancient tongue completely foreign to me; he let the sand spill from his small hand and into the dry water hole.

The sound of water splashing arose from the hole, within seconds it was completely filled with water. The boy called to his mother to join him, she stood, walked over to him and drank from the pool.

Now I have spent most of my life praying and believing in Christ, so there was no way I could let this opportunity pass me. I stepped forward and humbly introduced myself.

"Hello," I said with a smile, "I am Marcillie Benedict and I would be honored to speak with you.

The young boy looked at me and with a sly smile began to speak,

"The hurt in your heart has not healed, it has been there a long time, and would you be healed?"

"What hurt do you speak of," I asked puzzled.

"The loss of your mother and father, the pain of losing them, this is what drives you. The answers that you seek cannot be found through pain, nor can it be found through loss, it can only be found through understanding of what is, this very moment, in every moment, only through this can the answer be found," he said gently. Tears formed in my eyes and I started to cry. I thought of my parents and of their murders, the pain and confusion that I felt as a child. I thought of my obsession with the truth, and why understanding was so important to me. I looked into the eyes of the young Jesus and answered him,

"I would be healed." He looked at me with pure love in his eyes and said to me, "Then drink."
I reached my hand into the pool, brought the cool water to my lips, and drank. The water was sweet and cool, it tasted like nectar from a honey suckle. As I drank I could feel the water as it moved through my body, going into the very fiber of my being, bringing with it life. I could feel the hurt from my past as it gently melted away replaced by love. I bent over and plunged my head into the pool and drank until I could not drink anymore, savoring the sensation of peace and joy that flowed through me. I sat on the floor

laughing and crying all at the same time. Mary came over and brushed the hair out of my eyes smiling at me tenderly,

"You will be fine now, don't give up your quest it is important, more important than you know."

I smiled back at her thankfully.

"Thank you mother," I said over and over again, those seemed to be the only words that I could find. The young Jesus walked over to where John and Chris sat staring, stunned at what they had just witnessed.

"Hello," he said. He paused when he saw the holographic display looking at it with deep curiosity, watching the real-time images. I stood up and walked over to the stone bench where they were all standing open-mouthed.

"This is very interesting," Jesus said as he moved his hand through the images,

"It is almost perfect." He lifted the computer a bit and saw the images of himself and his mother in motion. He glanced at Chris and said,

"You should be proud of yourself." He placed the computer on the ground and placed his hand over it, a thin thread of light extended from his palm into the computer. The images grew larger until they were life size and extremely vivid. They looked as if they were alive. Chris was stunned and asked,

"How did you do that?" The boy Jesus looked up and replied,

"By improving one small microchip in your computers processor, often just one flaw can stand in the way of perfection." Amazed, Chris asked,

"What was the improvement?" Jesus laughed.

"Without understanding, information is useless.

"True, but can one not seek to understand information," Chris ruminated.

"I will give you an answer," the boy Jesus replied,

"But if you looked at all that is around you the understanding would come, for the answer already is given." Chris had a puzzled look on his face. The boy Jesus continued,

"Gold, silicone, carbon, and all other elements that you are familiar with exist within the same reality; they all have measurable mass and behave in accordance to your laws of physics. In order to create, you must step beyond those laws; you will find your new element in the space between matter and energy."

"What do you call your new element? Chris asked.

"I call this **element Q**," the little boy added with a smile. He turned around and walked over to Mary.

"We must go now," the boy said.
They walked back to the painting and it started to glow. They turned and smiled at us. The young boy raised his hand in a farewell greeting and said,

"Peace be with you and be in harmony with all," and then vanished.

Benedict stared off into the distance the memory of that night fresh in his mind.

"Are you feeling okay Father?" Charlotte asked concern tugging on the edges of her eyes.

"Yes child I am fine, this conversation has brought back lots of memories and I just needed a moment," Benedict cleared his throat and continued.

41

"After the boy Jesus and Mary left, the three of us discussed the relevance of the experience. The computer captured the events of the night perfectly; we reviewed the footage several times letting it all sink in. We talked long into the night trying to plan our next move. The hours went by and our eyes grew heavy."

"I am going to try and catch some sleep," John said lying down on the stone bench.

"That's a great idea," I replied. I stood and walked over to the sarcophagus and lay down, the lid was loose this time and kept wobbling so I got up and removed the lid. I removed my shoes and placed them next to the sarcophagus and climbed inside to sleep.

As I lay there trying to get comfortable my feet brushed against a groove on the far side of the sarcophagus, I followed the groove with my toes and found that it outlined a square I pushed it with my feet and suddenly I was falling and let out a startled cry. The fall was only a few feet so I was uninjured.

"What was that?" I heard John ask from the other side of the room.

"I fell; can you bring me a flash light?" I called to him. I heard the sound of someone rummaging around their bag and then saw the beam of a flashlight as it bounced around the dark room; a head peered over the edge of the sarcophagus. John peered down at me.

"You just won't let a guy sleep will you?" he said with a big grin on his face.

"Wow!" John let out a breath.

"Hey Chris you have to check this out, and

42

bring another light."

John handed me a flashlight, I looked around and was surprised at how big the chamber that I fell into was. The walls were adorned with beautiful frescoes and the chamber looked as if no one had been in it since it was built.

"Chris you might want to bring your camera," I called out.

I spotted an interesting monogram on the floor. 'This is one of the oldest **Christograms,** the Chi-Rho or Labarum,' I thought. The Greek letters Chi-X with the letter **Rho-P** in its center which stands for Christ in Greek. The letter X was intersected by a letter P in its center. The X lines were crossing at ninety degree angle which is equivalent to the solar ecliptic path and the celestial equator. Also Alpha and Omega letters were on each side. Everything referred to God in Jesus. The entire monogram was surrounded by a circle or rather a letter Omega.

It was an amazing discovery for me. I shined the flashlight on the stone that the monogram was painted on something about it just didn't feel right. As I sat there looking Chris and John approached.

"What happened?" John asked.

"That's not important," I replied,

"Look at this." I showed them the monogram and the stone.

"That's strange," Chris said as he knelt down. Bending over, he tapped the butt of his flashlight on the stone.

"Hear that? It sounds hollow."
I listened as he tapped the stone again.

"Yes it does," I agreed.

43

"We need to find out what's underneath."

"We need some tools to lift it up," John suggested in an excited voice.

"We don't have any tools," I said as I looked at the stone, "But maybe we don't need them." I placed my foot on top of the stone and rocked it back and forth; it barely moved, I continued to work it loose moving it back and forth like a loose tooth. The sand and mortar started to fall away encouraging me; I put more effort into it.

"I think this is going to work," I grunted, "Just a little bit more."

A few more minutes went by and the stone was now loose enough to get my fingertips under it. I tried to lift the slab but it wouldn't budge. John knelt down next to me and added his assistance.

"One, two, three," I counted down, and we lifted with all of our strength. The stone resisted us for a moment then all at once it was free, John and I stumbled backward and fell.

"There is a lever inside," Chris stated still filming with his camera; he reached his hand out and grabbed the lever and gave it a tug. The lever moved smoothly, there was a mechanical clicking sound and then silence. We stared at each other in silent anticipation, nothing happened. John was the first to break the silence.

"Now what!" The sound of grinding stone filled the passage way. The ground was shaking beneath our feet. We hurried out of the passage and climbed out, exiting through the sarcophagus. By the time we all exited, the ground had stopped shaking and the grinding noise had stopped as well. Chris jumped right back down into the passage without a second thought.

"What are you doing?" I asked.

"Finding out what happened," he replied and then disappeared down the passage; flashlight in one hand and camera in the other.

We followed him into the passageway and hadn't gone very far when he called out,

"I see a hole in the corner, it looks like small chamber." I looked in the small chamber adding the light of my flash light to his. It was about twelve foot deep and one point five feet tall by one point five feet wide. As we scanned the chamber I noticed a rectangular object in the far corner, it was completely covered with dust and I almost missed it.

"Chris, give me a hand will you," I asked and then I climbed into the small opening. I had to slide in on my stomach, the going was slow and I bumped my head several times on the hard rock ceiling of the passage way but finally I reached the box and dusted it off. It was a wooden box and had the **Chi-Rho** *monogram* beautifully carved into its surface. It was painted in beautiful pastels and the Fish and Anchor symbols were carved into the sides with great detail. It was a beautiful piece of art. I made my way out carefully dragging the box with me an inch at a time.

We were very curious to see what was inside the box. We carried it out of the passage way and into the cave; we placed it on the table and very carefully opened it. The box was unusually deep and on the bottom was another beautifully carved Monogram of a circle with the letter **D** delicately painted in gold. We were stunned by its craftsmanship and beauty.

"Why is it empty?" Chris said, "Maybe it's not, maybe the box itself is the clue. Notice the numeral 500 engraved under the circle and the **Q,** with the letter **D** inside." John interrupted suddenly,

"I remember the letter **Q,** is an abbreviation for **Quingenti** the Medieval Numeral **500** but in Roman Numerals and in Latin the letter **D** is equal to **500**? But what the number 500 states for; perhaps the year in which it was made or something very important happened in the past."

I smiled at him. "Now you see where I am headed, perhaps this could be the key to what we're searching for," I said. Chris interrupted,

"Sure, maybe this box held the real key once upon a time, but now it's empty."

"Maybe we aren't dealing with a regular key. As a matter of fact I remembered that something was written about the key in the oldest **Hebrew Bible** which I studied in Jerusalem a few years back. Before crucifixion, Jesus gave some kind **of key** to one of his trusted Apostles. He told him that the key will unlock the **secret** knowledge of the universe, and he should never abandon it. He shall pass the key to the next closest Apostle before dying. The key shall be hidden in a secret place. Thus we must find to whom exactly Jesus gave the key," I countered.

"Whatever it is we need to take it with us, so why don't I put it in one of my camera bags the box should fit quite nicely inside and I can just carry my camera. Now let's concentrate on our main task at hand." It was almost 4 a.m. and we hadn't slept yet. We packed the box and decided to get some sleep.

In the morning we were awakened by the monks as they entered the cave. They showed us their hospitality by bringing fresh crispy bread and water. After the meal we left the monastery and traveled to Munich to consult with Hans and Jorgen. They're accomplished scientists at Munich University. They welcomed us warmly and we all began working almost immediately. We spent almost one full week in Munich but didn't make much head way with the box. We decided to leave the box with them so they could study it further. Hans suggested that the box had at one time an important book or document and that we should look for any forensic evidence that remained within it.

After a week spent with them, we said our goodbyes and left Munich. Chris and John went back to their work at their respective universities in England. I went back to Vatican City and spent my time in the library working on the secret code. I found some more crucial pieces to the puzzle, evidence such as an ancient treasure map, various scrolls, and rare manuscripts. I decided to borrow them and left Vatican City. So now here I am, in this small charming town with you my two new young friends. I must tell you that the book you loaned me could be the missing link. It has the same letter **Q** on its cover. It is quite a coincidence Monk Salvatore knew exactly what he was doing when he took this book from the Vatican. I mentioned to you that there must be the second part of the book and it might possibly be at the Vatican. I didn't tire you out with my stories. Did I?"

"Oh, no, Father Benedict! As a matter of fact it was very entertaining," Peter said with a smile as he glanced at Charlotte for her approval.

"I like your stories too but I'm really tired," she replied.

"I'll tell you more stories tomorrow. Meanwhile, please show me the secret place you have for my treasures. Peter, can you help me with the maps and scrolls," he asked.

"Sure, I will," Peter replied.

"Okay, follow me," Charlotte announced then opened the attic door with her own key and they proceeded in.

"Where should we put these documents?" the Cardinal asked a bit nervous. "Right here, under the wooden floorboard," she replied. "Oh, it looks like a very good place," he said and smiled. They wrapped each piece with a linen cloth and put them under the floor. The Cardinal was happy as he announced,

"Good job my child. I am proud of you. I have a special plan for both of you; I'd say rather a **mission**! However everything is a bit complicated and involves a lot of work and some travel in the near future. This is why you must concentrate on what I'm about to tell you. The most important thing is to keep it a secret. Don't tell your friends about me or what I've told you either especially, in school. One more thing children, when I was in the Vatican I learned some ancient words from a dying monk, and it was purely by accident. He was a member of the **XII Templars** I told you about. When I speak in this ancient tongue, I can perform miracles. Just name anything. However, I don't fully understand the meaning of each word. But I wrote these words in my **Black Book**. That is why it would be devastating to me to lose it. Giving these

48

words to just anybody could mean imminent danger or even global disaster. I remember when I was only twenty; I lived in a small country-side monastery near Paris for three months in an old XVI century' church facility with other monks. I'll never forget how Monk Manuel performed a miracle by speaking in some unknown language. He made supper for twenty five monks using a piece of stale bread and wine. Manuel was guarded for twenty four hours by special police and wasn't allowed to speak to anyone. The police followed him everywhere from the private bathroom to the local shops. He possessed some knowledge of God's secret world. The **XII Templars** have guarded those secrets and the 'Holy Grail' for centuries somewhere in Vatican City.

The monks spoke rumors that Jesus himself visits the **XII Templars** and gives them new instructions from time to time. Jesus has the ability to materialize himself in a form of high visibility energy. It is difficult to believe until you see him for yourself. I remember the night I tried to spy on one of the XII Templars. I was so close to their headquarters that night. Then I saw some bright lights from the distance which radiated toward me and at the same moment someone knocked me down. I collapsed onto the floor and never knew what really happened to me. Later I awoke in the library sitting on the same chair I was previously sitting in. Isn't it strange? I learned a lesson and never tried it again."

"What is our mission then?" Charlotte asked.

"We need to find the second missing Holy Book. I feel there is so much to tell you but I know you'll find out for yourselves soon," the Cardinal added with an enigmatic look.

"What is the secret code about?" she asked again.

"With *this* **code** you could have access to the biggest secrets of the entire universe. I believe we'll know the beginning and the future of our existence and possibly of the exact location of the lost city of Atlantis. Maybe it will hold the lost map of the entire universe which no one has ever seen or quite possibly all of the historical information about how every single incident in the entire universe has taken place. I have found clues to some of those questions in those old ancient manuscripts which the Vatican has kept hidden from the public which never saw the light of day for thousands of years. I believe we would have knowledge of all of these things but somehow, something or someone has blocked the link of incoming and outgoing information into the human brain.

There is a gap between hundreds of civilizations, and we must find the links to connect them. It would be the sort of universal truth that we're searching for. The code could unlock not only our future but it can give us the knowledge buried under the stones for millions of years. With all of that information revealed, people would be free of diseases and would be self-sufficient. We could unlock **the DNA code** for every living species on the entire planet. We will be able to do that without going into manual laboratory procedures. Instead we would use the power of the **spoken code** and the power of the quantum world."

"Father Benedict this is so interesting! Please

teach me how to do the magic," Charlotte asked softly.

"I will my child but I need to give you one more thing. This is a key to my locker in the local post office. The number engraved on it is 1525 which corresponds to the same box number. I left some important instructions which I'd like you to read only if something bad happens to me. Do you understand that? I have some friends in Europe that you can contact in case of emergency. More than likely, they will contact you when the time is right. They will work with you. I have written them and they know my plans. Just be patient and follow their instructions and believe me your life will be beautiful. Of course there will be a lot of temptations along the way but if you persevere in your task, it could inspire you to do the right things. Trust me you'll be fine. The most important thing is your future education. Without that you can't go any further in this mission. I'll contact my friends in Rome and they will come and take both of you to a special Catholic boarding school in Rome, Italy. They will ask your parents for permission of course and as soon as they get it you must go with them. It's not just any school, it's a theological school taught by real *Alexandrian monks*. It will prepare you for the highest degree of education and your future mission in the Vatican City. Focus on your studies and follow my instructions and you will be fine," the Cardinal concluded smiling.

"I'll do exactly what you have told me to do. But what is our mission Father?" Charlotte asked with excitement.

"You and Peter must get the second part of

that Holy Book, which is probably in the North Tower where the **XII Omega Templars** reside. It is under the highest security and will not be an easy task. I must ask you again to be careful to whom you talk to and always keep this a secret. Now, I think it's your bedtime, you both have school tomorrow. Goodnight for now. Tomorrow, I'll show you the magic you asked for. Have a peaceful sleep," he said.

"Goodnight, Father Benedict," Charlotte said and left for her room downstairs. "Goodnight Father," Peter said as he ran to his room located next to Cardinal Benedict's. He jumped into his bed and threw his covers over himself hoping he would dream about his future mission.

Chapter 4. A Monk's Revenge

Cardinal Benedict sat by himself going over all of the things he shared with Charlotte and Peter. And the things he couldn't share with them because he didn't want to frighten them. He couldn't tell them the secrets were given to us by God himself but we haven't been able to access them. He couldn't tell them that the Vatican guarded some of those secrets for centuries because they didn't want people to misuse their power or use it against each other. He couldn't tell them that with the secrets, one person could destroy the entire universe. This is what he deciphered from the scrolls he took from the library.

The Cardinal sat in his room, decoding the book Charlotte gave him and writing the missing clues of what he had deciphered from other works. It became obvious to him that some of the facts he was looking for were hidden in this personal bible. The book was in excellent condition for its age. The pages were transparent like silk and beautifully handwritten. As he gazed over them, he imagined Jesus sitting and writing these pages. Each picture was hand painted with natural flower dyes. Having worked at the Vatican for so long, he knew they took very good care of their treasures.

His eyes were tired, his mind completely exhausted, he decided to put everything away and went to bed shortly after midnight. He peacefully closed his eyes and prayed giving thanks for all of the blessings he had in his life.

About two a.m. he heard knocking at the front door. He heard Henry muttering as he walked down the stairs. He heard Henry's voice for a moment then silence and suddenly a single shoot from a pistol. He sprung out of bed and ran downstairs. When he reached the bottom of the stairs, he saw Charlotte running to the door.

She took a look at her father lying on the floor, his body halfway out of the door, bleeding heavily. She began to scream. She looked out the doorway, into the night and saw a man running away. Cardinal Benedict reached her father, kneeled down, turned Henry over and saw blood pouring from his chest. Henry whispered "It was Muu" and then shut his eyes. Benedict checked his pulse but couldn't find one.

Alice and Peter came running. Alice screamed when she saw Henry and kneeled beside him holding him crying. Benedict grabbed Charlotte and Peter and held them.

The blood was all over the porch. Father Benedict leaned over and helped Alice up. He said a short prayer in Latin over Henry's body. Alice went to the phone and called the police. Charlotte and Peter knelt beside their Father each holding him crying. Alice went back to the door and pulled Charlotte and Peter away from their father and told them to go and wash the blood off of themselves. Obeying their Mother, the children left their father sadly. Benedict laid a sheet over Henry's dead body. A short time later, Charlotte entered the living room, dressed in a clean nightgown her eyes still swollen with tears. Benedict approached her and asked, "Charlotte, did you see the person who shot your father?"

"No, but I did see someone running down the street," she replied.

"Could you tell who it was?" he asked.

"At first I thought it was Monk Salvatore but I'm not sure he was too far," she told him trying to hold back her tears and not look at her fathers' body.

"If it was Salvatore, he came to get his book," Benedict added nervously. He sat Charlotte down on the couch and went to the kitchen. He picked up the house phone and dialed. He began speaking in Italian pausing momentarily and then continuing his side of the conversation. He hung up the phone and returned to the living room where Alice was sitting holding Charlotte and Peter.

"Don't cry children," she tried to soothe them.

"Alice, I can help you arrange Henry's funeral tomorrow," Benedict said with deep concern.

"Thank you father," she said choking back

tears. Carefully choosing his words, Benedict spoke to Alice,

"I know this may not be the best time to speak to you about this but I just contacted my best friend Emanuel. He works in Rome, in the monastery. I know your situation and I know without your husband, you will have a difficult time taking care of Charlotte and Peter. I would like to ease your financial situation. I would like to take Charlotte and Peter to the theological boarding school in a week or two. This is the best Christian school in Rome and its teachers are the Alexandrian Monks. They will be there for at least eight years until their graduation. I can assure you that they will be very successful in the future and you will be very proud of them."

"How can I live without them? I'll be so lonely," she whispered, crying.

"Don't worry, you can visit them once every Christmas and I'll send you a ticket each time," Benedict calmly added.

"Let me think about this. Please wait for a few days," she replied sadly.

"Don't worry, we'll talk another time," he said gently.

The police arrived and took everyone's statement. Tears flowed down Alice's face as the coroner wheeled Henry's body away. It was four a.m. and Alice put Charlotte and Peter to bed. As Cardinal Benedict lay in his bed, he heard Alice crying. He closed his eyes and said a silent prayer for her, Charlotte, and Peter. He opened his eyes and his mind began racing with thoughts of Monk Salvatore. Questions raced across his mind. Was it Salvatore? If he could kill Henry; what wouldn't stop him at to get his book back? It would be better for Charlotte and Peter to go to school in Rome where they will be safe. Benedict drifted off into a fitful night's sleep.

The following morning, Benedict woke up and got out of bed. He washed up, got dressed and made his way down to the kitchen. He found Alice, Charlotte and Peter making breakfast for everyone; fried eggs and ham sandwiches. Soon Cardinal Benedict came to join them. They sat in silence and ate their food. After breakfast, Alice and Benedict went to the local church to make all of the arrangements for Henry's funeral.

Charlotte and Peter had two more weeks of summer vacation. It wouldn't be the best vacation for them but Father Benedict promised to stay with them for the remaining two weeks. The church minister sent two workers and Priest Andrew to take Henry's body to the local chapel for a day before they move it to the cemetery. Cardinal Benedict paid for all the arrangements and Alice continually thanked him. She was devastated but left for work the same morning. Benedict and kids stayed in the living room grieving. Suddenly Charlotte interrupted,

"Father Benedict can you show me the magic you told me about? I have this little coin in my pocket. Look! You told me that you can make more money from a single coin."

"Sure, why not! Please, give me your coin and close your eyes." As Benedict spoke, Peter and Charlotte listened to his *ancient language* and waited for the miracle to happen. The Cardinal spoke in a soft voice and suddenly they heard the sound of coins falling onto the floor. They opened their eyes and shouted,

"Father, you did it! You did it!" There were a lot of coins on the floor. "Put them into the basket and give them to your mother as soon as she comes home from work." Benedict smiled and added, "I have to go into town and buy some food and then I have to pick Father Emanuel up from the local airport. His plane will arrive in 45 minutes. If you like you can come with me."

"I want to go," Peter said and Charlotte added,
"Me too."
The airport was a little over two miles away. They walked slowly and Benedict told them some funny stories from his youth. They paused for a moment as they spotted the small plane that had just landed. They went to the gate and Father Emanuel a tall, slender man walked up and greeted all of them.

"Hi everyone, you must be Peter and you are Charlotte. Nice to meet both of you," he said with happy smile.

"Hi father Emanuel. Nice to meet you too," Peter replied and Charlotte added, "Are you taking us to the boarding school?"

"Yes, if your mother agrees but in the meantime, let's do some quick shopping," he answered cheerfully.

"I like to shop. We only go shopping once a month," Charlotte replied.

"Now you can go more often with me and Father Benedict," Emanuel concluded, smiling.

"Sure, I would love to go more often," Charlotte told him happily.

57

"Tell me something about your school, Father," she asked.

"It is very old and its traditions are 2000 years old. It originated in Alexandria, Egypt and it was the first Christian school taught by the Apostles in the 1st century. You will like it! We call it an *Alexandrian Theological Academy.* It looks like really old monastery and is divided into two sections; the *Convent of Saint Mary* for girls and the *Templar's* division for boys. Our students are chosen by our Theological Committee. After eight years of study and successful graduation, a selected few are sent to the Vatican Headquarters working as a servant of God. We will discuss more details very soon my child," Emanuel said with a smile.

"Can I be a Templar?" Peter asked, excited.

"Yes, you will be one of them and we have a special plan for you Peter," Benedict added with assurance.

"But it takes commitment for life. If you think you're ready for that type of sacrifice then you're ahead of the game," Father Emanuel added.

"I think, I am ready," Peter replied.

"You must be a very brave boy, Peter," Emanuel said.

"Of course, I'm brave!" Peter exclaimed.

"Let's go into this supermarket for now and see what we can find for me to cook tonight," Emanuel said as he glanced at Peter. After two hours of shopping they slowly walked home, each of them carrying a few bags of food. It was a busy morning for all of them. They reached the house and sighed with relief as they placed the heavy bags on the kitchen table. Father Emanuel's spirit was high as he volunteered to make lunch for everyone. Charlotte offered her help and Peter arranged the table with plates and utensils. Father Benedict made sure the house was in pristine condition. He pondered who Henry's killer might be, his thoughts always returning to Monk Salvatore. To avoid any further confrontation with Monk Salvatore, Benedict decided to carry the **Memoirs of Jesus** with him at all times. Suddenly, his thoughts were interrupted by Father Emmanuel, "Lunch is ready."

"The spaghetti is perfect. I like fried mushrooms and asparagus with a bit of garlic butter flavor on it. I have to learn how you do it. We don't eat this very often. You're so good at cooking, you can cook for us every day Father Emanuel," Charlotte said happily.

"I wish I could but my brothers in Rome are waiting for me. I will however cook for you every day I am here. How about that?" he asked.

"It would be great," Charlotte said. Peter nodded his head in approval, his mouth too filled with pasta to speak.

"I saw that you have a volley ball net in your yard. I propose we play a game after lunch," Father Emanuel said smiling at the children.

"That would be fun," Peter said. "I want to play too wait for me," Charlotte added as she shoved a large serving of pasta into her mouth.

"Slow down Charlotte, we'll wait for you," Emanuel said.

"Maybe, I should play as well. I could stand to lose a few pounds," Benedict said. They all sat and talked and finished their meal, momentarily forgetting about the recent tragedy in their lives. As everyone placed their dishes in the sink and cleaned off the table.

"Great! Let's go and be sure you put the proper shoes on," Father Emanuel added energetically. They exercised for two hours and finally Benedict and Emanuel sat on the bench, reminiscing for another hour while Charlotte and Peter continued playing. Benedict looked at Emanuel and said,

"Tomorrow, they'll go to Henry's funeral," he said.

"I know it must be very hard on them," Emanuel responded.

"It's up to you to speak to their Mother, I'm afraid I may have jumped the gun and upset her about it," Benedict said.

"I will, I've always had a gentler hand regarding these kinds of things," Emanuel assured him.

"I've never acquired your knack," Benedict teased him.

Later that afternoon, Alice came from work and dinner was waiting for her. Father Emanuel showed his culinary mastery by making steak in tomato sauce and baked French style potatoes with garlic flavor mixed with green dill. She was surprised and complimented him on his cuisine. "Father Emanuel, you're really great cook. I would never have enough time or creativity to put together such a delicious dinner."

"Thank you, I'm flattered and happy that you like it. I never thought I was good enough to be a cook."

"How was your trip Father?" she asked.

"Good. Thank you for asking. How was your work today?" he replied.

"I'm a teacher and it's a hard job. I must work an extra hour or two everyday with the kids who have learning disabilities," Alice said nervously.

"Working so much and trying to take care of two children must be quite hard on you. Did you think about Father Benedict speaking to you about the boarding school for Charlotte and Peter?" Emanuel asked.

"I did, a little and thought it might be a good idea that my children get a better education than they would get here. However, I'll miss them very much," she replied with tears in her eyes.

"Oh, Alice you don't have to worry about anything. We will make all of the necessary arrangements for them and arrange your trips out to see them," Emanuel added with a big smile.

"If you can promise me that then I will give my consent. Do they have to pack all of their clothes?" she added.

"No, the kids will get special school uniforms. This is a Christian school. Trust us, they will be well taken care of," he pointed out, attempting to reassure her.

"Peter and Charlotte, are you ready to go to the boarding school? It's far away from here and we won't see each other very often," she said.

"I'd really like to go, I want to be a Templar, Mother," Peter said with excitement. "I want to go too, mother. I will make new friends and I promise to write you a letter every week," Charlotte said.

61

"I'll wait patiently for your letters, my dear Charlotte. I love both of you and I don't want to lose you," she added with concern.

"You are making the right choice for your children Alice. We will stay with you this week and then next week I'll take Peter and Charlotte to Rome with me. We will send you a postcard from Rome as soon as we arrive there. Please, do not worry about them. I will send you a personal report on them once a month," Emanuel added with confidence.

"Okay, then everything is arranged for them to leave next week. What about Henry's funeral?" she sadly asked.

"I have arranged it for 9 a.m. You should get some rest Alice," Father Benedict added.

"You're right, I should get some sleep. Thank you for everything," she said and went to her room.

"I have some work to do as well. Please excuse me," Father Benedict said.

"Can you tell us more about the boarding school, Father Emanuel," Charlotte asked.

"Yes, let's go have a seat on the sofa. Father Emanuel said kindly. They all got up from the table and made their way to the living room. Father Emanuel made himself comfortable on the sofa. Peter and Charlotte sat next to him and faced him, completely focusing on him.

"You will have lots of nice friends and you will learn many new things like martial arts, and different languages, and so much more. Let me tell you about the history of Rome," he said peacefully.

Peter and Charlotte listened to Father Emanuel telling his stories. As the night wore on, Charlotte and

Peter fell asleep next to him. He covered them with blankets and went to his room upstairs. Poor kids, he thought on his way out.

The next morning people gathered in the local Gothic church for Henry's funeral. Father Emanuel gave a short speech and then they all walked in procession to the cemetery. As Alice looked around at all of the people who showed up, she took comfort in the fact that Henry was a very likable man. However, it was also a very sad moment for her as she knew that she would be alone now; her husband killed and her children leaving her for school. The ceremony was short everyone lined up and threw fresh flowers on his coffin as they left. Father Emanuel and Benedict escorted Alice, Charlotte and Peter home.

As soon as they arrived home they sat at the table for coffee. Alice was contemplative and the three of them got into a long conversation about life and death. Father Emanuel had been a speaker for a long time and after his sad speech, Alice excused herself and went to her room to grieve. To ease the pain of the tragedy in their lives, Charlotte, Peter, and Emanuel decided to play ball in the garden. Father Benedict watched them from the distance. He had a lot of things on his mind lately.

First he must find out where Monk Salvatore was hiding and discover his plan. Because he is a dangerous Monk, a killer, and a skilled fugitive on the run and he must be stopped!

The evening was approaching fast, after supper Benedict had a friendly conference with Emanuel. They'd been long time friends for many years and belonged to the same secret organization, the **Christian Coalition of Knights,** known in the past as the **Secret Templar Society** in Rome for many centuries.

Today it serves the humanitarian ideas, they've spread throughout Europe. The members of the organization are direct descendants of the Templars and have inherited an enormous treasure which they've kept secret. They wear gold rings with a letter **T** engraved on it, which identifies them as direct descendants of Templars. Every new born descendant has the same letter T branded under their right foot. Soon after they were born, many of the children were sent to the Christian orphanages after their wealthy parents mysteriously died, disappeared or were killed by the members of the *Holy Confiscators in the past.*

Over the centuries, members of the old Roman Christian Society close to the Pope forcefully took wealth which lawfully belonged to the descendants of the Templars. Many properties including palaces, churches, land, gold, precious stones, and other treasures changed hands overnight as *blood* was *shed*. The true value of the Templars confiscated wealth could be estimated at billions of dollars. Many descendants are alive today, and they attempt to recover some of their properties but are unsuccessful. Cardinal Benedict and Emanuel are two of them. They travel extensively all over Europe looking for traces of real documents or books hidden in the libraries of old churches and monasteries. Cardinal Benedict had already collected a lot of evidence. However, as he'd gotten older, he'd lost interest in recovering his past wealth instead focusing on cracking the secret of the universe.

"Tomorrow afternoon, I have to do some business in town for a day or two. If you don't mind please take care of Charlotte and Peter. Hopefully, I will see you in Rome one day. Have a safe journey and give my best regards to our Christian friends in Rome. Thank you for everything," Cardinal Benedict said calmly with a smile.

"I'll take care of everything. I've already called our friends in Rome and they're waiting for Charlotte and Peter's arrival. They are good at their job and will train the kids for the mission to the best of their abilities. Before I forget, I came across an **ancient scroll** dated **68 CE**. You're not the only one searching after treasure. I bought it from a young *Bedouin* shepherd. He told me that he found them in the cave near the *Dead Sea* by accident. I translated those small pieces and you wouldn't believe what I found? It was written that a *secret of the universe shall be found in* **the 2nd Holy Book of Jesus** and the *Apostle* **St. Peter** *has the* **key.** We must find **the 2nd Holy** Book of Jesus and the **key.** Most of the writing was deteriorated for some unknown reason only small pieces survived. I thought it would be of interest to you since you work on decoding those ancient inscriptions. Do you believe that?" Emanuel asked.

"Sure, I believe it! Good job! After reading certain texts, I thought that St. Peter must have the *Holy Key.* As a matter of fact I'm looking for an answer myself. I think I'm getting closer and closer to solving this puzzle. I would like to see the scrolls. I got a phone call yesterday from my friend John, from

London. He will be here tomorrow morning. He told me that he's found some new evidence about the Holy Key. The same key you're talking about. He works at the ancient Christian monasteries, looking for hidden secrets codes in the ancient books. We traveled throughout Egypt last year looking for more clues. I suspect that he's found something important otherwise he wouldn't have called me," Benedict added.

"I'm very interested to see what he says. I'm getting tired. I'll go to bed and you should do the same. Goodnight!" Emanuel added with a smile. There was much more to be said but it was better not to say too much that evening.

"Goodnight!" Benedict replied.

The next morning Alice and Emanuel made a very tasty breakfast. Soon after breakfast Benedict went to pick up John from the airport, Emanuel kept him company. They didn't wait too long and immediately spotted John from the distance. Benedict approached him and said, "This is my fellow friend Monk Emanuel."

"Nice to meet you Emanuel, I'm John."

"Nice to meet you John."

"Benedict, it's been long time since our last journey to Egypt. I missed all the fun we had there. Do you have any good news for me because I have some great news for you," John happily announced.

"Not much from me but I'm waiting to hear your good news. Let's stop in the small cafe for a drink on the way. We can talk freely there," Benedict said with assurance.

"Good idea. I need to relax a bit. Let's sit at the

corner table near the window. After our last trip to Egypt, I thought a lot about that **Holy Key** we were talking about, I began to dig in the old books again and bingo! I found a new clue I think makes sense at least for me. I found that Jesus really gave the *secret* **Holy Key to the Apostle, St. Peter**, indeed, telling him to guard it with his life. Before Peter went to Rome to establish the Christian Church he passed the *Holy Key* to one of his closest and loyal *Apostles, Mark,* who went on a Christian mission to *Alexandria, Egypt; b*ut soon before his mission to Egypt Jesus gave also **Mark the Holy Book** and told him that it was a gift from God Himself to all the People on Planet Earth.

He told Mark that if he loses the **Holy Book** his enemy will destroy the entire *universe.* The Holy Book has the power to *build or to kill*. Jesus told him to hide the **Holy Book** soon after he arrives in Egypt. He told him exactly where to go and who he should speak to. St. Mark did exactly was he was told to do.

It was half of the 1st century before Mark was captured and killed by his enemies. Just a few weeks before he was captured, he passed the *Holy Key* and the *Holy Book* to a few trusted monks who hid the treasures in one of the oldest monasteries in Alexandria. It was hidden for almost two hundred years in a mountain cave guarded by two generations of *hermits*. Then in the 3rd century it was given to *St. Anthony* who carried the secret with him for almost one hundred years. Before he died in three hundred fifty AD at the age of 105 he passed the *Holy Key and* the *Book* to his most loyal monks, *Macarius and Amatas*. They kept the Holy Key and the Holy Book in

St. Anthony Cave near the Red Sea. Then finally a Monk named de Arturo *Beniciano* received the *Holy Key* and the *Holy Book from them* and brought it to El-Minya, the same church of the Virgin Mary where we found the empty holy box last year. But before he died in three hundred ninety five AD, he hid the Holy Key and the Holy Book in the same wooden box under the empty sarcophagus and told his friend, Monk Theodosius about it.

No one knew previously that such a book ever existed. However, the book was cursed and anybody who even tried to open it was cursed too. Thus on that memorable evening Theodosius was tempted. As soon as he lifted the cover page he died and was turned into dust. The **Holy Book** was never opened again. The box was found by a few members of the **Secret Hermit Society** *who lived there*. They were told that the *Secret of the Universe was written or recorded in that* **Holy Book**. There was **a Letter** attached to it which said it couldn't be opened. The curse was written on it. They didn't dare to open it; and then they hid it in their private collection.

Then a member of the *Secret Hermits Society* wrote a letter in which he stated the truth about the *Holy Book* and where it was hidden. They never thought anyone would ever see this letter. Soon after all of the members of the society died and there was no one to carry on the holy responsibilities," John said.

"Thus it was thoughtful of Jesus to give the **Holy Book** to *St. Mark*. Why he didn't give the Holy Book to St. Peter because he knew that St. Peter would be executed in Rome very soon and the *Holy*

Book would be lost forever or destroyed by His enemies. Do you imagine something like that? It was hidden deep in the cave for hundreds of years and no one ever thought such a treasure existed. It makes so much sense now. John, you did fantastic job. How were you able to find this information?" Benedict said, stunned by the great news.

John continued, "I dug for those books for ten years in one antique library which belongs to the small monastery in the outskirts of London. I don't have a clue how this book landed there, but I found a small volume which wasn't there before.

But listen to that. Then soon after came the era of robbers and plunderers. The leaders of Rome sent the Holy Expedition of Robbers all over the world to search for any type of treasure. They went to Egypt and Alexandria and plundered mainly the old monasteries, knowing they would find gold there. Accidentally the hermit's letter was found on the shelf by a robber named **Decius.** After he read the letter he went inside the cave to look for the hidden box. Without knowing exactly what he'd found, he took only the *Holy Book and the Holy Key to* **Rome.** Then quickly he sold the holy artifacts to a few rich monks, for a huge amount of money. When the monks found that the **Holy Book** and **the Key** were such a rare treasure, they made a deal with the Pope. The Pope paid them a lot of gold, precious stones, and other material goods, perhaps a hundred times more than they paid for it. Also he gave them huge estates in the countryside. Their names were kept secret and he made deals with them, not to talk to anyone about it. They lived in wealth and happiness for a few years.

69

But one day the Pope found out that the monks lived their life to the fullest and they were talking to other people about the treasures. He ordered them to be killed. Thus, the *Holy Book* and the *Key* ended up in the **Vatican Headquarters** where it still sits today. What do you think about that?" John asked with wonder, smiling.

"I think it is a fantastic story. More than I expected to hear from you, John. You've done quite a bit of research since we've seen each other last time. It would explain why the box was empty. We don't have any proof that your story is true, and to find an answer, we must wait a few more years. Also Emanuel bought 1st century scrolls from the Bedouins in Rome. They claimed that they found the scrolls in the old cave near the Dead Sea. The scrolls were in such bad condition that he was only able to translate a few fragments of the written text. It says that the ***Secret of the universe is hidden in the 2nd Book*** *of Jesus*. Perhaps they are both referring to the *Holy Book*. Also, it was mentioned that the key was given to St. Peter. Thus it would confirm what you said," Benedict concluded with an enigmatic smile.

"This is amazing news. I'm even more convinced that everything I've found so far is true. I would like to see those scrolls fragments," John said excited.

"I'll show them to you. Perhaps you visit me in Rome this year. What is our plan for now?" Emanuel asked.

"Our plan is to get that *Holy Book and the Key*. This is the reason you must take Charlotte and Peter to the boarding school as soon as possible. I estimate

70

it will take us at least six years to train the kids well," Benedict added with a bitter look. Then John continued,

"I also found some handwritten notes on the margin of the volume perhaps written by one of the hermits. He said that the book could destroy not only our planet but the entire universe. Now, I wonder myself how can that be possible?"

"Perhaps thousands of years ago someone tried to do that. You never know. Of course it could happen! Just imagine a crazy person who hates everyone on the planet," Emanuel said.

"He is right. This book must have the power to do that sort of damage, I believe. We must keep our finds secret for as long as possible. This is why Monk Salvatore escaped from the Vatican with the 1st part of the *Memoirs of Jesus*. I know why he didn't take the 2nd part of the **Holy Book**; because, it is under high security. It is watched 24/7 by a three of the *XII Omega Templars*. They guard the **Holy Book** with their own life. There is no way that anyone could go in or out without being noticed," Benedict said with confidence.

"I think that Salvatore must have jumped out of the window with the 1st *Holy Book* because there is no way he could have walked out of the North Tower alive. Salvatore was lowest in rank of all the *XII Templar Monks*. He must've felt fully ignored by the others and is angry at everyone. I know he was a highly trained monk. They call him one of the best of all the **Spider Monks**. He can easily climb walls like a spider. Those monks are trained in the *Alexandrian Theological Academy*, in Rome for very long time. I

71

heard that only three of the XII Templars have the power and the advanced knowledge of initiation. I think they are the ones that watch the *Holy Book and the Key*. It is possible that Salvatore is planning revenge," Emanuel added with big concern.

"It seems that he is our enemy and we have to take that seriously," John said. "You are right! He is a very dangerous man. I want no more debate on this subject in public places. We must be careful and keep all information strictly confidential. He could have spies walking around and listening. I worked hard to get to this point and I would feel very bad if someone screws up our plan," Benedict added with concern.

"What about Hans and Jorgen in Munich?" John asked.

"I think they are hiding something and I don't trust them. They haven't come up with any reasonable solutions in regards to our decoding plan," Benedict pointed out.

"Perhaps they're busy with something else. It seems like we can't count on anyone," Emanuel added, smiling.

"Trust me it is better that way. My mom always said if you want to do it right you better do it yourself," John replied with smile. "She was right. Let's drink that cold coffee now and go home," Benedict said.

"I always drink cold coffee because I never have time to drink it when it's hot," John replied and laughed.

"You're right old friend, I've never seen you drink a cup of hot coffee," Benedict smiled.

"If you don't mind, I would like to stay over the weekend. On Monday I will go back to London," John said.

"I'm glad that you decided to come in the first place. You can't imagine how important it was for me. You saved me another few years of hard research. I want to thank you for that, John," Benedict said.

"That is what friendship is about. It is my pleasure to contribute to our mission and only three of us know where we stand so far," John replied confidently.

"How is Chris doing with his quantum computer and that **element Q**?" Benedict asked.

"He is okay but still struggling with this element. He and his friends tried to analyze this new stuff but it doesn't fit any description of the existing ones. It is a big problem," John said.

"I'm sure he will find something very soon. He is a very talented scientist," Benedict added happily as they reached home.

"The house and the garden are very charming," John said.

"You will like it here. It is a quiet place and the air is filled with the aroma of wild flowers all day long, you will sleep like a baby," Benedict said laughing.

"I can feel the magic already," John replied.

"I will prepare an early lunch for us. Meantime, you take care for yourselves and relax," Emanuel announced as he went straight to the kitchen. He pulled from the refrigerator a few eggs, some tomatoes, bread, and butter. Then he reached for a few plates piled up on the shelf above his head. Charlotte and Peter ran excitedly into the kitchen.

"Hi Emanuel. Do you need any help?" Charlotte asked. "Sure, can you beat those eggs with a fork and Peter, can you bring fresh dill and parsley from the garden? When you come back I would like you to cut those tomatoes for me," Emanuel asked.

"Yes sir!" Peter rebuked and left.

"Did you pick your friend up from the airport?" Charlotte asked.

"Yes, we did. You will meet John soon. He went to change his clothes. We stopped on the way in cafe Mirabelle for quick coffee," Emanuel added.

"Mirabelle has very good chocolate cakes but they cost a lot. Once a month we shop there for good cake. Emanuel, I'm already finished mixing the eggs. What do you want me to do next?" Charlotte asked.

"You can slice fresh bread. It is crispy and smells really good. When I was young, my mother baked fresh bread every week. It was so delicious," Emanuel said smiling. Peter ran back to the kitchen and said, "Here is your fresh dill and parsley. Now I can slice the tomatoes and perhaps some green onion."

"I like your enthusiasm Peter. You will need this positive attitude in the boarding school. We are almost ready. Let's put plates, forks and knives on the table. I will call our friends to come over," Emanuel said and left. Peter set the table as Charlotte served everyone as they gathered into the kitchen and sat at the table ready for prayer. Emanuel and Benedict said a few words in Latin and then John was introduced to Peter and Charlotte.

"I heard that you're going to the boarding school in Rome. Are you excited?" John asked.

"Sure, I am. I will be one of those famous Templars," Peter exclaimed and jumped off his chair a

74

bit. "Me too and I'll have plenty of new friends," Charlotte added and clapped her hands.

"I'm glad that you're really excited about it. Your future will look even brighter from now on. I can see a lot of new opportunities for both of you," John added with bold optimism.

"It is the right choice for young people especially today. I would say it is the right place for both of you. Just remember, you must try your best!" Emanuel said as he glanced at both of them. Then he thought they don't know how tough it is going to be.

"Indeed, it will be a challenge for both of you. But you're brave kids, and I believe in you," Benedict added with a serious tone in his voice.

"I like challenges," Peter said.

"Me too," Charlotte added.

"That's good to hear but let's enjoy our food right now," Benedict said.

"You're a good cook, Emanuel," Charlotte said.

"Who will cook for us at the boarding school?" Peter asked.

"The school has professional cooks and a huge dining hall. They serve three meals a day, you will never be hungry," Emanuel said as he shook his head.

"I already like it," Peter announced with a happy smile.

"I think I'm finished. I have some work in town I have to take care of so please excuse me. Emanuel I will leave it to you to entertain John for the time being. Thank you again," Benedict said. He had something very serious on his mind.

"You should thank Charlotte and Peter as well.

They helped me with the cooking," Emanuel said.

"Thank you children," Benedict said with short smile and departed from the table.

"I'm done as well. Thank you to all of you. Please excuse me. It was as long trip and I would like to rest up a bit," John said and left to his room. Emanuel and the kids cleaned up the table and washed all the dishes.

Emanuel went to his room and took a short nap as well. Charlotte and Peter went to the garden to play ball. Cardinal Benedict headed into town, in search of Monk Salvatore. The time was an essence, he thought.

"Where are you going Father?" Charlotte asked.

"I'm going to town to look around. Don't worry, I'll be back soon. Be good!" he said, smiling.

"Can I go with you? I know my town very well and I can show you around," she said.

"That won't be necessary, my child. Trust me, I'll be okay," he added with a smile as he walked away, waving his hand at her. Charlotte watched him until he vanished around the corner. Just as he was about to cross the street, two other priests approached him and talked for a moment. It looked like they were friends. She recognized them it was Father Rafael and Father Dominique from the local church. But she remembered that he mentioned he didn't have any friends in town. Perhaps they met at the funeral. It seemed a bit strange, she thought. Charlotte became suspicious but reassured herself he would be back soon. A few hours had passed, and there was no sign of Father Benedict. Worried she thought maybe he got lost in the city so she went to look for him. She knew every restaurant and every shop in town but he was nowhere to be found. He just simply vanished into the proverbial, *black hole.*

Father Benedict didn't come back that evening. Charlotte worried that maybe he was kidnapped or even killed. He had disappeared the same way Father Salvatore did, she thought. Deeply concerned, she went to the post office with the magic key Father Benedict gave her and found the corresponding box number. She opened it, took out a small leather case and left for home. She checked to make sure no one was following her. Her heart was beating fast. As soon as she arrived home, she ran to her room, and locked the door. She realized that her little bible book was in Father Benedict's room upstairs.

She ran to his room and looked around but the book wasn't there. Maybe, Father took it with him, she thought. She noticed a few pages of the translation and took them. He said it must be kept secret. She looked around to see if she missed anything important but there was nothing there. She noticed that Father Benedict didn't have many personal items either. She ran to her room downstairs, and began to search on her own. She opened the black suitcase, and found a letter which read,

"My Dear Charlotte and Peter,
I write out of fear that my life may be in danger. Since I have entrusted and confided my secret too, I sincerely believe that it will stay with you. To show my appreciation, I'd like to pass on a little inheritance to your mother for your future. It will give you comfort for the rest of your life. However, one day you must learn

77

the *secret code*, I wrote in my **Black Book**, and you must memorize it. Do not write it on any piece of paper as it could be very dangerous. It will open a new window for your prosperity. My friends will contact you soon with a special assignment. You must trust them, and follow their instructions. It's important! When you're sixteen, you will join the **Secret Society of Knights**, *in Rome*, just be ready. You must become a monk in order to join them but this part will be taken care of by my friends. They're experts in this and they'll train you accordingly. After six years completion of the higher education, you'll be ready for your *mission* of *life and death*. Peter, you will join the **XII Omega Templars**. It is up to you on you how far you go. Charlotte will work undercover in the *Vatican Headquarters* as a liaison. I believe in you, and you should do the same. The details of your mission will be given to you when the time is right. I wish you a lot of luck. Remember to work hard! I'll miss both of you. Maybe, one day I can meet you in Rome when the time is right.

Your friend, Father Benedict."

She understood clearly the Cardinal's message. The new chapter of her and Peter's life has just been opened. With her mind set to success, she ran to Peter's room. "Peter, read this letter, from Father Benedict. He mentioned if anything happened to him we must get from his mail box the suitcase with the secret documents inside. We must hide this suitcase in a safe place. I saw him yesterday when he was on his way to town. He told me that he'd be back soon and he hasn't come back. Maybe, he isn't coming back. After you finish reading we should go to the attic and read his **Black Book**. We don't have much time. On Monday morning, we're leaving for Rome with Father Emanuel. Let's go!" she said. "What if he comes back tonight? We should wait a bit longer," Peter replied.

"Peter read the letter," Charlotte insisted.

"Okay, I'll read the letter," Peter replied.

Charlotte sat on the wooden chair and waited patiently. Peter concentrated on reading and as he continued to read, he smiled. He was excited at the idea of becoming one of those XII Templars. Charlotte interrupted with an enigmatic smile, "Don't be too excited Peter!"

"Why not, can you imagine our life will turn around one hundred eighty degrees?"

"All right Peter. I'm excited too but let's go to the attic!"

"Okay, let's go! But what if he comes back tonight?" Peter asked.

"I told you, he is not coming for at least a week."

"How do you know?"

"Just be quiet Peter. You better take the flash light and camera. We should take a few pictures in case."

"Just wait! Let me look for my camera in the closet. I got it!" Charlotte opened the attic and they quietly snuck in.

"Peter, lock the door! We don't want any intruders." Charlotte moved the wooden floorboard, and picked up the **Black Book**. Peter took out the ancient scrolls and a map.

"Charlotte can you open the scrolls and hold

79

them open. I'll take a few pictures. Then open the ancient map and hold it." The cameras flashlight was powerful. They took several pictures.

"Okay, I think we're done. Let's read the *Black Book* now."

"You read it, Peter. I like when you read."

"Okay, since you insist. It starts with Part One. 'My parents died when I was only six. Within a week I ended up in the local orphanage with hundreds of other kids. Some of their parents had also died in different type of accidents. One rainy day a few monks sent by the Vatican came and took me and a few others to the boarding school in Rome. At first they checked our right feet to see if the letter T was there. I was told later T stands for Templar. They saw my foot and whispered something to each other and then they took some of us with them. I had a distant family in town but they were scared to take me to live with them. I didn't know why they were so scared. The trip to the Vatican was long and I was tired. In a new school, I met a lot of nice friends. However, each day seemed like eternity for me. I thought, I would never grow up and always be six. Christmases were the only good time I remembered because my uncle and aunt visited me and brought me plenty of good chocolates which I shared with my friends. I always asked my uncle to take me home but he told me that I must stay there to become a man. I cried each night but it didn't help and I would run to my room, and sneak under the bed." Peter paused and said, "Charlotte I'll skip that part and go a bit further, maybe to another chapter. We don't have enough time to read his biography right now. "Okay, let's do that," she added and Peter continued his reading.

     '*Life in Vatican* City became more complicated than I could ever have imagined. I worked twelve hours a day in the Vatican Secret library. I was rather enslaved by the older ranking monks. However, I tried to enjoy every moment spent in the library. The languages I studied were different from the Latin or Italian used by the other monks or the higher priests. I was advanced in the study of languages and ahead of the average monk. I thought I was blessed and better than anyone else. Finally, one day I was asked to do the translation of a very old and rare piece of an ancient bible, and the secret scrolls. I did a good job and was proud of myself. But then I had to work longer hours. Many times I slept in the chair I worked in. No one noticed. Soon, by accident, I discovered the Secret Society called the *XII Omega Templars* which was operating in one of the two towers. I learned a little bit about them but it was taboo. No one ever talked about them.

     One night, around two a.m., I was still working in the library. I was asked to drive one dying monk to the hospital. He had high fever and needed an emergency surgery for his appendix. I found out later that he was one of the XII Omega Templars. While he was dying, I taught from him some of the oldest perhaps most powerful spoken words of God which at the time I didn't fully understand even though I was an expert on ancient languages. I didn't know what kind of language he spoke but I wrote every word on a napkin, I found in the car and then I hid it in my sock. Later when I got back to my room, I rewrote all the words in my *Black Book*. I put a note in the margin; do not copy these words under any circumstances. It could bring bad luck or even a curse to anyone who dares. It would be better to memorize them. I discovered later that these words can do miracles. If you spell them you'll be able to multiply any object including money, bread, wine, and more. I couldn't believe it. Then I remembered what I learned from the holy books. When Jesus spoke those words, he could feed five thousand people or more with one loaf of bread. However, whoever will abuse this secret code will be punished by death." Peter paused again and said, "Charlotte did you hear that?"

"Sure, I did! What are we going to do? I can't read this language. Father Benedict said it's like Latin or Aramaic."

"Maybe, I should take a picture," Peter suggested. "I don't think it is a good idea Peter."

"It's okay. I'll keep it secret and no one will ever see it only you and me," Peter said and took a few pictures of those magic words.

"Okay, you made your point," Charlotte said with approval. "Can you imagine that one day when we learn how to read these words we can do the magic ourselves?" Peter concluded.

"Sure, if we come back from Rome," Charlotte replied.

"It could even be earlier. Let me continue the story." Peter read more chapters but it was getting very late and finally they fell asleep.

The next morning Charlotte whispered, "Wake up Peter."

"I'm awake! Let's go for breakfast. I think Father Emanuel is making something good. I can smell fresh garlic bread and fried eggs," he replied.

"First we must put all these treasures back, and cover the floor with dust. I want to be sure that everything is secured," Charlotte said with concern as she took a duster to spread the old dust evenly. When they were finished, they ran downstairs to the kitchen where everyone was waiting for them at the table.

"Good morning," Charlotte said.

"Good morning Charlotte, good morning Peter. How are you doing on this great Sunday morning?" Emanuel asked.

"We're doing great! I'm very hungry," Peter replied. "Me too," Charlotte added with smile.

"Good, we have plenty of good food on the table. I hope you will remember this breakfast for a long time. I made my favorite spinach salad and I want you to eat everything because scientists say it is very healthy. Tomorrow we're leaving for Rome," Emanuel added decidedly.

"I will miss all of you. It's going to be hard for me to be alone in this big house. But I will visit you in Rome, every Christmas. Charlotte, Peter, be sure to write me long letters, every week. I want to know how you're doing out there and if you need anything," Alice said with sadness in her voice.

"Don't worry mother. We'll be fine," Charlotte replied graciously. "Yes, mother. Don't worry! You're the best Mother!" Peter added happily, and gave his mother a big kiss.

"I'm sure, they will be fine Alice. Trust me they will be in good and safe hands. You'll be proud of them one day," Emanuel said with self assurance.

"I want to believe you, Father, but it's a difficult

time for me," she said and shed a few tears.

"Kids, if you like you can each take a small suitcase. But take only a few of your favorite things," Emanuel added cheerfully.

"Okay," Peter said and ran to his room.

"Can I take my toys?" Charlotte asked.

"Just only a few; in school you'll be very busy and there will be not much time to play with your dolls. But you can have them at your bed side," Emanuel said.

Charlotte went to her room to pack a few favorite things. She will miss her room and her books. She sat on her bed and thought, what would happen if Monk Salvatore comes back and looks for his book everywhere, he might discover the treasure hidden in the attic. Maybe she should find a new secret place for them. She thought about her summer being cut short. There will be no more fun in her small town where she has grown up. Suddenly her thoughts were interrupted as Peter ran into her room and asked,

"Charlotte, do you want to go for fishing with our neighbor, Tom, to the local river? You know he does this every Sunday morning since his wife passed away. Let's go! We can have some fish for dinner and Father Emanuel will fry them. I'm going, anyway," Peter said. "You go and have fun. I'll pack my suitcase. I'm still thinking what to take," she replied. "Okay, but don't think so hard. Tell mom, I went fishing with Tom." "I will! See you later, Peter."

Everything was going by the book at least she thought that way. She went to the rose garden to pick some fresh berries for the afternoon cocktail. Soon she filled her basket with fresh fruit and then lay down

84

on the green grass under the huge pine trees. She felt good as her mind shifted immediately to the boarding school in Rome. She wondered what the new place would be like. She closed her eyes and imagined her new school and new friends. The sun was flickering between long tree branches touching and soothing her face. Crickets and grasshoppers played their familiar tunes and the birds performed their opera pieces over and over again. She was happy again. The strong invigorating aroma of fresh roses and the slight breeze put her into a short lethargic sleep. It was the perfect human-nature relationship. However, the moment didn't last long as she was awakened by Peter running into her with a basket full of fresh fish.

"Charlotte, open your eyes and see how many fish we caught. It was quick. I haven't seen anything like that for long time and we got some crabs too. Tom got another two buckets of fish. He said he will give us some more later."

"How nice of Tom; let's tell Father Emanuel. He will be happy to make something special for dinner," Charlotte said admiring his catch.

"Sure, let's do that," Peter agreed. Emanuel and John were coming back from their long walk around town. They came closer, wondering what Peter had in the bucket.

"Peter, where did you catch so many beautiful fish? Indeed, it will make a great dinner. I like trout and herring. I can help you carry the bucket. It must be heavy," John asked and took the bucket from Peter.

"Our neighbor, Tom, took me fishing at the local bay. He does that every Sunday morning. He has two more buckets full of fish. We better hurry and cook them, he is bringing us one more bucket in an hour, he said."

"How nice of Tom to share his fish with his neighbors, surely God will bless him for that," Father Emanuel added very seriously. "We caught a lot of crabs too. I think I got one hundred of them and I know how to cook them," Peter enthusiastically announced.

"I love crabs, and I will help you cook them. Sounds like we're going to have a crab party tonight and perhaps tomorrow too," Father Emanuel added with energy.

"Crabs are my favorite! I'm good at making crab salads. I'll be happy to help you," John added.

"I already picked fresh berries and I'll make a perfect cocktail," Charlotte said. "Okay, everyone get to work. It will be our last remarkable dinner together in this charming house. I'll miss it for sure. But trust me; there is nothing better than fresh fried fish with chopped garlic and a splash of oil with fresh squeezed lemon plus a bit of salt with pepper. Sometimes simpler is better," Emanuel proudly said. Meantime, Peter boiled the water with green dill, garlic, salt, and pepper for the crabs. Emanuel and John ran to the rescue as the crabs were very aggressive and were escaping from the big bowl. Obviously the crabs didn't feel as if they wanted to contribute to anyone's dinner. Within ten minutes the crabs were in the hot water and almost ready to be served. Everyone sat at the dinner table for this special crab-fish fiesta. Indeed, it was delicious and the aroma of fresh spices was improbable.

John and Emanuel were reminiscing their youth, and brought a lot of laughs to everyone at the dinner table. Then Mrs. Alice asked, "I wonder where Father Benedict is?"

"He had some business in town for a few days. He will be back sometime next week," Emanuel explained.

"Oh, I see. I thought maybe he left us without saying goodbye," Alice added.

"Alice, I would like to thank you for your hospitality. I really enjoyed every moment here. Please, do not worry about Charlotte and Peter. They will do really fine. They are going to the best catholic school. It has a great reputation," Emanuel added once more with confidence.

"I already miss both of them but as you said I'll see them for Christmas," Alice added with a bit of smile on her face.

"Everything will go well," Father Emanuel assured her with a calm tone in his voice. He sounded like he could convince even his own enemy.

"I have trust in you," she added confidently.

"Okay, kids, you can help me wash dishes and after that you are dismissed for the rest of the day," John said seriously but with softness in his voice.

"Okay, we're ready. Let's go Charlotte," Peter said and they ran to the kitchen pushing each other playfully. "Slow down!" John shouted and added,

"Peter would you put the left over fish, and the crabs in the refrigerator?" Charlotte rinsed each dish and Peter wiped them off with a paper towel. It didn't take them more than thirty minutes to clean, and restore the kitchen to its pristine condition.

"Thank you children, you did a wonderful job cleaning. I believe you won't have any problem adjusting in the boarding school," Father Emanuel said.

"We're easy to deal with; right Charlotte. However, I will miss those crabs," Peter replied, smiling. "Yes we are easy. I will miss those crabs too, Peter," she added.

"Don't worry. They serve crabs from time to time in the boarding school. Would anybody like to play tennis with me?" John asked politely on his way to the garden.

"I would!" Charlotte said and followed him. Peter glanced through the window and smiled. They played tennis together quite well. Charlotte was only twelve but was a good player. Peter went to his room to pack a few things; a few favorite books, a couple of shirts and two pair of jeans. He hesitated for a moment, wondering if he packed well. He had a few toys he liked, but was afraid that his new friends might laugh at him when they found he still played with toys. He thought it would be better not to take any. Indeed, he was excited about the trip and the new life awaiting him. He lay on his bed, closed his eyes and began to dream about his future school.

Monday morning the local birds began their ritual gathering on the chestnut tree branches for their morning chat. Perhaps they were discussing family matters or the neighbor's scandals. Soon everyone in the house was awake. Peter and Charlotte went about their usual morning ritual of getting ready for the day. Alice made breakfast for everyone and hurried about the house getting ready for work. She kissed Charlotte and Peter goodbye.

"Give my best regards to John and Father Emanuel," she said on her way out. "We will. We love you mother! Don't worry! We'll be fine," Peter shouted. Charlotte gave her a big hug to cheer her up. Alice turned around and hurried out of the door with tears flowing down her face.

Soon Father Emanuel and John joined Peter and Charlotte. "Good morning. Who made such a nice sandwiches?" John asked.

"My mother, she was in a hurry to get to work but she said goodbye to both of you and apologized for not doing this in person," Peter said.

"It's okay. All of us must make a living and today everything is expensive. I've always thought that this world should be different, better, not too materialistic. We've created so many unnecessary problems in our everyday life and now have a difficult time dealing with them," Father Emanuel said with a smile.

"I believe all people should live in harmony. What time are you leaving?" John asked.

"Our plane leaves at ten a.m. We have almost two hours before our departure," Father Emanuel said.

"I think mine is at ten thirty a.m. We can leave together to the airport. I always like to be early otherwise I get nervous," John said.

"Okay, it's a good idea. Kids, are you ready?" Father Emanuel asked.

"Yes but it is only 8 a.m. We still have plenty of time," Charlotte said.

"Maybe, one day, I can visit you in Rome for

Christmas," John said.

"That would be nice! We can play tennis," Charlotte said. "That would be great. I haven't been in Rome for at least two years. It would be a good reason for me to go back," John said.

"I think you should definitely come visit me. Our secret society has the annual meeting once a year in June. You will meet some interesting people from all over the world. You could stay in our guest house. Now, kids, would you help me clean again before we leave? When your mother comes home this afternoon the house should be in pristine condition. We have exactly thirty minutes and then we have to go," Father Emanuel said.

"Thank you Emanuel for your invitation. I will definitely try to be there for Christmas. We'll keep in touch. I will finish preparing for my departure to London. See you in awhile," John said as he rushed to his room. The time went by fast and everyone was ready to go. Charlotte locked her door and put the key in her pocket positive that she will need it in the future. "I'll miss this place," Charlotte stammered.

"I heard you Charlotte. You should think positive," Father Emanuel whispered. As he glanced at her, he saw a few tears in her eyes. However, he didn't make any remarks to her as he knew it was normal. They all put their bags in the car and took their seats. There wasn't much conversation in the car as each of them was lost in their own thoughts. Father Emanuel contemplated Charlotte. He knew that the freedom and wild life of this spirited, small town girl is probably over for good. She isn't aware of that yet as the new chapter of her life was just opened the moment she locked the door and put the key in her pocket. Who knows if the same door will ever be open again? Maybe, never! He thought. Then his mind shifted to Peter who was more determined than Charlotte. But he thought will Peter be able to face the real hardships of monastery life. Father Emanuel speculated for a moment. They arrived at the airport and John interrupted the peaceful atmosphere,

"Okay, here we are! I hope you'll have a pleasant and fast trip to Rome. Charlotte, Peter I'll miss you but surely I will see you in December. Remember, try your best despite the circumstances, I have faith in you and know you'll make it! See you Emanuel." John said with a big smile on his face.

"Have a nice trip yourself," Emanuel added on his way. Peter and Charlotte said goodbye. The small plane awaited them. They got in and sat in very comfortable soft armchairs. The steward served them soft drinks and soon the plane took off. "Are the two of you comfortable?" Father Emanuel asked.

"Yes! This is my first time on a plane," Peter said. "Me too," Charlotte added. "You will be fine. In four hours we will be in Rome. If you like you can take a nap. When you wake up we will be there and we will all be very busy soon," Father Emanuel said with a smile.

"When I am busy the time goes by fast!" Peter said.

"You are right Peter," Father Emanuel added. They were comfortable and watched the new world from the plane's windows. Soon they fell into a long nap which lasted until they landed in Rome. As soon as the plane touched Italian soil, Peter and Charlotte opened their eyes. They took a taxi to the center town of Rome and from there they decided to walk. Father Emanuel introduced to them all of the major historical buildings, the opera house, the best shops and nice restaurants on the way to their new school. They marveled as they heard the sound of the Italian language everywhere they went. The most popular words were; Grazie. Thank you, and Per Favore. Please. They stopped at the street kiosk to buy a mineral water and listened Father Emanuel spoke Italian to the vendor. Every time he spoke, he would translate it to Charlotte and Peter.

"Posso avere dell'aqua minerale?" Which means; May I have a mineral water? Then he asked again, "Ha una misura piu piccola?" Which means; Do you have a smaller size? Then Charlotte asked, "Can we send a postcard to our mother. She will be very happy to get one."

"Indeed a splendid idea. Let me ask if they sell one here," Father said. "Arete cartoline? Do you have postcard? Quanto costa? How much does it cost?" He paid the bill and they kept walking.

"Thank you Father," Peter said. "You're welcome," he replied.

"Peter, did you bring the camera?" Charlotte asked. "Oh, I forgot! I left it in the attic, hanging on the hook's wall." "How could you forget? It is so important. We could've taken a lot of pictures and sent them to mother," Charlotte said disappointed.

"I have a camera, and I will ask someone to take a few pictures. Don't worry," Father Emanuel replied. "How splendid" Charlotte replied happily.

"Potrebbe scattarci una fotografia, per favore?

Which means, Sir would you take our picture please? "Grazie. Thank you!" Father asked politely and then added, "I think we have some good looking pictures. Now we need to get to the school. It's just ten minutes away." It was a beautiful, sunny afternoon, perfect for a walk. A lot of people were walking by and laughing.

Chapter 5. Life in the Alexandrian Theological Academy, Rome, Italy
Boarding School

When they'd finally reached their destination, Father Emanuel said in a calm voice,

"This is the famous '*Alexandrian Theological Academy,*' the XIII century Monastery established by the Romans. In fact it is named after the real **Alexandrian Theological School** established two thousand years ago in Alexandria, Egypt. It was originally run by hermit monks and gained a great reputation.

Let's get into the monastery first and later I will show you your student's quarters. This beautiful carved wooden door was originally made in Egypt by a monk, very talented artist and brought to Rome in XIII century. At first glance you can see the church doesn't look modern. It was built from white heavy rocks and the walls are painted with Saints frescoes in bright and pastel colors. The stained glass depicts the holy family's life. To your right is a carved stone pulpit where the priest explains the Scriptures to students and other catechumens.

The church has a few different sanctuaries. You probably recognize this huge scene of the sacrifice of Isaac, and on the other wall is a scene depicting Abraham receiving Holy Communion. As you can see so many different holy paintings all over the walls and finally on each column you can see embedded stone crosses. We have two chapels here, one of St. Mary and the second one of St. Peter. Most of our students come here for their daily prayers. Finally we have a library here containing a few thousands ancient manuscripts and other books written in Coptic, Greek, Arabic, Hebrew and more. The most exiting thing right here is this tower called, *Tower of the Monks* for centuries it has been the abode of solitaries. Inside the tower is a very old well with fresh water which has the ability to give anyone full body renewal. We call it a miracle well. You must be careful not to drink too much because you could become too young.

We have also here two refectories accessible to church goers. If you look through the window you can see our guest house where our special guests stay from time to time. When your mother comes to visit, she can stay out there," Father Emanuel concluded with a big smile.

"Father, what are all those written inscriptions about," Peter asked.

"I'm glad that you asked. This one written above the door said; Regna Firmat Pietas means; Piety Strengthens the Nation; the other one to your right; Benedictio Domini Divites Facit stands for; The Lord's Blessing Gives Wealth. And that one above the altar; Justus and Judex stand for; *Let the Lord be the*

Judge. Okay! Now I'll show you to your student's quarters. They are separated by big walls. From this point on, you will only see each other once a year at our Christmas party. Let's go! I'll register you first, Charlotte and then we'll register you, Peter. We must go first to the Principal's office," Father Emanuel said.

They walked through the alley with beautiful chestnut's trees on each side. In the middle was a wild green garden filled with white aromatic gardenias.

"Here we are," Father said as they stood in front of an old, heavy, mahogany door with an iron door knob. Then he added, "I want you to read this inscription taken from the Genesis written on the door. Charlotte would you like to try?"

"Yes Father, '*Behold, I have given you every plant yielding seed, on the surface of all the earth and every tree which has fruit yielding seed.*'"

"Isn't it beautiful?" Emanuel asked politely. "It is," Peter said as they entered the principal's office. On the wall just above the principal's head the *Ten Commandments* were written in bold black letters. Charlotte knew them very well and hoped that Father Emanuel would not ask her to read them out loud. She knew she had sinned but couldn't think of any at that moment. Her thoughts were interrupted by Father Emanuel again,

"This will be your principal, Sister Agnes. This is Charlotte and her brother, Peter. My dear Charlotte I must leave you here with Sister Agnes. I will go register Peter on the other side of the wall in the boy's dormitory. I hope you like it here and do well. I must say goodbye to you. If you have any problems you can talk to me but first please, talk to Sister Agnes. Good luck, my dear!" Father Emanuel said briefly and left.

"Good bye Peter! See you soon," Charlotte added with a smile. Peter looked into her eyes and smiled back as he followed Father Emanuel.

"Nice to meet you Charlotte, please, follow me, I'll show to you your room. You've arrived a few days earlier than the other students. Don't worry soon you'll have a roommate. We have a very diverse group of students. They come from France, England and many other countries. You will meet them soon, my child."

Charlotte followed Sister Agnes upstairs to her new room. Sister Agnes was tall and slender, and spoke as if she was an army General giving orders to the soldiers. Charlotte thought it might not be easy to deal with Sister Agnes. However, the place was nice and she liked it. The corridor was wide with high ceilings and white Gothic columns on each side. There were beautiful flower's arrangements in almost every corner. Sister finally stopped next to a green door and pulled out a key attached to a long chain that was wrapped around her waist. She opened the door with her key.

"This will be your room and this is your key. Do not lose this key under any circumstances. You will share this room with one of the new students and I hope for your sincere cooperation. Breakfast is served everyday at six a.m. But you must report to the courtyard every morning at five a.m. for the morning exercise. Be sure you're on time. Your lunch is at noon and dinner at six p.m. There will be no other food served between meals. I hope we clearly understand each other, Charlotte. Also it is mandatory that you only wear school uniforms. Put your things in your room and I'll see you in twenty minutes in my office for your new uniform."

"Yes, Sister Agnes," Charlotte replied. Sister left quickly and closed the door behind her. Above the bed, on the wall was a fresco of the Virgin Mary and below it was written, "Mother of God."

Charlotte sat on her new bed and unpacked her small suitcase. She hung her two dresses, two pants and one jacket in a small closet. The bathroom was small but would be good enough for two people. She must adopt herself to a new life now. Twenty minutes had passed and Charlotte ran downstairs to Sister Agnes' office.

"You're late five minutes! If I say twenty minutes I mean twenty minutes. Do we understand each other Charlotte?" Sister Agnes pointed out with a dictatorial tone in her voice.

"Yes, Sister Agnes. I will remember that next time."

"Okay. Have a seat. I want you to try this pleated red skirt, navy blue jacket, and red hat with blue ribbons. You are very petite; I think size two will suit you well. Also I'd like to remind you that no other clothes are allowed in this school. You'll have three sets of school uniforms. Every Monday, Wednesday and Saturday at eight p.m. you must hang your dirty uniform on the hanger and put them outside your door, on the door's knob. Our cleaning service will pick up your old uniform and replace it with the clean one. What size shoe do you wear?"

"I'm a size six," Charlotte replied.

"Okay, here is three pair of the navy blue Oxford shoes. Please, go to the changing room and try everything on. I'd like to see how it fits you."

"Yes, Sister Agnes," she said and went to change her clothes. After a few moments had passed, Sister Agnes called out, "Are you ready, Charlotte? Why it is taking so long? I don't have time to fool around. I have plenty of work," Sister said.

"I'm ready," Charlotte replied as she quickly popped out of the dressing room. "Okay, it looks perfect! Now go to your room. Wait! I almost forgot. This is your exercise outfit, navy blue shorts and the same color t-shirt and blue socks. Also pick up your swimsuit for swimming classes. Now you can go to your room. We will see you at six p.m. for dinner in the dining room just around the corner. You will find it, you are a bright girl! Also, here is your bathroom robe. The towels are in your room. They will be cleaned twice a week. Just remember everything I said. I hate to repeat myself twice."

Charlotte smiled a bit and then quickly departed to her room. She undressed herself and took a quick shower. With relief she lay on the bed and glanced at the Saint Mary Fresco on the wall. It is beautiful, she thought. She set the clock ten to six and then closed her eyes for a short nap. She was exhausted and fell asleep quickly. She had a short but vivid dream in which the fresco of Virgin Mary walked off the wall and Mary spoke to her.

"Welcome my child. I'm glad to see you here; you will be a nice addition to our life in the monastery. I will be your guide to a brighter future. Just ask me for help when you're in trouble. She smiled and gently touched Charlotte's face. The clock rang at exactly ten to six waking Charlotte up from her dream. She opened her eyes, dressed herself in jeans and a t-shirt, and ran to the dining room. As she opened the door, she noticed a few nuns in navy blue habits sitting at the long table glancing at her suspiciously.

"Good afternoon Sisters," Charlotte said.

"Good afternoon Charlotte. Please join us. I would like to introduce you to Sister Cleopatra, Sister Eleonora and Sister Claudia," Sister Agnes proudly announced.

"How do you do?" Charlotte replied.

"Thank you, we are fine. How do you like our school?" Sister Claudia asked. "I like it," Charlotte replied.

"We hope you will do well," Sister Cleopatra added.

"Next time make sure you are dressed in your school uniform for dinner," Sister Agnes added despotically.

"Yes, Sister," Charlotte replied.

"Tomorrow new students will arrive and our student orientation will take place on Friday. We have very good cooks here. They make the best homemade soups and special dishes consisting of a variety of vegetables, baked potatoes, barbecue chicken, lamb, and other delicacies. I believe you shouldn't have any complaints about the food. We've never had any in the past! Do we understand each other Charlotte?" Sister Agnes asked with a cynic smile.

"Yes, I understand," Charlotte replied.

"Now, Sister Eleonora will say a thank you

99

prayer. Please close your eyes and pray with us," Sister Agnes asked. Soon after prayer everyone enjoyed food. The two cooks came in and out of the dining room with dishes full of aromatic delicacies from fried chicken and French potatoes to homemade salads with Italian dressing. Charlotte was happy and enjoyed every bit of it. The food was good like her mother would make it. There was no conversation during dinner. The Sisters were silent all the time and only occasionally smiled. Charlotte was really hungry and finished her dinner fast. Sister Agnes glanced at her and pointed out with wonder,

"There is no reason to hurry. Be sure you enjoy your dinner Charlotte. Life is so uncertain and perhaps too short. Now, please wait for all of us until we finish our food." As the sisters were done with their dinner, Sister Agnes spoke again, "Now, dear Charlotte, I want you to help the cooks with whatever needs to be done in the kitchen."

"Okay, I will help them," Charlotte replied and walked slowly to the kitchen. Indeed, they had a lot of work to be done from dirty dishes to peeling potatoes and carrots. She knew she would be busy for two or three hours. They gave her an apron and she began to wash the dishes. Soon after that the cook Andrew asked her to peel potatoes. He said at least ten new students will arrive the following morning. Charlotte did well as she whistled a few popular tunes from time to time. There were a lot of potatoes to be peeled. She was getting tired and around eleven p.m. Andrew finally dismissed her. She went straight to bed and was so exhausted, she didn't dream that night. Tomorrow will be a new day for her. She didn't have to report for the morning exercise as the school hadn't officially started yet. However, she must go for breakfast at six a.m.

The next morning her alarm woke her up at five thirty a.m. She was excited because it was Tuesday and the new students should be arriving. She thought she would have more fun with girls her own age. She put on her new uniform and slowly walked down the stairs to the dining room. All the nuns were sitting at the table as though they hadn't left it from the night before. "Good morning Charlotte. The uniform suits you well. Please, join us for breakfast," Sister Agnes said and the other sisters nodded their heads in approval. "Good morning sisters," Charlotte said politely.

After the thank you prayer everyone enjoyed the hot porridge soup and cold ham sandwich with two slices of tomatoes. Suddenly Sister Agnes interrupted, "Charlotte, if you like you can keep me company today. In forty five minutes, I will greet the new students coming from the airport by bus. Would you like that?"

"I would like to!" Charlotte replied with excitement.

"I like your positive attitude, my dear. Let's go then! Please, wait for me outside in the garden," Sister Agnes announced in a cold voice. Charlotte went out and sat on the bench under the pine tree and listened to the singing birds which reminded her of her own countryside town. She thought about her mother and missed her. She decided that tonight she will write her a letter. Then she thought of Peter and wondered how he was doing with the other boys behind the wall. She must find a way to communicate with Peter, maybe she will ask Sister Agnes about it. Her thoughts were interrupted by Sister Agnes alarmed voice.

"Charlotte, are you there? Oh, here you are! Please, follow me. We are meeting them at the first bus stop at the end of this square which we call, Saint Andrews Square. You see we're almost there. However, we will wait about ten minutes. At least, we have a nice and sunny morning."

"It is beautiful right here and I really like it. I don't mind waiting," Charlotte said with self confidence.

"Oh, I think, I see the blue bus in the distance. It's probably the bus we're waiting for. Sometimes they come earlier especially when the plane is on time," Sister Agnes said. "I'm excited," Charlotte said.

"Me too, every year our students come from every part of the world. Last year we had plenty of students from Asia, Australia and Africa especially from Egypt whose Christian traditions are as old as two thousand years. It was a student exchange program and I believe quite beneficial for everyone. After completion of their education in our Academy, most of the students return to their own countries. I think it is a nice contribution and every year here is a bit different. The bus just arrived. Be ready!" Sister Agnes announced with a firm voice. She was quite excited herself. She must be lonely here when the students are gone. Although, she is a nice lady-nun but she is a bit despotic, Charlotte thought for a moment.

The bus stopped just a few inches from

Charlotte's feet and the driver opened the door. The girls exited the bus one by one laughing and joking. Sister Agnes pulled a list from her pocket and began calling out the girl's names, "Anne, Amelie, Arabelle, Antoinette, Brigitte, Claudine, Emilie, Julie, Madeleine and Sophie." Each of the girls answered her in kind.

"Okay, you are all here. Welcome to the Alexandrian Academy. This is my assistant Charlotte, if you have any questions please ask her. We are now in Saint Andrews Square. Please grab your luggage, line up, and follow me!"

Meantime, Charlotte noticed Father Emanuel and Peter as they arrived at the same bus stop. Within minutes another bus arrived full of boys. Charlotte glanced at Sister Agnes and asked, "Sister may I talk to Peter and Father Emanuel for a second, please."

"Sure, we'll wait for you but be quick about it," she added.

Charlotte hurried over to Peter. "Hi Peter! Hi Father, nice to see you again," she said.

"I'm glad to see you too. Excuse me; I must make sure all the boys have arrived."

"Hi Charlotte, how is everything going for you?" Peter asked. "I've been very busy since yesterday. But tonight I will write mother a long letter. Peter, I like your uniforms, nice navy blue pants, jacket and a white shirt with red tie and navy beret with red ribbon around. It is really nice. Did you ever think you'd be wearing a school uniform?"

"No but I like it. I like your outfit as well. I told you everything would be different here. I will have new friends soon. I'll talk to you later," Peter said and gave her a hug. Father Emanuel was busy calling out all the boys' names from his list, "Dominique, Etienne, Jerome, Patrick, Robert..."

"They are French too. I must go Peter. I hope to see you soon. Remember to write mother a letter once a week. Bye now!" she said and left.

All the girls followed Sister Agnes and Charlotte. Within a few minutes they reached the Academy.

"Okay, girls this is your new school, the Alexandrian Theological Academy. The majority of you will spend between five and seven years right here. Form one line and come into my office to register one by one. The official orientation will be on Friday. Charlotte could you please help me, as soon as I finish, I want you to distribute to each girl a new uniform including a robe and shoes."

"Yes! I remember where they are," she replied. Charlotte spoke to each girl and thought they all seemed very nice. She gave each one their new uniform. However, she liked the last one, Amelie, the most. "Amelie, I'm looking for a roommate, would you like to share a room with me?" she asked politely. "Sure," Amelie said.

"We will have so much fun. You will like my room. It has a nice view from the window. You can see all of St. Andrews Square and the opera house across street. Maybe one day we can go to the opera for Joseph Verdi, it's my favorite."

"I like opera too. Okay, I'm ready to go," she replied.

"Let me talk to Sister Agnes for a moment."

"I'll wait for you right here," Amelie said. Charlotte ran to Sister Agnes office and asked if she could be dismissed.

"Thank you, Charlotte. You've helped me a lot today. You're a very special girl and I admire your spirit and positive attitude. Did you find yourself a roommate yet?"

"Yes, actually I did. Amelie wants to share the room with me. She seems like a nice person."

"I'm glad to hear it, dear Charlotte. I told everyone lunch is at noon. Don't be late. Tomorrow, another group of students will be arriving, if you'd like you can help me again."

"Sure, no problem; see you later Sister," Charlotte replied and went to take Amelie to her room. "Amelie, let's go!" Charlotte said happily. "Okay, I'm coming, Charlotte." Amelie followed her dragging her luggage and her new uniforms. "Here we are! I think you will like this room. I feel it's special and there is no other room like ours. Tell me something about yourself."

"Wow I love the painting. I grew up with my grandparents in the South of France, in a small town called Belleville. My parents died in a plane crash when I was five years old. Last year my grandpa was killed on the street by a car. My grandma always said that life is a gift from God and we should appreciate it."

"Nice thought Amelie. But it is very tragic that our loved ones have left us so early. My father was killed at home just a month ago by some stranger. It happened so fast and now I'm here. I came here with my brother, Peter. I promised my mother that I would write her a letter every week. I should write one tonight, please remind me."

"It is a sad story, Charlotte. While you write your mother, I will write to my grandma. I love her very much and we only have each other. Let's go for a walk before lunch. I like to exercise every day and if you would like to keep me company it would be great."

"Sure! But trust me, we will be very busy here and we won't have time for too many extra activities. Did you hear that at five a.m. we must be at the courtyard for the morning exercise and at six a.m. we must be in the dining room for breakfast? Maybe on Sunday we will have some free time. We only have a few days of freedom because on Friday we have school orientation."

"Don't worry Charlotte, we will find time for fun, I'm an expert on making impossible things happen. I brought with me a small record player and a few nice records of lyrics and love songs. You'll like them. Let's go outside now."

"Okay! But we must wear uniforms all day long. I suggest you change your clothes now because later you won't have time."

"Okay, just give me a few minutes." Amelie ran into the restroom and a few minutes later came out dressed in her uniform.

"It looks good on you. Let's go!" Charlotte said.

"I'm not crazy about this uniform but if I must wear it, I will."

"Amelie, you look fine. Let's see the opera house first. We have exactly one hour for exploring. We have to be careful of the cars. As Charlotte and Amelie ventured out, they were amazed at all of the wonderful sights. Look at this beautiful Baroque

Rococo palace. I think it's a perfect place for the opera. Can you sing? Let's sing something from Verdi, perhaps Traviata will be good."

"I can sing and this is my favorite piece. Just listen, Pa, pa-aaa-aa-aa-o-la-la-la-o-o!!!! How do you like it?"

"It is splendid but a bit crazy. Look! Those boys stopped just to listen to your soprano voice. It's nice. Keep going Amelie." "You're not serious. Let's run! Crazy boys! I don't want to sing for them. Come on, Charlotte! Why are you laughing?"

"Those boys like you, Amelie." "But I don't like them. Let's go, Charlotte! Do you like ice cream? I see an ice-cream shop at the end of this square. I will buy you one. I speak a little Italian."

"Sure, I love ice-cream. Let's run!"

"Which one do you like? Pistachio, coffee or strawberry"

"I like pistachio!" "Okay! One pistachio in cone and one strawberry, please. Fate sconti per studenti? Do you give a student discount? Quanto costa? One hundred fifty liras. Grazie. Thank you. Charlotte, we got a twenty five liras student discount."

"It is good. Hm, the ice-cream is perfect. I can eat it every day. Thank you Amelie for being so generous."

"You're welcome, Charlotte. Would you like to sit on the bench out there?" "Okay! Let's sit and finish our ice-cream. What time is it?" "Eleven thirty don't worry. We still have plenty of time. Let's enjoy ourselves; we don't know when we will get another chance like this."

"You're a pessimist, Amelie but I understand

107

your point. How old are you?"

"I'll be twelve next month. How old are you, Charlotte?"

"I'll be twelve in December. Let's walk back we have only ten minutes. Thank you! It was a fun escape but I wish we had more time."

"Next time, trust me."

"Hello girls. How was your walk? Next time, be sure you let me know where you are going. Last year we had an unpleasant accident right here. Two girls went for a walk and never came back. They are still missing and the police haven't been able to find them. Just be careful out there with so many strange people walking on the street and not all of them are your friends. I will recommend you always walk in small groups for your own safety. However, next week you will be very busy and there will not be any time for walks. Now go and enjoy your lunch," Sister Agnes said with a smile.

As Charlotte and Amelie entered the dining room, they smiled as they saw all of the girls sitting at the table, and soon lunch was served. They sat next to Sister Eleonora. The cook Andrew brought out mushroom pizza, green salad, and orange juice. It tasted delicious. After lunch Sister Agnes called all the girls for a meeting in the auditorium.

"I would like to bring to your attention a very important safety issue in our campus facility. You must report to me or Sister Claudia if you are leaving the campus. Last year we lost two students. They left for a short walk and never came back. Be sure you walk in groups of four and always with Sister Claudia or Eleonora. Just a reminder for all of you, on Friday morning, at ten a.m. we will have our student orientation. Please, be on time. Now you are dismissed."

"Amelie, did you hear? No more solitary walks. There could be a kidnapper out there. I'm afraid, we have to be careful. I wouldn't mind walking with Sister Claudia. Don't you agree?"

"Sure! I didn't know about kidnappers here but I'm not afraid of them," Amelie replied. "Amelie, kidnappers are very dangerous. Back home, my teacher told me that there are rapists and killers in the world. I would rather put our adventures on hold for a few years. Don't you agree?"

"Okay, I'll agree with you for now. Perhaps we can do something else."

"I'd like to stay in my room for awhile and write a letter to my mother. I promised her."

"Okay, let's go and relax for a few hours. I can tell you some funny stories." "Great, I'm dying for really good stories," Charlotte replied, smiling.
The girls run upstairs to their room. Charlotte sat at the desk and wrote a long letter to her mother.

"**Dear Mother**, we're finally in Rome and I believe this ancient city has a spirit. Our school is very old and has character and personality. From my window I can see the opera house and hopefully one day I can go to see one of my favorite operas. Peter is in the boy's quarters in a separate building from mine. I saw him yesterday and he is very happy about the school and his new friends. I'm not going to see him often but I think we can trace messages between the buildings. I'll find a way. So far, I have plenty of French friends. I found a roommate and her name is

109

Amelie. She is nice and she likes adventures. I think we will do well together and become good friends. Our principal's name is Sister Agnes and she is very strict about discipline in our school. This Friday we will have student orientation and I will find out more about our new teachers. I will let you know more details in the next letter.

Don't worry about us. We love you and are looking forward to hearing from you soon. I hope you're doing well and everything is okay at home. How is Father Benedict doing? Is he still looking for Father Salvatore? Please write soon.

Love Charlotte."

"Amelie, I'm done with my letter. How about you," "I'm almost done. It always takes me some time to make sense of my writing. I must be careful what I write because my grandmother is very sensitive and doesn't like to hear any bad things. So, I can only write about good things. Maybe it is better that way. Don't you think so?"

"It depends, but if she is really sensitive it is better to not worry her too much. If she is old she could have a heart attack and we don't need that."

"Definitely, we don't! I want to see her on Christmas if possible. Sure, I already miss her very much."

"How do you feel about the school so far?" Charlotte asked. "I don't know yet. I came here to make my grandma happy. She said I must get a good quality education. She told me that it was her dream to put me in a good school. When she was young in her twenties she wanted to be a nun. But her mother asked her to get married and have children. She did but was unhappy whole her life," Amelie secretly confessed.

"How sad, I think that life is so uncertain for most of us. We can't predict our future but we can create it up to a certain point. With a bit of luck we can be very successful too."

"I like your optimism, Charlotte. I hope we can be good friends forever."

"I hope so too. Let's go for dinner. It is almost six p.m. Sister Agnes doesn't like when we're late."

"Let's hurry up."

Everyone was already in the dining hall sitting at the table. The cooks ran in and out with aromatic plates filled with barbecue ribs and mashed potatoes sprinkled with green dill and cucumber salad. The waiters served different juices and very appealing fruits cocktails. The most popular among the girls was the black berry one which they called the *Devil's Eyes*. This strange name wasn't welcomed by the nuns but they smiled and accepted it after awhile. Dinner was turbulent from loud conversations and excitement. The girls laughed freely and joked as they exchanged their school experiences and life stories. It was understandable as it was their first day in the boarding school. The nuns know it will not last as school starts in a few days and discipline will prevail. There will be no more talking at the table during breakfast, lunch or dinner. The nuns liberally accepted the noisy evening atmosphere but with a bit of bold skepticism. Soon all the girls left to their rooms and silence overtook the dining room and entire school for another twelve hours. Tomorrow everything will start all over again.

The morning was welcomed by the singing of exotic birds and the alarm clocks set at five a.m. for the morning exercise. The hall was filled with the cacophony of running girls. Sister Eleonora would be conducting the morning exercise routine and was already waiting for the girls in the garden. Everyone arrived wearing their shorts and t-shirts. Sister Eleonora gave the girls commands using her private whistle. She ran with them for fifteen minutes around the field and put them through different types of exercise routines. She was in great shape for a woman of her age. She was P.E. teacher for almost twenty years. The girls liked her and her liberal point of view on emotional and personal subjects. She was strict and tolerable at the same time. After 45 minutes of intensive exercise she dismissed them and the girls had fifteen minutes to play on their own. The girls would gather together and pick their favorite game to play, from jumping rope, hula hoop, and hide and seek.

Charlotte and the other girls would rhythmically repeat some popular kid's rhymes. Meantime, other girls would sit on the bench or into the circle and wait for their turn to play hide and seek. They had a lot of fun and learned more about each other.

After the games, the girls would run into the dinning room for breakfast. Charlotte mailed the letter to her mother on her way back. As soon as she slipped the letter into the mailbox, she felt some relief. She met Sister Agnes and asked her if she could call Peter from time to time. Sister told her that she has one phone in her office and would let Charlotte use it once a month and for no longer than ten minutes.

"Why for only ten minutes?" asked Charlotte.

"Because there is no reason to call anybody except in emergencies and it is important to work on your penmanship, so you should write letters more often," Sister Agnes replied and then she explained that the phone would be picked up accordingly on the other side of the wall by Monk Emanuel or his assistant Monk Antonius and then Peter would be called to the phone.

Charlotte was excited but couldn't express it. Wednesday and Thursday came and went by fast. Amelie and Charlotte went to town again but were accompanied by Sister Claudia. They went for a long walk and stopped for ice-cream on their way back. Sister Claudia was friendly and told the girls lots of exciting stories of Roman history, especially the Julius Caesar and Augustus era. Although she seemed exhausted, she talked all the way back to the school's facilities. Charlotte and Amelie were stunned by her youth, energy and enthusiasm.

Finally came Friday and at ten a.m. all the girls and nuns gathered in the auditorium for the orientation. Sister Claudia gave all the girls a tour of the classrooms and went through every single subject which will be taken by each student. She began her speech with a bit of a history,

"Welcome everyone to our famous Alexandrian Theological Academy. I like to tell you that our school is the younger sister to the oldest Catechetical School of Alexandria, in Egypt. The first Christian School of Alexandria which was originally founded by St. Mark himself around 180 AD. This school has been an important religious institution for many years. The

113

scope of this school was not limited to theological subjects, but science, mathematics, and astronomy were also taught. We were told that many famous scholars and many great teachers came out of that school. The native Egyptian Origen, who is considered the father of theology, was one of them. He wrote over six thousand commentaries of the Bible and his famous Hexapla as you may already know.

They spoke the Coptic language which spread throughout Upper Egypt. Today not only the Coptic priests but other qualified girls and boys are taught theology, languages, history, art, music, iconography and much more. This is only a little taste of the history you will be able to find in almost every book in our library. Now please follow me and I'll show you your classrooms. You will have many different subjects and teachers. Most of them are monks but some are sabbatical Professors coming from different universities and different parts of the world.

Trust me you will have a lot of fun. You'll have twenty different subjects you can choose from but twelve of them are mandatory. On the left side of this corridor are; science, math, physics, chemistry, geography and biology classrooms. On the right hand side are; Latin, Coptic, Greek, Aramaic, Hebrew, Italian and French classrooms. French was optional but we decided that this year it would be your mandatory language for the next four years. Also you can choose swimming, dancing, or ballet classes.

We also have in our facility a special program where the majority is the pure classical martial arts. We put a few students on this program each year. I don't see anyone yet qualified for this type of program but we are open and flexible, and we do make exceptions from time to time. Then for the next four years you will be advanced on every subject. You will start with level one and the second year you will move to level two, in the third year level three, and in the fourth year, level four. You will be sixteen when you finish your last level. Then after that the next four years will be advanced study on only six subjects. You will master these subjects to perfection and I believe apply them for the rest of your life. Just be ready for this adventure and good luck to all of you. If you have any questions, ask now or talk to Sister Agnes later. Each class will have only twelve students and be forty-five minutes long. You will move from one class to another within the fifteen minute intervals. Your classes will rotate every week. Here I have a copy of your classroom program for the first six months. Please, pick it up and be sure you put it on the wall in your room. We don't want to have any misunderstanding. I believe that you are going to study hard this year. Also I believe that this is the reason why you came here at the first place. You're dismissed now. Please, go to the library and pick the first set of your weekly books and notebooks. Be sure you are ready for the Saturday morning Latin classes. Have fun and see you for lunch."

Sure, it was a lot of information and the girls were exhausted. They went for lunch and tried to enjoy every bit of it. They thought maybe in the future there will be no time for lunch either. Indeed, they were overwhelmed by the weight of their future responsibility. However, soon after lunch each of them went to the library to take the necessary books

115

out. Then they walked to their room with heavy loads of books. Amelie asked Charlotte what she was thinking of all of that they'd been told so far. Charlotte replied in calm voice,

"Don't worry Amelie, we will make it! We are young and have nothing else to do in our life. This will definitely be a challenge for each of us and this is what I like about it. Perhaps the unknown is giving me more excitement after all. Can you imagine how smart you will be? And then it would really take a man to compete with you. Just think positive and think about all the privileges you will have in your life. Also you will posses all the privities of the higher knowledge which you will get right here."

"Charlotte, it sounds very simple and easy that you almost convince me that I can make it. But how I can handle all twelve subjects which come with stress, it requires a lot of discipline and self confidence. I am not sure if I have those two."

"Amelie, stop you are afraid and talking nonsense! Just think that you will be able to do it and without stress. Just imagine you are very successful and everything is easy. How about that," Charlotte said, laughing.

"You sound very convincing and I like your positive attitude. Yes, I try to think that it will be very easy for me. Thank you, Charlotte. It would help me focus. Let's talk about something else now. How is Peter doing?"

"He is doing great! I think he likes being here and he will make it. He has a lot of new friends and he seems very happy." "This is good news! I want to feel that way too."

"Let's go out just to relax and have fun talking. Amelie, would you take the blanket. We can lie down on the green grass and get an hour suntan. Put your swimsuit on. The weather is gorgeous," Charlotte said. "It is great idea! Let's go! I desperately need some fresh air and sun too. I can clearly hear Sister Claudia's voice in my head telling me that I will be too busy and have no time even to walk."

They walked to the garden and put the soft blanket on the green grass and then lay down with comfort. It felt good with warm sun rays flickering over their faces and the fresh aroma of wild flowers. Charlotte whispered, "I wish this precious moment would last forever." "Me as well, I love those lazy moments."

Chapter 6. Inside the Mind of Monk Salvatore

Monk Salvatore paused for a moment next to a tall pine tree to catch once more glimpse of Mrs. Alice's house. It was past midnight. His heart was excitedly pumping like an oil drill searching for black gold.

He thought to himself, '*Now or never.*' He must get inside the house to search for his **Holy Book** *Part 1* which he left with Charlotte. He'd found out that Cardinal Benedict stole some priceless documents before his escape from the Vatican Secret Library.

What could they be? Salvatore constantly weighed these questions in his mind. He looked around for safety. Only the lonely moon smiled at him.

He walked to the door turned the knob but it was locked. He glanced at the open window just above his head, on the second floor. It was the same window of the room he'd rented a month ago. He climbed with ease. He knew he was the best Spider Monk in the entire Vatican City.

Within a minute or less he was inside the room. He stood for a moment and thought of his new plan. 'What shall I do next? I must hurry before Benedict comes back.'

He peeked through the open door and spotted Mrs. Alice room downstairs. The door was half ajar and he could clearly hear her loud snores. He closed his door and looked frantically for his book. It must be here, somewhere, he whispered to himself constantly; talk to me, talk to me! He went through every single place he could think of. He found some of Benedict's belongings. But the book had seemingly vanished or perhaps someone stole it, he thought.

He sat on the wooden chair and tried to think where Benedict would hide his treasures. He got up and walked back and forth. Suddenly something clicked in his mind. He remembered there was an old attic at the end of corridor. He must go there.

The wooden floor was squeaking under his feet. He was a bit nervous. The beads of sweat formed on his forehead. He reached for the iron knob of the wooden attic door. He smiled and then slowly turned the knob to his right only to find out that the door was locked. 'Not good,' he whispered. He reached to his pocket for a flash light and a small metal pin he'd used to open almost every single door in the entire monastery. The door lock clicked easily.

He opened the door and looked around. The dust collected over many years covered the entire attic. The moon light penetrated through the partially falling roof. He searched every corner, every shelf and every hole. 'Where are you?' He whispered to himself. As he walked back and forth before he noticed that one wooden floor piece was moving under his feet. He picked the loose piece with his pocket knife and bingo! His eyes grew large when he saw many different pieces wrapped in leather waiting to be retrieved.

Still stunned he picked each piece one by one. He knew the pieces were priceless. They'd probably never seen the day light. He wrapped everything in his frock and returned to his former room. He found an old linen sock hidden in the closet and carefully placed each piece inside. It was time to go, he thought. He tightened the sock around his waist and was ready.

Then the unholy thought came to his mind. "No witnesses! They are thieves!" He whispered. "They stole my Holy Book. I hate them all and they never meant to give it back to me! I have no mercy for any of them; men, women or even children."

He pulled the matches from his pocket, ignited few and threw them onto the carpet, in the living room. The fire grew exponentially immediately spreading in every possible direction. He stood for a moment looking at the fire, smiling. He heard some noises in Mrs. Alice room. Why should he save her? So he decided to leave and quickly. She was part of the conspiracy against him also. As he was about to climb down he hesitated for a moment, thinking, maybe he'd forgotten something of value from the attic but now there was no time.

He climbed back quickly through the same open window and as he was about to hit the ground one of the neighbors came out and spotted him. The neighbor shouted,

"Thief! He must have ignited the fire! Call the police!" Then he grabbed his old rifle and began shooting at Salvatore. Salvatore run between the bullets climbing a wall, and leaped into the trees.

All the neighbors ran toward the burning house with buckets filled with water and a few hoses. They heard Mrs. Alice screaming for help but they couldn't do much as the roof suddenly collapsed. It would have killed anyone foolish enough to enter the conflagration hotter than the great gates of hell.

Meantime, Salvatore short of breath leaned against an old tree in the darkness. He heard the last bullets flying by him one after the other. 'I lost him,' he whispered to himself and ran off to the local mountains. Nearly safety he put his hand on the stolen treasures. He knew no one saw him in the attic and no one noticed for sure that he set the house on fire. It was dark. 'They just saw my shadow only!' He whispered to himself over and over again perhaps feeling a bit anxious. He had to do that there was no any other way to get these priceless pieces from Cardinal Benedict. He was lucky. Maybe it was luck that saved him. But if he must kill again he was ready.

Now sitting alone in one of the abandoned caves in the mountains he could study carefully the **Black Book** of Cardinal Benedict and examine the ancient maps, and *2000 year old scrolls*. Luck smiled on him again as he discovered an old forgotten tongue written by Benedict's hand in the **Black Book**. He repeated the sentence over and over again without understanding or knowing what that meant.

Unbelievably tired, his last thought was to make a wish. He spoke the wish aloud.

"I wish I have a twin brother that I can talk to." To his great surprise the image of Salvatore's twin appeared in front of his eyes. He didn't know if it was real. As he touched it he noticed that the image was transparent. He read the secret sentence again and made the same wish over and over. Several Salvatore's images appeared. He looked with disbelief and thought maybe he can use soon this new discovery to his advantage. He made successfully different wishes and he received them. His hands were full of gold and other precious rare stones from sapphires to emeralds. It was so easy, he thought. Now he had achieved endless power. No one can compete with him. He got what he'd always dreamed of. He will no longer be on the second plan like he'd always been.

Now, who dares to try and keep him behind the scenes? Now, he is the master of his destiny and he could manipulate others with great ease. Maybe he can even be equal to God. Perhaps he thought; he could be in charge of the entire universe from now on. The thoughts were running throughout Salvatore's head and made him even more exhausted. He fell asleep only to dream more and more. He cried for his lost childhood and past misery which followed him all the way to Vatican.

Whom to blame for everything? In his dream

he was the valiant man fighting for his long lost rights. He was pleased with himself. He justified the four killing he'd committed. They are unlike so many other serial killers who kill for passion or for pleasure, he thought, my murders were of necessity to aide and further the pursuit of my inheritance and my revenge! I am fully justified then. Therefore negativity brought about by these acts should not cloud my mind after all and slow me down from my quest. So if I must I'll kill again, and again, to the last witness.....

Suddenly his dream was interrupted by a strange noise. He ran out off the cave only to find alone coyote angrily howling at the lonely moon. Reassured he returned to the cold stone cave floor, lay down, talking to himself for hours, making new plans. Now, since he'd found pertinent information in Benedict's Black Book he was content, at least for awhile. He will go to Paris not only to find the last descendant of the real Templars, mentioned by Benedict on a piece of an ancient scroll, but he must translate his secret letter hidden in the wooden box for fifty years. He must find out what kind of **inheritance** his ancestors gave him and where to look for it.

Everything was still a puzzle but its pieces were slowly falling into one solid piece. However, there was still a long way before he would achieve his glory. It will take most of his time and more effort not only to find what he was looking for but mainly to fight Cardinal Benedict but not killing him yet. Salvatore knew that without Benedict he would be unable to solve many of the mysteries. Thus he still needed him until the last puzzle could be finally solved and then he can kill him at the end.

Chapter 7. Sister Agnes' Devastating News
The Boarding School, Rome, Italy

Suddenly their idyllic time was interrupted by Sister Agnes.

"Hello girls! Charlotte I must talk to you. Please, see me in my office in five minutes," Sister announced and left. "Okay, I will do that," Charlotte replied.

"What is going on? What does she want from you? Can't we have one peaceful moment without interruption?"

"I don't think it is anything important. Maybe, she needs some help in her office. I will find out soon," Charlotte replied and left.

"Come in! I have a letter for you. Please, sit down," Sister Agnes said.

"This is good news because I'm waiting for a letter from my mother."

"This letter is from Father Benedict, my dear. He said that he will call you tonight. I don't know where I should begin to tell you what happened. But this letter is rather very sad. He said that it was an accident and your house was burned down. The people tried to help but it was a bit too late as the fire broke out suddenly one night. Father Benedict wasn't there when the fire started and he couldn't save your mother. He came too late. But someone said that it was probably arson. The neighbor saw a man running from your house with a small bundle of things and soon after that the fire rapidly broke out in a huge flame. It was around two a.m. That night was hot when the neighbor went out and then he saw the fire. He called the firefighters. He screamed for help and the neighbors came out and tried to break the door down but the fire cut them in. Suddenly part of the roof collapsed before them. The fire looked like a monster and moved so fast. They barely escaped. Soon the firefighters came and fought the intense fire. Within twenty minutes half of the house vanished with no trace. They looked for your mother but couldn't find her. It was too late! Everyone stood there for a few hours and prayed to God. He is really very sorry about what happened to you my dear Charlotte. The north side of the house including the attic only partially survived. The next morning people came and dug out a few objects from the ashes. They found some pictures and a few toys. He will help you, don't worry. This school will support you as long as you are here," Sister said and then added with sadness.

"As soon as Cardinal Benedict calls, I'll let you know. He asked me to put you in our special program." She embraced Charlotte and they cried together for a few minutes.

"Oh, my child, my heart is broken for you. You are too young to be on your own. But I'm sure that God is watching over you right now. I hope whoever did this will be punished forever!"

Charlotte was in shock and couldn't speak she wanted to be alone.

Sister Agnes went to the garden to talk to Amelie.

"Amelie, Charlotte will not be joining you. She went to her room to grieve. Her mother died in a house fire a few days ago. They think someone set the house on fire deliberately. Everything is gone and there is nothing left. I'm sorry to tell you but give Charlotte some time to recover. I'm sad myself. Why has everything gone so wrong for this poor child?"

"This is horrible news, Sister! I'm more than terrified. Oh my God! Poor Charlotte. What can I do for her?"

"I'm terrified myself! I don't think there is anything in this world that could replace her mother, my child. Just leave everything as is. Try to talk to her and give her support. I must go now."

Sister left with disbelief on her face. Amelie stayed in the garden for another hour and thought about what she would say to Charlotte. She must find something really nice to tell her. But what would be nice in a situation like this. She stared at the blue sky and daydreamed.

Meantime, Sister Agnes received a phone call from Cardinal Benedict. She went to Charlotte's room and knocked on the door. "Charlotte, may I come in?" There was no answer. She pressed the knob and the door opened. Charlotte was lying on the bed with a pillow over her face. Sister Agnes walked over to her and removed the pillow. Charlotte didn't move. Her eyes stared at the ceiling. Sister Agnes shook her.

"Charlotte, are you okay? I came because Cardinal Benedict is on the phone and would like to talk to you. Come with me!"

125

"If I didn't come here my mother would have never died," Charlotte whispered in low voice.

"Please don't say that my child. I know it is hard to understand but perhaps the unknown is the purpose of life. We never know what is going to happen tomorrow. We are like flowers with a spirit. We can't escape death. Some people believe that death is only the transformation of human energy to another state of existence, perhaps the exodus to a new and better life. Maybe she is watching you right now and wants to tell you don't cry my dearest Charlotte. I'm fine and happy."

"Do you think the flowers have spirits too?" Charlotte asked.

"You never know, maybe they do."

Charlotte followed Sister Agnes to her office and picked up the phone. "This is Charlotte. How are you Father?"

"I'm okay but I feel so sorry that this happened and that I was unable to save your mother and catch this bastard. I believe it was Monk Salvatore. I also believe all of our treasures in the attic survived the fire and he stole them. I don't know where he is right now. For the past two weeks I've searched every hotel in town, every mountain's cave, one by one, so far no trace of him. How can I recover those treasures? I put my life on the line for all of that. Salvatore is a very dangerous man and I don't think he is alone in this. Perhaps he has some secret friends in town who support him. It is an incredible loss and I don't know how I can recover it if ever. Now I'd like to talk to you about your school. Both of you are on this special program I mentioned to you previously. I want you to

126

try your best. This mission of life and death means absolutely everything to me, to all of us in our secret organization. You can't fail! I've already talked to Peter about everything. I gave instructions to my best friend Father Emanuel he is taking care of Peter's future. Please, do not talk about our relationship to anyone including the Sisters there or any of your best friends. My life could be in danger. Also do not mention Monk Salvatore's name. Who knows, he could be in Italy one day and if he finds you there, your life will be in jeopardy. After the murder of Mrs. Alice I'm just beginning to understand the murderous depths of this man's soul. He is diabolical, vicious, malicious and cunning.

I think I must take off the hat I have worn for so many years; the supremely studious religious researcher, and replace it with a new hat; a skilled deceptive hard nosed detective willing to do anything to find and stop this man forever. For all eternity; he must be stopped. If you see him you must call me immediately or talk to Father Emanuel. He will know what to do. Only Sister Agnes has my phone number. I instructed Peter about this as well. What I can do for you, my child? I can promise to you that I will rebuild your house soon. I feel so bad!! God will watch over you from now on. I will talk to you soon."

"I'm glad that you will rebuild my house. Thank you for that Father. Father Can you tell me if you spotted Peter's camera hanging on the wall near the attic's exit door."

"I didn't see any camera. After the fire, the neighbors were digging through the ashes and possibly took it. Otherwise Monk Salvatore has it.

Why is it so important?"

"We took some pictures of the ancient maps, scrolls and the secret words written in your Black Book. We forgot to bring the camera with us to Rome."

"Holy Ghost! This is not good! I hope if your neighbors took it then I can take it back from them. It is very important. I must look for it. But the worst of all is that my **Black Book** vanished too and we don't have anything for now! Tomorrow, I will dig for more things in the ashes. So far I've only found the medallion which belonged to your mother. Okay my dear Charlotte, I must say goodbye to you for now but I will be in touch with you, I promise!"

"Goodbye Father Benedict."

"Goodbye my dear Charlotte and be brave especially right now."

"I promise," Charlotte said whimpering as she hung up the phone. Then Sister Agnes spoke to her,

"Dear Charlotte, you'll be on our special program starting tomorrow. Just ignore the old handouts. Tomorrow you will have martial arts training for half a day. On Monday, Tuesday and Wednesday morning you will study languages, on Thursday you will have physics, chemistry and biology, on Friday math and astronomy classes. You will have martial arts and swimming classes from four to six p.m. on a daily basis with Coach Louis. He has been teaching here for twenty five years and he is the best in this field. You will meet him tomorrow at eight a.m. in my office. He will take you to our special sport facilities. Trust me after four years of his intensive martial arts technique; you will be the master of your own destiny.

However, this program could be a bit hard on you and you must not give up.

Otherwise, you will be not able to do your mission. This is the only way to do it right. I wish you good luck and if you have any problem in the future please talk to me. I never ask my students any questions. I know your mission is strictly confidential and I will not ask you any questions about it. I was instructed by Father Benedict to follow his plan. He earned his respect among the members of the secret society and I will do as he's asked of me."

"I would like to study French if possible," Charlotte said. "Yes, you can choose whatever you like, my child. You will have special privileges in this school but you must continue to earn them. I believe in you and pray that you'll make it. Now, you are dismissed. Go to your room and get some rest for tomorrow. Be sure to come for dinner at six p.m."

"Thank you for encouraging me, I'll do my best."

"I know, you will, my child."

Charlotte went to her room where Amelie was waiting for her.

"Charlotte, I heard from Sister Agnes about your Mother's death. I feel immensely sorry for your loss. Let me know if I can do anything for you right now."

"I will be fine. I need more time to think about it but thank you for your considerable support. I was told by Sister Agnes that starting tomorrow I will be on that special program. We will only have French class together. But maybe you don't need French. You already speak perfect French."

"Charlotte, I was never good in French and I would like to retake it again. I would like to be with you in this special program if possible. Do you think Sister Agnes will let me?"

"That's a great idea! Please ask her."

"I will tonight, after dinner. It would be very cool if we could be in the same program. Maybe, I'll need a recommendation letter. I wonder who can give me one."

"Maybe, it won't be necessary. Let's hope for the best. Just be bold and smile fearlessly when you ask her for permission. You must have a convincing attitude to win her heart," Charlotte suggested with a smile.

"Thank you! I'll do exactly what you say Charlotte."

At dinner time, the girls run to the dining hall. They spotted Sister Agnes sitting at the table with other sisters; Amelie greeted her with warm smile. Sister Agnes smiled back as she glanced at her then at Charlotte's sad face.

The servers quickly run in and out of the dining room with trays of food. They served smoked salmon, French fries, cucumber salad with fresh basil, fresh boysenberries and fried banana. The food is class A, Amelie thought as she whispered something in Charlotte's ear. She began preparing herself for her short speech with Sister Agnes. She waited for the right moment to strike. Sister Agnes was talking to the other nuns and took her long time to finish her dinner. Maybe, she is confessing her whole life to them, Amelie thought, and decided to wait patiently. It was getting late and everyone left the dining hall.

Only Amelie, Charlotte and the sisters remained at the table. As soon as the Sisters finished they went to the garden to relax. The evening was very pleasant. Sister Agnes noticed that the girls followed her and she finally asked,

"Did you enjoy your dinner, girls? Is there something on your minds?"

"The dinner was fantastic. As a matter of fact I would like to ask you if it would be possible for me to join the same program with Charlotte."

"Why do you want to do that?"

"I want to be with Charlotte. We are good friends and roommates. I like challenging the unknown. Please let me be in this special program with her."

"Okay, let me think about it. Come to my office at eight a.m. tomorrow and I will let you know."

"Thank you Sister! I will be there for sure," Amelie enthusiastically confirmed and returned to Charlotte with a bit of hope. Sister Agnes glanced at her with a cool smile and left pondering.

"Charlotte, she asked me to come tomorrow morning. Do you think that I have a chance?"

"I think so. I have to be in her office early, she is going to introduce me to the martial arts coach Mr. Louis. She said he's been teaching here for almost twenty five years. You better bring comfortable shorts and a t-shirt with you just in case she says yes. It would be very wise of Sister Agnes to let you join the special program. Let's hope for the best."

"His name sounds very French. Let's sit on this soft green grass for a while. It feels good especially in the evening. I'm glad we still have summer. I don't like winters, they are too cold for me. I'm a hot blooded creature, how about you Charlotte?"

"Me! I'm definitely a cold blooded 'creature.' Close your eyes and try to relax now. There have been too many things that have happened today and I have so much pressure in my head. I must learn how to cope with it all."

They shared a moment of silence that lasted more than half an hour. Only the matting birds sitting above in the tree branches kept them company whistling their love songs. A cool breeze reminded the girls that it was time to go.

"Amelie, let's go! It is getting chilly. It is almost eight p.m. I don't feel well," Charlotte said.

"I'll make you some really good French tea and you'll relax. Whenever I'm down a bit, I drink different teas. It helps to lift my spirit."

"Okay! Let's try your remedy." The girls went to their room and Amelie quietly boiled the water for tea. She brought her own ceramic tea cups decorated with colorful flowers from Paris. They were very elegant. She put a few different teas into the ceramic teapot and poured hot water over.

She said, "We shall wait three minutes. I call this tea, *Peace of Mind.* I've created a different tea for different occasions depending on the mood I'm in. Tonight, I am in a peaceful mood. It is ready." Amelie poured a cup for Charlotte and served it to her.

"It tastes really good. What kind of teas did you mix?"

"It is my secret recipe but I will reveal it to you. I mixed a bit of mint, black tea, and some aromatic tea such as; rosé, jasmine, and earl gray. The proportions are the real secret. I'm glad you like it. This is my favorite one too."

"I'm sure I'll sleep like a baby. May I have another cup please?"

"Sure, here it is. Enjoy!"

"I'm quite exhausted. You wouldn't mind if I go to bed early?" Charlotte asked. "No, you've had a very difficult day. Goodnight!" Both girls went to bed at around ten p.m.

On Saturday morning they woke up before six, showered, dressed, and ran to the dining room for breakfast. Everyone was busy with their new classes and assignments. At eight a.m. Charlotte and Amelie went to Sister Agnes' office for their meeting.

"Good morning girls! Have a seat. Amelie, tell me, is there any particular reason that you want to be in this special program?"

"Only friendship," Amelie replied.

"Good reason. But are you sure that there is no other reason?"

"I'm quite positive!"

"This program is very difficult and you might not make it."

"If Charlotte is able to do it, I will make it too! I am adamant and strong-willed."

"You are very confident. I like that! You have convinced me. Congratulations! Get ready for a roller-coaster ride in the years ahead of you."

"Thank you Sister Agnes. You've made me really happy."

"We'll see how it goes! Both of you will go through an experience of rebirth. Now follow me, we'll walk to the exercise facilities to meet Coach Louis. I hope you'll work well together. It takes exactly five minutes to walk there. We have a beautiful gym and spa facilities, I'm sure you will enjoy them. Okay, here we are! Good morning Coach Louis, these are your new girls. Good luck girls, I will see you later."

"See you later Sister Agnes and thank you," Amelie happily replied.

"Good morning girls. I will be your coach. You already know my name. And you are?"

"I'm Charlotte."

"Nice to meet you, Charlotte."

"I'm Amelie."

"Nice to meet you, Amelie. I'm glad that you are dressed properly let me show you the training rooms. These facilities are huge and you can get lost alone. My focus is on a few things this year. As you have already figured out, you've been chosen for this special program for a purpose. I am your teacher, please pay close attention. We will meet here every day and Saturday we will meet from one p.m. to six p.m. Today you will start two different exercise routines. The first we call, the **Bat** routine. I'm sure you are imagining why it is called that name. The other one is called, the **Spider** routine. On those chained rods you will exercise the Bat position. It is very simple. You will hang upside down on the rods like a bat. We will start with ten minutes intervals and extend a few minutes more each day. At the end of the 4th year you'll be able to hang for twenty four hours without interruption.

Now let's move to the other training facility which is equivalent to a ten story building. As you can see part of the hall doesn't have a regular roof. The plastic dome above protects it from the rain. You will climb those tall poles every day which will enable you to become like a real spider one day. Every year I train many monks. In the future, you will climb those poles within a few minutes. It takes quite an effort and the right techniques but as you know, nothing is impossible. No one can ever catch my spider-monks, any questions."

"We are ready," Amelie announced. "We are," Charlotte said with convinced attitude.

"I like your determination, girls. Let's start with a warm up. Can you run for fifteen minutes around the field? It is the size of a regular athletic field. Please stretch for five minutes before you start running. I will show you a few of the finest ones. Flexibility is a very important factor. Your muscles must be totally relaxed in order to avoid even the slightest injury. Under my supervision it shouldn't happen at any time. Try these few things and repeat each one ten times. Watch me carefully and then you should run freely." The girls followed their new coach's instructions.

"Okay girls! Good job! Now I want you to do the Bat position for ten minutes. In the beginning I will let you use the towel under your legs. After ten minutes you will learn how to climb the poles. Are you ready?"

"Sure, I'm ready," Charlotte confirmed.

"Me too," Amelie said.

"You know how to do it, I'm sure you've done it many times in your back yard when you were younger. In the future when you become familiar with the Bat exercise you will learn how to jump up and down from different levels of the rods. Everything will happen in motion after you build up the strength in

135

your legs and stomach. Okay, it's good. How do girls feel?"

"I'm fine," Amelie said, hanging upside down on the rod.

"I feel great! I used to do this all the time when I was five. In our back yard, we have a few long wooden rods which we used for hanging carpets," Charlotte said with a smile.

"Okay girls ten minutes have passed. Let's walk to the other room. I will give you a special plastic device that acts like glue. You will stick it to your fingers and toes. Now you'll be able to climb the poles. Are you ready? Just try and don't be discouraged if you don't make it the first time."

"It is hard! I can't do it," Amelie said with disappointment.

"Oh my goodness I can't do it either! Perhaps I'm too heavy!" Charlotte added.

"It is okay. Don't panic! I will show you, just watch me very carefully. You move your hands upward alternating them like a salamander does. Then your legs go accordingly as you pull them up a bit one by one. You will catch the rhythm after awhile and it will go smooth. Now, try again."

"Coach Louis, you're very good and quick! How fast can you go like that?" Charlotte asked with excitement as she moved a few inches up on the pole.

"I've been doing this all of my life and can go very fast. Trust me, you will do it even better when you learn the right technique," the coach replied, laughing.

"Let me try again! This hand moves up then the

136

other leg up and left hand up then the other leg up. It is working, I moved up one inch. However, it will take me a century to learn how to do it right," Amelie said with a smile.

"It's not so hard, believe in yourself and you will make it. Okay girls! Now, let's switch to the other room for the Bat exercise again and then we will come back here once more. Don't worry we have all day long."

"It is much easier the second time in this Bat position. Now, I can do it for twenty minutes," Charlotte said.

"No Today, you will only do it for ten minutes according to our basic plan. However, if you like you can do it tomorrow for twenty minutes. The intervals for each day must be the same because you want to train your muscles the intelligent way and you want them to memorize every movement and duration of each one. Your muscles have long term memory. It is important you don't confuse your own muscles. Give them some time, I can guarantee that you will be more successful when you listen to my instructions."

"Coach Louis, do you have any other exercises for us?" Amelie asked with concern.

"Sure, you will have basic sword and Karate lessons that you can use for self-defense in case of an emergency. Of course you will take mandatory swimming class. But hopefully you already know how to swim and you will only need to master your craft. Believe me, you will be very busy here if you want to achieve your mastery. Okay, ten minutes is over and we are going to the other room again. I hope it will be a little easier for you to climb. Just remember the basic move, you are now a salamander and in the future you'll become a spider. Try to memorize this simple routine."

"Okay, I am a salamander now. I am a salamander now," Amelie repeated and climbed up at a good pace. Charlotte took the other pole and did the same. In that slow pace they moved up a few feet and then slowly slid back to the ground. They began to enjoy their lessons. They repeated their routines over and over again for another six hours with a short break for lunch and finally left for dinner at six p.m.

"I'm hungry and extremely tired," Charlotte said.

"Me too, do you think we are going to make it?" Amelie asked with deep concern.

"Sure we will, especially with coach Louis. He is very determined and knows exactly where we are going. I like that! I couldn't imagine a better teacher than him."

"You're right. He is very experienced and excellent at what he does. I already like him," Amelie added.

"We forgot to ask him about a massage."

"What are you talking about Charlotte?"

"I'm serious because tomorrow morning our bodies will be in pain and we will not be able to get out of bed. I know and I already feel it."

"Are you joking?" Amelie asked.

"Amelie, I'm not joking. Have you ever exercised for six hours non-stop? I haven't!"

"Let's hope this will not happen to us. In the meantime, don't worry and enjoy your dinner," Amelie said in a calm voice then laughed.

"Hello girls! How was your new coach?" Sister Agnes asked politely as she passed by them.

"He is very good and we exercised non-stop for six hours. Hopefully we will be okay tomorrow," Charlotte replied.

"I hope so too! Tomorrow, let me know how you feel. It is your day off. I'll be in my office most of the day. Now, you should enjoy your dinner and try to relax a bit."

"Thank you Sister for asking," Amelie said.

"You're welcome my child," she added with a great smile. The girls finished their dinner and returned to their room.

"I am not going to take a shower tonight. I will brush my teeth and then go straight to bed. How about you Amelie"

"I'll take a shower and brush my teeth because I think you are right, and I won't be able to move tomorrow morning."

"Good thought. Maybe I should force myself to take a shower too."

"You should!" Amelie suggested.

Soon after their showers, the girls fell hard on their beds and went right to sleep. It was a peaceful and cozy night. The beautiful aroma of jasmine trees sneaking through the opened windows woke the girls early Sunday morning. It was quiet and seemed as if everyone was still asleep. Charlotte opened her eyes and asked, "Amelie, are you awake? How are you doing?" she whispered knowing that she wouldn't be able to get up easily. Her muscles felt stiff.

"Yes, I am awake but I can't move. I think we've got an emergency situation. We need a special retroactive massage and fast." "You're right! A miracle would help. But how are we going to let anyone know what is happening to us. I wish, Sister Agnes would visit us now," Charlotte said in a still voice.

"Maybe if I scream loud enough she will hear me." Amelie said desperately.

"Sister Agnes! Please. Help," Amelie screamed as loud as she could but there was only silence. She screamed again, "Sister Agnes! Please help us!" Within ten minutes someone knocked at the door. "Come in!" Amelie energetically shouted remembering that she had forgotten to lock the door last night. Sister Agnes and Sister Claudia stood at the door.

"How are you doing girls?" they asked with a big smile on their faces.

"Pretty bad I would say, I'm rather dead," Amelie replied with a heavy voice.

"We can't move much. My muscles are sore and stiff like rotten wood. Sisters can you please help us? Is there a cure for our symptoms? Or do you think we must suffer like this for a week or two," Charlotte asked with sadness.

"It's okay, girls. We hear the same story every year. Don't worry we will help you. Your coach, Mr. Louis gave us this special remedy, a sort of miracle balsam and told us to apply it to every single muscle for thirty minutes. He knew that you would need it. I brought Sister Claudia with me because she has a lot of experience with this sort of thing and she will take care of you Charlotte. I will take care of Amelie. Are you ready?"

"Sure, I'm ready," Charlotte said painfully as she tried to turn her head a bit to the right.

140

"Thank you for coming Sisters. You are angels. I hope I will be able to walk again soon," Amelie whispered in a painful voice as her eyes asked for mercy.

The Sisters energetically began their difficult task. The balsam was thick and sticky and smelled like old horse manure. Their entire body was covered with it and they couldn't breathe easily because the stinky aroma overwhelmed them. They wondered if this stinky balsam would actually cure them. They watched as the Sisters put the plastic gloves on. Charlotte thought they looked like butchers ready for autopsy. They were told that the sticky balsam must go inside their muscles and it would take hour or two. They assured the girls that they had done this type of treatment previously and there would be 'no harm done.' As the Sisters began the intensive body massage, the girls thought they were enduring a method of torture and they began to scream. Every touch was like a tooth extraction without anesthesia.

Amelie thought the Sisters were karate experts as their fingers felt as though as they were made of steel. The girls shouted many times. To ease the pain the Sisters gave them each a small piece of bread to bite in case the pain persisted longer than ten minutes during each session. It was a crucifixion-like experience for the girls. Meantime, Sisters told them how the first Christianity began, and how the first hermits and Saints suffered of so much pain that finally they gave their lives up. The stories didn't build the girls self esteem.

Soon Sister Eleonora came into the room with dark glass bottle filled with some strange looking fluid.

As if to make their feelings more miserable she told them that she will put this solution on their bodies soon after the two Sisters finish with their massages. The girls were terrified; perhaps they must kiss goodbye this earthly paradise for good, they thought.

Sister Eleonora pulled her frock's sleeves up and leaned over Amelie's body. She poured the cold fluid over her back and began the intensive massage. Next, Sister Claudia pulled hot towels out from the thermal container and fully covered Amelie's body. It gave her a bit of relief and she sighed. Charlotte was next, and they worked hard and tried to be polite at the same time. Sister Claudia called Coach Louis for a quick conference. He told them that the girls should take a cold shower and they would be fine tomorrow. Now, the Sisters discussed amongst themselves if they should try to convince the girls or just carry them into the shower and decided that they would carry them. The Sisters lifted each girl and placed them in the shower. Sister Agnes turned on the cold water and the girls shivered uncontrollably as the water fell on them. Sister Agnes turned off the water and the Sisters wrapped the girls into hot towels. It was a moment of relief for everyone. The Sisters stood over them like angels. Sister Agnes said with a bit smile,

"Girls, don't worry anymore! You will be fine tomorrow. Now Sister Claudia will make a hot herbal bath for you, you'll really enjoy!"

"Thank you Sisters," Charlotte whispered in pain.

"Oh God, thank you," Amelie stammered. The Sisters walked out off the room leaving a glimpse of hope behind.

The girls slept in intervals as they discovered it was much easier to handle the pain. Soon the Sisters returned with an herbal revitalizing drink. They instructed the girls that the drink smelled and tasted terrible and they should hold their breath as they drink it. Sister Claudia spoke in low voice,

"This is a remedy that has been used for two thousand years. This drink is known by the monks as the **Black Angel**. They said it would put you on your feet within twenty four hours. It is very promising and if you believe in it, you will be well."

Sure Sister quite convinced herself of the magic power of this ancient elixir. The other Sisters agreed with her, nodding their heads in approval. The girls drank slowly and when they were about to finish, Charlotte remarked, "This is the worst drink I've had in my entire life. It must be worse than horse urine. Oh, God please help me not to throw up!" and then she lost consciousness. Sister Agnes ran to the rescue and slapped her face a few times. She opened her eyes but still struggled to keep the drink down. Finally she lost the battle and threw up.

"Oh, St. Peter. Don't do that! It's a very expensive drink; it is a gift from the Egyptian's monks. People call this special plant a **Virgin Mary Heart.** They said when Mary traveled with her family through the Egyptian desert; she became thirsty, sat on the sandy land and began to cry. The *Black Angel* appeared and the spring water erupted from the well. Red flowers began to bloom near the well. Every year since, the flowers bloom and the fresh water still flows from the well. It serves anyone lost in the desert. The monks found that the water and the flowers have

143

healing properties. Whoever drinks the water and eats the flowers will become healthy and young again. It will take months for us to get a new supply of this elixir again," Sister Claudia shouted angrily.

"I think the girls should sleep for a few hours and they will be fine. We'll check on them this afternoon. Later, we will prepare another hot herbal Jacuzzi. Let's go and let them rest," Sister Agnes announced and they left quietly.

It was a sunny Sunday afternoon. Everyone was busy with cleaning and organizing rooms, getting library books, and visiting the campus facilities. The view was very picturesque from almost every window of the room as the buildings were situated on the hills between tall pines trees and jasmine gardens. Coach Louis talked to Sister Agnes about Charlotte and Amelie's condition.

"I'm sure they will be fine. I train students every year and from my experience I know that the first day of training is hard on them. Trust me, tomorrow when they'll train again, they'll experience a little pain or no pain at all. But as you mentioned the hot Jacuzzi should make them feel good. Good luck and let me know how they are doing."

"I will. We will take care of them. Thank you for your concern Mr. Louis," Sister Agnes replied. Meanwhile, as the hour passed, Sister Claudia went to tell the girls that the herbal Jacuzzi was ready. Charlotte asked for a robe and Sister Claudia handed it to her. Amelie announced that she felt much better and she would walk to the closet for her robe.

"You're doing so well. It looks like the medicine is working. Perhaps, I can walk myself too," Charlotte said proudly and put her first foot on the floor. She rose from her bed and slowly made her way to the door. They followed Sister Claudia to the sauna and spa area where the hot herbal Jacuzzi was waiting for them.

"Okay girls, I know it was hard day for you and for us as well. I will be here in two hours with Sister Eleonora and we'll give you the final massage. See you later."

The girls entered the Jacuzzi and sighed with relief. "Thank you for everything Sisters. It feels so good," Amelie happily announced. The Sister looked at the girls and smiled as she left.

"I can exercise my legs now. I never really thought that the Sisters were serious about all the stuff they were doing. They said the elixir would rejuvenate us and I think it works. Don't you think so?" Charlotte said with disbelief. "At first I thought that they were joking or just having fun at our expense. But I think that since they go through the same procedure every year, they know exactly what they're doing. I think this herbal drink really worked a miracle on us," Amelie added with relief.

"I'm happy too. However, my heart is still broken. I feel like my whole life has vanished in that vicious fire. I can't understand why my mother couldn't escape on time. Perhaps something else happened out there and she was unable to. Maybe, someone knocked her down and the fire broke out before she woke up. Or maybe she never woke up because someone killed her. It is bothering me so much. I must find out what really happened. It will haunt me for the rest of my life. It could be the same person who killed my father. I try to understand his motive, but so far I don't have a clue. We didn't have any enemies in our small town either. I just don't understand why?" Charlotte said.

"Whoever did this horrible thing must be a vicious psychopath. I will help you catch them. You can count on me at any time Charlotte. You are my best friend," Amelie said seriously.

"Thank you, Amelie, but I must do it myself. It will become too complicated and probably dangerous. This person is determined and probably a serial killer. It won't be easy to catch him."

"Just think without limits Charlotte. We are young and able! This is what counts the most, and the other things will come. As we learn martial arts no one can stop us, we will simply be unbeatable. Do not underestimate our future abilities," Amelie added bravely, laughing.

"I like your bold attitude Amelie. It will really help us to focus on the right stuff. But you do realize we just started martial arts and there is long way to go? After our terrible muscle pain, I can hardly believe, I will ever make it to the end."

"Be an optimist! In Paris we say, "Live well, laugh often, and love much." I can promise you that you won't be disappointed. What would you attempt to do if you knew you wouldn't fail? Just think that way."

"I would go crazy! Stop talking for a moment and let's enjoy the pleasure, Amelie. It feels so good and we don't know how long will last. Perhaps this Jacuzzi has a spirit and makes me dream more. I don't want to leave it anytime soon. I could stay here all day and that would be exactly 86,400 seconds. I wouldn't mind one massage a day from Sister Claudia," Charlotte said, smiling.

"I'm glad that you are yourself again Charlotte. Happiness is in the heart, not in the current circumstances. Abandon the bad things and free yourself from them. Seek out small indulgences for yourself and feel the pleasure of this precious moment once more. Later you should make a date with your favorite book and fall asleep," Amelie concluded with a diabolic gesture.

"Amelie, you are a spirited girl and I am glad that I picked you to be my roommate. It is fun to be around you. I will never be bored with your companionship."

"Thank you, Charlotte for your honest opinion! I wouldn't find any better roommate than you, for sure!"

Suddenly their idyllic moment was interrupted by Sisters Agnes and Claudia coming in with towels and hot oil for their final body massage. It was rather a luxurious time for the girls which will most likely not come again anytime soon. The girls enjoyed this special massage and wanted it to last forever. It felt so good they fell into a short nap.

One hour later the Sisters left and the girls didn't even notice. Charlotte opened her eyes and whispered,

"Amelie, wake up! The Sisters are gone and we didn't even say thank you. I feel so good now. I think this amazing elixir will put us on our feet again. We will go by Sister Agnes's office to say thank you. Can you believe that after almost twelve hours of the body agony we are ourselves again? This is really great news and we have reason to celebrate."

"I feel fantastic too. I didn't notice when the Sisters left. But they did a great job. Let's say thank you to Sister Agnes!" They knocked at the door on their way out.

"Come in! Nice to see you girls in one precious piece, how are you? I'm glad that the miracle formula worked for you," Sister Agnes said with happiness on her face.

"We came to say thank you to all of you our Dearest Sisters, with a capital and bold letter **D**. We wouldn't be better without you. This unusual herbal drink worked a real miracle on us. I believe that there must be a Holy touch to it. We should celebrate the good news," Charlotte said with excitement.

"I'm glad that I could be of service to you my dear girls. This is only a part of my job. I have great satisfaction that I was able to help you," Sister said, feeling special at that precious moment.

"I would like to say thank you for all the things you have done today to make us feel better. Now, I know that there is something unusual about this school and why everyone wants to come here. You are simply the best!" Amelie proudly said, closing her final speech.

"You flatter me too much girls. It is only a part of my duty here. It was my pleasure to help you. You're such brave girls and I will keep my eyes on you. Ask me for any help at any time and I'll be there for you. Now go to your room and rest. I'll see you for dinner at six p.m." Sister said with a tear in her eye. She was indeed flattered too much and knew that she was only a servant of God.

"See you later, Sister Agnes," Charlotte said.

The girls changed their clothes. It felt good to be without pain. Sunday dinner was very special as there was an open buffet and everyone was picking whatever they desired. It was fun to be relaxed and without pressure. The girls were happy to find out that every Sunday would be an open buffet. The reality of their new lives would start on Monday and there will be not too much fun only study and homework. Charlotte packed her plate with fried fish, mashed potatoes, green veggies, and fresh fruit salad. Amelie filled her plate with so many different foods giving an impression that she hadn't eaten for two days in row. Charlotte made a remark,

"Amelie, you must be very hungry."

"We haven't eaten all day. Don't you remember? We were in pain for almost twelve hours. I'm hungry like a wolf," Amelie bravely admitted and laughed.

"Let's sit there at that empty table. No one will bother us. I just want to enjoy my food," Charlotte said. "Great, I want to relax and delight with mine as well. I don't want to think about tomorrow."

"Tomorrow will be an easy day. We only have morning languages and afternoon martial arts with two breaks for lunch and dinner. Amelie, do you think we will make it?" Charlotte asked with a serious tone.

"Yes, just don't worry and enjoy your food before it gets cold. Can we talk about something really pleasant like flowers or stars? We have to learn how to separate pleasure from duty. It would be very beneficial for our relationship. I want you to think seriously about that," Amelie clearly underlined her point of view.

"Okay, I will try my best!" Charlotte replied trying to sound positive.

"I like these boneless chicken kabobs and my favorite veggies; zucchini, asparagus, green beans and cauliflower. I'll bring more when I finish this platter."

"Good luck with all of that, Amelie. Seems like a lot! I hope you won't throw up! Bon Appetite!" Charlotte pointed out with a big laugh.

"So far I'm enjoying every bite."

"This is good. I'm finished but I'll keep you company. However, I would like to have some orange juice."

"Can you get me one too?" Amelie said and was determined to finish all her food. They talked and laughed as Amelie told a few French jokes.

"Can we walk around the garden? I feel so full. You were right, I ate too much," Amelie admitted with concern. "Sure! I like to walk as well. It is very healthy. Take your shoes off; we can feel the soft grass beneath our bare toes."

"Okay, I'll do that. Then we can listen to the whispering wind and perhaps be the first to dance to the sound of singing birds. I like that."

"Do you miss your home?" Charlotte asked.

"Yes! My grandmother must be lonely. She asked me to come here so I did but I missed my friends and all the fun we had. Now I know I won't see them for many years. I feel like it is a sacrifice I had to make? In the future I would like you to visit me and stay as long as you like."

"Thank you Amelie. This is more than generous of you and I'll never forget that," Charlotte replied with a tear in her eye and glanced at Sister Agnes standing near.

"Girls, don't forget we have curfew every night at eight p.m. You shouldn't be alone outside of the building after eight p.m. Do we understand each other?"

"Yes sister," Charlotte replied. "Yes, no problem. But it is a very pleasant evening," Amelie added cheerfully.

"I agree with you. It is a beautiful night. I'm glad to see you both in a perfect shape. But you can get cold from walking barefoot on the cold grass."

"Okay Sister, we will be careful," Amelie said boldly.

"I wish you a pleasant evening, girls and see you for morning exercise."

"Okay, we will be there. Goodnight Sister."

"Goodnight girls!" They walked to their room and Amelie set water for hot tea.

"Every evening I like to have a different tea. I made several combinations of tea which I put in those little goblets. I choose the type of tea by the mood I am in each day."

"Amelie, then what mood are you in tonight?" Charlotte asked.

"I'm in a 'witch' mood tonight so I will drink this special tea called, *Magic Wind*. After that I feel like I could fly with the wind. You will see for yourself."

"Sure, only if you have a magic broom. Let me have some of your tea then maybe I can keep you company on this long journey," Charlotte added and laughed.

"Don't laugh Charlotte, maybe we can really

fly."

"Okay! Give me that tea then. I'll be back in five seconds," Charlotte calmly said and went to the bathroom, looking for something.

"The tea is ready. Where are you, Charlotte?" Amelie shouted.

"Here I am! Dear Amelie! I found only one broom in the bathroom so we must share it."

"You are funny. Try it and you won't have any regrets," Amelie said laughing.

"It tastes like a dried evening wind," Charlotte said in an enigmatic tone.

"Can you really taste a wind? I've never thought of that possibility," Amelie wondered.

"In my world you can taste it."

"Then tell me how it tastes?" Amelie asked.

"Hmm, I would say something between winter and summer wind. Let's say like a very dry autumn wind," Charlotte concluded, smiling.

"I see! You sure about that, let me try again. Maybe, you're right! I will try and remember your expertise about my **Magic Wind** tea. You are quite a *persuasive raconteur*. It took me a long time to find the right name for this creation. Now I've learned it has the real flavor too. I'm really trilled."

"It really does!" Charlotte replied as she elevated her eyebrows with amazement.

"I'm tired already and I'm not sure if I can wake up at five a.m."

"I set the clock and I will wake you up. Let's go to sleep then. It was a hard day but at least your tea will allow us to dream again," Charlotte replied and glanced at Amelie's happy face.

"Charlotte, you wouldn't mind if I listen to a few French songs with my head-speakers on. They are my favorite ones. I'll listen quietly, under my blanket. I won't bother you at all. I promise," Amelie said with a convincing tone in her voice.

"Sure, I wouldn't mind and I'm tired myself."

"Okay sounds good. Goodnight! Charlotte." Everything was set for a peaceful and quiet night with only one exemption; Amelie was quietly singing to every single song she listened to. Charlotte tried to be polite and didn't say anything but she couldn't sleep. How in all the heavens they could wake up at five a.m., she thought. Then she got the strange feeling that her fate with Amelie as her roommate would be a mixture of joys and sorrows. She got out of her bed, switched the light on, and pulled Amelie's blanket off of her to reveal her body moving in a cobra style to the rhythm of the music.

"Amelie, open your eyes! I can't sleep! You've been singing in French for the last thirty minutes. I like French but look what time it is. There is no way we will wake up at five a.m."

"Charlotte, don't be so negative! Just listen to this song and hopefully you will change your mind. It is a true love story and it is on the black list because it is too sexy even to listen to. Put the headphones on and feel the moment."

"Amelie, you're crazy! I don't even know a word in French. Give me the headphones but you have to tell me what they're singing about." Charlotte put the headset on and listened. "The music and their whisperings are indeed very sexy. How did you get this tape if it was on the prohibited list?"

"My friend, Charles, recorded it and secretly gave it to me on my birthday. Isn't it something to put a chill in your stomach, I wonder how it really feels," Amelie whispered in an enigmatic voice as she still moved in her cobra style. "Amelie, be realistic! You are hypnotized by that music like a real Cobra. We are in a catholic school and we can't even think freely about this kind of passionate love. You must grow up to it! Try to suppress it inside of you with all your strength," Charlotte said with a slight frown.

"I can't! I tried many times but whenever I listen to this song something special awakens inside of me. It is spontaneous and simply inevitable. I don't know exactly in which part of me but I feel sick to my stomach always. It feels like the drummer strikes the rumba rhythms in the middle of my body each time," Amelie bravely confesses still moving in the same odd way.

"Then don't listen. Perhaps you should talk to Sister Agnes about it. Maybe she can help you. I don't have a clue what this is about. My mom never spoke to me about these things except that I would learn everything in biology class and I was too shy to ask and deeply in my heart I didn't show much interest in this subject. I played with dolls instead. Perhaps, I am too young. I suggest you wait until we learn this year in our mandatory biology class. We will probably learn everything we want to know about the human body!" Charlotte seriously advised Amelie. However, she didn't have a clue as her secret chord had never been touched before in anyway.

"Maybe you're right. I'll wait! It sounds to me like a tragic whisper, Charlotte, and now I am in a grave mood indeed. Perhaps, you're planting a seed of doubt in me. But you must admit that this song is very special. There is everything in it; finesse, fantasy and sophistication! The sort of innocent love which cannot be explained by any means or action, it must simply be felt. A true love deepened in the subtle imagination of the human mind! My heart is almost broken," whispered Amelie, frowning. Then she stared in the air with amazement and laughed.

"Yes! There is a sensible point to it, a bit of passion in that romantic spirit of yours, Amelie. But it could have a tragic end. Enough of this, we have to get some sleep now! It is enough! Please, turn off your music now. Look at my eyelids. They are so heavy. Goodnight!"

Then the next morning and exactly at five a.m. as the clock struck the hour Charlotte jumped out of the bed and shouted, "Amelie, wake up! It is five o'clock. We will be late."

"I'm tired. I can't go," murmured Amelie.

"Amelie, you must get up," Charlotte said as she pulled her blanket off.

"Okay, okay, give me a minute," she stammered.

"It seems like you are in a sulky mood, Amelie. I told you yesterday that it would be almost impossible to wake up so early. I'm tired myself. Let's go! No time to waste."

The girls put on their exercise shorts, white shoes, and t-shirts and ran to the backyard where everyone was ready for the morning jog. Surely, they would wake up fully as they ran. The last fifteen minutes they played seek and hide again. Exactly at six a.m. they walked to the dining room for breakfast.

"I don't really know what classes I have today. I already feel like a martyr," Amelie shortly concluded with carelessness.

"You look like a careworn virgin, Amelie. It is a bad sign. Remember, this afternoon we have class with Coach Louis," Charlotte whispered, smiling.

"I wouldn't worry about that too much if I was you. I am in excellent spirits."

"Good. At eight a.m. we have Hebrew class and then we have a one hour break. Meantime, I need to go take a shower," Charlotte said in a low tone. "Perfect, I can listen to more music," Amelie murmured.

"I don't think so. Amelie, I want you to be serious for a moment and stop that nonsense. Music and your cobra dance are only on Sundays. Do we understand each other? I must concentrate on my classes," Charlotte said with a cold voice.

"Sure, you've got yourself a deal. I need a shower too. Let's go!" Amelie added in a chirping tone. They put their uniforms on and went to Hebrew class. As they entered the classroom they saw Sister Agnes at the teachers' desk. The girls were relieved to see Sister Agnes was going to teach the class.

"Good morning girls. I will teach you Hebrew and I hope you will learn it and find it useful in your life." Someone knocked at the door.

"Come in!" Sister replied.

"I'm sorry to bother all of you but I have a new student. This is Lady Lily from London," Sister Claudia announced and left.

Amelie whispered to Charlotte, "She looks

rather like a lady Parsley with her puffy hair."

"Please sit down in that empty seat," Sister Agnes said as she glanced at Amelie with amazement.

"Amelie would you like to say something?" Sister added with a frown on her forehead.

"Actually not I am dreadfully sorry about my peculiar behavior. I shall be sorry for having said that," Amelie added with a candid smile.

"I want to believe that you are really sorry, Amelie, and it won't happen again."

"I will be awfully obligated to it," she confirmed with penitence on her face. Then she threw herself down onto her chair.

"I will hold you to your promise, Amelie. You can sit down but in a quiet manner. You bewilder me. Some of you have a lot to learn," Sister added in a cold voice.

It was silent for a moment as sister Agnes looked for her notes which seemed to have disappeared in somewhere. She murmured to herself mockingly. "I don't think that they could walk away. Charlotte, you are apt girl. Can you go to my office and check my desk? I must have left my notes there."

"Yes Sister." Charlotte replied and hurried out of the door.

"I want to tell all of you that youth is unpredictable and must be controlled especially in this facility. You came to this Academy to study and get the best values life has for you. I want you to grow up to these standards," she paused for a moment with her somber thoughts, as though she was reflecting on her own past nobody knew about, at least not yet. Her hands quivered a bit. It was rumored that she ran away from the deepest love of her life, many years ago. A man named Richard who was madly in love with her. After she left him, he committed suicide. Her heart was broken and she still lives with many regrets about that fatal day. Her thoughts were interrupted by Charlotte's entrance. "Sister, I found your notes."

"Thank you, Charlotte. I would like to talk about the Masoretic Text which by definition is the Hebrew text of the Jewish Bible. It was widely used as the basis for translations of the Old and New Testament and recently also for Catholic Bibles. It was a group of hard working monks and scholars of the Masoretes with great prestige and reputation. With their accuracy and error-control techniques, they contributed too many translations of the fine second, third, and fourth century manuscripts. Without them this ancient language would be lost forever. The Masoretes would not alter the sacred consonantal text. I would like to mention just a few of the many; Ben Asher and Ben Naphtali as their names are written in almost every modern dictionary. What great spirits!

Also, lately found is the Nash Papyrus, all world is talking about it, the second century BCE, contains a portion of a pre-Masoretic Text in regards to the *Ten Commandments*. It was a very important discovery by many dedicated monks and scientists who put their lives on duty. But the most excited discovery lately was of the Dead Sea Scrolls at Qumran caves, dated from 150 B.C. to 75 AD exactly covering Jesus Christ and his family life. The scientists said it is written in a prototype of Masoretic text. Very few manuscripts survived the destruction of

158

the Holy place, Jerusalem in 70 AD. We should be very thankful for what we have. I will teach you this ancient language which is not so difficult but it will give you the ability to read and translate the oldest texts. With a bit of luck, some of you will work for the Vatican library and you will find it very handy. Also I would like to point out that the language of the Masoretic notes is partly Hebrew and partly Aramaic. Jesus spoke both but mainly He used Aramaic. This is what most historians say and you should remember that. Here are some handouts for you to read and remember what I've told you. With this in mind, class is dismissed. I will see you next Monday. You have a great day!"

The girls went out for a fifteen minute break to relax and stretch their bones before the next class begins.

"We have French class now. I wonder who will teach us. Learning French is going to be a great experience for me," Charlotte said happily.

"Sure, you will have fun," Amelie added without much concern.

"I'm glad that each classroom door is marked with different letter. It saves us time finding the right class. Then here we are at the door with the letter F, surely for French. The bell is ringing, hurry, get in," Charlotte said in earnest tone in her voice. The girls sat at their desks patiently waiting for the teacher. He seemed to be running late. Five minutes later, he showed up.

"Bon jour. Good morning. Je m'appelle Bertrand de Mondi. My name is Bertrand de Mondi. I will be your French teacher for the next four years. I sincerely believe our relationship will be astounding. I'll mostly be speaking French so you can get used to the sound. Are you ready?" he asked with a masculine smile.

Amelie whispered to Charlotte as she gestured putting her right hand on her heart, "He is dreadfully handsome, my dream man, tall and slender with black hair and secret dark eyes hidden under thick eyebrows. His gorgeous face with carved marble lips ready to embrace a kiss; I could die for it!" she stared at him in amazement.

"Be quiet! Amelie, be serious and behave yourself. I hope he didn't hear you," Charlotte said as her face turned instantly purple red and then she added with a bitter smile,

"Amelie, I am embarrassed for you!"

"Don't worry! I'll be fine if one day he asks for my hand."

"Amelie, you are being childish. I must remind you, we are in a catholic school and most of us will probably become nuns. You must forget about it. He is a Monk himself and he can't marry. But I must admit that you have quite an imagination and good taste."

Their chatting was suddenly interrupted, "Let's introduce yourself, girls. In French we say; Je m'appelle. My name is...Let's start from the left row," he replied and wrote the sentence on the blackboard. "Je m'appelle Lady Lily."

"Very good, now write this sentence on the blackboard, the accent is on the second word which we say quickly. Next please," he confirmed with the same charming smile.

"Je m'appelle Charlotte," she said with a frightening voice and turned red again as she thought her first words in French sounded horrid.

"Excellent!" Bertrand said as his brown eyes scanned Charlotte from head to toe. She was shy but full of grace. She was tall and slender. Her perfect face, blond curly hair hanging freely over her shoulders, startling green eyes full of feminine charm put a magic spell on him instantly. He didn't smile but there was something special in his facial expression, a sort of unspoken desire which had been suddenly awakened from a long lethargic sleep. Even Amelie noticed this special moment as she whispered to her,

"Charlotte, I can read his mind. I think he likes you."

"Amelie, stop!" she whispered.

Then Bertrand suddenly asked as he faced Amelie, "Comment vous appelez-vous? What is your name?"

"Je m'appelle Amelie," she gracefully replied. She was a tall and pretty brunette with blue eyes and a good sense of humor. He glanced at her and asked, "Are you French?"

"Yes, I am," she replied softly.

"Why are you taking French then?" he asked.

"I was never good in French. I think, I can improve it with you," she added with a devilish smile on her face.

"If you think so then I will help you," he added with a smile and then asked, "Comment allez-vous? How are you, Amelie?"

"Tres bien, merci. Et vous?" "Fine thanks and you," she replied.

"Would you write this on the blackboard

Amelie?" he asked politely.

"Sure, I will," she confirmed and walked spontaneously to the blackboard. He said, "I want you to practice this simple task between each other. Veuillez vous asseoir. Please sit down, Amelie."

"Je me suis tres bien amuse. I have enjoyed myself very much," Amelie answered as she walked back to her seat. Bertrand looked at her and shook his head with approval.

"Thank you, Amelie. Let's continue our introduction. What is your name?" Bertrand asked the next student sitting in the same row. "Je m'appelle Brigitte."

Bertrand began to write simple expressions and a few sentences on the blackboard and then read each one very carefully. "Yes. Qui. Please. S'il vous plait. Thank you. Merci. You're welcome. De rien. Good morning. Bon jour. Good evening. Bonsoir. Good-bye. Au revoir. I want each of you to repeat after me each word," Bertrand said in a calm voice. It was a lot of fun for each girl as the words sounded very cute to them.

"Please, rewrite every single word in your notebooks and exercise at home with your roommates. Be sure to remember everything you learned today. I will write a few more words for you as they are very easy to memorize," he said and began to write again and repeat each word a few times for them.

"How do you do? Enchantee. How is your life? Comment ca va? Excuse me! Excusez-moi! Sorry! Desole! Je voudrais. I want."

Someone knocked at the door. It was Sister

Agnes. She interrupted for a moment and excused Charlotte from the class. There was an important phone-call from the Cardinal Benedict. "We will miss you Charlotte. Be sure to copy every word from Amelie," Bertrand said as he looked deeply into her eyes for approval. "Yes sir," she replied with an electrifying voice and then left.

"I don't have a clue what happened, but Cardinal Benedict said it was very important. He will call back in five minutes, he said. Have a seat," Sister added with a low tone in her voice. Within five minutes the telephone rang. Sister picked the phone up and handed it to Charlotte. It was Cardinal Benedict. He was very frightened as he spoke.

"Charlotte, I think, soon after the fire, someone stole your camera with everything in it as I mentioned to you last time. I discovered that it wasn't Monk Salvatore. He simply missed the camera hanging on the wall as he was in a hurry to get all the hidden treasures from under the attic floor. It was your local neighbor who stole it. He is living just a few blocks away from you. I conducted an undercover observation of his house for a few weeks. Obviously he must have developed the film. He learned those magic words by accident and discovered the power of it. Now, using that knowledge he is building some strange looking structures around his house which has brought attention to all of his neighbors. They are wondering how he got the money for it all. I feel very uncomfortable about it because I asked you specifically to keep the contents of my **Black Book** confidential. I never thought that you would photograph these particular secret words. I didn't want anybody to learn that magic formula except for you and only when the time is right. These words are powerful and I knew people would abuse the power of it and this is exactly what has had happened now. You didn't leave me much choice Charlotte. I must do whatever it takes to confiscate the pictures from this man. I might even have to demolish some of his new structures. They will just disappear the same way they got there. It is absurd what he has done to his house.

Now, I must risk my own life. He lives alone and on the weekends he fishes in the local creek. With a bit of luck I can do it in this weekend. I hate thieves. I also wanted to let you know that I am slowly rebuilding your house. At the end of this year I will complete this project. I have made some more plans regarding your future mission. In the meantime, I will stay where I am. I spoke with Peter, he wasn't happy about his camera. The Monk Salvatore contributed greatly to all this mess and our misery. I will be sure that he pays for this dearly. How are you doing, Charlotte?"

"I am doing great! I've learned a lot so far and I feel good about the school and myself. The martial arts are a bit tough but I think I can make it. I have nice friend, Amelie, she is my roommate. She is funny and I like her very much."

"It is good to hear that you are happy out there and everything is under control. Good-bye my child and be a good girl. I don't want to be disappointed. Next month, I will call you back hopefully with good news. I must find out for sure who killed your mother and why? I'm conducting a special experiment to find the answer. I will let you know soon."

"Good-bye and thank you for everything," Charlotte said as she was concerned deeply about the bad news. She couldn't do much and neither could Peter but she trusted Cardinal Benedict. She wasn't sure if it was better that Monk Salvatore had the camera or that strange neighbor. It was a big dilemma left in her mind after she hung the phone up. She left Sister Agnes' office and went to her next class.

The hours passed by fast and it was almost twelve noon, time for lunch. She rushed to the dining hall and Amelie was already sitting at the table.

"Hi Amelie are you hungry?" Charlotte asked.

"I can eat a horse. What do we have left for today, Charlotte?" Amelie asked curiously.

"The martial arts class only. I am happy because I am a bit exhausted after everything."

"You must admit that the French teacher is a cute guy," Amelie pointed out laughing.

"Yes, indeed he is good looking but you should not think about that anymore. Maybe, I haven't grown up yet but you better wait for me. I like your excitement Amelie. You bring life to our shadowy atmosphere."

After lunch, they went to the martial arts class. Coach Louis was waiting for the girls with a new fencing instructor.

"Hello girls! Today you will meet your new fencing coach, Mr. Gautier. Then in one hour, I will show you the basic karate moves and after that we will do our regular exercises. See you soon. Do your best," Coach Louis said and left. The new coach was French. He was handsome and it didn't escape

Amelie's attention. He was toll, blond and had blue eyes. He gave the girls swords and gave them a few important rules on how to handle them. Then he spoke,

"I will teach you an unconventional fencing technique which will give you the ability of self defense in a case of group attack. You will be able to use two swords at the same time. It is a bit difficult but I will teach you how to do it. You will work to attain perfection. This kind of sport requires the highest discipline which I assume both of you have. Let's get to it." They didn't waste any time. Coach Gautier worked hard with the girls on every single move. The moves were spontaneous but very accurate. An hour later coach Louis showed up. They began karate dance with music. It looked a bit unconventional but he said that the music helps to coordinate each move. There were hundreds of single repetitions. It looked easy but was actually hard work. One hour later, exhausted the girls lay down on the wooden floor.

"I feel like I have exactly three hearts; one in my head, one in my chest and an additional in my thighs. My whole body is pulsing," Amelie whispered with closed eyes.

"I feel the same way. Isn't it weird?" Charlotte added, gasping. Within ten minutes Coach Louis showed up and they moved to the other facilities. The regular exercise appeared to be easier than a few days ago. Even coach Louis gave the girls a compliment. "Girls, I must admit that you're doing pretty well today. I hope there will be no more pain in your muscles. If you can overcome the pain then your muscles will forget about suffering. You will be

166

surprised that they have their own memory and they will remember this as a sort of pleasure," Louis said laughing a bit.

"It is an interesting theory, coach," Charlotte pointed out.

"Did you ever lie to your muscles?" Amelie asked.

"Sure, many times and I don't suffer any more pain. Okay girls, now we move to the swimming pool facility for the remaining hour. This is an Olympic size swimming pool. You will like it and no one will bother you. A regular class is about twelve students and it is a bit crowded. The two of you should consider yourselves very lucky. I believe you can swim and you will learn new styles today. In the meantime, put the swim suits on. I believe we have some extra ones in the changing rooms. You have five minutes to get dressed and come back."

"Let's hurry," Amelie said.

"We have quite a busy schedule today, coach," Charlotte said with disbelief.

"You are young and powerful, girls. I wouldn't worry too much," the coach added with a smile. The girls ran to the locker room.

"Charlotte, I found some swimsuits near the lockers on the shelf. What size are you?"

"Size two should fit me."

"Okay, I got it! I need a size two for myself as well. They are nice and have the school logo on the front. Here you go Charlotte. Let's change quickly and finish this final hour. I am getting tired."

"Okay, girls, now that you are ready. Let's warm up for about twenty few laps and after that you can do some diving," he said and watched them very carefully as he continued to check his watch. Charlotte wondered if he was watching them and keeping their times. The girls finished the last lap.

"Good job girls! I must admit both of you are quite good swimmers. I would like for you to dive five times each and try to hold your breath for at least thirty seconds each time."

Charlotte loved to dive. Amelie followed her. They enjoyed themselves and had a bit of fun when they discovered a secret bridge under the water. It was quite a mystery. The girls wondered why anybody would build a bridge in the middle of a deep swimming pool and they needed an explanation. Soon after they emerged from the pool, Amelie asked bravely,

"Coach Louis, do you know anything about this mystery bridge beneath the water?"

"Sure, it was built by monks four hundred years ago between these two monasteries as an escape road from invaders. Years later an earthquake happened and the bridge collapsed. It was too heavy to lift it back up. In recent years, the swimming pool was built over the stone bridge which connects these two facilities as well as the two different swimming pools on each side of the monastery. However, an iron gate was built beneath the water between the two swimming pools and you can't swim freely to the other side."

"This is quite an interesting story," Charlotte admitted with a smile.

"I love those secret paths especially when they come with a bit of history," Amelie added ready to go.

"Okay, girls, you are dismissed. Enjoy your evening," coach said and left. The girls ran into the shower, rinsed the swimsuits and walked to the spa for a short body recovery.

"Let's take a hot Jacuzzi with a water massage like we did yesterday," Amelie said.

"I love your idea. What about our dinner?" Charlotte said with a bit of disappointment.

"I totally forgot! Actually, I am not very hungry. Let's get our food and have it in our room later on. Let's do it and fast."

"I think we worked too long and our body will reject food right now," Charlotte replied.

"There is always that possibility. Also we must get as much rest as possible because later on we will be too busy," Amelie said as they entered the dining room.

"I agree with you one hundred percent. Look I see some plastic containers over there on the shelf. Let's get one for soup and one for the second dish and the little cup for fresh salad," Charlotte said and asked the cooks to fill the containers. It was full service in that facility and the girls walked back to the Jacuzzi. It was perfect timing and no one will bother them. The other girls were already busy with their homework.

"This hot bubbling water feels like paradise. I can stay here and dream all night," Amelie said.

"There is nothing better for stress than a hot Jacuzzi," Charlotte added as she fully relaxed.

"Forget about your stress Charlotte. You are too tense. You should dream about something or someone you want to have," Amelie suggested.

169

"I don't have any needs. I prefer simplicity in my life. That way everything is less complicated and very easy."

"I'm sure you have some dreams Charlotte. I have some and as you can easily guess my dream right now is the French teacher. You know, I've never been in love and have no clue what it is about.

"Me neither and I don't want to think about it now. I think my life can go on without it," Charlotte said, laughing.

"You wouldn't want to know what you're missing. I think that love is like a life engine. Just think of a car without an engine and you will get the picture." "I think he is too old for you Amelie." Charlotte said as she closed her eyes and enjoyed the swirling water.

"I found out that he is only twenty four and has a Ph.D. in French. He must be really good at it."

"Amelie, wake up! You are only twelve. You must be crazy to fall in love with an old man like that."

"This is what excites me; his experience and his gorgeous looks. Simply put, he is my type," Amelie replied laughing.

"You're too young and I can forgive you your fantasy. I know when you wake up ten years later you will think that everything was crazy and you will laugh," Charlotte pointed out seriously. "I'm not sure about that. Maybe my heart will be broken, you never know," Amelie said, laughing.

"I don't think so! You will meet a new prince charming and maybe get married."

"And then I will have regrets," Amelie added.

"About what?"

"My past love," Amelie whispered.

"Maybe your platonic love only. Be serious Amelie," Charlotte said laughing.

"Do you think I am not serious?" Amelie looked at her seriously.

"Yes, I do. Look at the clock. It is almost nine p.m. It feels so good to be pampered like this but we better go."

"Okay, time to go! Let's abandon god's pleasure," Amelie said with an exciting gesture as if she was acting on the stage.

As they passed by the Sisters quarters, they heard loud lamenting coming from one of the rooms. The girls paused for a moment and listened carefully to where the scream was coming from.

"Whose room is that?" Amelie asked.

"I don't have a clue. Maybe we can knock on the door and find out," Charlotte said and knocked at the door. There was no answer. She turned the knob and the door opened. Amelie follow her. They saw Sister Agnes lying down on the floor lamenting over some objects. They walked closer. Sister held a picture in her left hand and a knife in the other. She didn't notice the girls. She was crying and calling the name, Richard over and over again.

The girls were trapped in her room and a bit embarrassed by the awkward situation. They were not sure if they should stay or run away. Suddenly, Sister Agnes noticed their presence and stopped crying. She stood up and immediately apologized for her behavior. She was in shock not only by the state of her mind but also by the embarrassment at the girls' presence.

"Sit down on the sofa. I am really sorry for my strange behavior. I get into this emotional state from time to time and I can't control myself. This is like a disease for me I suffer every year at the same time. There is no cure for it. I've tried to take my own life but I always fail. Today is his birthday. Richard was my love once and when I left him, he committed suicide. I have had regrets ever since. I can't forget him either. I should have never left him. Now it is too late to fix the past. Oh, God please forgive me! I never knew what price I would pay for that loss. He was my life and my love. Once there was a great passion between us which died with him forever. I didn't have enough courage to accept his love the way he wanted to give it to me and I ran away from him." She paused for a moment and then dropped the knife on the floor. She put the picture on the table and sat on the wooden chair. She looked terrible. The girls were terrified. Amelie almost passed out from the emotional distress. Charlotte was intimidated and speechless but tried to put a few supporting words together,

"We're sorry that we just plunged into your room without an invitation. We didn't know how serious it was. We thought maybe something horrible had happened."

"Don't be sorry, my dear Charlotte. I'm glad that you stopped by. I was thinking of doing something bad to myself. I can see everything clearly now. I should be thankful to you for this blessed intervention. Perhaps God sent you here. I've become intolerable to myself lately. I've been asking myself the same question over and over again, for thirty five years. Why? Why did this happen to me? I can't live like this anymore. You've opened my eyes tonight and I see myself as a foolish old lady. Thank you girls, I will make some tea. Would you like to have a cup?"

"Certainly sister," Charlotte replied as she glanced at Amelie's frightened pale face. Amelie shook her head for 'yes' and whispered with a frigid voice, "Yes, the hot tea will do us good."

Sister served the hot tea and tried to be polite. The atmosphere was stiff like at a funeral gathering. A stigma of melancholy hung over the evening and it would be remembered for the rest of the girl's life.

"How's the Egyptian tea?" Sister asked.

"It's really good," Charlotte said. Amelie squeezed out a short, comfortable smile to impress Sister Agnes with her self-esteem.

"It's a gift from my Egyptian friends, from the *St. Anthony Monastery*. They said it will make your worries go away. I drink some every day hoping that one day I will be free of worries," Sister Agnes proudly announced and served the girls more tea.

"You should try Amelie's tea selections one evening. She makes a different tea for every occasion, depending on what mood she's in," Charlotte said and glanced at Amelie.

"I would love to try your tea Amelie, maybe next Saturday night. I'm a heavy tea drinker," Sister added with a smile.

"Sure, it would be my pleasure," Amelie added with a convincing smile. "However, it's getting late and I think we should go Charlotte. Sister Agnes must be tired too and it's been a long day for all of us. Thank you for this special tea, Sister Agnes."

"Oh no I'm fine girls. I'll have some more tea. I

must do some reading for tomorrow, but thank you for stopping by. Hopefully we'll see each other during the week. I feel much better now. Girls, I need to ask you to keep this evening's incident confidential. Goodnight!" Sister said as the girls were about to leave.

"Don't worry about that part, you can count on us. Goodnight Sister Agnes," Charlotte said with assurance. "Goodnight!" Amelie said with a smile.

Sister Agnes looked at them for a long time until she could no longer see them as they headed to the other part of the building. She would now be lonely again. The girls walked to their room and lay down on their beds with a look of disbelief in their faces.

"What an evening! I'm stressed out even more after tonight. Did you ever imagine that something like this would happen? I was so relaxed after sitting in the Jacuzzi," Amelie asked. "Maybe we saved her life; everything does happen for a reason. You know, this is what could happen to you if you fantasize too much about your French teacher. You don't want that to happen, Amelie. Do you?" Charlotte said, laughing.

"I don't think so. This is only a platonic fantasy. I would never kill myself for love, at least I don't think so," Amelie said startled.

"People say; love is blind, Amelie, and never say never. We can't be sure what we're really capable of doing until that final moment finally arrives. We're still too young for that kind of experience and I think we're really blessed. Just enjoy the moment."

"Sure, I will, but I feel sorry for Sister Agnes. She does that tragic scene every single year and without spectators until tonight. Maybe, I'll make some of my own tea to relieve our stress. How about *Blue Fantasy*, would you like to try some?"

"Sure, any tea is a good tea for me and especially tonight, later I'd like to read my science book," Charlotte exclaimed.

"Go ahead, I promise not to bother you. In fact, I have a good story I'm reading myself."

They spent the rest of their evening drinking good tea and reading their science 'stories.

The next morning was repeated with the same exercise routine, breakfast, and language classes. However, at nine a.m. there was an interesting biblical study on the Codex Vaticanus subject taught by a new teacher, Lord William Green. His amusing appearance brought Amelie attention as she whispered to Charlotte. "His name should be *Green Dill* instead. He's so skinny and with that long hair of his, he looks rather like green pickled dill, doesn't he?"

"Amelie, maybe you're right, but please no more joking. He looks just fine," Charlotte whispered back with a little bit of a laugh. Despite everyone's opinion, Lord William Green continued his lecture.

"The Codex Vaticanus is one of the oldest manuscripts of the Bible, dating back to the 4th century. It is written in small, neat Greek. However, the origin of the text is uncertain. The manuscript has been housed in the Vatican Library since the 15th century."

Everyone listened to him as he spoke about the Old and *New Testaments* and a detailed discussion followed after that. Following a fifteen minute break, they went to Sister Claudia's class where she began speaking about the various miracles in the Bible.

"The definition of a miracle can be explained as when God intervenes in the laws of nature, from the old Latin word *miraculous* meaning something wonderful. In other words, it is a divine intervention by a supernatural being in the universe. For example: God may suspend or speed up the laws of nature to produce a supernatural event or God can create matter out of nothing. He can breathe life into inanimate matter, and so on. In small town, Lanciano, people witnessed the visible transformation of the Eucharistic bread and wine into the Flesh and Blood of Christ. It has been scientifically proven to be real, non-deteriorated human heart muscle despite its one thousand, two hundred year presence in the church. I hope you enjoyed today's lecture and will be able to tell me next time if you have experienced any miracles in your own life, class dismissed."

It was around eleven a.m. when Charlotte decided to talk to Peter and find out how he was doing. She went to Sister Agnes' office and the Sister dialed the number to Father Emanuel's office and they waited for a moment. Father Emanuel picked the phone up and said he would find Peter. After five minutes, a voice spoke on the other end.

"Hi! This is Peter. Charlotte, how are you? I spoke with Cardinal Benedict; he's rebuilding our house which will be done by the end of the year. He said he spoke to you about the camera and some other stuff, so I won't bother to repeat what you've already heard, but I have some good news for you. It seems I'll be accepted to join the Omega Templars, that is, if I pass the special test. I don't know the details yet, but I've heard it has something to do with Christ's crucifixion. I'll let you know as soon as I find out. If I'm not able to reach out to you, then I'll have Patrick contact you. Christmas will be here soon, and I'll know everything by then. But most of all, I miss Mother. I just don't understand who did it and why?"

"I miss Mom a lot too, but don't worry, I'll find out who did it. I'll get this bastard, just watch me. My coach has been teaching me a lot of different techniques and he said I'll be good and fast like a spider monk within a few years. I'll be able to climb a ten-story building within a few minutes. Yesterday, when I was swimming, I discovered an opening at the bottom of the pool by pure accident. Our coach told me that the two swimming pools between the two monasteries are connected by an underwater bridge. There is however, an iron gate that was built between them a few years ago. I thought it would be a perfect place for our future contacts. We can exchange information without being seen. I think the gate may not reach all the way to the bottom and I could swim under it to the other side, but I'll check this out tomorrow. That's why I've been practicing my diving so much lately. Slowly, the pieces of the puzzle are falling into one place. Peter, what do you think about it?"

"I think this is really great news. I swim, dive and climb a lot too. In the meantime, I'll let Patrick know about the underwater bridge, so that in the case of an emergency you can meet him there. I trust him, so tell me exactly, what time do you swim? He wants to be one of the XII Templars too. I think he'll make it. He's really good at everything he does. I've been very busy lately, so I don't have much time for any entertainment. I'm sure you can imagine something like that, huh? It's been so long since I've seen a movie or played a game, just simply too busy with my studies and homework."

"Me too; I have swimming class between five and six p.m. on Mondays, Wednesdays, and Saturdays. How about you, what time do you swim?"

"What a coincidence, the same times as you. This is perfect! We can synchronize our meetings. Let's meet this Wednesday for a minute," Peter said with curiosity.

"Okay! I will meet you at exactly five thirty p.m. It's my diving time and for almost thirty minutes."

"Okay Charlotte, see you there. I must go now. Bye!"

"Good bye Peter," Charlotte said and left the office. Sister Agnes was no longer there as she had a class to teach. Soon it will be 12 noon and time for lunch. Charlotte went to her room to change her clothes and went to lunch. Amelie was already there.

"Hi Charlotte! I'm ready for our afternoon exercise. How is Peter doing?"

"He's doing great. He has a new friend, Patrick. He said that they're so busy and they have no time for any entertainment."

"Same like us, I'm not surprised. Christmas will be here soon and we'll have a few days of vacation. Maybe we can do something special together. What do you think, Charlotte?"

"Sure, we can visit Vatican City together. I've never been there. I will talk to Sister Agnes about it."

"That sounds like fun. Maybe some of the other

girls can join us," Amelie said excited.

"Sure, it's a good idea. What are they serving for lunch today? Let's take a look," Charlotte said as they paused in front of the buffet and picked a few fried pike-fish with potatoes and spinach on the side.

"Charlotte, look at this drink, it seems like it's made for lovers."

"You wish, Amelie. It's just pink lemonade. You're a frenetic girl, aren't you?"

"It looked like a real love potion to me, at least in my imagination," Amelie mocked.

"You better try this crispy fish, it's excellent," Charlotte gibbered with a full mouth.

"Sure, but I would prefer the steward serving us a wild crispy pheasant. Wow! It could be fun! We should go hunting one day. Maybe we can ask our French teacher, Bertrand de Mondi. He's a real Frenchman and I'm sure he loves to hunt like most European men. It would be fun to get lost in the wilderness and only to get one precious moment together."

"Amelie, I'm sure if that moment came, you would run away."

"You're right, I probably would," Amelie said giggling

"Then stop talking nonsense. You're irritating me with your giddy imagination. It makes no sense to even talk about it, because it will never happen. Amelie, you must focus and be more realistic," Charlotte pointed out with a laugh.

"You're funny Charlotte with that uppity attitude of yours. I've never met a girl like you. You can be my utopian usher and I will be a valorous vagabond, following you day and night," Amelie said with Gallic gesture.

"Amelie, you look like an undismayed virgin right now."

"Charlotte, don't stab my heart," she said snickering.

"We better go to Coach Louis' class, it's almost one p.m. You can finish your creative play later. Maybe you'll need a pinfeather," Charlotte added with a mocking tone in her voice. "You're funny, Charlotte," Amelie concluded as they entered the gymnasium. Coach Louis was already there.

"Hello girls. How are you doing today, any complaints about muscle pain?"

"So far so good, no pain," Charlotte replied positively.

"No complaints here either, coach!" Amelie added with a soft voice.

"Good then. Today we'll start with a few karate kicks. Later we'll increase our time on bars to thirty minutes followed by our regular routine. I will be observing you, so be sure to ask any questions you might have," the coach said in a peremptory tone while he walked away to his coaching armchair. He sat in comfort and watched the girl's karate moves.

"Sure, coach. No problem," Amelie confirmed in pensiveness. They performed their best karate kicks in sets of twenty in constant repetitions. An hour later they ran to the other rooms and continued Bat and Spider exercises. "What are you thinking about, Amelie?" Charlotte asked hanging upside-down on the rod.

"I'm commemorating my past freedom. I think I

will stay like this forever. I feel like I'm in a cocoon and soon I will spin a silk," she whispered shrugging her shoulders.

"This is good. I'll have a new silk scarf. You're too stressed out. Aren't you? Think big!" she sighed.

"I'll try, however, I'm clinging to this wooden rod and it feels like I'll be here permanently," Amelie chortled.

"I'm glad that you laugh," Charlotte said.

"Okay, girls, you can finish your chit chat later as the thirty minutes had just passed. Let's switch to climbing now. You're making progress and it seems like you got a fix of new energy. I'm glad."

"Thanks coach, it definitely helps our self confidence. It is an auspicious sign; right Charlotte."

"Oh yes! I feel this glowing energy in my heart," she added with a smile.

"I'm glad that you have a good sense of humor, girls," Coach Louis admitted with an attentive look. The girls trained hard for many hours and were getting better and better each time. However, often it felt like an avalanche was coming over their heads.

Soon after training they sneaked to their favorite spa. On their way back they paused near Sister Agnes room but heard nothing. With a sigh of relief they walked straight into their room and enjoyed one of Amelie's new teas.

Wednesday would be exciting, Charlotte thought. She was supposed to meet Peter that afternoon in their newly established secret place at the iron's gate, beneath the water. On that morning she went to her Greek language class, followed by Italian and French. Amelie sighed in her French class each time Bertrand spoke with his charismatic voice. The hours flew by fast and then it was time for the Coach Louis' daily exercise. The girls made hundreds of repetitions which would build their strength and flexibility; they switched from their karate kicks to the sword's lesson. Then at exactly five thirty p.m. they swam to the iron's gate. Charlotte spotted Peter and his friend Patrick, who she had first met when he arrived by bus. They were so happy to see each other; they exchanged hugs over the iron bars. Charlotte swam to the surface to catch some air and then dived again deep beneath the iron's gate to the other side. Indeed, there was a gap under the gate as she originally thought.

There was a small pocket of air above the underwater bridge between the water surface and the concrete columns. They each swam there and spoke freely for a few minutes. Amelie quickly followed everyone.

"Amelie, this is Peter, my brother and his friend, Patrick."

"Nice to meet you, guys," Amelie replied.

"Nice to meet you too," Peter said and shook hands with her.

"Nice to meet you, Amelie. How do you like your school so far?" Patrick asked with a smile.

"We have the same programs like you and we like it. So far so good! We learn a lot. What about you?" Amelie asked.

"I like it too. Peter and I have been having some fun together, especially in the martial arts classes."

"I know, it's hard, but definitely worth the pain,"

Amelie said and laughed.

"We have to go now, but we'll see you on Monday. This is our final week before Christmas," Charlotte said. "Okay! Bye girls. See you on Monday at the same time." Peter added and vanished in the water.

The girls successfully swam back. It was almost six p.m. The coach noticed their long absence and asked, "You've been under water for quite a long time. I can't imagine that you two have been holding your breath the entire time. How did you manage it?"

"We found an air gap beneath the concrete above the water's surface. We can easily breathe down there," Charlotte said with confidence.

"Well congratulations, but I knew about that gap which I discovered myself a long time ago. It didn't take much to find it. Okay, girls now go and enjoy your dinner and I'll see you tomorrow," coach concluded with satisfaction and left.

Soon after dinner they enjoyed the spa for thirty minutes. It was the only place in the entire school where they could rest and relax.

"Charlotte, I like Patrick. He's a very cute boy. Peter is good looking as well," suddenly Amelie interrupted the lull.

"I'm glad that you like him, at least he's your age."

"But an older man excites me in a different sort of way. Bertrand is a very mature man and that is what I like about him. All of my luscious fantasies are about him," Amelie cheerfully announced.

"I'm glad that he doesn't know that. Then it seems we're going back to square one with you, but hey, that's fine with me. Amelie, just forget about Patrick for now. You know, I like listening to you; it's as if I'm listening to the perfect symphony. Talk to me some more as I enjoy this nice Jacuzzi. There's no substitution for a nice bath like there's no substitution to Amelie's love stories. I must admit you've got a knack for these types of stories. Don't you?"

"I know Charlotte you've never even been in a platonic love. At least you should try. You don't know what you're missing out on. Just imagine; it's like an incandescent fire in the middle of your stomach and an inaudible confession of love in the air at the same time. I wonder how it would sound if Monk Bertrand professed his love. He must have been in love once or twice in his past. How anybody could ignore a man like him. Don't you agree with me?" Amelie said with a languishing voice.

"It is apprehensive and unapproachable for me. How do I put this, a sort of incantation which I don't understand and on top of that, love is also uncertain don't you agree, Amelie?"

"To a point, yes, I do. But love is also spontaneous and unplanned. At this point it's the best, a sort of incantation as you said. I agree so far. Unfortunately for me, it's also only platonic or a lackadaisical experience," Amelie said lingering.

"Fortunately for you, Amelie, someone also said that love is silly and dull like a sort of phantasmagoria."

"Don't be ridiculous! You're wrong! What would life be without love and excitement? There would be no people, no you and me. Love is like a breath of fresh air for your spirit. It can be pure lustfulness. It

184

can touch each nerve of your body and make you feel excited. You can get lost in love and sometimes it can be forever," Amelie said with keenness.

"You definitely aren't aiming to become a nun then; so you don't have to worry about keeping your feelings in check," Charlotte said with apprehension.

"You're right! I want to be madly in love. How about you," Amelie asked.

"I don't know yet. If I fall in love with some sexy man and go crazy with my feelings like you, then probably not. But at this point, it's difficult to say."

"You mean, if you freak out! I'm still waiting to be swept off my feet by my knight in shining armor on his white stallion. Hopefully, I won't have to wait very long," Amelie whispered in a romantic mood.

"What about a Scottish knight wearing cute kilt? It would be more romantic, wouldn't be?" Charlotte asked with a laugh.

"I prefer a traditional knight, but I would consider a cute, Scottish knight dressed in a kilt," Amelie whispered again with nobility of movement.

"You need to watch out for what you wish for as he may just kidnap you and maroon on an unknown island where you'll live and die alone. However, you can always cast your own story. Amelie, our time in the spa is over. Put your robe on. Let's go and do some homework, I have plenty of reading to do," Charlotte added and got out quickly. "Thank you for the advice. I'm ready to go," Amelie added with a sour tone. They put their robes on and walked slowly to their room. It was a quiet night, but very busy. At midnight they turned the light out and went to bed.

Finally, December came and the Christmas Holiday was just around the corner. On Sunday morning, the Sisters were decorating the Christmas trees with holy angels, bright stars, angel's hair, lights, candies, and rainbow ribbons. The girls were busy wrapping their presents for each person and gathering them around the trees. It was a lot of fun and a lot of laughs.

The Christmas music was heard in each speaker on every floor. The atmosphere was enchanting and very relaxing. It reminded everyone of home and family. The cooks were working on a special Christmas menu and the girls were getting ready for their last week of school and their final exams. It would be a time to remember for the rest of their lives, indeed.

Also there would be a big party on the last day of December to celebrate the New Year. Everyone was very excited. The Sisters had already picked the pastoral music for this special occasion. Sister Agnes was personally involved in most of the events. She asked a few of the girls to help her organize this big party. It was a tradition to invite the boys from the neighbor's Monastery to the party, so Sisters would tighten the security a bit. But there was enough time to handle that.

It was another Monday, Charlotte and Amelie went to their French class for the final exam and later the same morning took also a few different tests. They agreed that the tests weren't so difficult and they should pass them. At noon they met for lunch and were a bit excited. "Charlotte, how did you do?"

"I think I did fine. Maybe today wasn't my best

day, but I should pass all my tests. However, I'm not so sure about French. It was a bit tough for me, for some reason that particular subject wasn't so clear for me."

"What was it?"

"*Describe your best friend*. I'm not good enough at French to write a whole story like that, but with a bit of good luck I'll make it," Charlotte said with a bit of disappointment.

"I'll help you with your French tonight. I promise! I feel guilty that I've been ignoring you. French takes a lot of practice, so maybe if I cut down my love stories a bit I'll be able to help you," Amelie admitted with a guilty look on her face.

"Thank you, Amelie! You know it's going to be a great sacrifice on your part. I'm not sure if I will let you do that," Charlotte said with a laugh.

"Sure, I can do it! You must not know me very well," Amelie said in defense, smiling.

"Okay, I believe you. Let's enjoy today's lunch, it appears to be something different. It looks like fish fillet and spinach," Charlotte whispered.

"I'm glad that we have a few choices today, and you're right about the spinach. The cooks fried it up with some eggs, and that's why it tastes so good. My Grandma always made it that way," Amelie added while enjoying every bite of it.

The girls were done with their lunch and had some time to relax a bit before they had to change their clothes and go to their martial arts class. Their coach was very happy today as he'll have soon a week vacation. He'll be traveling to London to spend Christmas with his family. His brother is a well known lawyer for an international law firm in London. They always spent Christmas together.

The hours of training seemed to go by so slow. The Bat position was getting easier each time and they extended their time to an hour. The climbing was still very difficult, but they were improving their technique each time. The karate moves came so easy for the girls, just like fencing did. They quickly developed powerful legs and shoulder's muscles. Their coach complimented on their progress that afternoon,

"Girls, I must admit that you are some of the best students I've had so far. I can see that you're working very hard and have made a lot of progress in such a short period of time. It's unusual for girls of your delicate size. I have high hopes for your future. Just keep working! After you're done here you can move on to the swimming pool. One hundred laps today. You know your routines, so I won't bother you very much."

The girls completed their required laps in the pool and were ready for diving. Today they were to meet again with Peter and Patrick. They should be there in exactly five minutes. They took a deep breath and dived deeply to the gate. They saw only Patrick waiting alone. He was calling them over with his hands to swim under the gate. Charlotte thought that something must have happened to Peter. They took a final breath and dived under the gate, to the air pocket where Patrick was waiting for them. Charlotte looked at Patrick and asked,

"Where's Peter?"

"Peter couldn't come today. He's taking a

special test. It came earlier than we previously thought."

"What kind of test?" Charlotte asked.

"I think he mentioned to you that he wants to be one of the three **Omega Templars**. He can become one of them only if he passes this test. But this test is no an ordinary test. How can I explain it to you?"

"Don't worry, just tell me," Charlotte pressed the issue. Her face became pale. Amelie was terrified by the unexpected news.

"The test began for him yesterday. I saw him today and he asked me to bring you there to see him. He said he may not make it. But you're going to be in a shock when you see him in this condition, so I'm going to tell you what's happening to him and where he is right now. Here it goes: he was crucified yesterday evening to a wooden cross. The monks said that the nails were put between special muscles in his hands and feet and that he wasn't likely to feel much pain. They've been doing this procedure every year and have a lot of experience. To ease his pain, the cross is not immediately put in a vertical position. It begins by leaning him against a wall at a 60 degree angle. He must suffer through the pain for exactly three days. Every day, three monks come to check on him and each day they move the cross a bit higher. They put special balsam on his feet and his hands to prevent infection. Then, on the third day the cross will be lifted to an exact 90 degree angle.

It will be the most painful position for Peter and he must stand his pain for an entire day. While on the cross he cannot eat or drink. This swimming pool is connected to the St. Mark Chapel where Peter is right now. It is an ancient stone grotto. The monks have already seen him this morning. We have only five minutes to swim out there and about five minutes to speak with him. Just follow me."

They took off from the gate and swam straight into the grotto. Patrick opened the XI century, heavy wooden door with an iron knob. Charlotte and Amelie followed him inside. They stood in a half dimmed, almost dark stone cave. Peter was half conscious and sweaty, hanging on the cross. His hands and feet were bleeding. The iron nails were long and big. His head was bleeding from the iron wreath that was placed on him. It was frightening how he looked, like a waxen sculpture in pain. He was speaking in an unknown language. He didn't notice his visitors arrive.

"What is he saying? He didn't even notice us. What should we do? Patrick, here's a wet towel. I want you to squeeze some water on his lips. He looks terrible," Charlotte said with tears in her eyes and gave the wet towel to Patrick. He approached Peter and squeezed the wet towel over his face. The drops of the water moistened Peter's lips. Peter had been speaking in an old Aramaic language,

"Eli Eli lema sabachthani," My God, my God, why have you forsaken me?" It was the same words Jesus spoke when He was crucified. Patrick was stunned by what was happening.

"This is incredible! We must leave now. I want you to be strong girls and pray for Peter. He must survive this great ordeal. It is a life and death situation for him. Do this for him. He must pass this test."

They looked at Peter for the last time as he lost

190

total consciousness. Then suddenly they heard a voice,

*"**Peter, my child; do not fear**. I will make you strong and I will give you **wisdom** with which your adversaries will not be able to contradict or resist. Just follow my path. I will open your eyes to see the **truth** hidden around you. I will give you the **key** to open **the secrets** of the universe. I will open the gate of heaven for you. **Just listen to my voice**."*

"Whose voice is that?" Charlotte asked as her face became as white as pearl powder. Amelie and Patrick were terrified and wanted to leave. Charlotte looked at Peter and saw his eyes opening slowly.

"**God** talks to Peter!" Amelie said in a low voice.

"How are you Charlotte?" Peter suddenly whispered.

"I'm fine Peter. What can I do for you? How is your pain?" she asked with tears in her eyes.

"I don't feel any pain. I'll be fine. Don't worry," Peter spoke in a chilling voice.

"I will pray for you, Peter. You'll pass this test, just believe in yourself. I love you, Peter."

"I love you too, Charlotte. See you soon," Peter said and passed out again.

"We will pray for you, Peter," Amelie said and Patrick added, "Be strong man! You must make it."

Charlotte ran to Peter and put the wet towel on his face for a moment. Then she squeezed a few drops of water onto his mouth. They rushed back. It was already after six when the girls emerged from the swimming pool. The coach was sitting on the chair, still reading his newspaper. "I'm glad to see you're back, girls. That was a long dive, indeed. See you tomorrow and enjoy your evening."

"Thank you, coach. Enjoy your evening as well," Charlotte replied and they left. They walked fast to the spa. It was cold outside and the emotions they had were too much for one evening. The spa gave them some relief and soothed their cold bodies with a new energy.

"Charlotte, what do you think is going to happen?" Amelie asked.

"I have faith in Peter and I know he'll make it, even though he looks so terrible. This test will make him stronger and more focused on his goal. I have faith in God and I believe that all of this is happening for a reason," Charlotte said.

"Let me pray for Peter. Oh, Dear Lord Our God please let Peter stand the pain with dignity and allow him to get through the next two days. Amen," Amelie said sincerely.

"Thank you, Amelie for your deep concern. Certainly, God listens to your prayer and He will make this happen. I will pray for him tonight. I know it is the only way for him to achieve what he wants. There are no short cuts in our lives unfortunately. Each of us must carry an invisible cross on our path in life, and when the cross gets heavier we must pause for a moment and take a deep breath, and then keep going. With all the temptations on our path, the load seems too big to carry on, so we feel like giving it up, but we can't!"

"Charlotte, that was nice. I know this can't be easy for you right now, after all the bad things that have happened to you recently, but I will stand by you and Peter. You can count on me; it's very difficult for me to understand all of this. There is Peter suffering on that cross and God is talking to him at the same time. Everything is sounded so real, but no one would believe it until they saw and heard everything with their own eyes and ears. I believe we're blessed to be here right now, at this school; otherwise we wouldn't have experienced anything like that. However, I must admit that being in that chapel was very scary for me, but at the same time it was so beautiful. You see all that stuff only in the movies. Don't you agree Charlotte?"

"Sure, I agree. I have a feeling that the time we spend at this school will have a significant impact on our lives forever. Tomorrow, we can check on Peter again. I'm pretty sure Patrick will be there too. He's a nice guy. Peter told me that he wants to be one of those Templars too."

"He may change his mind after what he saw today and how much sacrifice is involved," Amelie said. "You are right, we never know. People can change their mind when they realize and see how much pain is involved, but if Peter makes it through, Patrick will go for it. I'm quite positive about it," Charlotte said with confidence.

"I agree. It's getting late and we should go. We should get some food on our way back home. I don't know if you remember, but we've skipped dinner two days in a row."

"You're right Amelie, we better go, it's almost eight p.m. and hopefully the dining room is still open."
"I'm pretty sure it's open until nine thirty p.m. The cooks are usually busy with baking bread and cakes

for the next day. Soon, they'll be even busier with the Christmas party coming in just a few days, to be more precise on Friday. Who knows, they could be even open until midnight. I wouldn't worry about that, Charlotte."

They put their robes on and left the spa. They stopped in the kitchen to pick up their dinner. The cooks were very busy indeed, preparing the Christmas menu. Chef Andrew showed the girls some secret specialties which will be served at the party.

"These are different types of gingerbread: Italian, German and French. You can try a few samples and let me know which ones you like the best. This one is an Italian cake made of a mixture of fruits, nuts, and spices, we call it Panforte. You can also get a small sample of that right now. These crispy cookies are made with pictures of different animals and they are flavored with anise, some with mint, and some with basil. Thus, you have a choice of three to choose from. We will have ten different courses on our menu to choose from for the New Year celebration party; everything for your discerning palate," Chef Andrew said. The girls were enjoying each cookie.

"I like this Italian one. How about you Charlotte?" Amelie asked.

"I love the Panforte and this anise cookie is like heaven in my mouth. Thank you so much Andrew," Charlotte said.

"You are the best cook, better than my Grandma, and that's quite a compliment," Amelie added on their way out.

"I'm glad that you like everything. I've been

194

doing this for almost twenty five years, right here in this kitchen. Goodnight girls," Chef Andrew said with a smile.

"Goodnight Andrew," Amelie said and they left with their late dinner packed carefully into boxes.

"I will make some tea for us and we can listen to some jazz. I'll help you with your French tonight if you like. Tomorrow we find if we passed the finals. I hate taking tests because you never can be sure of what they'll ask you to write. I especially don't like grammar; I was never very good at it. Alright, I've made my favorite tea; it's called **Arabesque**. I call it after the famous Degas, Ballet Dancers. This tea is sophisticated like the dancers in that painting and will put you in a positive mood," Amelie proudly announced.

"I'm looking forward to it; you know I can't resist your famous teas." "Here you go. Please, do enjoy Charlotte. I know it will wash away your stress for the moment as I speak."

"Amelie thank you." She took a sip and smelled inside the cup. "The flavor is very flowery and aromatic. I like it! What would I do without you?"

"Thank you, Charlotte. Try this cookie. I like our cooks. They cook like my grandma. Let me delight in their specialty of the evening," Amelie said with a soft voice.

"Sure, I will do that as well. May I please have another cup of tea, Amelie; since you're the specialist on teas I will ask you to do the honor?"

"It's always my pleasure. Let me know when you're ready for that French review. I'll be ready too," Amelie replied.

"In a few minutes, Amelie," Charlotte announced. A few minutes had passed and Amelie asked again,

"Are you ready, Charlotte? Let's begin! In French; Puis-je vous aider means; Can I help you? Repeat!"

"Puis-je vous aider," Charlotte repeated ten times.

"Good! Do you understand? Comprenez-vous? I understand. Je comprends.
Please repeat at least twenty times."

"Okay, I can do that! /Compre-vu; Je kompren/. I understand," Charlotte said.

"Now say with me, I'd like. Je voudrais. We'd like. Nous voudrions. I'm looking for. Je cherche. I'm hungry. J'ai faim. I'm thirsty. J'ai soif. I'm tired. Je suis fatigue. See you later. A tout a l'heure. Good night. Bonne nuit. Okay, Charlotte, you're doing better. We must practice more tomorrow," Amelie said yawning.

"Merci. Thank you, Amelie. If I practice every day for ten minutes with you, within a few months I will be almost fluent."

"De rien. You're welcome, Charlotte." The girls were tired and went to bed at close to midnight. Tomorrow would be another challenging day. But most importantly; they would see Peter again.

The girls awoke to a cold, snowy morning and they glanced through the window at beautiful snowflakes pouring heavily from the sky. Perhaps the snowflakes were announcing the arrival of Santa Claus. Everyone was excited about the Christmas atmosphere and the upcoming winter break. Some believers, indeed, were pertinacious waiting for the real Santa Claus to come. The Sisters were busy decorating every corner of the school with Christmas ornaments and they seemed like they really enjoyed their Samaritan's like work. Happiness was flying through the air.

Charlotte and Amelie went to French class to find their test's result. Teacher Bertrand made a few peculiar comments, "Amelie, I'm really surprised you almost failed the grammar section part of your test. I thought you were French."

"Indeed, I am French, but as I mentioned to you I wasn't very good at grammar and that is why I'm retaking French again. I'm just terrible at grammar!"

"Charlotte, I really enjoyed how you described friendship in a few words. You wrote that *'friendship is like a touch of bleeding heart'.* You almost brought a tear to my eye. It is a beautiful expression, indeed," Bertrand said with his masculine voice as he slowly approached Charlotte and looked deeply into her eyes and then added,

"Can you explain to all of us how you got your poetic inspiration?"

"Maybe, Charlotte is a poet," Amelie whispered, laughing. Bertrand looked at Amelie seriously but didn't comment.

"These were the only three words I remembered in French," Charlotte replied. The girls burst into laughter.

"I see, so it's very fortunate for you that I still like it. It was a very poetic phrase, indeed. I am impressed by the way you put it," Bertrand replied with a short smile.

"I think it was rather frenetic," Amelie added.

"I didn't ask for your opinion, Amelie," Bertrand said caught by surprise.

"I know but I must express myself," Amelie added with a smile.

"Are you satisfied right now, Amelie," Bertrand asked.

"Indeed, I am," Amelie whispered as she looked deeply into his black eyes.

"Okay Charlotte, you can sit down. I want to tell all of you that French is a very romantic and sophisticated language. It has this amazing flexibility like no any other language. It is definitely the perfect language for expressing your inner thoughts. Let's practice a bit more and you will be free to go. I want you to repeat each word after me. Repeat it, please. Repetez-le, s'il vous plait. /repete-le sel-vuple/. Again. Encore. Write it down, please. Ecrivez-le, s'il vous plait. Do you want? Voulez-vous? I should like. Je voudrais. I have lost my friends. J'ai perdu mes amis. I'll be seeing you. A bientot. Come to see me. Venez me voir.

Be sure to practice these common phrases and as always please come see me if you have any questions. Have a great day!" Bertrand concluded as he dismissed the class.

"Did you have fun in class, Amelie? You made me nervous and look stupid in front of everyone," Charlotte asked as they were going to Italian class.

"Sure, but I didn't mean anything by it. I'm telling you that he is in love with you, Charlotte," Amelie concluded.

"I highly doubt it. You're having fun with this, Amelie. Aren't you?"

"Why isn't he in love with me?" Amelie replied with a smile.

"Why don't you ask him yourself? You're the one with the fantasy about him or maybe, you're just crazy my dear friend. He's too old for you and you're definitely too young for him," Charlotte said, laughing.

"Geeeez! Love is blind!" Amelie shouted.

"Amelie, you're watching way too many movies. Am I right?" "Maybe, you are. Maybe I've seen one too many romantic movies. But this doesn't change my feelings at all."

"Alright, your time is over now. Our Italian teacher is coming in. It's good that he looks like Cyrano de Bergerac with that big nose of his, so he's definitely not your type. We'll talk later, after class is over," Charlotte replied. Peter was the only thing on her mind at this point. She was worried if he was still alive, but she would find out that afternoon.

"I love the guy, Depardieu, who plays Bergerac, but you're right, he isn't my type," Amelie whispered when the teacher entered.

A few hours went by. The classes were over. Every Tuesday the cooks made the same lunch and Amelie always made the same comment, "I hate the food on Tuesdays, it's always the same. The same chicken wings in the same slimy sauce. I'm finally going to complain to Sister Agnes."

"Amelie, I don't think it would be wise. You can always skip Tuesdays and keep your body in shape. I remembered what the Sister Agnes said the first day I met her, 'no complaints about food.' Just forget it. I personally don't mind," Charlotte said.

"Okay, maybe I should just accept it."

199

"You should, Amelie, and it's only on Tuesdays. Trust me it will make you more sensible and a bit thinner."

"You always find the good in everything, Charlotte. Thank you for making my life a bit easier."

"Sure, you're very welcome. My concern today is only Peter. You know this is the second day of his ordeal. I need to see him tonight, but I'm very nervous," Charlotte replied.

"You're right. We better concentrate on Peter instead of my crazy love-games. Please forgive me, Charlotte. Now I can see how my fantasies pale in comparison to what Peter is going through. We will swim to his grotto tonight. Let me pray again; Dear Lord, I sincerely ask you to extinguish my fantasies and replace them with my deep concern for Peter's survival. Amen."

"Amelie, with your exuberant imagination it is difficult for me to distinguish your fantasies from reality. But at least you show remorse in the end, and from all of that I can extract the real truth."

"I'm glad that you've discovered the real me," Amelie said with a silly giggle.

"You are a gimcrack gosling, Amelie," said Charlotte as she laughed.

"I'm done with my lunch and I'm ready to go," Amelie said.

"Me too, let's change our uniforms and go to Coach Louis' class." As always, Coach Louis was waiting for the girls. There would only be two more classes before the winter break. "Hello girls! Are you excited about winter vacation?"

"We sure are, we can finally catch up on some

long overdue sleep," Amelie remarked.

"Don't forget, you must always study hard, Amelie, even when there's no school," Coach added spontaneously.

"Sure, but I'm also very tired."

"Well then girls, this vacation is coming at a very good time for you. Today we'll do the same routine, but the time has been extended to two hours for the first position and so on, you know the rest."

"Yes Coach, we got the rest," Charlotte replied, smiling.

"You're on your own today, but I'll be around and keeping an eye on you." It was their regular routine for each exercise, except a bit longer, and the girls were in a hurry to get to the swimming pool. After a few hours of hard work they walked over to the pool and Coach Louis said, "Girls, today we'll do one hundred five laps and after the holidays we'll increase it to one hundred twenty."

"Okay, no problem," Charlotte replied.
It was around six p.m. Patrick was already waiting for them at the iron's gate. They made a last jump up for some air and dived deep to the other side of the gate. They followed him until they reached the grotto. Peter was still hanging on the cross and the two burning candles were on each side of the cross. He looked like he was sleeping peacefully. The cross had been lifted up another twenty degrees. Peter suddenly opened his eyes.

"Oh, guys, thank you for coming. Don't worry, I'm okay! Only one more day left. I think, I'll be fine," Peter whispered as he tried to squeeze a little smile on his distraught face that was filled with pain. Patrick lifted Charlotte up so she could put the wet towel over Peter's face. Then she poured some water over his lips. "It feels good, thank you," Peter mumbled.

"Peter, are you sure that you'll make it? How are you feeling?" Charlotte asked, crying.

"I don't feel any pain, it only hurts when the monks lift the cross, and then the pain goes away. Each morning they put more miracle balsam over my hands and feet. Tomorrow, after the last lifting, I'll be happy," Peter whispered slowly.

"We will pray for you Peter, just keep your faith," Amelie said.

"Are you ready Patrick for the test?" Peter asked.

"I'm not sure yet, I'm still thinking it over, maybe I'm not ready. You're very brave Peter," Patrick replied with deep concern.

"Thank you for coming, I love you," Peter whispered with a quiet voice.

"We love you too Peter. Be strong and believe in yourself. Your feet are very cold. I will warm them up a bit," Charlotte said and began to massage his feet. "It feels good Charlotte, thank you!" Peter said. Amelie came to join Charlotte and Patrick was blowing the hot air from his lungs onto Peter's feet.

"Thank you guys, I'm warm now," Peter said with a slight smile.

"It is very cold in here," Patrick said.

"It's a stone cave, that's why it's so cold. It is five past six p.m. Peter see you tomorrow and don't give up! I think we should go," Amelie said.

"Bye Peter! See you soon," Patrick said.

"Bye guys see you tomorrow," he replied with

solace.

After they said goodbye to each other they departed in different directions. The Coach was there waiting for their return. The girls said goodnight to him and hurried up to the spa. It was freezing cold out there and with pleasure they soaked in the hot Jacuzzi for almost an hour.

"Amelie, I have to ask you for a favor."

"Sure, anything!"

"Please, do not talk to anyone about what Peter is going through, this has to all be kept a secret, I hope I can trust you."

"You can count on me, I can keep secrets. I would never mention to anyone about it, even if teacher Bertrand never talked to me again," Amelie said with equanimity.

"Amelie, you're one of a kind, you know that."

"Perhaps I am," she said smiling.

"I like your fairy-like nature; it brings a bit of sunshine to our life." Charlotte concluded.

"I'm so grateful for that my dear Charlotte," Amelie said, giggling again.

"We better go and practice some French, Amelie. You promised that we would practice every day for ten minutes," Charlotte said.

"You're right. Let's go then." The evening went by fast there was not much time left after the French review and other final assignments. With the taste of a good tea in their mouths the girls fell fast asleep.

Wednesday morning's bright sun woke them up earlier than usual. The birds were chirping a beautiful morning serenade to Mother Nature and woke everyone up. There was no way anyone could steal an additional thirty minutes of sleep. Amelie opened her eyes, walked to the window. She scanned the noisy birds and said,

"They look like old satyrs who try to make a joke with their saucy noise. I hate those birds. They do this routine every morning. Maybe I can keep them company and play the saxophone to their morning tunes. But I would prefer to shoot them."

"Sure, Amelie and everyone will scream at you. You look like an old shrew in that morning outfit. I suggest you better relax and forget about those birds. They don't have much of a brain, indeed."

"You don't know me yet! I'll kill those scavengers! I can't sleep; they've scorched my nerves. Bastards! Screw them! They don't even sing, they're screeching. I can hunt them for the evening barbecue. I'm sure they'll be tendered than the chicken wings the cooks serve us every Tuesday," Amelie shouted, scowling.

"Amelie, just remember that those little creatures are a creation of God."

"What about me? Are you looking for an excuse for them? I don't think so; those scum birds are not excused! I can't sleep in the morning because of them," Amelie shouted furiously.

"Amelie, you need to relax, have some tea. I hope you have one with a sedative in your tea-selection; you're making too much fuss about nothing. Now you're sounding like you're possessed."

"I brought a sling with me and I swear I will kill those beasts! I need some beans as missiles; I guess I can do it later."

"Amelie please come to your senses before

you become one of those Sepoys known in the legendary English army shooting at the ghosts. Let me look at those innocent birds," Charlotte said as she approached the window. "Oh, look at this cute little Serin, doing his everyday bath, isn't it adorable? Amelie try to be more liberal and be a mother to them."

"Are you serious? Me, be a mother to those little bastards? I'll put a muzzle on their beaks first" Amelie said still excited.

"Don't be a shad, Amelie! Put your anger aside and you'll feel better. Let's go to breakfast instead."

"I'm so angry, look into my eyes."

"Amelie, that's enough. Don't you think you're overreacting? Show a little compassion."

"They don't deserve compassion, why should I give them compassion? I'm hungry, today after lunch I'll finish the job, as soon as I get some beans from the cooks," Amelie admitted, being complacent.

"Amelie, what am I going to do with you. It's pointless to even argue with you."
They went for breakfast and later attended their Greek, Italian, and Hebrew final classes. They took a few tests, but nothing too difficult. After their last test they took a twenty minute break. Charlotte was exhausted and said, "I don't know why I'm so tired, I feel like my brain wants to jump out of my skull."

"Me too, for some reason I'm so aggravated, I think this morning's unfinished business with those birds is the cause of my misery," Amelie concluded. "I was hoping you forgot about them."

"No way, not a chance! As I already mentioned to you this morning, I'm going to take care of those

205

birds, once and for all, then I can rest in peace," Amelie bravely added.

"Okay, whatever you say. We should change, and go to lunch. I don't want to argue with you again."

"Okay! You're right, I should conserve my energy for later," Amelie said smiling.

Soon after lunch Amelie talked to the cooks and asked them for some dried beans, they gave her plenty without any hesitation. The girls were content, as the food was excellent. "Let's go Charlotte. I have only forty five minutes to kill those birds before our martial arts training."

"Please, give me just a minute; I'm almost done with my drink. You can't be serious about those poor little birds."

"I'm deadly serious! Indeed! I must take care of it now, before everything starts again tomorrow morning."

"You are serious, indeed! Then let's continue your undone work."

"Charlotte, do you imagine that I'll sleep better tonight after I exterminate those little beasts?"

"Okay Amelie, we're home. You're on your own. In the meantime, I'm going to take a short nap."

"Okay. I'll let you know about each successful shot and if or when I attain my final glory."

"Okay! I will keep my ears open."

Amelie put the dried beans in a big bowl on one side of the window; she grabbed the leather sling and with the grace of a trained archer sent a few bean's missiles straight across the yard into the birds sitting on the branches of the big pine tree. To Amelie's dismay the first several missiles were unsuccessful. The little Serins were still milling about as if they were auctioning off their goods for sale at the local exchange corn market and singing their old songs. Amelie was furious. She walked nervously in front of the window from left to right looking for the best solution. More than twenty shots were aimed at the tree, but without any visible success. Then with a renewed determination she focused on her task, but from a different angle this time. She would also put more force in her shots by stretching the sling a bit more she thought.

"Damn, bastards. They're playing a game with me," she grumbled. Another twenty beans passed between the window and the pine tree. Suddenly she spotted a big heron sitting on the top of a tree. He was a quiet hermit and she accepted him as a sort of art object. But those little Serins were on her last nerve and they must be eliminated. She must get rid of them now before it gets dark. She sent more than thirty beans flying again and it looked like one finally hit a bird. She screamed with happiness.

"Charlotte, I got one! Yes! I've successfully killed one little bastard!" Then she was shooting more and more. Charlotte jumped off the bed and asked,

"Are you sure? Where is it?"

"I'm positive, just look down there somewhere. That bastard must have fallen down onto the green grass below thanks for the gravity. Perhaps he's singing his last epitaph of life and death on his way down."

"Amelie, look! Don't you see our beloved Sisters standing under the same pine tree and staring at our window? How long have they been standing out there?"

"Sure, sure; I don't have a clue maybe they have a serious staring problem. You would never know. I'm very busy now don't bother me." Amelie didn't know that the same little bird she shot landed on Sister Claudia's head, on her freshly starched white hat. She wasn't too happy about it and called the other Sisters for help.

Soon they were marching straight to Charlotte and Amelie's room to solve the enigmatic bird's mystery. This didn't stop Amelie from sending several more beans across the yard. Suddenly someone hysterically knocked at the door. It was Sister Agnes.

"Come in!" Charlotte said with a terrified look on her face.

The Sisters marched forward and Sister Agnes asked nervously,

"Are you running some kind of con-fraternity right here girls? Or maybe you're just throwing bean's confetti out of the window, but I'm telling you it is too early for a New Year's celebration. This is a rebellion act. You're not confounded. I need to confiscate all your weapons at once."

Suddenly, Sister Claudia took her hat off and there he was, the little beast Serin lying down comfortable between the brown beans and the white starched edges of her hat. It gave an impression that he accepted her hat as his own coffin or perhaps graveyard. Then Sister Claudia said calmly,

"God created this little creature for our enjoyment and you dared to kill it! What demon told you to commit such a crime! What should I do with it?"

"We could congeal it in the freezer;" Amelie

208

answered and shocked everyone in the room. They looked at her with disbelief. She glanced through the window and spotted more beasts gathering on the tree branches. They must be grieving over the death of their fellow Serin, she thought. The sister was speechless and stood in silence for a moment.

Suddenly Sister Agnes burst into a hysterical laugh. Sister Claudia looked at her and laughed too.

"We must not be too harsh on you, my child, but indeed this is very funny," Sister Agnes whispered as she continued to chuckle heavily.

"Then what should I do with this little Serin," Sister Claudia asked again, still giggling.

"What do you suggest, Amelie?" Sister Agnes asked.

"If we can barbecue it, it would be better than the chicken wings in slimy sauce the cooks serve us every Tuesday, or we can give the little guy a perfect funeral," Amelie proudly replied and thought how much she still hated those little noisy beasts.

"I will choose funeral. Until then I will put it in the freezer," Sister Claudia said with acceptance and reassurance.

"Whose idea was this in the first place?" Sister Agnes asked.

"It was my idea. I didn't sleep well for at least two months because of those noisy bastards. Then I decided to shoot them with dried beans," Amelie confessed.

"You're right. I haven't been able to sleep either since those birds moved into that pine tree at the beginning of the school year. I was thinking about buying a sling shot myself," Sister Agnes admitted with a hearty laugh.

"Okay girls; let's put this case to rest. This case is officially dismissed due to lack of visible evidence that the Serin was actually murdered by any reason. Please be sure to consult with me any future problems you might encounter, let's reconcile our feelings for this coming Christmas. Amelie, no more sling shots and no more beans. We have plenty of beans in the garden now and perhaps they will sprout soon," Sister Claudia announced as she was leaving laughing heavily on her way out.

"Goodbye for now girls. I believe you still have a martial arts class today," Sister Agnes said as she was closing the door behind her.

"We're lucky that the Sisters have a good sense of humor about these things, or we could be in some serious trouble," Charlotte concluded.

"But the case is still open, at least for me. How are we going to solve this singing bastard's problem? It needs to be taken care of."

"We can get some cats. They like to chase the birds," Charlotte said.

"This is a brilliant idea! It would be a reciprocal benefit; the cats get the birds and we get peace of mind. We can bring all the street cats right here. I saw a lot of them near the trash cans. However, they're difficult to catch. We must make a special net. I'll start hunting for them tonight. Are you in?"

"Sure, I'm in with you, my dear Amelie," Charlotte confronted.

"Let's go to our martial arts class, we're late," Amelie said.

Their Coach was already there but he didn't

say much. Their routine began like it always did followed by karate and fencing exercises. The girls were exhausted a bit before they went for their final swim. Today was their last class before the winter recess. The girls were in a hurry to see Peter. Tonight was his final day too. If he survives this ordeal, he will be one of the three Omega Templars', something he wanted to be. They dived to meet Patrick at the iron's gate.

They followed him to St. Marks' cave. Peter was still there hanging on the cross unconscious. They began to revive him slowly. Patrick poured water over Peter's face. Amelie and Charlotte massaged his cold feet in what seemed a hopeless situation.

"Patrick, maybe he's dead," Charlotte said with tears. "I think he's just sleeping. He hasn't eaten or drank for three days. He must be very weak," Patrick sadly admitted. "We should pray for him right here! Oh, Dearest God, please give us a miracle right here. Please make Peter rise from the cross alive. Make his heart hot and his eyes blue like the sky. Give him his precious life back. Amen," Amelie said with tears. Charlotte and Patrick whispered after her.

They were very sincere in their prayers and believed that Peter would open his eyes again and begin speaking to them. It was eerily silent with the candles still burning, giving flickering shades on the stone's walls. Suddenly a warm wind picked up from nowhere. They stood there like night watchmen and observed what was happening.

"Guys, look! Peter's heart is burning red and pulsating so fast. This must be God's divine work," Amelie shouted with surprise.

"He's opening his eyes. Wow! Look! They're bright and blue like the sky. Amelie your prayer has been answered," Charlotte said with happiness.

"Hi guys! Thank you so much for coming. I feel great and tonight at midnight the monks will bring me down. Soon I'll be sleeping in my own cozy bed," Peter said in a clear voice.

"This is great news Peter! We are so very proud of you. You made it! We will wait for you and tomorrow we'll see as you'll walk again on your own," Patrick said calmly.

"Thank you heavenly father for giving me my life back, I am your Messenger and Servant from now on. Thank you for bringing my best friends and family and their kind words. Amen," Peter said and closed his eyes. Charlotte touched his feet and they were still warm. They glanced at Peter and then left quietly knowing that he was in good hands.

"Patrick, thank you for your friendship, it is priceless! Please, call me tomorrow and let me know what happened to Peter," Charlotte said. "I will, goodnight girls. At midnight the monks will do a special ceremony over Peter's body. I don't know exactly what it would be, but I'll call you tomorrow around noon and let you know," he said and left.

"Goodnight, Patrick!" Amelie shouted on her way out. The girls swam back and slowly departed from the pool area saying goodnight to their coach and wishing him a Merry Christmas.

It was cold and rainy outside. They jumped into the warm Jacuzzi with a huge sigh of relief. "This feels great, almost like paradise," Amelie peacefully said.

"Oh, yes! I'm so happy that Peter is alive and

will be okay. Thank you God for every moment of his life," Charlotte whispered with reassurance. "Don't forget Charlotte that we have a rendezvous with those cats tonight. Do you think that I can make a net from the mesh window curtains? It would be a perfect fabric for it."

"Sure, it would be but you should ask Sister Agnes if it would be okay with her."

"Okay, on our way back we'll stop by her room," Amelie said.

The pleasure of a hot water bath and a massage came to an end and it was time to go. They dropped their robes over their bodies and left. As they were passing by Sister Agnes' room Amelie knocked at the door but there was no answer. Sister Agnes had gone somewhere but there was no time to waste. They ran to their room and Amelie pulled down one of the curtains and cut it in half. She would make a double net for the cats. She'd pinned each corner and stapled the edges. It would be strong enough to handle any size of cat, she thought.

"Charlotte, are you ready? Let's go! There's no time to waste. It's getting dark. We must take some food as bait for them."

"I'm almost done. I need to get my jacket. It must be freezing cold out there," Charlotte said.

They left their room and went hunting behind the building where all the trash was collected. There were plenty of cats climbing over the open trash cans, picking over the food's scraps.

"Charlotte, hold the net with me. When the cat goes into the trash can we'll put the net over and grab it."

"Okay, I got it! Let's move on."

"Two cats are already in. Let's throw the net over the can. Now, we must turn the can upside down and the cats will go into the net. Hooray we did it!" However, the cats screamed like someone was murdering them. "Be quiet beasts! Charlotte would you give them some food to quiet them down."

"Where are we going to put them?" Charlotte asked wondering.

"Well, we'll have to put them in our room for the moment. I'm going to have to give them some lessons on how to catch the Serins. We're going to have to bring the dead Serin from Sister Claudia's freezer. She mentioned that she was going to keep it in her freezer until the time of the funeral arrangement."

"Okay, Amelie we're already at our door. I'll open the door, but be sure to close it quickly before the cats run away."

"Sure, no problem, the doors are closed. Let them run free. Kitty, kitty, come here. Oh yes, you're so cute and I'm going to teach you how to hunt those little bastards. Charlotte let's go find the dead Serin now."

"Okay, I'm ready. Did you remember to bring a small plastic bag for the creature?"

"I did, and I took a long string too. I will use the Serin body as bait for the cats. If this works, maybe we can bring two more cats," Amelie spontaneously declared.

"Amelie, stop right there. I think Sister Claudia lives in this room. I will knock on the door. Hmmm, nobody's answering. What shall we do?"

"We should get in and see what happened.

214

The door is not even locked. Sister Claudia, are you here? I see a refrigerator in there. Let me look in the freezer. Hmmm, I see a little bundle of paper, maybe this is it. Oh, yes! It's the frozen little bastard. Indeed, it looks better dead than alive. At least it can't talk."

"We should find her and let her know that we got her bird."

"Charlotte, this is not her bird. This is my bird; let's make this perfectly clear, we'll tell her that we went ahead with the funeral without her. I hope she won't mind," Amelie added.

"What will happen if the cats eat the bird? Then what's next on your agenda, Amelie?"

"I don't let them do that. We will need this bird for later. I have very detail plan. Don't worry. Now we'll go out to see if we can bring more cats. I'll tighten the string around Serin's neck and we can use it as bait. It should be easy. Here kitty, kitty, here kitty, kitty, come here kitty. I see two more cats near the trash cans. They're coming closer. They must smell the little beast. We'll walk slowly and just wait and see if they'll follow us."

The cats followed Amelie and the bait to their room upstairs. The new cats enjoyed the company of the first couple of cats. "Perfect job Amelie, what's next?"

"Just watch me. Here kitty, kitty. You see how they run around after the bait." Amelie picked up one cat, opened the window and said to him,

"Look at that pine tree. Do you see those little bastards out there? They are your precious food and your enemy. Tomorrow, early morning I want all of you to run onto the tree and catch those beasts! I

215

hope you'll enjoy your delicious breakfast. Do we understand each other?" Then she took each cat to the same window and told each one the same story. For the next hour she ran with the bait around the table and all cats followed her.

"Amelie, you must be tired already with your freaky show, aren't you?" Charlotte asked.

"No, I'm okay, I want to be sure that they clearly understand their important mission. I have perfect plan for them. Now, we shall walk them to the pine tree on a leash one by one. I will hang the little beast Serin on the tree branches as bait for them. The cats will spend the night with us, they are sociable creatures indeed. Early in the morning I will walk them straight to the pine tree. They will smell the dead Serin and climb the tree and then hunt the birds. Just look at them, they're like little tigers. The cats will scare the birds away for good and we'll be able to sleep well again."

"How are you going to hang that bird on the high branches of the tree? You're going to have to climb the tree together with the cats and if that's the case, then you won't need the cats since you can scare those birds yourself."

"I've thought of that already. I don't have to climb the tree. I'll tie a small stone to the other end of the string attached to Serin and throw it over the tree branches. With a little luck the string will entangle within the smaller branches and our lovely Serin will be quietly hanging in the air, waiting to be discovered."

"You've got quite a splendid plan Amelie. I hope everything works out for you."

"This is not only for me. This is for you too and for Sister Agnes and everyone else. She said, those birds are bothering her too much."

"Actually, you're right. I stand behind your plan one hundred percent."

"I'm glad we're finally in agreement about those birds. Now, let's walk those cats to the trees. I've cut some ribbons into long pieces. If you don't mind, you can tie it around cat's neck into two knots. I'll hold them for you."

"Okay, give me the ribbons. Come kitty, come to me, now, with all the rainbow-ribbons you just look like a Christmas ornaments," Charlotte said as the cats purred happily. "No time to waste, let's go Charlotte!" Amelie shouted as they marched straight to the pine trees.

"Charlotte, hold the cats, they must sniff the dead Serin before they run up the tree. I'll throw the bird into those branches above us. It looks tempting. Let them run free."

It was a wild chase. The frightened Serins flew into different directions. The cats quickly climbed onto the top branches but their prey had already flown away. A few cats jumped onto the grass and Charlotte was able to hold them. However, one cat got stuck on the single branch as he tried to get the dead Serin. He jumped but missed the bird. His ribbon entangled with the tree's branches and he accidentally hung himself. He gyrated around the red ribbon with this horrified grin on his face just next to the dead Serin. It was a gruesome scene and the girls were terrified by the event.

"What are we going to do? It looks rather grim."

217

Charlotte asked

"Don't worry! I'm going to climb up there and get them down."

"Are you sure you can do it?"

"Yes, I've climbed trees my whole life. I'll be fine," Amelie confirmed with assurance. Gracefully she climbed to the closest branch just next to the dead cat. She was about to grab the ribbon but the branch broke and she landed with it on the green soft grass. The cat was still hanging out there on the higher branch just next to the stiff Serin.

"Amelie, are you okay? You almost killed yourself. Maybe, I should call Sisters for help."

"No, no Sisters! I'm fine. This branch saved my life. I felt like a witch on a flying broom. I have just a few scratches here and there. Don't worry I'll be fine, just my butt hurts a bit. Damn cat! Let's go Charlotte, just forget about this beast. Take those four cats, still plenty for tomorrow. I'll take the branch with me."

"It's quite a chunk, Amelie. I can hide the branch near the trash," Charlotte said.

"No! There is no need for that. The Sisters will find it tomorrow and question it. I'll take it to my room and put it in the bathroom. Trust me it is better that way. Oh damn bastards, I hate them." After that grotesque scene they walked in grief to their room. Charlotte was supporting Amelie with her shoulder on their way back.

"The Sisters will find out sooner or later," Charlotte added.

"Don't worry about it. There's always some kind of explanation for everything. At least we'll get rid of the Serins. They really get on my nerves."

218

"We're almost there. Where I should put those cats?"

"Let them run freely in our room. In the morning we'll get rid of them. Everything is under control. I'll need some of those miracle balsams from our coach, Louis. Do you think we can get some? I'll have a lot of scars all over me."

"I can go see if the coach is in his room. I'll ask him. You just stay here. No more new ideas," Charlotte said and went to see the coach. She was lucky as the coach was in his room ready to leave for the last plane to London.

"Coach, I'd like to ask you if you still have that miracle balsam. I'll need some for Amelie. She took a bad fall from a tree."

"What was she doing up there? Let me look, I had a small jar of it in the freezer. Oh, yes, is still here! I can give it to you but when I come back from London next week you must bring it back to me."

"It is long story coach but for sure I will bring it back to you. You can count on me. Thank you so much and Merry Christmas again."

"Be sure to use the clean glass spatula. Do not contaminate the balsam. It is very special. See you soon."

"I will coach. Don't worry!" Charlotte said and left in a hurry.

"Amelie, I'm back! You're a lucky girl, coach was about to take off to the airport. I got the balsam. You look terrible. Have you seen yourself in the mirror? You got at least twenty cuts all over your face. You must stay here until you heal. Otherwise, when the girls see you they'll think that someone beat you

219

up. I will put the balsam all over you. Just stay still and no talking."

"I consider myself rather lucky to be alive. Those bastards! I hate them!" Amelie shouted.

"Amelie, I said be quiet! I can't concentrate. Yes, you're lucky, indeed. I think you better stand up until the balsam sinks into your skin. Total cuts; fifty-six. Thanks God the Sisters didn't see anything tonight. However, tomorrow they will likely find out everything."

"You're too sensitive Charlotte. Don't think about tomorrow; think about how much fun we had today."

"Indeed Amelie a lot of fun. I'd like to remind you that it's just past midnight. No school tomorrow. You can stay in bed all day long."

"I don't think so! I'll put some make-up all over my face and no one will see anything."

"Rather, no one will recognize you anymore, Amelie. I'm going to sleep and I think you should do the same. Goodnight!"

"This is what friends are for?" Amelie murmured.

The night was peaceful. The cats slept under the beds quietly, like dogs. At five a.m. the alarm woke everyone up. The cats were alert. Amelie put a winter coat over her pajamas and walked the cats to the pine trees. The cats ran onto the tree and scared the birds away. It was exactly as she planned it. She abandoned them out there and came back to her room, got dressed and put make up all over her face. Charlotte woke up and went to the bathroom to take shower. She got dressed and sat at the table for the morning tea Amelie was about to serve.

"This tea I call **Blue Angel**. It's perfect for your spirit; I mean to put your spirit up."

"Oh heavenly God, you look like you just performed in a pantomime' show Amelie. Where did you get this white powder?"

"I didn't use any make up. This is just regular flour that I mixed with a bit of water. It is okay, no one will even notice."

"You better stay here. I'll bring you breakfast."

"Don't worry! We'll take the last table in the dining room near the window. Let's go earlier so no one will see us."

"Okay, as you wish!" The girls went to the dining room. No one was there yet. They took some fresh crispy bread, fried eggs with salad and sat at the table near window.

Everything was going well and no one noticed them. Everyone was busy with their own stories. Soon the Sisters showed up and sat far away. Everything was by the book. Breakfast was splendid and the girls finished a bit earlier and were about to leave. As they passed by the Sisters' table they noticed a terrified look in their eyes. However, they were in a hurry. It was better to avoid them they thought. Perhaps they didn't notice the missing Serin yet and the hanging cat on the tree's branches. It was better to stay in their room for the rest of the day Amelie thought. She rushed upstairs and quickly opened the door then ran to the window only to find out that the cat and the Serin were still there fully frozen and covered by hoarfrost.

The sun rays were glittering and scattering

221

back and forth from them. Soon everyone will find out what happened out there. They looked more gruesome than yesterday; she lay down flat on the bed with her heart almost leaping out of her chest. She closed her eyes and listened to the silence whispering to her with an unfamiliar voice, murderer, and murderer. Then she fell asleep for almost two hours.

Suddenly she was awakened by the lamenting voices of the Sisters. They appeared at the door followed by the cats who gracefully accepted Amelie's room as a permanent shelter. Amelie almost had a heart attack. She sat on the bed her face completely pale. Sister Agnes spoke,

"Oh, Holy Ghost! Amelie, in all the heavens what happened to your face? And can you tell me why all of the neighbors' cats are in your room?" Amelie was speechless and then with the terrified look in her eyes she glanced at the Sister Claudia.

"Amelie, we came to investigate what happened to the frozen Serin. I was getting ready for its funeral. The poor thing vanished from the freezer last night without a trace. I personally put the bird there and I know it couldn't walk off by itself. I thought maybe you knew what happened to it?"
Amelie couldn't get her voice out of her chest and then Charlotte interrupted, "Actually we were thinking of the funeral ourselves. Last night we knocked at Sister Claudia's door but she wasn't there. Then we decided to find if the bird was there and accidentally discovered that it was in the freezer." She paused for a moment and was searching for the best story to tell but she couldn't find the right one. Then Sister

Claudia asked,

"Then what happened?"

Meantime Sister Agnes walked to the window and as she glanced through it, she said,

"I know exactly where the bird is, Claudia come here." Amelie grew pale and red spots popped up on her cheeks.

"Oh heavenly Father Who would dare do such a horrible thing to this poor cat?" Sister Claudia asked nervously.

"I need an explanation from you girls," Sister Agnes said.

"I don't know where I should begin. But as I already mentioned to you everything happened because of that noisy Serins," Charlotte said but Amelie interrupted,

"I will tell you exactly what happened. Everything started because of this little beast Serin. I would blame this bastard for everything that happened to me. When we took the little beast from Sister Claudia's freezer last night we decided to use it as bait for the local cats. We brought five cats here and I taught them how to scare the birds from the pine tree using the dead Serin as bait. We brought them to the trees on a leash last night and I decided to give them live training. I threw the dead Serin over the branches and let the cats run after the real birds. They successfully scared them away but one cat decided to go after the dead Serin. Unfortunately, his ribbon entangled within the branches and he involuntarily hung himself on that branch just next to the dead Serin. I climbed the tree to get them out of the branches. Unfortunately the branch broke and I fell to the ground with it. Actually, I was lucky that I landed with the branch, it saved my life, but I have fifty six cuts all over me. Charlotte already counted all of them. I put some white flour over my face to hide it but as you can see it didn't help much. That's the story. And I put the broken branch in the bathroom as a decoration." Amelie concluded her story with satisfaction.

"One more question, Amelie. What happened to one of your curtains? It's missing," Sister Agnes asked again.

"Oh, yes! I forgot to mention that last night we passed by your door but you weren't there. I wanted to ask you if I could use one of those curtains as a net to catch the cats. That's how we caught them."

"I must admit that indeed it was very quiet this morning. I was surprised by what happened to all those birds. Now I must thank you girls for all that. I am speechless indeed. You almost killed yourself, Amelie. God must have watched over you last night. You're a trouble maker and you look like an Egyptian mummy today. You need some miracle balsam from Coach Louis."

"I already got some from him, and Charlotte put it all over my cuts."

"This is good news my girls. I don't know what to say to you but it is very funny, indeed. I will ask the gardener to take those creatures out of the tree and then you can make a funeral for them," she said and laughed then added,

"I've never heard a story like this in my entire life. Oh, heavenly God! You probably brought this child to cherish and enlighten our miserable life in this monastery," the Sister said, laughing heavily in the corridor. She arranged with the gardener to remove the animals from the tree. Meantime, students gathered around the pine tree with disbelief in their eyes. One of the girls asked the gardener,

"What happened to this poor cat and Serin?"

"I was told they hung themselves, and worse, on Christmas Eve," the gardener replied with sadness as he was cutting the strings. The girls looked at him terrified.

"They will have a funeral for these poor creatures. This is what I was told this morning," the gardener added.

It was around eleven a.m. when Charlotte got the phone call from Patrick. Sister Agnes called her to her office.

"Hi Charlotte this is Patrick. Peter is okay. He sleeps for almost twenty hours. When he gets his strength back he will call you. They branded on his chest and left hand the Omega letter. This means that he is one of the three highest ranking Templars. I hope to see you soon. Say hi to Amelie for me. How is she doing?"

"This is fantastic news. Thank you, Patrick. Amelie is doing great! However, she fell out of a pine tree."

"What was she doing in the tree?" Patrick asked.

"It was about the cats and the Serins, anyway it's a long story. I will tell you later when we meet."

"But is she okay?"

"Oh, yes; just a few cuts here and there. Hopefully she will recover fast. Thank you Patrick for the good news and see you soon!"

"Bye Charlotte!"

Charlotte walked back to her room. She paused for a second near the window and glanced at the pine tree. The cat and Serin were gone and she was about to announce this news.

"Amelie, the cat and Serin are gone and for good. I talked to Patrick. He said hello to you. Peter is still sleeping but he is okay."

"This is the best news so far!"

"Amelie, what did you put on your face again? You look like a shaman after performing a bloody surgery."

"It is the iodine, just to prevent infection."

"You can't go out like this for lunch. The Sisters will have a heart attack when they see you like that. Can you wipe this stuff off your face? Otherwise, I will bring you lunch right here."

"Okay, you better bring lunch here. I can't clean it right now. I just put it on five minutes ago."

"Okay Amelie. What's next?"

"Charlotte, you exaggerate, just calm down and everything will be fine."

"I will go for lunch. See you in awhile."

On her way she met Sister Claudia. "I am glad to see you, my child. Tell Amelie that we can do the funeral for the cat and Serin this afternoon. I found some wooden boxes in the attic just perfect for the occasion. You can come at two thirty p.m."

"Sure we will be there." Charlotte got their lunches and went back to her room. "Amelie, I brought lunch for you and me. I decided to keep you company. I met Sister Claudia and she told me that the funerals for those two vagabond beasts are at two thirty p.m. We'll go and keep her company. She seemed very serious about it. She even found some nice wooden boxes in the attic for them."

"It is sensible news. Finally we'll get rid of those bastards for good. They became my nightmare in the last few days. The food smells good. It's my favorite, shrimp and fries. Thank you Charlotte, you just read my mind. Tomorrow is Christmas Eve and the cooks made those delicious cakes. I can smell them now! I can't wait."

"I'd like one of your teas to drink if you wouldn't mind."

"Sure! As soon as I'm done with eating I'll make it." Twenty minutes later, Amelie made her newest tea called, *Galapagos Islands.* Someone knocked on the door. It was Sister Agnes and the cats.

"Hello girls. I came to put a new curtain in your window. Also, we must get rid of those cats running around your room. They're like locusts, if you don't get rid of them for good they will come in by the hundreds. They must stay outside, in the garden."

"Hello Sister Agnes, I agree, the cats must go! I'm glad that you came. We have a very good tea and you're invited." Amelie agreed with a smile.

"Oh, yes! I remember that I promised to have tea with you one day and today is the perfect day. Amelie, what in heaven did you do to your face at this time?" The sister asked laughing.

"I put on some iodine to sterilize my wounds. It'll wash off. I'll clean it later," Amelie announced.

"The tea is delicious, much better than the tea I

227

make for myself. I should come more often. What kind of tea is it?"

"I call this tea *Galapagos Islands.* It consists of dried berries, which gives it this spectacular flavor and some acacia honey. I like this new exotic creation myself."

"I must have another cup. I really enjoy it. Sister Claudia would love your tea, too. I shall bring her next time."

"She asked us to come to the funeral at two thirty p.m. and we promised her that we'd be there," Amelie said.

"Okay girls, you go and meanwhile I'll install your new curtain. It shouldn't take more than a few minutes. I'll meet you there," Sister said with a smile.

"Amelie, let's go! You should wash your face. It looks horrific."

"I'll do that when I come back. I want those little bastards to remember what they have done to me."

On the way to the garden they met Sister Claudia and she asked for help with the little coffins. Her mind was so busy with the funeral that she didn't even have time to look at the girls when she asked them for help. Amelie took the little box with the dead Serin in it and Charlotte carried the big one with the suicidal cat. The gardener was already waiting for them near the pine tree where he dug two big holes. Then Sister Claudia took from her pocket a little vademecum bible and read a chapter on creation. She was almost moved to tears in this valedictory act to the beasts. Sister Agnes soon came to join her. There's a bitter irony to it.

The gardener stood with the shovel next to the

228

holes looking like a valiant solider ready to die for a cause. After the final explosion of the Sisters emotions on the life and death issue, the beasts were finally put into their permanent gravesites. Everyone looked into the pits. The bird coffin was so small that no one could even notice it.

The gardener was suddenly awakened by the Sisters voices and he began to put the soil on top of each coffin, and then flattened it down. Sister Claudia laid a small garland on each grave, still in an emotional state. The case was finally put to rest and Amelie was contented. She was officially exonerated from any potential future guilt and there was a moment of relief for her. Then suddenly Amelie noticed the horrified look in Sister Claudia's eyes. She hesitated for a moment like she was still emotional about the funeral.

"What have you done to your face, my foolish child?" Sister asked strangely as her eyes widened.

"This is only iodine. I wanted them to remember what they have done to me, those little beasts. They have no consideration for my life whatsoever! I must say. I got fifty six cuts because of them." Sister looked at her with disbelief and said,

"Oh Saint Clara!" Then she turned around, laughing.

"Girls, tomorrow is Christmas Eve and I want you to restore yourselves to pristine condition, especially you, Amelie. Do we understand each other? Otherwise you will scare all the girls and the cats too," Sister Agnes said, laughing.

"I'll try my best Sister," Amelie replied.

"Thank you for the delicious tea. I'll try to come

more often," she said.

"You're very welcome, see you soon, and thank you for the new curtain," Amelie said gracefully. Sister looked at her and smiled.

The girls left for their room and tried to relax after a gloomy day. Amelie lay on her bed and said,

"How am I going to restore myself for tomorrow? I don't have any clue. Do you?"

"Let me think how we can do that. I have an herbal mask. We'll see if it really works. It has some minerals in it and it should heal the wounds. Let me read the instructions. Here, it says; mix two spoonfuls with warm water to a thick consistency and then apply to the face, avoid eyes and lip area. It sounds very simple. I will do it for myself too."

"Great idea I want to look fantastic! Do you think French teacher, Bertrand will be there tomorrow for dinner? Amelie asked without reserve. "Sure, he will be there. Amelie you must wash that iodine from your face before I put on the mask. It smells like lavender flowers but it has that strange green color. Are you ready?"

"I can't wash this iodine; just put the mask all over. I'll wash it all later together."

"Okay, let's do it! You must lie down on the bed, but first put a towel on the pillow. I have this nice soft brush I can use for your face. How does it feel? You're almost done! You look like an alien right now. Can you do it for me, too?" Charlotte asked.

"It was fast but it feels really good and smells fantastic. Where did you buy that mask?"

"I bought it in a cosmetic's boutique. They sell only beauty masks there." "How long must we keep it on?" Amelie asked.

"At least thirty minutes. I'm ready! You can apply it on my face."

"It takes thirty seconds to put it on. You look like an Irish Leprechaun, Charlotte. Let's lie down and relax in the tranquil atmosphere just like they do in a professional beauty salon," Amelie proclaimed. "Let's do that!" Charlotte agreed.

They closed their eyes and relaxed for more than thirty minutes. They could only hear the tick-tock of the clock, hanging on the wall. They fell asleep for exactly two hours. Amelie awoke in a big panic,

"Charlotte, wake up! We fell asleep. This is not good. We were supposed to wash that mask off a long time ago. Let's do it and fast. It's so dried now! We need some kind of scrubber. Let's try a toothbrush. Okay, I'm almost done, how do I look?"

"You look green, Amelie. But maybe it's only temporary. Let me wash my face. Oh holy cow! I look green too! What the hell is that? Just let me read the instructions again. Maybe I missed something." Charlotte read from the package, Caution: do not keep on for more than thirty minutes or you may see a temporary discoloration of the skin which could last a day or two. This is terrible news, Amelie!"

"Oh, my goodness I'm horribly disappointed! It's less than charming news for sure! Maybe we can put some bleach on it," Amelie cried, as she was immeasurably devastated. "No more experiments! We should leave it as-is and it will slowly go away. Don't worry, Amelie. Our skin will look perfect in a day or two and your cuts will vanish too. Let's drink some good tea instead before we leave for dinner."

"The Sisters will be shocked when they see us. It's an immense mistake on our part," Amelie said in a bitter voice as she glanced in the mirror. She felt hopeless and threw herself on the bed covering her face with her hands. "It's not so tragic. They'll understand. Just ignore everyone for the time being," Charlotte said in a convincing tone. They sipped Amelie's new tea in a quiet atmosphere. Amelie nervously sauntered from one corner of the room to the other.

"I look like a saurian creature in a jungle. What'll Mr. Bertrand think when he sees me?" Amelie said in an imperious tone.

"You worry too much. His feelings towards you are imperishable and he won't notice anything because of the dim lights, which will diminish the effect. We look fine. I'm already accustomed to my new face. Don't try to spoil our evening! We'll laugh about it in the near future and remember it as the best time of our entire life," Charlotte concluded. "Okay, I'm convinced Charlotte. Let's go for dinner now," Amelie replied.

They walked to the dining room feeling renewed. They gracefully took the dinner plates, filled them with all the best food, and sat at the table next to the Sisters.

"Why are you so green tonight?" Sister Claudia asked and then brought it to Sister Agnes attention.

"Oh Holy Ghost you look like little green lizards," Sister Agnes said with restrained joy.

"I'm awfully sorry about our greenish look, dear Sisters. We put on these beauty masks to restore ourselves to a pristine condition and we turned green after that. We overslept, about two hours, with the mask on. The instructions said no more than thirty minutes. We will be like this for at least two days. All the intrinsic beauty and the pleasure will come later! This is our story for tonight," Amelie concluded with a big smile and shrugged her shoulders. She didn't feel like apologizing for her look anymore. Then she noticed a frozen imperturbable peace on the Sisters faces, which didn't last long, and suddenly they burst into hysterical impetuous laughter.

"Girls, maybe, I can help you with that a bit. It was my idea originally when I asked you to restore yourselves to a pristine condition. I have a cucumber mask with a whitening effect; all natural, no chemicals added. You'll come to my room after dinner and I'll put it on your faces," Sister Agnes said, still laughing. Then she added, "I just want to remind you that tomorrow all of us will spend the morning and early afternoon in the church with one break only for lunch. Then at six p.m. we will celebrate our Christmas dinner. Be sure you're on time. Are you ready girls? If you've finished your dinner we'll go to my room for the beauty mask. Sister Claudia will help me."

The girls followed the Sisters and soon found themselves sitting in the soft comfortable armchairs with cucumber masks on. The Sisters assured them that they'd look one tone lighter. The beautification wouldn't take more than the traditional thirty minutes. Sister Claudia was reminiscing about her youth and laughed with Sister Agnes about some Santa Claus' jokes circulating around. Then twenty minutes later Sister Agnes made good tea and served everyone. She removed the mask from the girls faces and said,

233

"You see for yourselves just exactly what I said, one tone lighter."

"Oh, yes, now I'm reincarnated from a green lizard to a gray mouse. But it is much better, indeed," Amelie announced happily.

"I wonder what kind of mask you used. But whatever it was, please dispose of it immediately. When I was young, I studied cosmetology for a year. This is why I never had any problem with my skin," Sister Agnes cheerfully announced, smiling.

"Thank you Sisters for the delicious tea and a beauty mask, we shall go. We'll be there tomorrow for sure," Charlotte said and left.

"Charlotte, I'm glad that we have vacation. Tonight we'll enjoy a spa to restore our inner beauty," Amelie said.

"I wouldn't mind. It's so cold and it'll be fun. Sister Agnes is one-of-a-kind but deep inside I think she's had a tragedy."

"She was probably very unhappy when she was young. We really don't know much about her except her broken love story. She must have loved this poor guy, Richard. Why didn't she marry him?"

"We never know what's hidden inside someone. Everyone has happy moments and dreadful moments too. One day you're an angel and the next day you can become a killing monster without any explanation. It's scary and perhaps some unknown force manipulates our behavior. It is very strange," Charlotte said. "Well, we call them angry people. Sometimes, I feel very angry inside and I want to run. Perhaps one day I'll become a killer too," Amelie stated.

234

"Stop talking nonsense Amelie. It could be contagious. I feel an electric shudder passing through my body now. You are crushing the positive image of yourself and you don't want the Sisters to find out about it, especially your beloved French teacher, Bertrand," Charlotte said jokingly.

"I know it feels awful. Let's forget about it and enjoy a moment of a true pleasure. Since I look very gray I don't expect much attention from Bertrand tomorrow. What will he think of us when he sees our faces?" "Amelie, you think too much. He'll probably say two silly geese."

"You're right! He will think exactly like that. Oh silly me, and my harum-scarum fantasy. I just imagined myself as a High Priestess on a gondola with Bertrand as the gondolier."

"Amelie, let's grow up first and later we will have our fantasies."

Chapter 8: The Secret Life of Cardinal Benedict

Cardinal Benedict stood looking at the charred remains of the house; they stood like dark sentinels vigilantly standing watch. Thoughts of the family that he had grown to love swam through his head bringing tears to his eyes. He closed his eyes for a moment clearing his mind of all negative thought thinking only of the happiness and love given to him by this family, a smile lifted the corners of his lips; he took a deep breath and started to speak, the ancient secret words flowing from his mouth, the words known only to God Himself.

The hair on his neck rose as the feeling of power moved in him, he raised his hands, thin streams of energy flowed out from his out stretched fingers. The air in the room seemed to glow as the ash lifted from the ground. The ash moved through the air going back to its original place in the house and reforming the burnt out structure.

Benedict walked through the newly resurrected house looking fondly at the photos on the wall. He smiled to himself thinking of the children "at least they will have a few pictures of their mother and father," he said aloud. "Any little thing helps." He walked into the backyard and sat down on the swing that hung from a large oak tree, as he swung he went over the details concerning the night of the fire.

The camera with the pictures of the secret documents had gone missing the night of fire. Peter and Charlotte had told him about the photos they took right before their departure to the boarding school in Rome, they told him the camera was in the attic and the film was still inside. Only one person had been in the attic since the fire and that person was Oliver.

Oliver a middle-aged man lived by himself and for the most part kept to himself. He would only leave his house for the Sunday morning mass at the local church, and later for fishing at the local river. Sunday morning would be the perfect time for Benedict to pay a visit to Oliver's house.

Thus on Sunday, early morning Oliver left his house dressed in a black suit and white shirt for the morning mass. Cardinal Benedict waited until Oliver disappeared down the street; he walked to the back of his house. An array of strange works of art littered the back yard that had the feel of magic to them; Benedict opened the back door and went inside. The house was huge and cluttered with a variety of collectible items. "How could one person collect this many items," Benedict said to himself.

But it was not his concern at the moment. He was looking for the camera and the pictures. He went to the bedroom and searched but with no success, he went to the library and searched still no luck. Benedict went to the basement and found a locked door, he spoke a few of the ancient words and the lock opened. Inside he found a dark room for developing photos, strings were stretched between the walls and freshly developed pictures hung drying.

Benedict searched everywhere and finally found the camera. He opened one of the drawers and spotted an envelope of developed film; he checked the contents and discovered that it was the right one. He confiscated camera and took all of the pictures, however, the picture with the secret code was missing.

'Where could it be?' He thought. If Oliver already knew the importance and the power of the written words he discovered then he would likely hide this particular picture but where?

"Perhaps he took it with him," Benedict whispered to himself.

He left the house and locked the back door behind him. He decided to destroy the structures and pieces of art that Oliver had built the same way they were constructed, using the power of the secret words. The newly constructed facilities brought attention from neighbors.

After he was finished Benedict went back to his place, changed the clothes and went down to the river carrying a bucket and his fishing pole. He stopped in the garden dug some worms for bait then made his way to the river. It was sunny and the weather was perfect for fishing. He cast a line into the water and waited. He sat on the grass enjoying the pleasure it brought.

In the distance he spotted Oliver walking towards the river. When he was close enough Oliver introduced himself,

"Hello my name is Oliver. How are you?"

"I'm fine, thank you," Benedict replied.

"Today is a beautiful day, great for fishing."

"It sure is," Benedict agreed with a smile. Oliver sat on the small blanket; he stared at the blue sky for a moment then glanced at Benedict. His fishing-rod moved sharply. He jumped from the blanket and picked it up setting the hook expertly.

"Didn't I tell you it was a great day," he said, laughing as he reeled in the fish. Oliver took the fish off the hook and threw it into the bucket. He glanced at Benedict then lay down on the blanket and stared at the blue sky again; he put his hand into the pocket and pulled out a picture. Benedict glanced at Oliver,

'I need to get that picture back,' he thought to himself.

Suddenly his pole bent over as a large fish took the bait, he reeled in the fish, he tried to unhook the flopping fish but it slipped out of Benedicts hands and flew through the air towards Oliver. The fish hit

Oliver in the face scaring him. He jumped up and ran several feet away wiping his face off. He was so startled that he left the precious picture behind. The Cardinal apologized and picked up the fish grabbing the picture at the same time. It was a very convenient situation. He put the fish in his bucket and excused himself.

"Nice to meet you Oliver, I'll be back again in the afternoon maybe I will see you then. Good luck with your fishing."

"Thank you, it was nice to meet you as well," Oliver replied, smiling, and continued on fishing.

The Cardinal hurried home, he couldn't believe his luck.

"I could not have planned that any better," he whispered to himself. Once home, he pulled the picture out.

"It's the right one", he said sighing with relief. He retrieved a book of matches from over the mantel and struck a match, he held it to the picture and watched it burn,

"That fixes that," he said to himself. He picked up the bucket and took it to the kitchen sink,

"Thank you Mister Fish," he said as he slit its belly.

The next day Benedict sat on a wooden stool; he picked up his cell phone and dialed Chris's phone number.

"Hello Chris! This is Benedict. How are you doing?"

"Hey Benedict, I'm doing well," Chris replied, "However I have been very busy with my project. What's new?"

239

"I am going to try an experiment in resurrection and will need your help for a week or two; I will fill you in on all of the details when you arrive. Could you bring your quantum computer with you?"

"Of course, just give me an address and I'll be there. I can leave tonight."

"That's great," Benedict said with excitement in his voice then he continued, "I really appreciate your assistance in this matter and I promise that you won't regret it. Have a pleasant flight and I will see you tomorrow." He hung up the phone and then called John.

"Hi John, This is Benedict. How are you?"

"I'm fine. What's up, it must be important for you to call so late," John replied yawning.

"I would like you to join me here in Kalin tomorrow if you are able, there is an experiment that I am going to perform and I want you to be here for it, you won't regret it I promise."

"What kind of experiment?" John questioned.

"An experiment in resurrection," Benedict replied.

"How could I miss it," John said sounding a little more awake.

"I'll explain the details to you in person when you arrive, good bye for now, have a safe trip." Benedict hung up the phone and went for a walk to think about the implications of the experiment that he would soon be conducting. "What have I gotten myself into"…?

The next day Benedict headed to the airport, it was a long ride in a taxi but he finally reached the airport. He waited in the lobby for a few moments and then saw Chris coming from the baggage claim. Benedict walked over and they exchanged hugs.

"Nice to see you Benedict, it has been long time."

"I'm glad to see you too, it has been long time. John will be landing shortly as well, in the meantime let's go to the *Monet* Cafe."

"It sounds really good, I'm hungry," Chris replied.

"Have you made any progress solving the problem with the **Q element**?" Benedict asked.

"I wish. I showed my colleagues the recorded images of Mary and the little Jesus and they didn't believe my story, but when I showed them the Q element they were stunned. We tried to analyze it but it doesn't fit into the periodic table of the elements. I have an element which has not only been discovered but it is working perfectly. How is that possible?"

"There are some things around us which we will never understand." Benedict's phone rang. "That's John, he just sent me a text telling me that he has arrived, stay here and enjoy your coffee we will be back in five minutes."

"I'll order some sandwiches for us. Chris said. Benedict left the café and walked to the baggage claim, John was already there waiting for him.

"Hello Benedict, it's nice to see you," John said in greeting, and added, "It has been too long." Benedict replied warmly,

"Chris is waiting for us at a café not far from here." As they walked Benedict asked,

"How is your research going?" John took a deep breath and explained,

"I found some information in regards to the Apostle Peter that would confirm that the key existed, but its location is still a mystery." Benedict thought for a moment and then spoke in a soft voice,

"I'm convinced that it's in Vatican City." They walked on in silence the rest of the way to the cafe, Chris was sitting at a table near the front entrance eating a cookie. He stood up from his chair and waved,

"John, Benedict! Come here," Chris exclaimed walking toward them.

"It has been a long time since we were all together… too long." He continued reaching out his hand as he approached them.

"All for one," John said reaching his hand out.

"And one for all," Benedict concluded adding his hand completing the stack. They laughed and the three walked over to the table.

"Have a seat, I ordered you both a sandwich and coffee. I ordered it to go so we can eat at the house. Also I ordered you both cookies as well; they looked so good I couldn't wait so I ordered us an extra cookie for the ride to the house."

"Thank you," John said picking up his sandwich bag and removing one of the cookies.

"Any time Brother any time," Chris replied. Benedict spoke up,

"I have a cab waiting we can leave as soon as you are ready."

The ride to the house was silent, each lost in his own thoughts. When they arrived at the house Benedict unlocked the door and they all walked inside.

"Looks like it got a makeover," John said looking over the house,

"I thought you said there was a fire."

"There was, several months ago, I wasn't here at that time. I was trying to track down Monk Salvatore in town; I believe that he set the fire. One of the neighbors said that one night he saw a man looking like a Monk at the front door, it was around two a.m. and Mrs. Alice likely was sleeping. He left shortly and soon after that the house burned down."

"This is really terrible news!" John replied fully stunned.

"The neighbors could hear her screams as she was engulfed in the flames. Everyone in the neighborhood was devastated. I lost everything too. He stole the ancient maps, my personal memoirs I wrote in the **Black Book**, and much more. I must get the book back." Benedict sighed then continued, "A week after the accident I called the children and told them the whole story, they were devastated. I promised them that I would rebuild the house so I did.

"You did a great job Benedict, but we can't let the bastard get away," John added angrily.

"I'll help you to get this son of a bitch," Chris exclaimed adding his support.

"The worst thing is that before Charlotte and Peter left for Rome, they took some photos of my treasures including my journal so not all was lost. They were in a hurry and Peter forgot his camera he left in the attic. I wouldn't have ever known about it, when I told them about the fire Peter asked if his camera was in the attic. He hoped that it had survived. I told him that everything was gone and that

243

I suspected that Monk Salvatore had stole the camera. But listen to this. One day I noticed that one of my neighbors had strange structures popping up around his house just over night. I observed him for two weeks watching his patterns. So one Sunday morning when he left for mass I sneaked into his house, and confiscated camera and film. However the most important picture, the one with the secret code was still missing. I figured that he must carry the picture with him since he knew of its power.

Soon after the mass he went for fishing and I followed him. I pretended to be a fisherman as well actually I was fishing and even caught a fish.

As I suspected he had the secret picture and I was able to recover it in a mysterious way." He relayed to them the advents of that day taking time to describe in great details the fish incident. Then he continued,

"This morning I found out Oliver was killed likely last night. I think that Salvatore killed him. That means that he is close bye and is extremely dangerous, we have to be careful."

"What was his motive?" John asked.

"I think that he has a few spies in town. They saw the huge structures which Oliver was building over few weeks. They got suspicious and told Salvatore about it. Moving on to the matter at hand, I'd like to perform a resurrection... I want to bring Mrs. Alice back to life."

John and Chris looked at Benedict like he had lost his mind.

"How are we going to do that?" Chris asked in wonder.

"You will just have to wait and see," Benedict replied mysteriously. "I asked you both to be here to witness this miracle. Chris I want you to set up your quantum computer in her bedroom. Be sure that you record every moment of this phenomenon I don't want to miss anything."

"Neither do me," Chris added and went to the bedroom to set his computer up. Chris finished and Benedict dimmed the lights and began his meditation. He spoke in an ancient tongue that Chris and John couldn't understand. He spoke slowly and distinctly holding the medallion in front of him.

The energy in the room intensified as the air before the medallion formed into the shape of a human. Benedict repeated each word once more and the image became more visible.

They could easily recognize Mrs. Alice, she looked confused. Benedict opened his eyes and began to speak to Mrs. Alice.

"Do you recognize me?" he asked.

"I do," she replied.

"What happened to me?"

"Someone set your house on fire. Do you remember anything from that night?" he asked.

"Kind of, I heard some noise in the attic but I thought perhaps mice were chasing each other. Do you know who set my house on fire?" she asked sadly.

"I think that it was Monk Salvatore, no one saw him but I believe that it was him," Benedict replied.

"I thought he was such a nice man, I rented a room to him you know," Alice explained.

"I will catch him and he will pay with his own

life," Benedict promised.

"That won't bring me back will it?" she said crying.

"But at least justice will be served."

"How are my dear Charlotte and Peter doing, I was going to visit them on Christmas?"

"They are doing great!" Benedict exclaimed glad to be the bearer of good news. "Peter passed his test and is on his way to becoming one of the Omega Templars. He is very proud of himself. Charlotte is also doing very well; they both miss you very much."

"Thank you for this moment of happiness. I'm so proud of them; will you tell them that from me? She asked crying.

"Chris is recording everything in his quantum computer. You'll be able to tell them yourself through his computer, please come closer, look into the camera and tell Charlotte and Peter how much you love and miss them."

"Sure! Charlotte, Peter I will love you forever. Study hard for your future and never give up our or perhaps now your dreams," she said her tone growing weaker.

"Your image is depleting as we talk," Chris said watching the controls.

"You're becoming invisible again. Rest in peace," Benedict said as she completely vanished still holding her medallion.

The next morning they made plans to look for Salvatore. They decided to look downtown where Benedict had seen him previously.

"If Salvatore is there we will try to follow him," Benedict said. Within twenty minutes they reached their destination, a classy night club named *Tiberius* where only the most prominent individuals of the city go for dinner and social interaction. The atmosphere was very calm and elegant with dimmed lights and the scent of wild flowers mixed with aroma of fresh coffee.

They spotted Salvatore sitting alone at the corner table, reading a newspaper and slowly sipping his coffee.

"Let's wait here until he leaves," Benedict said lowering his head. A few moments later Salvatore emerged from the club, he walked through the alley and down a road lined with big pine trees on either side. He was walking in his serpentine manner moving in-between the trees. They followed him to a gated estate; he paused for a moment and looked around then swiftly climbed over the tall fence.

The three friends followed him over the fence keeping their distance. In the distance they watched as the monk entered a house, they crept up to a window and peered in. Salvatore was packing his things into a large bag; he placed the bag on top of the table. He sat at the table and wrote on a piece of paper, then he reached in to his bag and pulled out a book, he opened the book and leafed through a few pages. Benedict recognized it was his journal, the **Black Book**.

"That's my journal," he whispered, "Let's go get it, there's three of us against one of him."

They walked around to the front of the house and quietly opened the door; quietly they made their way through the house searching every room. "He's not here," Chris said as they searched the last room.

"He must have escaped through the back

247

door." Benedict went to pick up the note he left on the table and read it out loud,

"I know you are following me; and I know why. Soon the entire world will be mine! Catch me if you can."

The Black Knight."

"Son of a bitch," Benedict cursed, "Black Knight indeed, I told you that he is smart, even diabolical. I thought we had him for sure."

"Let's follow the bastard," John said with more than a little anger in his voice.

"It will be difficult to follow him; the hills around here are dotted with caves and now that he has my journal he will be able to do real miracles for himself. There is only one way to stop him," Benedict concluded.

"And what is that?" Chris asked.

"We must kill him," Benedict coldly explained.

The next morning Benedict woke early and made coffee, he sat in a rocking chair smoking a cigar, John and Chris joined him.

"Good morning guys," Benedict said cheerfully, "Have some coffee." The two sat down as Benedict poured them coffee.

"You know I have been thinking about my scrolls, one of them is almost two thousand years old and the second one is dated to the XII century. I secretly took them from the Vatican library. I thought that it was a major discovery at the time and indeed it was. I marked on the map two of the places mentioned in the scrolls, were I would likely find coded instructions as to where the key is located. I thought for a moment that the key must be in the

248

Vatican City as we discussed previously, John found some evidence which confirms these suspicions but now I am having second thoughts, maybe it is still in Egypt hidden in some basement in one of those monasteries or maybe it never left Jerusalem.

One of the *scrolls* mentioned *the name of the Templars* who *were in possession* of the **Secret Letter.** I don't know who wrote the names on the scroll maybe it was one of the last Templars who actually had possession of the same *secret letter* and was afraid what would happen to it when he'd die. I traced some of the names from the scrolls, and found few addresses for one of their *descendants* alive today living in France."

"Maybe we should arrange a meeting with those *descendants*," Chris said.

"That is what I am thinking," Benedict replied and added, "If they have the **Secret Letter** they need to be warned of the threat that Monk Salvatore poses, and maybe they could help us recover my stolen items. We can leave for France in the morning. I will make a few calls and make our arrangements."

After breakfast Benedict made a few phone-calls tracking down one of the Templars' descendants by the name of Jerome, he agreed to meet with them in Paris in two days. They spent the afternoon preparing for their trip, later in the evening they sat on the front porch sipping tea and talking about their adventures together.

"We have an early flight tomorrow so I'm going to bed," Benedict exclaimed yawning tiredly.

"That sounds good. Hopefully, we can relax a bit in Paris. I need a short vacation; my work at the university has been overwhelming lately. Good night Chris." John replied.

"Good night guys!" Chris said staring at the moon.

The next day they landed in Paris, retrieved their bags and went to the front door. They saw a man holding up a sign with Benedict's name written on it. Benedict walked over and introduced himself.

"Hello I'm Benedict and these are my friends, John and Chris, you must be Jerome."

"Yes, indeed. Nice to meet you," he replied as they shook hands.

"Please follow me. My friend is waiting for us in the car. I would like to invite you to my house where we can discuss the matter in a more secure environment."

They followed him to the black Bentley. A large man was standing next to it. He smiled and waved at them.

"My name is Jacques but please call me Jack. How was your trip, Gentlemen?" "It was quite pleasant, thank you. I'm Benedict and this is John and Chris."

"**Gentlemen**, please, get in and relax," Jack said. Benedict noticed a tattoo on Jacques' right hand the same tattoo that was on Jerome's right hand. They must belong to the same Templar Secret Society, he thought for a second. They drove to the outskirts of Paris; the landscape was beautiful; orchards and gardens stretched out as far as the eye could see on each side of the huge French Chateau. The Bentley stopped in front of a large estate. Jacques got out and opened the rear doors.

"Please follow me," Jerome said walking toward the entrance of the house. An iron door decorated with a lion's heads opened automatically as they approached. They stepped into a lavishly decorated living room, the interior was splendid, the walls were painted with colorful frescoes, the aroma of fresh gardenias and lilies filled the rooms. Jerome asked the butlers to bring them some drinks.

"Gentlemen, make yourselves comfortable," Jerome said as he took his seat then he continued with a smile on his face,

"Tell me, what can I do for you?" Jerome asked.

"We have reason to believe that you have something very important to our research," Benedict stated coldly as he continued,

"We have found information hidden within a *secret code* and after almost twenty years of hard work we are unable to complete our research because a piece is missing. We believe that with a bit of your help we will be able to do just that."

"What kind of code," Jerome asked interested.

"It is hard to believe but it is the key to understanding the universe," Benedict answered.

"This is getting interesting; tell me more about you?" Jerome asked.

"Chris is a computer specialist, he built a *quantum* computer and with it he has been able to record much of our research including our last trip to Egypt. John specializes in ancient Christianity specializing in translating ancient religious manuscripts. I also specialize in ancient languages and I am an expert in hidden forms of communication.

I have worked for the Vatican Library for over twenty years."

"This is very interesting indeed. Chris would you please show me your quantum computer, I would love to see it?" Jerome asked.

"Sure, I'll be glad to," Chris replied, he opened his computer case and removed the computer, then he uploaded the images from the Egyptian monastery. The holographic emitter hummed, and then an image of a fresco materialized hanging seemingly in thin air. Jerome waved his hand through the image.

"Chris, this is a masterpiece indeed. I am impressed with your talent, you truly are a genius!" Chris uploaded the footage taken in the cave.

"Can you dim the lights?"
Jerome walked over to the main switches on the wall and turned them off. Chris started the display; the room went silent for a few moments as the images moved around the room that was now transformed into a cave.

"Are those images real?" Jerome asked.

"Yes, they're very real even though they look like they were made for a movie. We stayed for one night in the cave while in Egypt. The local monks told us that miracles are witnessed in the cave from time to time, I was lucky to be able to record everything," Chris said.

"I believe you," Jerome said visibly shaken, "I never thought that I would witness anything like that." He paused for a moment took a deep breath then continued, "What exactly do you want from me?"

"We're looking for a letter," Benedict said

matter-of-factly.

"What kind of letter?" Jacques asked.

"You know exactly what I'm talking about. Don't you?" Benedict said looking into Jerome's eyes. There was silence for a moment.

"Do you really know what you're asking for?" Jerome asked breaking the silence. "Yes I do," Benedict answered, "And I sincerely believe that this letter is the missing key or link to the answer, the final truth about our universe, about all of us. When I was at the Vatican, I translated a few ancient scrolls which I believe are part of the key. The first scroll mentioned that shortly before Jesus was betrayed, he gave a very important letter to his closest Disciple and asked him to guard it with his life. That Disciple did as Christ asked and before he died he passed the letter to another trusted Disciple. It went on like that for almost ten centuries. The letter changed hands and locations many times throughout the centuries; it was moved from Israel to Egypt and from Egypt to Syria and then back to Jerusalem. It stayed hidden in Jerusalem in a cave of an old Monastery for almost two centuries. In XI Century a Holy Crusade went to the Middle-East with a new religious mission.

One of the honorable Templars discovered or rather found accidently the **Holy Letter** in the old cave with several other documents that were of great value. He brought the letter to a small town in southern Italy. He hid it at the local church where his younger brother was a Priest. They buried the letter beneath the marble flooring. A Holy Cross engraved in green marble marked its hiding place for the next two centuries. The church was in disrepair and had

253

been looted by thieves. They removed marble, brass, gold and anything else they could haul out. For almost two more centuries the church was abandoned, part of its structure had collapsed and only the large marble slabs remained.

Then one day a wealthy Knight George II moved to the town and bought the church ruins. He began the renovation of the entire structure. When he inspected the interior flooring a loose piece of the marble laying near the altar caught his attention, he removed the marble piece and found the purple velvet pouch with the hidden letter in it. He never opened the letter, there were clear instructions written on the envelope asking that it not be opened.

He traveled to South of France where some of his best friends who happened to be the descendants of the real Templars were living. They called themselves the **Knights**. They recognized the value of the letter, there had been whispers of its existence for a few hundred years. They secretly hid the letter, and only passed the knowledge of its existence down to very few and select individuals, few today would know of its existence let alone its location. I have feeling that you're one of them," Benedict said with self confidence.

"Very impressive, indeed, I must say. You are a very brave man, however how you can be so sure that I am in possession of such a letter?" Jerome asked.

"We accomplished a lot so far; only this letter is missing key. Do not underestimate me or my ability, Jerome. Give me some credit. Will you? I am on a quest to solve our destiny which was already engraved in the Holy Stones by God himself and now He is leading me," Benedict spoke seriously.

"Tell me Benedict, why a man like you, would want to do such a thing? Why would you risk your life and the lives of others, for humanity?" Jerome asked.

"Because it is in giving that we receive, it is in forgiving that we are forgiven, and it is in dying that we are born to **eternal life**," Benedict spoke the words of God.

"You sound like a priest," Jerome said smiling.

"I'm a Cardinal and a priest too," Benedict confirmed and added,

"This world is so *materialistic*; we are the masters of man-made injustice and misery. God through his Son, a man of flesh and blood, wanted to build a better life for all of mankind, without regard to the color of skin and beliefs. He said,

"*I will die for a better you*. People are beautiful, and each one can bring something new and unique to our society. We can build a better future together, we can share knowledge with others, we could be free of diseases, we can develop advanced science, build new spaceships that run on antimatter and travel to the other galaxies. This knowledge was given to all of us by God himself, two thousand years ago, but we rejected it. We rejected Him and His knowledge. If we would have accepted His knowledge at that time, we would be a different people today, we would live in peace and harmony, we would learn how to love, respect and understand. There would be no doubt only faith and humility. His secret knowledge was lost with his death but it can be resurrected; I deeply believe that it is not completely lost yet,"

Benedict said, smiling.

"You sound like a philanthropist, Benedict. Do you think that mankind is honest enough to receive such a treasure?" Jerome asked honestly.

"I think that each of us deserve to know truth," Benedict stated matter-of-factly.

"Where do you keep the scrolls that you discovered?" Jerome asked.

"I kept them at the house I was staying at. I had them hidden under the wooden floor in the attic. I had to leave town for a few days and when I returned I discovered that a Monk named Salvatore stole all of my hidden documents. He is very dangerous man; he has already killed a few people and burnt down the house where I was renting a room. I tried to capture him but he is very skillful and always escapes. He is known as a Spider-Monk."

"I am familiar with Spider Monks, the Vatican likes to use them as assassins, they are very well trained," Jerome commented.

"He will try to contact you to obtain the *Holy Letter*, he will offer you money first and when that fails he will try to steal it. He also has stolen my personal journal; I kept all of my notes in it including powerful ancient words written in it. He uses these words like a magician to create his own miracles, using them for his own personal gain, he will likely destroy any one that stands in his way and will stop at nothing to get his hands on your **Holy Letter**," Benedict sighed, staring off into space a troubled look on his face.

"You can't imagine what this letter means to me and to my society, we are honorable men, direct descendants of the Templars. *We will protect the Will*

256

*of **God** at the cost of our own blood*. We are a separate entity from the Vatican, and we answer to no one but **God,** they don't have a clue that we are in possession of the letter. We have guarded this secret for almost 1,000 years and it will stay that way. I will wait for *God's instructions* Benedict," Jerome said, standing. "His 'Will' will be done; he will tell me when the moment is right. He will show me the way. There is too much to risk for me to hand this letter over to anyone. Although I would be glad to finally relieve all my fellow Knights from this duty. They would be pleased that they were able to contribute to a good cause at the end. Gentlemen, I thank you for coming, and it was an honor to be of service to you. I will be in touch. Please, have another drink with me," Jerome said and his butlers served a dark red drink to his guests.

"I would like to thank you for the promise you made today. I know that you're an honorable man, and I can count on you when the moment comes. I'm convinced that you will keep your oath to God, surely this is our destiny," Benedict said as he sipped the red drink. It was very sweet and pleasant.

"I like your ***quantum computer***, it's got a lot of marketing potential, we should meet one day and talk about a business venture together," Jerome said turning towards Chris.

"I would like that. I'll call you from London," Chris said.

"Good luck! Guys, I'll be there for you when you need me. Our hunger for knowledge could build the inner strength and confidence in each of us for sure. Jacques will take you back to town. Goodbye!"

Jerome said, smiling.

Within thirty minutes the black Bugatti stopped in front of the hotel, **Le Solei**. Jacques told them that he and Jerome owned the hotel and they could stay as long as they would like to, the food and drinks would also be provided as well as a taxi service.

"Thank you, Jacques. It is more than generous of you. Please send my regards to Jerome," Benedict said.

"I will," Jacques said with a smile and drove off.

"It looks like we get a special treatment tonight," Chris said. A tall man came out to greet them and then picked their bags.

"My name is Antonio," the man, dressed in an elegant red suit with dark blue strips on each side, said, "And I will be your host, if you will please, follow me." They took the elevator to the penthouse. "This is your key; please call if you need anything. We will serve you breakfast at eight a.m. lunch at noon and supper at six p.m. You can also eat in the dining room downstairs if you like it. We have a jazz band, every evening. Please enjoy our hospitality," he said and departed.

The living room was huge and provided a 360 degree view of the city. Everything was spotless and perfectly placed. There were three separate bedrooms each a master suite in its own right. A large kitchen and a fully stocked bar completed the list of amenities.

"What do you think of Jerome and Jacques?" Benedict asked.

"Nice fellows. They seemed very serious, especially Jerome, I think we can trust them. How long are we planning to stay in Paris?" Chris asked.

"At least a week, I need a vacation. I haven't had a break for years, I work hard and I deserve it," John said, waiting for their confirmation.

"We all deserve a vacation and we will take advantage of this opportunity, we will stay at least a week. I'm going to bed. It is after midnight and I'm tired. See you in the morning guys," Benedict said and walked into his room closing the door behind him.

The first night in Paris was peaceful, in the morning they woke to the smell of breakfast being prepared. The sound of soft jazz music was coming from the speakers hidden in the walls. After eating they decided to explore Paris. They began with the Louvre and ended with a fancy cafe called **Madeline.** The three ate a small lunch enjoying each other's company.

The serenity of the moment was suddenly broken when Benedict spotted Monk Salvatore who appeared outside of the window. Salvatore glanced in and then quickly vanished. "Guys, did you just see Salvatore through that window or am I just paranoid?"

"I saw him as well," Chris said looking more than a little concerned.

"I can't believe he's following us," John said, frowning.

"He's not following us. He is after the same information that we are. All of the information that he needed was in the documents that he stole from me. He doesn't need us at least for the moment. His next move will be to call Jerome regarding the letter. I'm glad that we arrived before Salvatore had a chance to make contact.

"I would call Jerome and see if he was contacted by Salvatore," Chris said.

"Good idea Chris let me call him and ask," Benedict said and dialed his number. "Hello Jerome, this is Benedict, we are at the cafe *Madeline* eating and we just saw Monk Salvatore look in at us through the window. It seems that he is following us and will probably try to contact you."

"He already did," Jerome said confirming their concerns. "I fully ignored his offer, which is probably why he is following you, to get an idea of what you know. Just forget about Salvatore for now, everything is under control just enjoy your vacation. I have instructed my staff at the hotel not to allow him on the property and have also increased security. If there is anything else that I can do for you just give me a call."

"Thank you Jerome, for everything you have done. I really appreciate it," Benedict said.

"It is my pleasure," Jerome replied and then continued, "I would like for the three of you to join me at my chateau tomorrow morning, I will arrange for a car to pick you up, you can stay with me for the next few days it will be safer. If the three of you would like to tour the city or the country side my personal driver and a security will accompany you."

Benedict hung up the phone, he than relayed the details of the conversation to Chris and John, the three spent the remainder of the day reviewing the information that they had gathered with the quantum computer. They ate a light dinner and went to bed.

Benedict had trouble sleeping that night his mind restlessly was going over the information that had been recorded in his now missing journal. The

260

next morning the three gathered their belongings and went to wait in the hotel lobby, they did not have to wait long.

"Gentlemen," a large burly man said approaching the three. "My name is Comodo. I am here at the request of Jerome; if you would please follow me."

They exited the hotel and got into a waiting car. Within an hour they arrived at a gated estate somewhere deep in the French countryside. It took an additional fifteen minutes to arrive to the main house. They entered through huge mahogany doors into a pergola decorated with live acanthus' leaves and exotic orchids, splendid Doric columns ran along each side. They walked till they reached a large iron door.

Jerome appeared and greeted them warmly, "Nice to see you, gentlemen welcome to my home. Before we go in, I must ask you to put these sandals on your feet." He handed each of them a pair of Roman style sandals and masks. The masks covered the face from the nose up, it also covered the eyes with a screen allowing the wearer to see out but no one could see in.

"This is to protect our anonymity, remember don't introduce yourself by name to anyone as we don't use our given names, just simple hello will do. If you are ready please follow me.

They entered a huge ball room, people were standing around talking to each other and waiters were serving trays full of appetizers and exotic fruits. Jerome spoke to a few friends as they walked in; they made their way through the ball room and into the library. One of the men in the library spoke with a masculine voice.

"We have heard quite an interesting story about the three of you," the man said offering them a seat. "Some kind of humanitarian mission that you are involved in, we would like to hear more about it, there is always a possibility that we would like to be a part of it."

Benedict took a deep breath and looked at Jerome for approval, Jerome nodded his head and Benedict explained, "The mission doesn't concern any financial reward just pure dedication and faith to God's Will. It would take place in the Vatican City."

"Our reach wouldn't go as far as that, we'd never mingle our interest with that of the Vatican. The two have never worked well together and we still have some unpleasant memories from the past. It is beneficial for both parties to stay away from each other. However, this is an unusual circumstance and I assure you that I'll protect your interest and promote your gratuitous mission. We will deliver the letter that we posses in order for you to complete your mission when the time is right. I have trust in you and your mission; I want to see peace and happiness achieved in my life time. If you are indeed correct and I do believe that you are then this can happen through the revelation of this secret of the entire universe and will be revealed to all of us. On another note I heard of your childhood and how you came to work at the Vatican, there is one thing that I would like to ask of you."

"Of course," Benedict replied, "What can I do for you?"

The man stood and walked over to stand in front of

Benedict and asked,

"Show me your right foot." Benedict took off his sandal and held his foot out for inspection revealing the letter T, branded into the sole of his right foot.

"Just as I thought," the man exclaimed and whispered,

"You are one of us! Many of us came from similar backgrounds. Many years ago, the Vatican sent out missionary assassins, who were called the *Holy Collectors*, they were given a list containing the names of all the Templars' descendants and given a mandate to execute any that they found. They went from town to town all over the Europe, looking for any Templars or their descendants. When the *Holy Collectors* found them, they would kill the parents and abduct the children. They would send the children to be indoctrinated into various secret societies. The Vatican then would confiscate their wealth including all palaces, castles and farms. They became known also as the *Missionaries of Death* and they terrorized our people for generations. Cardinal, you abandoned the Vatican because of your beliefs and dedication to your mission. You did the right thing. Now, your eyes are opened to a new path in life and new freedoms, I don't know much about your mission but I deeply believe that you are a true man of God; I feel that I am fortunate to meet such an honorable man." Benedict nodded his head in agreement, he thought for a moment than he spoke.

"I would be glad to share the details of my mission when the time is more favorable for both of us. My immediate concern is Monk Salvatore; he is a threat to all involved. There is one thing that I do need to share with you in regards to this monk I will tell you the story now if you are so inclined." The man nodded his head and Benedict began.

"During my time at the Vatican I was fortunate enough to meet one dying monk. I'd say everything was just a pure accident. He was a member of the XII **Omega Templar Secret Society**, living in the North Tower of the Vatican. I was asked to take him to the hospital one night. He was very sick near death. We spent some time together talking and I tried to absorb every single word he said to me. He'd gotten a high fever and was near death it was then he shared a secret with me. It was the real power of the spoken word, the same spoken words that Christ Jesus used to perform his miracles. There is an unexplainable and immense power in these words and whoever possesses their secret can accomplish great things. I wrote these words down in my journal the same one that Monk Salvatore stole, now he poses this power and there is no way to take this power from him and let him live."

"Then he must be eliminated," the man said coldly.

"I wouldn't worry about him at the moment, but I agree that he is a potential threat." The men in the room agreed and decided to work towards that end.

"Enough doom and gloom," Jerome said, "You are my guest and I want this night to be enjoyable, allow me to show you around. Our facilities are quite large; the chateau has belonged to my ancestors for almost ten centuries. Every year each of us receives a small sachet of golden coins. The coins came from the treasure that our ancestors left for us, the treasure is immense. We calculate that today, the historical value of each coin is equivalent to one million Euros. You could sell the coin to a museum or private collectors and live comfortable for many years. Since you are one of us, you are entitled to the same inheritance as each of us. I would like to present you with one of these sachets. It lawfully belongs to you. Please, take this gift as our appreciation for your hard work."

"Thank you for your generosity. I will accept this sachet; it is a privilege for me to be counted as one of you." Benedict replied humbly and thought it would be a perfect inheritance for Charlotte and Peter. Jerome placed his hand on Benedict's shoulder and said, "Tonight you will be daubed a Knight."

The ceremony was held in a small auditorium adorned with large wall coverings, a small platform covered in red velvet rose from the floor. Beautifully crafted swords with scarlet and golden scabbards' sat on a stand near the podium. Three Knights dressed in historical regalia approached the platform each holding a different type of sword. They called Benedict to the platform.

One of the Knights placed a red velvet pillow onto the floor and asked Benedict to kneel on it; the second knight made a short speech informing Benedict of his entitlements, the third Knight placed a long sword on Benedict's right shoulder, and proclaimed him a Knight. They sang an old song of the Knights, when they had finished the Knights said in unison, "Rise Sir Knight and embrace your calling."

Then soon the first Knight said, "Welcome to the world of Knights. I hope you will enjoy every moment of it." To celebrate this special moment waiters walked in with glasses of red wine. Benedict was proud of himself. For the first time a new feeling awoke inside of him. Feelings he would usually hide from the public eye. He would always remember that he grew up in the orphanage. The second Knight approached him and asked, "Don't you feel like a different man now?"

"I feel great, but I'm still the same man. Although I must say that it is definitely a very impressive custom," Benedict said, laughing then added, "Indeed, you have a lot of fun here."

"Isn't that what life is about?" the Knight said, laughing.

"Perhaps, I feel I have missed so much fun in my life. I've never given it much thought. You've opened my eyes to it," Benedict said with concern.

"I'm glad that I did. I've heard one of your friends is sort of a computer's genius. I would like to meet him. I have an interesting proposition for him," the Knight said.

"Sure, he is right over there," Benedict said as he pointed at Chris. Benedict and the Knight walked over to Chris.

"I would like to introduce you to..." The Knight cuts Benedict off before he could finish.

"Hi! I've heard a lot of good stuff about you. You've built a quantum computer. I'm a scientist myself and I would like to talk to you about my proposition. Perhaps, you will find it interesting. I hope, you don't mind."

"It would be my pleasure," Chris said.

"I would like to talk about your computer. Can

you demonstrate it for me before you return to London? If it works as well as I've heard, I would like to make you a business proposition."

"I can demonstrate it for you but I'm still looking for this one element which is called the **element Q** and I can't figure it out. It doesn't exist yet in the Mendeleyev standard chemical table. It is too early to say much. But I believe that one day it would be discovered," Chris said.

"I'm a chemist and scientist myself, and maybe I could be of help to you. Do you think you will have time tomorrow? I will send my driver to pick you up right there. We don't have to wear sunglasses for our meeting. Surely it would be much more comfortable for both of us," he said.

"I think, I can meet you, tomorrow," Chris said.

"Perfect, I'll prepare everything for our meeting. What time is the best for you?" "Let say, two p.m.," Chris replied.

"Okay! See you then," he said, sipping his red wine. Chris walked away and searched for Benedict and John. They were laughing and talking to Jerome.

"Hi, guys! It seems like you're having fun," Chris said. "We were just joking. Then tell us what happened," Jerome asked.

"Well, he wants to meet up tomorrow and talk about my computer. He said he has a business proposition for me," Chris said. "He is a great scientist and is always working on new projects. I must say, he is a very successful man," Jerome added, smiling. "We will see if he likes my quantum computer," Chris said.

"Good luck on your project! Please, let me

know if you need anything. The open buffet is in the other room, please go and get something to eat, the party will be over at midnight. My driver will drive you back to the hotel just let me know when you're ready. But if you decide that you want to stay please let me know. See you in awhile," Jerome said and departed to continue mingling with his friends.

The boys went to the buffet room for a special treat. There was plenty of food, from several different styles of mini-fish to a few stunning barbecues, and fancy desserts to finish off the meal. The next table served plenty of Bordeaux. Everything had been laid out neatly, expertly, in a masculine way known only to the Knights.

"I haven't had an evening like this for at least half a century. I have immensely enjoyed myself," Benedict added, laughing. As they got ready to leave, Jerome approached them and said, "Gentlemen, I hope, I have given you the enjoyment you deserved."

"It was more than enjoyment, it was rather an adventure for us and especially for me," Benedict said with comfort.

"I'm glad that I delivered and I might say you've earned it! Thank you for coming. We will be in touch, for sure," Jerome added as he signaled his driver to come over.

"Thank you for your hospitality. It was quite an evening for me. Perhaps the next time we'd like to stay in your chateau for a day or two," Chris said.

"You're welcome! At any time you can stay with me. Goodnight gentlemen!" Jerome said, smiling.

They left the party fully content and drove back to the hotel. It was after midnight and they simply went to sleep.

The next day brought another opportunity to explore a part of Paris they'd not seen yet. They have been engaged in discovering new sites. They stopped for coffee and sweet cakes at small café *Chevalier.* Chris remembered his appointment with the Knight. The opportunity for him was fair and tempting. It would be an imprudent thing to let it slip by. Thus he interrupted their peaceful walk.

"Guys, I must keep my appointment with the Knight. If you would like to keep me company then we must go now," Chris said.

"Okay, you go ahead. I would like to keep walking and relaxing. If John wants to go with you, I wouldn't mind," Benedict said.

"I'll pass too. I like being here, in the sun. It feels really good and soothing. Good luck out there and give us a call if you need us," John said, smiling.

"You got it! See you later!" Chris confirmed and walked back to the hotel. He passed by the beautiful XVI century Gothic Church in the best part of old, charismatic Paris. He ran into his room and put his computer into the leather case. Then he walked back to the lobby and waited for the driver. He arrived within a few minutes and they took off. They arrived at the front entrance of XIII century enchanting estate and waited. The Knight greeted them from the distance,

"You're indeed on time. That's a rare quality in people that I appreciate very much. Please, come in. My name is, Etienne. Nice to see you again hopefully, no one will bother us. Please, sit down on this chair and I'll bring you some good coffee."

"Thank you," Chris replied as he unpacked his computer preparing for the presentation. Soon Etienne showed up with two cups of coffee, and said,

"Try these freshly roasted beans. You'll be stunned by its irresistible blend with the taste of hazelnut. If you drink this coffee every day you won't have to wait too long for your dreams to come true. Please indulge yourself." Chris took a big sip.

"You're certainly right. I love good coffee and this is a very good coffee indeed," Chris confirmed as he took another sip. "Are you ready to show me your computer," Etienne asked confidently. He was a tall, gray headed man with green eyes, in his late forties.

"Okay! I am ready. Look into the images which I recorded in one of the Egyptian's monasteries. As you see they are alive and can walk and talk freely," Chris said.

"This is almost incredible! We will make a fortune! I'll sponsor all your projects, cost is no object. I want to have this computer. Can you sell it to me?"

"I can build one for you but this is not for sale. I'll need it for our future mission. This piece is very special to me as it was blessed by the holy Jesus and St. Mary. Those images are real and priceless."

"You're telling me that this is a real picture of the baby Jesus and Virgin Mary?"

"Yes, it was a miracle. We waited in the Egyptian cave all night long and it was my first recording using this newly built quantum computer. Originally these images were small but the six year old baby Jesus made some kind of improvement to it. He changed one of the elements, in the computer memory to an unknown element; he called it a **Q** *element*, which doesn't exist in the chemical chart yet. That is why the images are so big. I tried to analyze this element with my fellow friends at the university and it simply doesn't exist yet."

"I know what you're saying, Chris. I'm a chemist myself and maybe together we can find this imperceptible element in my laboratory. I'm a born optimist. Lately, I'm working with new synthetic chemicals. There is always the possibility that one of them could fit into it."

"We can try. Maybe you will be the lucky one who can find this element," Chris replied a bit concern.

"How long do you think it will take you to build a new quantum computer?" Etienne asked.

"Perhaps, a few months if I am in a good mood," Chris replied.

"Can you imagine the faces of the Knights when they see this computer? When can we start our venture?"

"I don't know. I could take one year sabbatical leave from my work. However, I must arrange everything," Chris said briefly.

"Would you do that please? I will pay you ten times more than what you make right now plus fifty percent of our venture business. I've already made a written contract and my lawyer will be present when we sign it. I'm confident that everything will work the way we want it to. Let me know when you are ready," Etienne said politely.

"Sure, I'll call you from London in a week with an answer," Chris said.

"Please, join me for lunch," Etienne said

politely.

"Absolutely," Chris replied. They walked into the small room with the table set perfectly for lunch. The butler lit the two candles on the table. Soon the cook brought a few dishes filled with seafood in a spicy sauce and a fresh salad on side. Then the bartender came with a variety of different liqueurs and French wines. There was more than enough for two. Later the chef brought delicious cakes and pastries.

"As you see this castle is quite big and we can open our own laboratory right here. You will build your computer and I'll solve the element Q mystery. I can't wait to see it in the electron microscope."

"Etienne, I already looked into the electron microscope, you must trust me; it is not a regular element. The composition showed a sort of symbiosis between the two different elements. It looks like a vibrating miniature-brain. The peculiar thing is that these two unknown elements are connected with strange looking spherical bonds, like a bridge. Now I think the bonds could be made of antimatter.

The element is in a high energy level and in constant motion. It could be an electromagnetic energy in a quantum state. However, the element Q is still in a sort of equilibrium state. This is as far as I went with my research," Chris said.

"You suggest that the element Q is partially built of antimatter? Yes, it could be true. It is possible that the energies surrounding the element are converted from one state to another, back and forth, depending on the elements needs at a particular time. It could be a sort of revolution in physics. I would like to see the element myself. Can we take it to my lab for analysis? I have a key for the entire institute. I will call my friend, Gautier; he is an expert on quantum physics."

"That sounds like a good idea," Chris replied smiling.

They went out and the driver took them to the Chemistry Institute where Etienne has worked on his research in inorganic and organic chemistry for over twenty years. They arrived in fifteen minutes and Gautier was already there waiting for them in his car.

"Gautier, this is my new friend, Chris. We would like to examine a new element and maybe you could help us," Etienne said.

"Nice to meet you Chris. Of course I will help you," he said. "Nice to meet you, too," Chris replied.

Etienne opened the door and they took the elevator to the second floor where all the heavy scientific equipment was located. He turned the lights on and set on the electron microscope to the maximum magnifying power. Chris put the element Q into focus, and each of them examined this phenomenon. Chris glanced again to be sure that he is seeing the same element he saw last time in his lab. Indeed, it was the same element but it behaved a bit strange this time. It was shaking like a gel, or rather dancing. Chris was surprised but didn't say anything and just waited for their opinion. With doubt in his eyes Gautier interrupted,

"I've never seen anything like that. It looks like a little bomb ready to explode. But it is definitely a bundle of high energy, trying to escape. It is bubbling like an active volcano. Where did it come from?" he pondered, fully stunned and almost speechless. Then

Etienne added,

"I don't know what to say. It is unlike anything I have ever seen, in my long career as a chemist. It looks like a bundle of DNA to me."

"How does it work?" Gautier asked.

"I'll show you," Chris said as he put the element back into his computer. He connected all the parts together and the show began. It was spectacular watching the magnificent motion pictures moving in and out of the computer. Gautier was really stunned. "Chris, this is a sort of miracle element. It really does something amazing and I have never seen anything so perfect. Let's go to my physics lab. I want to look into it in a partial low-speed accelerator."

"We must be careful not to destroy this precious element. Let's go then," Chris said.

They left the Chemistry Institute and drove to the physics lab at the local university where Gautier was doing his research in a quantum application of new atoms in high and low speed accelerators. He was at his post for over thirty years. It didn't take them too long to reach their destination. With freshly birthed enthusiasm they jumped out of the car and headed straight to the lab. He switched the lights on and sprightly began his work. He turned the accelerator on and asked Chris for the element Q which he placed inside the chamber and said, "Chris, I will apply a low temperature to it with the infusion of a low speed nonflammable helium gas. I want to see if this element has any memory. I've never done this before," Gautier announced.

"I think, it must have some kind of memory otherwise it would not replay the same pictures each

274

time. But let's find out," Chris replied, smiling. "Guys, I hope you know what are you doing? Do not destroy this precious element because if you do, I will have a heart attack," Etienne said with a shaking voice.

"Okay! Are you ready?" Gautier announced.

"Yes! Let's do it!" Chris said.

"I'm not ready. Wait!" Etienne cried out.

"Calm down, Etienne. Nothing will happen to it!" Gautier shouted as he glanced at him, and then turned the machine on.

"You'll destroy it! You'll!" Etienne lamented.

"Forgive me but shut-up! Etienne. I can't concentrate!" Gautier shouted again. "Look! Something strange is happening," Chris said as his eyes opened widely. "Oh yes! The bundle is untangling slowly. The spherical bridge structure is breaking apart. Now, it looks like a spider web. What will happen next? I don't have a clue," Gautier said still excited.

"I told you guys you'll destroy this precious God given element," Etienne cried. "Be quiet! Etienne. You don't know anything about physics," Gautier shouted nervously.

"Now, what! I hope it comes back to its original form when the temperature drops again," Chris pointed out, wondering if it was possible.

"Etienne, you're an expert on coffees aren't you? Could you please make us some, I'm getting a bit nervous now," Gautier said looking at the changing element with deep concern.

"Okay, I can do that," Etienne said and went next door, to the small office. He spotted the coffee maker on the table, in the corner.

"I have a feeling that something amazing will happen soon. The bridge-bonds which protect the element **Q** look as if they are made of antimatter. The high energy is trapped inside of the bridge structure and tries to escape each time causing the element to vibrate. It looks like it is going to explode in a second. I've never seen anything like this!" Gautier said in a low voice, still excited inside. "It feels like sitting on dynamite. Look at this. I don't believe it! The spider's net, I mean the bonds, multiplied or cloned into two exact looking bonds and replicated in the center where the main brain of DNA is. It is a sort of reproduction process. Perhaps the element has its own DNA. Maybe, each bond has its own genes like real DNA does. You see those strings in the net; they must carry the miniature memory coded inside of each gene. It looks like someone trained the memory of each gene and asked it to memorize each movement; very interesting, indeed. The element **Q** can think!

This independent DNA' microchip could be implanted into quantum particles, combined with antimatter or perhaps a different type of energy and it can tell the particle what to do. With its unique ability we can train any dead object into a moving or talking factory. Isn't it fantastic? Maybe we can even teach the element **Q** to talk to us soon," Chris shouted loud, laughing.

"What is happening?" Etienne asked carrying coffee for everyone. "Look! Etienne, this structure reproduced itself like a regular animal DNA does, perhaps a sort of spontaneous cloning. What will be next? We've already witnessed a revolutionary event right here. Give me that coffee, Etienne," Gautier asked nervously. He took a sip of the fresh coffee and sighed with relief.

"This is good news! But how could it be?" Etienne said, excited, sipping his coffee and staring at the elements.

"Wa-wa, don't move! Just look! Each spider net is wrapping back into a bundle again. Now we have two identical *elements Q,* miraculously we cloned them, like babies and in such a short time. This is exactly what we wanted to happen. I still can't believe that we witnessed this phenomenon," Chris shouted with excitement.

"Let's clone them again! You see the temperature dropped rapidly. This is why the elements didn't multiply once more. But they can do it again. Okay, Chris, you can take the first *element Q,* and place it into your computer. Now, we will do a recording session on cloning another new *element Q,"* Gautier announced, as he injected a new dose of helium gas, and increased the temperature to its desirable degree. The computer recorded every step of the new cloning procedure.

"Okay! The bundle is opening again into the spider like net. Now it is cloning, beautifully. I'll keep the constant temperature in the accelerator a bit longer then we can obtain a few more copies of the *element Q,"* Gautier added happily.

"It is fantastic! I can't believe what I am seeing!" Etienne cried again, sipping his already cold coffee.

"We need more fresh coffee please," Chris asked as he glanced nervously at Etienne. "Don't worry. I'll be back in a minute," he said as he quickly ran to the office. Exactly four minutes later he emerged with three cups of fresh aromatic coffee.

"Thank you Etienne," Chris said.

"You're very welcome!" he replied.

The cloning went smoothly and they repeated the process until they received eight new Q elements.

"Guys, I think, we have enough elements for now. We can do a few more tomorrow. This is a miracle," Gautier added with disbelief. "Guys, now we're ready to start a new business venture. Chris will build quantum computers, Gautier and I will make the elements Q," Etienne said. "I'm in, definitely without a question. When will we begin our business?" Gautier asked, looking at Etienne. "Don't look at me you better ask Chris when he will be ready for that. I don't have a clue how to build a quantum computer, and you can't do it either. Am I right, Chris?" Etienne replied.

"You are right! We can start within two weeks. I must return to London and make arrangements at my physics department. I must take a sabbatical leave. Soon after that, I'll return here," Chris replied.

"It sounds good to me; let's look at those images you recorded, Chris. They're spherical, and still moving in every possible direction, between these two computer's screens. We can see even better now, and from each angle, how those strings untangled step by step, and how they replicated. Guys, I'm getting tired. I have three couches in my office. It is already three a.m., we can sleep here tonight!" Gautier suggested with a happy smile on his face. They were exhausted and fell asleep fast.

The next morning, they woke up with new

energy. There wasn't a better night for them than last night. Etienne already made coffee and they cherished every moment. The elements Q were removed from the accelerator and packed nicely into the plastic containers, and then placed into a low pressure refrigerator.

"Did you sleep well?" Gautier asked. "The couch was very comfortable. I slept like a baby," Chris said, laughing.

"Me too, no complaints," Etienne said, sipping his morning coffee. "I must return to the hotel, my friends are waiting for me. But we will meet very soon. I would like to take with me to London one of our newly birthed cloners, if you wouldn't mind. It would be a big surprise for my friends in my department. They didn't have a clue where to find this secret element Q. Thank you for your brilliant input," Chris said. "I'll drive you back, Chris. Thank you Gautier for everything, and especially for being smart," Etienne said and laughed.

"Okay, guys see you soon! Thank you for bringing this element Q with you. We will find a new application for it very soon. I will build a new engine that runs on antimatter, using your element Q," Gautier said happily as they shook hands goodbye. Etienne drove Chris back to the hotel. He extended his invitation for him and his friends to come over for dinner on Saturday, to his castle. Chris promised to call him if he needed a ride. Chris walked to his room upstairs, but the guys were not there. He took a shower and decided to take a quick nap. He was exhausted after last night. Around noon, John and Benedict came back with nice crispy French pastries.

"Wake up! Chris, we brought you something special," John announced happily.

"What's that?" Chris asked with a sleepy voice.

"Just the best French pastry in France, crispy, sweet and straight from the oven," Benedict said.

"It smells fantastic! Give me one. Thank you, guys for thinking of me. Hmm…, it is delicious," Chris replied as he sat on the sofa, enjoying the pastry. "Then tell us Chris, what really happened yesterday? Did you get a reasonable proposition from your Knight?" Benedict asked.

"You won't believe what happened last night. His name is Etienne, and he offered me a partnership in a business venture. I will build computers, and he will sponsor all the production, and then we will split the profits 50/50. But the most important thing was that we examined *the **element Q*** with his best friend, Gautier, who has been doing quantum physics research for over thirty years.

We moved to his physics' lab last night where he conducted a new experiment with my *element Q.* He put it in the low speed accelerator, and then applied constant temperature and helium gas to it. We witnessed an amazing thing, as our **element Q** began to *clone* itself.

I'll turn my computer on then you will see for yourselves. Just look very carefully. It didn't take too long for the element to clone. In this way, we obtained several identical elements Q. It was an amazing discovery. I brought one of the clones with me, and I will take it to London to show my friends at the university. They won't believe it! I am so excited! I promised Etienne and Gautier that we will start our new business within the next two weeks. Gautier will clone the element Q, and I'll build the quantum computer. Etienne will hustle business arrangements. He will pay me ten times more than the university does, he said. I like that idea," Chris said, laughing.

"This is great news! You deserve every bit of it. You've work so long to build this quantum computer. I'm very glad for you," John said, as he observed the cloning of the element Q. "Yes, finally luck has smiled on you. I'm happy for you. This element seems to have a brain!" Benedict said, staring at the images and laughing.

"Etienne invited all of us to his castle for dinner this Saturday. I am going, what about you, guys?" "Sounds like fun," John said.

"Sounds like a great way to spend our last night in Paris," Benedict replied.

"After the dinner I'll go straight to London," Chris said.

"Perhaps, I'll do the same. There is no point in going back with you, Benedict, since Monk Salvatore is in Paris at this moment. Probably he is watching us from a distance," John said.

"He is very smart. I personally think that he came to Paris after his own business. Boys, I have a bad news for you," Benedict said sadly.

"What is that?" Chris asked. "Do you remember that night when Salvatore was in our room? He made some noise in the living room and we woke up. I didn't tell you that I found his foot print in the bathroom. He took of his shoes and quietly walked through the shower room to the living room. And guess what I found out?" Benedict said with a puzzling smile.

"I have no clue!" Chris replied.

"I thought that it was a ghost, anyway," John said, laughing.

"Not exactly, I examined his right foot print on the wet floor, and noticed a letter T on his heel. He is a descendant of Templars. I was stunned by my discovery. I've been thinking about why he is looking for revenge. Yesterday, afternoon, I was walking in the park. The weather was great and I wanted to relax. From the distance, I spotted someone who looked like Salvatore and decided to follow him. There was distance between us and he couldn't see that I was following him. He went to the public library, and searched the old **encyclopedias.** I looked through the windows and saw everything he was doing. However, he saw me with his fox like eyes, and quickly vanished in his odd way without a trace. Then without much thinking I went into the library, and sat at the same table. He was in a hurry, and the book was still opened, on some old Templars' pictures. I stared into them, one by one, and one of the pictures struck my attention.

In the picture was a man who looked exactly like Salvatore, and I thought he must be his great grandfather. I read half a page about that man. He was a very wealthy man and almost one tenth of France and Italy was in his possession. His father was a Bishop at that time. Then it was written in small print that he was brutally killed by his enemy and his body burned to ashes. It was so bad I thought. Then all his properties, castles, gold, treasures and hundreds of acres of land miraculously went under the Vatican control many years later.

However, his great grandson survived. He was hidden in another city by the Bishop's best friend, whose name was not mentioned. But the man, who took the child, was a priest. He couldn't take care of the baby and after a few days, gave him the name Salvatore and put him into an orphanage. He also left for the child, a secret letter with instructions written in codes, in a small wooden box. Also he left a ring with an engraved monogram, the letter T, which belonged to Salvatore's father. Then when I turned to the next page to read more, I notice that the page was ripped off. I was wondering, why Salvatore would take this one particular page with him? There must be something very important written on it, I thought. I went to look for another copy of the same volume. I was lucky, the last XI volume, was hidden on the shelf between some old manuscripts. I opened on the same missing page three hundred sixty five, and I was stunned to see hundreds of Latin numerical codes. Each number was accompanied by a different alphabetical letter. I wondered what this meant, and why did Salvatore need those codes? Then something clicked in my brain.

Salvatore must be in possession of his wooden box, I thought. When he got the box back he found inside the written instruction in Latin codes. He didn't know what the numbers stood for until today. He was waiting all his life to discover the truth about himself and today he made sense of it. On that missing page, were written the Latin codes which corresponded to the same code number engraved on empty graves. Then I discovered in my mind that the treasure must be hidden in each grave instead of a dead body. It was very common in XVIII century that the Templars hid their treasure in empty graves and they did that for many centuries as they were constantly running from their enemies. This is why the codes existed and why they were widely used. On the head stones or marbles the specific inscription in codes was engraved. Some of those highest Templars would have the list of those graves with the hidden treasures inside them. For example, XVNEP would stand for a grave located in one of the northeast sides of those old cemeteries, in Paris.

Then it would explain why Salvatore is here. I bet you that he already visited the oldest cemetery in Paris and looked for those empty graves and possibly found one. I left the library and slowly walked the streets. I passed a few old window displays where I paused for a moment and looked around. On one corner I noticed the antique shop and I decided to go in. I always liked to look into these things; it relaxes me in such a way. I collect those little amber silver spoons. In the showcase, I found a few old spoons with the yellow amber in, and bought them. I was about to leave and then noticed behind the curtains, a private dimmed room. At the round wooden table, Salvatore was sitting with two men. They were trading some old pieces of ceramics and miniature sculptures. They must be valuable, I thought. Salvatore took a lot of money and put it into his pocket then quickly left through the back door. I thought, maybe he saw me with his back eye and this is why he left so fast. I followed him. It seems to me he knew Paris very well perhaps better than we do. He knew all the shortcuts through the alleys. I thought that I lost him in the dark back alley but he suddenly emerged on the other side of the street. It was amazing how flexible he was.

He paused for a moment at the corner of the street, and seemed like he froze there for a time. I watched him for ten minutes, and he still didn't move. I suspected that there must be something wrong with him. He was still standing when I approached him. However, he didn't look at me. When I touched him, my hand went through his body; I noticed that he was transparent. I was stunned and stood there with disbelief. Where did he go? It was another high-tech trick. But how did he do it?

Then I recalled our last session on the partial resurrection of Mrs. Alice. Salvatore using the same holy words I used to build his own doubles. Why? He can escape faster that way. He dumps his doubles behind each time he runs. Brilliant! We didn't think of that yet!

Now you can see how smart he is. I think he is a mastermind in disappearing. I have a plan for us. Tomorrow we're going to follow him to the oldest cemetery in Paris. I'm positively sure that he is looking to recover his grandfathers' treasures," Benedict concluded.

"Maybe, we can make our own doubles," John said.

"Very interesting, I would never think that this little man has so much past left behind," Chris added with a smile.

"Maybe we will need our own doubles, after all he is a dangerous man. Don't forget he can kill in the most mysterious way," Benedict added with concern.

"You're right and we shall take this possibility under consideration. Then what is our plan for now?" Chris asked.

"I suggest we follow him. I know where the oldest cemetery in Paris is. Let's go! We shouldn't wait until tomorrow. We can stop for a quick meal on our way out," Benedict said.

They went out and stopped in a small cafe to pick up a few sandwiches and then caught a taxi that drove them to the cemetery. Within twenty minutes, they were at the oldest cemetery in the outskirts of Paris. They asked the driver to wait for them.

The cemetery looked like one big gated estate with huge pine trees growing on each side of the walls. The monuments were built with splendor by rich aristocratic families, priests, and important government politicians. It was like visiting a local museum. They decided to walk between the alleys and read the old inscriptions on each tomb. Some of the gravestones were dated to the 10th century.

Benedict felt Salvatore would more than likely be interested in these tombs. People were bringing beautiful fresh flowers and colorful garlands and placing them on the X or XV Century tombs. Benedict found that odd as it gave the impression that their ancestors died recently. Maybe these people are the descendants of Templars and in these graves are laying not the bones of their loved ones but the gold stored by their great grandfathers.

"A very unusual place indeed, there is an enigma hidden in the ancient marble crosses," Chris pointed out as he wandered around.

"Guys look at this tomb. It is dated to 12th

century. However, no names of the deceased or loving epitaphs but someone just placed fresh and expensive garlands with beautiful colorful ribbons. Isn't it strange a bit? I wonder what XIIcp2 stands for? I bet you that this grave is empty. Perhaps, Salvatore is looking for such tombs. But even if he finds it, he must have special tools to lift the headstone. It is a two person operation," Benedict pointed out with a smile of a sleuthhound detective.

"Sure, he can't do it himself. But if he has a partner, he must share the finds with him. He would endanger himself by revealing his secrets to any strangers. Isn't it a risky business? I'm fully convinced that he acts alone," John spelled out as he dazzled everyone with his point.

"You've made your point John. I suppose, we'll meet him here, digging alone," Benedict pointed out.

"Guys, don't move! Lower your heads! I see Salvatore digging in the third row to my right. We shall hide right here, behind this headstone. He wouldn't see us, for sure. We better be fully undercover," Chris whispered.

"Okay! Let's see what he finds. Whatever it is, try to be calm. No excitement!" Benedict whispered.

"Sure! Whatever he finds wouldn't be for the betterment of the world," Chris added jokingly.

"It would rather be a liability. How long do you think it will take him to open the grave? It is rather laborious work. He doesn't even have the proper equipment for digging," John noticed.

"If you are so worried, you can help him," Chris added with a smile as he glanced at John.

"It could take him a few good hours. We better

figure this out, maybe we should watch in shifts," Benedict said in serious tone.

"I can take a short nap on this gravestone. You wouldn't mind. Would you?" John asked.

"I don't think you can sleep here. It is cold and unpleasant but if you insist, go ahead," Chris said.

"You could have a nightmare. I brought a newspaper with me so I'm going to read. Let me know if anything happens," Benedict concluded and put his nose into the newspaper.

The digging took him almost two hours. Finally, Salvatore was able to pull out a few objects from the tomb. Benedict peered through his portable binoculars with curiosity. "Guys, I think, he found something of value. Looks like he was preordained for this mission," he whispered.

"What is that?" Chris asked.

"I'm not sure, but look for yourself," he said and handed the binoculars to Chris. "I see a small sack. He just took out a coin and it looks shiny and gold," Chris confirmed with a smile. "Let me look into it. Oh, yes! He just pulled out a box from the pit. I can see a man with demonic fury in his eyes. I just wonder how he is going to carry this heavy load of gold. Wait guys! He opened the box and poured the contents into a big sack. He didn't even look at it. I'll call this action, an essay on gold and greed," Benedict said laughing.

"We must follow him. I just wonder what he is going to do with that. You would never know what this type of insidious character is able to do," John said as he opened his eyes from a short nap.

"What would you do on a rendezvous like that and with pure gold? Likely you will sell it. I bet you, he will go to the same antique store where I saw him before," Benedict commented ready to leave. They followed Salvatore and he indeed stopped at the same antique store. They observed how he traded the priceless pieces for very little money. It was shame to sell treasures like these for peanuts. "I have a feeling that he doesn't have a clue how much this stuff is really worth. This is simply upsetting! We must stop this kind of behavior. We must talk to Jerome about it. Who knows maybe this is a part of their treasure too," Benedict said frustrated.

"I don't think so! It is more intricate than we think. Salvatore inherited this stuff from his grandfather. He has only those codes which were given to him when he was four years-old. It must be in his favor. But it seems like he doesn't care for those treasures anymore. He is just trying to get rid of them and fast. He could sell them to museums for a lot of money," John concluded with disappointment. Salvatore vanished as fast as he got there. They try to look for him but simply he remained brilliantly nowhere to be seen. He has been an irritating character since he escaped from the Vatican.

"Let's go home! I believe that with this divine sense of immortality set to rest in our minds, we may close our adventure as undercover explorers at least for today. I'm tired and cold," Benedict said. A bit exhausted they tried to accommodate their egos and ambitions toward their future mission; they finally walked back to the taxi and drove to the hotel.

Dinner awaited them in their cozy penthouse, next to the roaring fireplace. Everything was just on time as they were very hungry. The waiter served hot exotic cocktails and black hot tea just to relax and warm them up. Then soon after, he served French ravioli with butter and fresh basil, a Renaissance style with orchids on each side of the plate. The red wine accompanied this luxurious set up.

"Choose to relax or choose to hunt. I prefer to relax. I'm getting tired of hunting for this shrewdly monk. He is like air lately, and his vagabond like behavior makes me uncertain. Obviously, he frantically maneuvers to avoid us and he is wasting our time too. I always thought I had better things to do in my life. I don't know about you guys," Benedict said, still irritated but with no obligation to entertain the audience anymore.

"I have my own plan too but he suddenly appeared as a freak of nature into my life. Now, I must find the time for both; my virtual plan and Salvatore's snarky adventure. His pragmatic attitude makes me sick. However, I consider him a specimen on extinction and perhaps this excites me a bit," Chris said laughing.

"Definitely, he is not one of those zeitgeist or moralist thus he is not going to last. We have two choices; leave him alone with his cynic attitude or catch him before he destroys all of us. Ultimately, we have the choice between peace and strife. Surely, he is not prone to cooperate. I didn't find any merits in his sloppy behavior. I personally must pursue the second option," John said, smiling coldly.

"I got your point, boys. It seems to me that we have the same striking fulcrum, so far. I agree with you, there have always been a tragic wisdom and a tragic bitterness some where in the spectrum of human behavior. Let's enjoy the rest of our evening otherwise I will not be able to sleep. Tomorrow is our last day in Paris," Benedict said quite content but still sober-minded.

"Just remember that we're invited for dinner to Etienne's castle, tomorrow at six p.m. It will be a fun evening. I like to rest in different atmosphere. This constant running is killing me. I'm not twenty anymore," Chris said.

"I'm looking forward to going as well. At least it will be one day without hunting for Salvatore and I'd consider this as my personal success," Benedict said.

"Guys, if you wouldn't mind I'm going to rest in my room. I want to read a book. I brought with me a fictional book on ancient civilizations," John said as he walked away.

"Sure we wouldn't mind, would we Benedict?" Chris said, smiling.

"I want to rest too. I must say goodnight to you," Benedict added as he walked straight up to his room.

The night was peaceful without any major interruption. The sparkling sun brought the morning glory and woke them up. Benedict sat at the piano by the fireplace and struck a few tunes while Chris and John sipped wine on the patio overlooking the Eiffel tower. Soon the cooks served artichokes with king crab and blueberries. It was quite a whimsical morning fare, they thought. The aroma of French coffee opened their nostrils, bringing them unexpected comfort. They were definitely in a perfect mood for the morning conversation. Fresh green salad with homemade dressing, crispy bread, garlic olive oil dip, and chopped basil were a great addition to it.

"I feel like I just escaped to the fabled garden for a moment. Breakfast is really delicious. My dear friends, I don't know if you would be interested to go once more to the cemetery just to see if Salvatore is hiding between the tombs. I thought it would be wise on our behalf to stop him from excavating any more treasures. He is a lost man and doesn't know what he is doing. I don't understand why he suddenly needs a lot of money; it doesn't make much sense for a single monk. He must have some secret plan behind his own black curtain. Thus if he is still pursuing this way, he will destroy all of his inheritance very soon. On top of that, much of the great Templars' treasure will be lost forever in some raven ravish hands of the antique shops' owners. I would call this a crime!" Benedict said with a raucous voice.

"It is upsetting. But what can we do? There is not much we can really do. You can't stop him from digging after his own inheritance. Maybe it looks like a very odd way of doing it but he has his point too!" John concluded, aggravated a bit.

"I wouldn't mind going with you again. Just to watch him. John is right, we can't do much. If we try to stop him he will go underground again. I would leave everything as is and keep joy in a breath of moment for ourselves," Chris pointed out, smiling.

"Okay! Maybe, you're right. Soon after breakfast we shall take off. It is a pity for us to let go of such an opportunity without knowing what will happen next," Benedict added impatiently.

"You're like a warrior with an enticing option.

You simply can't resist. Can you?" John pointed out.

"I would say it is rather an event that taps you into a burgeoning curiosity about the monk's discovery. You can't sit still! Can you?" Chris interrupted with a laugh.

"Yes! I wouldn't say no! Indeed, it sparks my imagination to a certain point of curiosity, and there is an exuberant passion underlying in it, for me. I would say, a symbol or odyssey of primordial consciousness," Benedict said and paused for a short intermission then he added in an unobtrusive manner,

"I'm an extroverted type of man thus this type of Scotland Yard work gives me satisfaction."

"Sure, you're a determined man! You ache for adventure, something dangerous keeps your adrenaline surging," Chris threw in an exciting conclusion, staring into Benedict eyes. Everything sounded just right to him.

"Sure, I might need a buzz in order to keep up with all of that. So, let's go! I don't want to waste anymore of my time," Benedict paused.

"Maybe I am thrilled with the chase. Perhaps I would rather return to my research, but for now a serial murderer must be caught…stopped before he kills again!"

Chapter 9. Life in the Alexandrian Academy December

The next cold and snowy morning brought a lot of excitement for everyone. It was Christmas time.

The students rushed to the beautifully decorated dining room for dinner. The lights were dimmed. The tables were covered with green and red linens and lined up in rows like an army of soldiers in a battlefield. The students from both monasteries came with teachers, priests, monks and nuns. It would be a party to remember. Charlotte and Amelie were waiting in the corridor for Peter to appear when suddenly they spotted him dressed in a long chocolate brown frock looking like a ghost. Patrick kept him company. She saw a sweet smile on his painful grayish looking face. He lost some weight during his three-day ordeal. He was a different Peter than she remembered but she knew she loved him all the same.

"Hello Peter! How are you?" Charlotte asked as they embraced warmly. Amelie gave him a hug too. "I'm okay! Thank you oh Mighty God for sparing my life on the cross. I made it Charlotte! I'm the number One," he said, showing a deeply branded letter Omega on his left hand and in the middle of the chest. It looked grossly terrible and Charlotte trembled. Amelie held her shoulders before she hit the floor. Amelie was devastated herself and her limbs were shaking too. Patrick gave her a hand before she collapsed.

"What a price you must pay for your honor to God," Charlotte whispered with tears. "You're a very courageous boy, Peter. You've already got Angels wings," Amelie added in a low voice.

"I'm next! I'm ready for the same sacrifice. I must keep my promise to God," Patrick said in a strong masculine voice. "Sure, we'll support you, Patrick," Amelie whispered. Suddenly, she noticed their teacher, Bertrand coming toward them.

"Merry Christmas, are you ready for dinner?" he asked. "We were just about to go in," Amelie said, smiling, trying to look her best as she stood up firmly. She followed him, looking for a suitable place to sit. The best place would be next to him but he walked away to join the other teachers. She didn't have a chance to be close to him. Disappointed she joined Charlotte and the boys. They found a nice table not too far from the teachers' table.

Amelie could see Bertrand's face clearly. Her gray colored face suddenly took on nice rose shades and her cheeks turned red as she looked at Bertrand each time. Charlotte noticed and said,

"Amelie, take it easy. Try to relax and focus on your dinner. We'll be served a special menu today." Amelie looked at Charlotte but didn't reply as her soul was anguished and perplexed within her own fantasy world.

"I feel like the treasure of my soul has been stolen and exhibited to scorn. I'm ashamed of myself now."

"Amelie, stop lamenting, you have a powerful imagination. Bertrand doesn't even know about your fantasy. Be more realistic! Stop looking at him. The servers are running with trays of delicious food. Be ready! Today they're going to serve twelve different dishes like the twelve Apostles according to the Christian tradition. The first one is my favorite; they call it the Czar Crown or Fox Ears a sort of high-end fried dumpling. The difference is that the first one is filled with a precious forest truffles or wild mushrooms with unbelievable aroma. The other ones are filled simply with potatoes, cabbage or cheese. You should really enjoy this precious menu."

"I'll try, Charlotte," Amelie confirmed with a scanty smile.

"This is my favorite one as well. Peter, you should try it," Patrick said.

"I'm not hungry, yet. Maybe later," Peter said weakly.

"Peter, you must eat! You must get your strength back. You haven't eaten for almost four days," Patrick said.

"We worry about you because you've lost several pounds. I can feed you," Charlotte added and Amelie shook her head in approval.

"I can do it myself just give me a bit more time," Peter replied and slowly ate one dumpling. Soon, the wild hot mushroom soup was served. After awhile, delicious fried fish in rosemary oil, baked potatoes with roasted garlic and green dill were brought and then cooked cold-fish with veggies in a clear gelatin. The new dishes were coming accordingly every thirty minutes until midnight including the best cheeses, poppy-seed cakes, pumpernickels, gingerbread cookies, and much more. It was nice and everyone was chatting at the table listening to Christmas Carols.

The next day, the official winter break began. It would last almost two weeks. The silvery snow covered all of the campus and it looked like it had been put to sleep with a touch of a magic wand. The rising sun scattered back and forth from the white soft snow into the rainbow and made every morning glorious.

Then finally a New Year arrived and a special dinner menu will be served for this occasion at 7 p.m. Also the ballet dancers were invited not only to perform the classic *White Swan* show but also to teach the students how to dance waltz and tango. There would be a fun entertainment. The girls and boys were dressed in their best outfits. Amelie made herself a new ballroom dress with a bit of XVIII Century touch from the purple velvet curtains. She looked stunning and secretly hoped for at least one dance with French teacher. It would be a special party to be remembered by everyone. As soon as the girls were dressed and ready to leave Charlotte whispered,

"Amelie, you look like Ophelia. Your dress is stunning. Let's hope Sister Agnes wouldn't notice and cry about her precious purple curtains. It was worth such a great sacrifice. How do you like my black dress?"

"It is very classy and it suits you well. I can give you my white pearls. Just put it on!" "You're right. It is a perfect match. Thank you Amelie."

"I should take my favorite French love tape. I'll switch the tapes in a right moment and then ask Bertrand to dance with me. He will understand the true meaning of love. It would be a surprise for everyone too," Amelie said, laughing.

"Amelie, I'm not sure if your clever plan will go smoothly tonight. Think twice! Also, I'm not sure if you're serious or just making fun of this poor French guy, Bertrand. Maybe, you should go over your splendid plan with Sister Agnes first. I don't want you to get into trouble."

"But if I tell Sister Agnes everything then it

wouldn't be a surprise anymore," Amelie pointed out.

"Okay, you got your point. Let's do it your way," Charlotte said with a bit of skepticism. The girls ran to the big ballroom where everyone was waiting for ballet dancers. The lights were dimmed, the music was on and the dancers showed up on stage looking like they just jumped out of a Degas painting. The show was very picturesque and everyone enjoyed. Soon after the show the open-bar dinner was served. In the meantime the ballet dancers were teaching girls and boys how to dance to the famous tunes of Waltz and other classical pieces.

Each person received a beautiful cotillion, made of colorful ribbons, which was pinned to each person's costume by the party host. Each cotillion had a different name written on the ribbons such as cat, bunny, king, rose, lily, and other names of flowers or domestic animals. Each cotillion had its double, the girls and the boys walked around trying to find their match based on their cotillion names. King dances with queen, princess with prince, cat with dog, etc. It was a sort of a fun game. Even the Sisters were dancing with the monks and the priests. In the middle of the party Amelie snuck into the music room and switched the tapes to her favorite French love song. Soon after that she approached the teacher, Bertrand and asked him to dance. The teacher was in shock as the music was too emotional for his ear, and he refused to dance. Amelie was embarrassed and her face turned purple-red. It was a good thing that Charlotte was around and asked Amelie to dance.

"I hate him! He refused to dance with me. He didn't get it! I made a fool of myself," Amelie whispered into Charlotte's ear and laughed.

"It's too much for this little man to handle. I told you that it could be a problem," Charlotte whispered back as she glanced at Bertrand. His eyes met hers with deep desire for her. He scanned her up and down and then walked away. However, the music brought much more attention than Amelie originally anticipated, especially from Sister Agnes who was stunned by the erotic sound of the whispering love song. She walked toward Amelie and Charlotte and asked,

"Amelie, you look like Madonna from the Baroque era, like you just walked out of a XVI Century Caravaggio painting. Your pretty dress also looks very familiar to me. Did you make it from the window curtains? That wasn't so wise. It will be difficult to get a replacement for that. One more thing, do you know who put this nasty tape into the record player and spoiled the party?"

"I wanted to surprise everyone with this emotional, beautiful French music," Amelie replied with a devilish look in her eye.

"You certainly did," the Sister said and looked into Charlotte eyes then added, "Charlotte, I thought you had more sense than Amelie. I'm very disappointed in both of you. You will be punished for this transgression, which is unacceptable in our facility. It is a violation of academic rules. You'll spend two days in the basement facility. Now go to your room and change your clothes. I will meet you there within five minutes."

The girls walked to their room with mixed feelings. Then Amelie interrupted,

"What do you think is in the basement that we haven't discovered yet?"

"We're going to find out in just a few minutes. I wouldn't worry too much about it. We better get into warm outfits. Surely, it will be freezing cold out there," Charlotte said with serious concern. Soon Sister Agnes knocked at the door and walked in with a terrible expression on her face.

"Your tape was confiscated! I'm sorry girls that you will celebrate your New Year in the basement alone. Hopefully, it will be a practical lesson for you and teach you common sense in the future, let's go."

The girls followed her to the basement, which at first glance looked like a cave. It was quite dark and chilly in there. Sister opened the first cell for Amelie and then the other one for Charlotte. Only iron bars separated the two cells. There were no beds and no benches either. The holy cross hung on the stone wall and iron chains. The Sister locked each cell and put the key into her pocket. On the way out she said, "Happy New Year girls." "Happy New Year Sister," Charlotte sadly replied.

There was quiet. Suddenly, Amelie said,

"Charlotte, we can exercise on those bars the Bat position. Coach Louis would be proud of us."

"Certainly he would. Let's do it then. Why is so dark in here? Is there any light around?"

"I don't have a clue. But I see a little flashlight in the distance."

"Amelie I have a bad news for you. Those little lights you see are nothing other than rat's eyes."

"Oh, holy cow let's jump on the bars! I can already smell those beasts and I don't like the

300

feeling."

"Amelie, just relax! We can hang on these bars for at least six hours. Soon it will be midnight and we can celebrate a New Year together."

"Sure, it is something to remember for the rest of my life! I'm very grateful for that!"

"Amelie, don't panic. You asked for that! You should be happy that I'm here to keep you company."

"This is the price we must pay for true friendship Charlotte. I'm thankful for that." "I'm glad that at least you appreciate that. Try to sleep a bit and save your precious energy for later. I think you'll need it soon." They closed their eyes and were ready for a long nap. Half an hour later they heard a noise. Someone was coming to pay them a visit. A few clicks in the lock and the door opened. From the distance they saw a bright flashlight and then they heard the voice.

"Happy New Year, girls!" the voice said. It was Bertrand.

"What are you doing here?" Amelie asked as she jumped off the bars.

"I felt guilty that you had to spend the New Year right here all alone. I decided to keep you company for awhile if you don't mind," he said and paused for a moment.

"This is not like you, tell us the truth! Why are you here?" Amelie said, irritated.

"Trust me! This is the only reason," he insisted, sipping wine straight from the bottle.

"You came here because you want to drink, secretly!" Amelie added, laughing.

"I came to pray for you. I'm really sorry," he

said and pulled the bible from his pocket and read a few psalms aloud so the girls could hear them. He was very sincere and Amelie was about to forgive him almost everything.

"Do we have any light here? We saw a few rats running around. I hope they are not going to eat us overnight," Charlotte said quietly.

"I will not allow anything like that happen to you, my dear Charlotte. I'll bring you a small lantern. It will keep the rats away. I know those bastards come down here all the time. They must have found some underground tunnels. I'll be back in ten minutes," he said and left.

"Did you hear how nice he talked to you? My dear Charlotte, I'll not allow anything like that happen to you. He is obviously in love with you. There isn't any other explanation for it! I don't believe it! Why doesn't he ever talk to me like that," Amelie shouted angrily.

"Amelie, be quiet! You're irritating me. You're crazy! He's just trying to be nice, that's it!" Charlotte said, laughing. Within exactly ten minutes, Bertrand returned with a lantern and two bottles of water and said,

"Try not to drink too much then you won't have to go to the bathroom. The lantern has enough kerosene for at least two days. I asked Sister Agnes for permission to come here and she agreed. Tomorrow, I'll bring you lunch. See you then," he said and left with a narrow smile on his face and big concern in his eyes. He thought the girls went a bit over their limit.

The night was peaceful and went by fast. The

girls were hanging on the bars in the Bat position all night long. Amelie opened her eyes in a panic attack screaming,

"I don't feel my legs! Maybe the rats ate them!"

"You scared me. You have your legs. Be quiet! Try to flip over off the bars onto the floor."

"Okay, I did! But I don't feel my legs much," she replied.

"Me too, we hung on the bars too long. Just stretch and exercise your legs a bit. I'll do the same. I'm glad that one night is done. It is nine a.m. and we'll get lunch at twelve noon. I'm not hungry," Charlotte said with a bit of disappointment.

"I'm not hungry either. I ate a lot last night. Don't you think that Sister Agnes overreacted a little? I didn't know she would be so angry at me."

"Amelie, what would you do in her shoes? You're a bit rebellious in nature."

"Maybe I am, but that doesn't mean I should be punished for it."

"Be more objective, Amelie. You were punished for the curtain and for the tape. Be a judge of yourself for a moment. You're charged with two counts from the criminal stand point."

"Are you playing lawyer with me, Charlotte?"

"Certainly not I am just trying to be fair. On top of that, I was punished just for being your friend. Don't forget that! Now, I'm stuck here with you, trying to be nice. You know, I could be in our comfortable room reading an interesting book."

"Do you have any regrets then?"

"I don't, but I don't want you to talk crazy. Show a bit of repentance, not to me but to Sister Agnes and to Bertrand. Trust me it would be beneficial for you, and maybe for me too."

"I get your point! Let me revise my behavior while we are here, in this stinky cave. I know I can do better. Obviously, I can't change my wild nature but at least I'll try to correct it a bit!"

"Oh Holy Ghost finally we're coming closer to an understanding. You try to keep your promise. Now you'll see for yourself what a waste of time it is. Two precious days are taken away from my short life. I'm not happy about that. How will I explain to Peter what really happened to us? He'll think that both of us are very crazy. I feel really bad about it."

"Oh, Charlotte don't exaggerate, I feel like a criminal. As a matter of fact everything is my fault. I'm sorry that I dragged you into my crazy fantasy. You shouldn't be punished for that. It's me who should be punished. I must talk to Sister Agnes and she should let you go."

"This is my fault too. I should have stopped you from doing it, but at least we should talk to Sister Agnes about our plans. I had bad feelings about it from the beginning. I thought it could be a scandal. She is a nice person after all, and she even offered us her hand a long time ago. We should have taken advantage of that. It's me to blame for everything now."

While the girls weighed their crime and punishment issue, teacher Bertrand arrived incognito.

"Hello girls! How are you doing? I brought you a big lunch. But it seems like you're very busy."

"Thank you, teacher Bertrand. But I want to admit that everything was my fault and Charlotte should go free. She had nothing to do with it. She is with me here because I'm her friend. Unfortunately the devil is inside of me telling me what to do. Trust me, I'm the bad one and I alone should be punished," Amelie admitted bravely, still laughing. Bertrand looked at her with disbelief in his eyes and said,

"My child, I'm shocked by your truthfulness. I'm really impressed by it. However, when we deal with the friendship issue it's difficult to judge our behavior. We do many crazy things in the name of friendship, and we're punished for the things we've never done in most cases. Charlotte made her own judgment in this case. But whatever she has done for you, it is more than generous of her. I would consider it a blessing. Thank you for your confession. I'll pray for you, my poor child and may the Lord have mercy on you. I must leave now but I'll likely see you tomorrow again for lunch. Goodbye for now girls."

"Goodbye!" Charlotte said. Amelie was speechless; however she held a gravel of joy on her almost horrified face.

"Then at least he'll pray for me, isn't that fantastic! While I have confessed to him my little crime, I'd do better with confession of love! Am I so bad? I'm a great egoist and an immense liar," Amelie cried out.

"Well Amelie, as for me you're not so bad, and it's not necessarily egoism or a lie as you said. But I'm not sure about that love of yours, obviously. However, everything depends on which angle we look at it from. On top of that, this little crime of yours, as you said, is just a small thing in comparison with the whole universe, so we should definitely disregard it. Try not to talk about it anymore, as there is no capital punishment for what you have done. Let's just put an end to these self-inflicted wounds of yours, promise."

"I promise! I'm glad that you think of me that way. I'm sorry that I dragged you all the way into this terrible cave with me, even though you haven't done anything wrong. It's supposed to be my punishment only," she answered with a visible humbleness on her face.

"I don't mind being here with you. Maybe, I need to better understand other people's problems, perhaps simply for the sake of a higher purpose," Charlotte concluded with a mysterious smile.

"That's very generous of you, as Bertrand said, and I thank you for that. You've got some remarkable qualities that I'll always admire. Now forgive me, but I must contemplate my sorrow alone," Amelie added with mockery look in her eyes.

"Sure I understand that," Charlotte replied. No words were spoken for hours and the silence hung in the air. Perhaps, Amelie was defining evil and good or even tried to separate them in her own mind. Confused, after finding that the distinction between evil and good began to fade, and finally disappeared in front of her eyes, she began to cry. It was more than remorse; it was the disgrace of her soul. How would she face the world tomorrow? She thought. She hung onto the bars and tried to forget all. The rats were running around as soon as they discovered the left over lunch-scraps. Amelie was furious and began to scream but no one heard her voice. Soon Charlotte interrupted as a subtle smile flitted across her lips,

"Amelie, pull yourself together and think positively. They're not going to harm you. Just hang onto the bars a bit longer. They are after the food."

"Those creatures stink like old pig manure. I hate them. Look…so many of them! Where are they coming from? I don't like this place!" she said with a horrified look in her eyes. She was deeply shaken. In the meantime, the rats were consuming left over food from the plastic containers abandoned in the corner of her cell.

"You'll be fine. Just look at their cute faces, they're not so bad after all. You see, they just finished their lunch and are about to leave. They're survivors like us."

"You're right! They're leaving, indeed. I'm relieved," Amelie pensively agreed, however, her lips quivered and then she added nervously,

"They're definitely not cute, but rather ugly."

Charlotte smiled and whispered, "It wasn't so terrible after all. But for sure, we're not coming back here again, right Amelie!"

"Right, Charlotte. Never again!" she said as her voice broke frequently and she began to weep.

The night was peaceful. The heavy dampness of the ancient cave woke them up. Then around noon there was a click at the door lock. The teacher Bertrand appeared as though from the mist with two boxes of lunch. He announced cheerfully,

"Hello girls! You should be happy as within exactly six hours you'll be free to go. It's good reason to celebrate! I brought you lunch." he handed them boxes and then sipped the wine straight from the bottle.

"How was your night girl's?"

"It was terrible! The rats were running around one after another like crazy. They were hungry. It was awful! I want to be out of here and fast!" Amelie spoke ardently.

"Sure, you will be out very soon my child. However, be patient," Bertrand added as he emptied the wine bottle.

"I beg your pardon! Are you already drunk?" Amelie asked him imperiously. She became totally bewildered by his behavior.

"Not necessarily!" he murmured with a burlesque laugh, burping occasionally.

"I'm sorry. See you later, girls," he added as he was leaving, whistling his own tune.

"Did you see that, Charlotte? He amuses me. A total lack of respect for the ladies; I don't like him anymore!" Amelie was exasperated.

"Just ignore him! He acts foolishly. But finally, you got his full image today. I'm glad that this happened. On the top of that we have better things to do in our short life. He is already a lost man, I'm telling you," Charlotte said calmly and precisely, putting a smile on her face.

"I just wonder why he's drinking all the time. It's really scary! Devil knows what he's up to," Amelie said with disbelief. They sat on the ground and waited. Time moved fast. Amelie threw a nasty joke occasionally. Charlotte was stunned by the content of each one.

"Amelie, where did you learn those dirty jokes?"

"I had a friend, Charles. He used to love to tell

dirty jokes. He grew up in orphanage and picked them up on the streets. When he was sixteen he ran away and found his first job in a nightclub. Perhaps he picked them up there."

"I see. Is he still your friend?"

"Not any more. The police arrested him for killing a neighbor."

"Poor guy, I believe he wasn't the right friend for you, Amelie."

"But he was nice guy when I knew him."

Around four thirty p.m. the teacher Bertrand came and let them go free. It was earlier than they expected. Sister Agnes didn't show up, perhaps she was embarrassed about her quick judgment. The girls ran to their favorite hot Jacuzzi. The water was soothing and the pleasure was all theirs. "Do you believe it? That was fast! We're free spirits again!" Amelie screamed with happiness. "It feels like heaven. Nice to be back, and still on vacation," Charlotte said firmly. There was a long silence hanging in the air. Perhaps, they couldn't believe that the burden of guilt was lifted of their shoulders and for good. It was like a dream too beautiful to understand. But it was real.

"It seems strange that I'm still happy after all of that we just went through. Perhaps it would make us stronger. However these two days felt like a century for me. No more rats!" Amelie raised her voice suddenly and put a big smile on her face. Then she confessed,

"I'm glad this criminal act of mine is finally over. I should learn how to resist most of my temptations. They're really bad! On the top of that I'm so stubborn.

I should try to revise my behavior, Charlotte, you must help me."

"I will if you let me. You must learn how to resist. I believe it shouldn't be so difficult. Just consider it as an open option."

"I will, I promise," she added.

The hour slipped by without even noticing. The girls put their robes on and walked slowly through the long corridor. They paused for a moment near Sister Agnes' door and heard the same French love song that got Amelie into trouble. They gazed through the small keyhole and spotted Sister Agnes, dancing alone. They couldn't believe what was happening in there. She was frightened but still emotional. With a fearful face she whispered like she was possessed.

Suddenly she picked the picture of her beloved Richard from her desk and kissed it. She stared at the picture constantly and her tears were pouring like a heavy rain. She was in a state of shock or perhaps ecstasy.

She collapsed onto the floor and lamented her existence. As soon as the song finished, she elevated herself off the floor, put the picture back on the desk and then lay down on the bed. It was a perfect act. She performed like in the real theatre. Indeed, she was a great actress, without knowing that. The girls were stunned, looked at each other with disbelief and then they left, laughing on their way out. They didn't have enough courage to knock at her door this time.

"It seems like Sister Agnes gave a new performance tonight but unfortunately without any audience. Since she likes my song so much I don't understand why she was so harsh on me in the first place!" Amelie added, still laughing.

"Maybe, she misjudged you and now she has some regrets or even guilt. You would never know. Just forget about it," Charlotte said, smiling.

"I don't think that she has any regrets at all! She's just an old hard-headed maid," Amelie said with satisfaction and laughed out loud.

"I want to ask you to forgive her everything," Charlotte said seriously.

"Why should I do that? Give me one good reason!" Amelie said exasperated.

"Just for the sake of integrity my dear Amelie, it would be the best position for you at this moment of uncertainty."

"I'm not sure if I can do that," Amelie said disconcerted.

"You must try otherwise it would be an unceremonious act on your behalf," Charlotte said with tenderness.

"Perhaps I'm deprived of any integrity!" Amelie said impatiently with a devilish look in her eyes.

"I'm not sure about that! I personally think that you're full of integrity just you don't want to admit it. Don't be angry, please. Try to use your reason at this time, promise."

"I'll try," Amelie replied with a bit of reserve.

"Now, Amelie, make some of your favorite tea. I really enjoy drinking it. Let's be at peace with ourselves while we're here." They looked at each other and laughed.

"I think I'm back. I'm me again. I thought it would never happen," Amelie whispered.

"I'm happy for you, Amelie."

They entered the room. Soon they found a small envelope on the floor. It was from Peter and she didn't have a clue how it got there. Someone must've slipped it under the door. But it was sealed, and the letter P was engraved in the middle of the purple seal. She sat on her bed and opened it. It read:

Dear Charlotte.

I'm doing great! I heard that you and Amelie were imprisoned in the basement of the monastery for two long days. I believe it wasn't anything serious and I won't ask you about the details. I hope when you read this letter you'll already be out of trouble. Now, I have bad news about Patrick. He is dying in the same cave where I was previously crucified. His crucifixion went smoothly and he was okay for two days.

Suddenly, something happened today. The monks don't know what to do. If they take him off the cross he'll fail the test. He is unconscious and won't open his eyes. He is still breathing. I want you to come and see me in the same cave tonight around six thirty p.m. before the monks come to check on Patrick again. They put the miracle balsam on his body just two hours ago. Please, hurry!

Love, Peter."

"Amelie, take your swimsuit and let's go to see Patrick in the cave. He is dying, Peter said. Read this letter quickly and hurry up! We have only fifteen minutes to swim there. Take the flashlight with you. It's so dark and cold there."

"Okay, let me read it fast. Oh, no, Heavenly Father! Please, save our friend Patrick. Charlotte, I have the left over balsam from Coach Louis. I put it in the freezer. We'll take it with us. Maybe, we can help

312

him. Let's go! I'm ready!" They dove in and swam straight to the cave. The water was freezing cold. Within five minutes they were already in the cave. Peter was waiting for them with warm towels. The two white candles were burning in each corner of the cave, giving a bit of warm light.

"Charlotte, help me put the balsam all over Patrick's body. Let's start from his feet first. Peter, you should massage his heart. Let's pray for his life. Dear Lord our God. You have the power to revive Patrick from the darkness of death. We're sincerely asking you to give the precious life back to our beloved friend. You put him through the test of restitution and loyalty to you. He is giving you his life right now and what else could be more precious than his own flesh. Please return the spirit of life into his flesh and give him a second chance to prove his loyalty to you. Bring the fire to his heart and the light to his eyes and then he can see you again and be grateful for the gift of life. Certainly you will be not disappointed! Amen."

"That was a nice prayer Amelie. Thank you for that," Peter said.

"I think Patrick's feet are getting warmer," Charlotte said, still rubbing the miracle balsam into his feet.

"I think his heart is beating faster too. He only has six hours left on the cross in order to pass this test. If he opens his eyes likely he will make it," Peter said.

"Maybe our prayer was received by God. Peter, take some balsam and rub it into Patrick's chest. It would help him for sure," Charlotte whispered.

"We must hurry! In fifteen minutes the monks will come to check on Patrick to see if he is still alive," Peter added nervously.

"Patrick, open your eyes! It's me, Amelie! Patrick, try to open your eyes. Please! Please! We love you Patrick! Be strong! Don't give up! Never give up!" Amelie cried aloud.

"Patrick, you've almost passed the test. Please, open your eyes. Don't be stubborn," Peter shouted in his ear.

They felt hopeless and were about to leave. Suddenly Patrick raised his eyelids and blue light came from his eyes, which spread into golden rays. It was a spectacular scene. He was coming back in full glory. They screamed together in disbelief. Then he muttered,

"I had a strange dream that I was dead. Then from the distance I heard your voices, calling me, and I woke up. If you hadn't called me, I don't think I would be back. Thank you, I already feel much better. I love you all." A tender expression appeared on his slender and fearful face. He was trembling and looked like he had just returned from a long trip.

"We love you, Patrick. Be sure you fight to the end. We must leave now. The monks are on their way here. We'll see you later," Charlotte said and jumped into the pool. Amelie followed her. Peter ran around the corner, just barely missing the noisy monks. They glanced at Patrick and one of them said,

"Oh Holy Spirit; you're alive." A small smile stirred timidly on his face.

"This must be a miracle," the other monk added with disbelief.

314

In the meantime, Charlotte and Amelie swam back and quickly jumped out off the freezing water. They put their robes on and ran into the hot Jacuzzi. It would be their second one that evening. As soon as they got into the soothing water they sighed with relief.

"Oh, God and Saint Mark thank you for saving Patrick. It was an impossible mission from the beginning. I was afraid he wouldn't make it. He was weak and powerless. Now I believe that he'll be able to stand on his own two feet tomorrow," Amelie said with faith.

"He will! I think that he is strong enough to recuperate the temporary loss of his power. Give him a few days and you'll see for yourself," Charlotte said peacefully.

"I want to be sure that he'll be fine. This is the only concern I have now. They are our best friends, like family and we don't want to lose neither one," Amelie added with a smile on her still cold face. They enjoyed the bubbling Jacuzzi for another hour. After that it was a peaceful night for both of them.

The next day Patrick was regaining his power. He was so happy that his ordeal was finally over as it seemed like an eternity. He will be one of the three highest Omega Templars like Peter. This good news made him even stronger. Now the two good friends will be bonded for life, working together for their secret mission, which will be given to them after four years.

Chapter 10. Cardinal Benedict the Detective.

It was sunny Saturday morning. They marched on the cobbled streets, and then walked through the park, with the perfectly lined up colonnade of oak trees on each side of the alley. They passed the golf course, the crowded park, and then turned uphill with slopes full of enchanting wildflowers with their aroma still hanging in the air. They passed the vineyards and olive groves then finally they reached the cemetery.

From the distance they spotted a narrow shadow sneaking between the old tombs. This must be Salvatore, they thought. Positively inspired, they pursued with a fiery enthusiasm and focused on the object. There was an unspoken moment which seemed to last a bit longer than they thought. It felt like the participation in a crusade expedition against an insane evil.

Salvatore was enthusiastically digging in the newly found grave. One long hour had passed as he pulled out of the tomb many strange looking objects. Some of the findings he couldn't recognize as a potential fast profit, he threw them behind the grave and ran with boisterous energy between the alleys, looking for the next tomb to explore. He moved like a wind with unknown cosmic power which was quite impressive. There was a lot of fuel in his engine, so he didn't have to worry about running out of it.

This man didn't have any fear even death wouldn't shake him, at least it seemed that way. Why was he so determined? This was a constant question in Benedict's mind.

They lost him for a moment and Chris decided

to follow him alone. But for reasons known only to the monk, he cloned his doubles on different pathways and finally ran away.

Benedict and John went to investigate the abandoned tomb's treasures. They were stunned by their discovery and couldn't believe why Salvatore neglected such precious pieces of science. He was ignorant for sure at least in their minds. Indeed, it was quite upsetting. Obviously he was looking for easily sellable items only. On top of that, he wasn't a scientist, and he didn't care for something that didn't look exactly like a shiny piece of gold. One of the abandoned items was an old map of the entire universe made and signed by Galileo himself. He drew the planet Earth and Venus orbiting the Sun and Jupiter having exactly four moons. He also knew that Venus moves between Mercury and Earth. He showed on the diagram the universe running into infinity.

He put many other planets without names however at the exact position we see them today. This is why the pope, four hundred years ago, summoned Galileo to Rome suspecting him of heresy. Their minds were too small to comprehend the brightness of Galileo's sky revolution.

The other map was a strange looking piece of art, an older version map of the universe, dated to ten thousand B.C.L.; whoever made this map was very accurate, and perhaps a mastermind of the entire universe, Benedict thought. The numbers were written or rather etched on a hard, unknown material. The calculations of the distances between each planet were written on the edges of the map and the sun was in the center of the universe. It was a sort of phenomenon. This map would entirely revolutionize our world, they thought.

But the question is who made this brilliant map? The edges of it were worn out but for an unknown reason very well preserved. A strange looking seal was in the top left corner of the map, with the letter Ω pressed in the center of it. They were speechless for the entire time as they looked at the map.

How could it be? Perhaps God made it himself! They thought. It wasn't made of gold this is why Salvatore abandoned it. But it was priceless, indeed and had the holy touch. There must be a divine power behind it. The possibility always exists that a lost ancient civilization was entirely wiped off the Earth by the disaster and only the map survived. However, the described precision of each calculation would require advanced astronomical instruments and the knowledge of physic's and math's laws. They were exhilarated by this great discovery. Soon Chris showed up saying,

"I lost him completely. He produced at least ten of his own doubles and finally vanished somewhere. Why are you so excited, guys?" Chris asked breathless.

"Chris, you wouldn't believe what we found right here? Just look for yourself. I believe we have a few more items to look over. John, would you please open up this scroll?" Benedict asked, still excited inside.

"This map is a sort of geographical one. It was made a very long time ago. All the continents are in one precious piece. However you can distinguish vertical cracks between those big lands. It shall be examined in better light. Do you see this small island, right here in the middle of this crack? It is written, Atlantis, the legendary continent described by Plato. How did Plato, the Greek philosopher know about the island?" John asked curiously.

"Perhaps Plato found those old maps purely by accident between the old manuscripts hidden in the private library, one of those wealthy individuals, descendants of the real Atlantis' survivors. They guarded those precious artifacts with their own life and kept them in secret places. Then Plato decided to copy the original pieces. He wanted to tell us that the great and highly educated civilizations existed many thousands of years ago. Those individuals must have travelled around the Earth in order to make those kinds of maps. However, we're unable to see most of them. Why? Perhaps, they were destroyed by natural or man-made disasters or still hidden somewhere waiting to be discovered. There is always the possibility that they engraved their greatest maps onto the stones, now lying on the bottom of the oceans.

There are a lot of gaps in our history. Who knows if we'll ever be able to find out what really happened to all of them. We're talking about civilizations that existed maybe millions of years ago, and their uncanny transformation embodied in the stones, waiting to be discovered again. I'm positive that they were in possession of an advanced knowledge. How will we be able to find out in such a short time of our existence on this planet before we destroy ourselves again, and maybe one day soon?"

Chris said pondering into the future.

"Perhaps, there was intervention by another civilization from another planet. Guys, look at this funny object! What is that?" Benedict asked, gazing into the wooden piece with wonder.

"It looks like some kind of mechanical device. These two horizontal surfaces are functioning as electromagnets. In the electromagnetic space between them is an object floating in the air. How did they make such fantastic thing? Definitely, those scientists wanted to tell us something, but what? Maybe, their secrets of life; they were a prodigy type of people, for sure. However, this looks to me like some kind of lifting device. They're telling us that we could lift any object using a certain power of the electromagnetic field. It would be an ingenious idea if it could really work the way they had built it.

Thus we can move any heavy blocks of stones in any desired height or direction. It would be quite interesting. Wouldn't be?" Chris said thoughtfully as he recalibrated his point slowly.

"I admire your kinetic imagination. Finally, it would explain how the Egyptians built their great pyramids. I've always been fond of their concept. Exquisite observation Chris, indeed! By the way, you said that Salvatore already left the cemetery. I wonder if he already traded his newly discovered pieces in the same antique store. His irreverent approach is very irritated. I hate his oddity. We better go! We're invited for dinner at six p.m. tonight. Aren't we?" Benedict concluded with a meticulous look in his eyes. They were ready to leave.

"We must go," Chris said deadpan as he

carried the electromagnetic instrument. John took the maps and they slowly walked back to the first taxi and drove to the hotel with accomplishment. They were ready to share their news with Jerome and Etienne.

As soon as they entered the lobby, they spotted Jerome talking to the host. He noticed them as well and asked,

"Gentlemen are you ready to go? My car is waiting for us out front."

"Sure, we're ready." Benedict said, scanning friendly Jerome. They drove to Etienne's estate in the secluded area. He greeted them with a friendly smile.

They walked through the French garden filled with life-size bronze sculptures of ferocious wild beasts in combat.

"The beasts are fantastic and scary. They feel as though they are alive," gibbered John.

"Perhaps, it's the creative impulse to everyday life. Definitely a triumph over the feral," Chris added as waves of change rippled through his mind. They walked into a huge house decorated with a notable collection of French art, personifications of virtue, they thought. A heavy framed painting of secular versions of rusty-green saints hanging on the walls gazed at each other across the living room, and finally reflected in the mirrors on opposite sides. The crystal chandeliers hung on the axis cast into glittering infinity. Perhaps it spoke of plutocracy, their hopes, fears, and aspirations, Benedict thought. They approached the dinner table set up with the remarkable silverware, porcelain, and red-white linen. New faces without masks, gathered around the table to the sound of soft jazz music. The candles were lit by the servers at each corner of the table as the guests took their seats. The servers ran back and forth with the varieties of international wines, drinks and cocktails. Then the entrées of wild truffles to escargots were served followed by the final course of each one choice. Thus plenty of shrimp, fish and beef kabobs with fresh salads, artichokes, asparagus, and the forest true grilled mushrooms were consumed. Modest conversations followed between and after each course. Everyone was quite content. As the atmosphere got a bit loose, everyone walked to the conference room. It was like magic, all the members sat on the chairs in conjuring order, ready for the speaker. Jerome walked slowly behind them, as he constantly whispered to Benedict,

"They're the highest in ranks of our secret society. You can trust them with your own life. I trust them with mine, and they have never failed me."

"I believe you," Benedict whispered back to him. Soon they got in, and the doorkeeper closed the door behind them. Jerome stood on the platform and began his speech.

"Gentlemen, thank you for coming. I'm proud to be a member of our intelligent society. Lately we're facing new challenges and some of them are quite complicated. I would like to welcome our newly appointed Knight, Benedict. He is one of us and he is coming with a new peaceful mission for the betterment of the world. However, there are some obstacles on his way to this global glory. Perhaps, those obstacles will soon become our obstacles as well. We must find a solution to this newly acquired problem, and I will need your help. Benedict, would

322

you briefly describe the problem we're facing today."

"Sure, it would be my pleasure, gentlemen. We're chasing an individual named, Salvatore, the monk and fugitive from the Vatican, a member of the Omega Templar Secret Society. He is a serial killer and a thief. But the bad news is that he is one of us too. Lately, I have found out that he is a descendant of the wealthy Bishop, the Templar, who owned almost one third of France and Italy or perhaps even more. Bishop and his close family were assassinated or rather slaughtered by the group called, the *Holy Confiscators.* It happened a few centuries ago.

As time went by all of his descendants were liquidated, with the exemption of the last one, the baby renamed Salvatore who was saved by the family best friend, who happened to be a priest. The baby was hidden in the Christian orphanage. The monk left him a little wooden box with a handwritten letter in codes, hoping one day Salvatore would discover the truth about himself. The box was hidden by the priests in the basement of the monastery at the orphanage, in a small town near the Baltic Sea for almost half century. The Bishops wealth was confiscated; part of it was given to the popes as a gift by the members of the confiscators who vanished later with the most valuable treasures without a trace.

There was a conspiracy behind those *Holy Confiscators* and *their mission.* They moved from town to town like a storm and destroyed every potential enemy of the holy church; at least they thought they were their enemies. Soon after, the confiscators went under public scrutiny, and they turned out to be the most corrupted people simply thieves and killers themselves.

Some plead insanity, and their charges were dropped. The church denied any association with those groups. There was no connection whatsoever, they said. Isn't it an amazing story? When Salvatore was six, the monks from Vatican City came and took him to the oldest Alexandrian Theological Academy in Rome for higher education. Soon after his graduation, he was working for Vatican Headquarters and became a member of the Templars' Sect called, the XII Omega Templars. However, he was a lower ranked monk whom everyone disregarded. At least he felt that way for almost forty years. Last year he decided to escape from the Vatican. He brought the wooden box back to Paris. Just a few days ago, he visited the public library, in the center of old Paris. I followed him. He successfully decoded all the codes written in the letter. He is a very intelligent individual however, diabolical, dangerous. He also walks like a spider, and it is almost impossible to catch him. We call them Spider Monks. They were trained in the Alexandrian Academy. I would consider them as the most skillful individuals on the planet Earth.

He can vanish in the snap of a finger without a trace, and the worst thing lately is he uses his doubles to confuse everyone. Just yesterday, I followed him with Chris and John. He went to the oldest cemetery in the outskirts of Paris, looking for the treasures hidden by his ancestors in the old tombs. He was rightfully looking for his inheritance, obviously.

Thus this letter was a key to his family's greatest hidden treasure he didn't know about for the most of his life. However, Salvatore is thoughtless, and taking only the gold pieces from his newly discovered treasures, and selling them immediately in a local antique store for pennies. You wouldn't believe it!

The worst thing is that on the top of this misery, he is throwing away the most valuable pieces of the past, like those we found today on the side of the tomb he was digging in; the ancient maps of the universe, and some amazing instrument dating maybe to ten thousand B.C. Please look at these priceless pieces which we brought with us today. They are worth more than all the gold money he found out there. My deep concern is that he will destroy the most valuable Templars' treasures. It is rather a sad irony! Isn't it? He must be stopped. At least this is my opinion. Gentlemen, thank you for listening."

"Very interesting indeed, Can we look into it?" Jerome asked with disbelief on his face.

"Sure, here it is!" Benedict said, opening the treasure map on the table.

"Gregoire, you're an expert on these types of fascinating old pieces. Would you glance at this?" Jerome asked politely.

"Absolutely, I've never seen anything like that. It is definitely an original map, and you were right, dated to at least ten thousand B.C. How in all the heavens has a piece like this survived after so many natural and man-made disasters? It is almost unbelievable! However, the instrument you brought, I can't say what its purpose is," he replied and everyone gathered to look over each piece.

"Chris, what do you think? You're a scientist,"

Jerome asked with a blaze in his eye.

"Sure, I think of it as a miniature model of a bigger device which was used to transform a heavy object to the desirable location or to build new structures perhaps even pyramids. Since most of the stones have magnetic properties this would make sense," Chris pointed out with stark clarity.

"Very brilliant Chris perhaps it was a great discovery at that time but is still wrapped in a mystery. Where did all those great scientists vanish to?" Jerome flushed with a question in his mind.

"Perhaps they traveled with their secrets to another planet in our universe," Gautier added and then continued,

"I want you to look into this map of the universe very carefully. Perhaps you're already noticed that it has more than two planet Earths on it. How is it possible? But it also shows a few different universes. Hmm! Chris, can you recall our antimatter experiment? I think it has something to do with the antimatter state. The second planet Earth is likely made of antimatter only, and it is a mirror image of the Earth. At least I think it is. But how do I explain this phenomenon? Is there any life out there? We need a brainpower consortium to answer this dilemma otherwise it will always remain a question. What do you think, Chris?"

"I think you're right. Antimatter has a mass and it responds to gravity as ordinary matter. Thus this second Earth could be built of antimatter which accumulates into dense gases, just like the planet Jupiter. Because the antimatter must go some place. It couldn't just vanish without a trace. Also since we

326

have gamma radiation that naturally occurs in space, there will always be antimatter. We call this the particle's attraction.

There must be a balance in space in order to keep all those planets running around the sun. I also believe that we could have another perfect planet like our Earth filled with atmosphere however, in a different universe. Perhaps people like us live out there too. They could have all the technology we've only dreamed about," Chris underlined his point with a smile.

"Good point, gentlemen and very interesting at the same time. But coming back to our issue, where did we stop?" Jerome asked a bit confused. Someone from the crowd interrupted, "How dangerous is Monk Salvatore?"

"He wants to destroy the entire world. He told me that in writing before he escaped. I was about to capture him," Benedict added with concern.

"I know some of those Spider-Monks. They can be very dangerous. We must save ourselves first in order to make our planet safe. What shall we do?" someone shouted from the crowd again.

"I have an answer!" one person replied.

"What is that?" Benedict asked.

"Kill the monk!" he said. There was silence for a moment and then Jerome suggested, "We must catch him first. Let's set a trap at the cemetery."

"Good idea. Do we have gunmen?" someone asked.

"Of course!" the voice confirmed.

"I don't think it would be an easy task but let's give it a try and play detectives," Benedict said with a smile on his slender face as his eyes scanned everyone around.

"Okay, I'm glad that we've agreed so far. Tomorrow morning, we shall meet at the cemetery, sharp at ten a.m. be sure to be on time and don't forget to wear your tactical camouflage clothes. Meantime, please have something to drink," Jerome added and then walked back to Benedict.

"I was impressed by your speech, Benedict. But this Salvatore is one of a kind. Isn't he? We'll have some trouble getting to him. However, I feel bad that he is one of us. How unfortunate it is. Isn't it? It is really pissing me of!"

"I know, it bothers me too or rather irritates. He really stepped on my nerve many times when I tried to catch him," Benedict said, laughing.

"At least you laugh. This is a really good sign! I know you're under tremendous stress. Hopefully, tomorrow will be a good day for all of us. I would never suspect that he could find the key to his treasure so easily. It must be a coincidence."

"Did you know about the type of treasures hidden in the tombs?" Benedict asked.

"I thought many times of that possibility but I never had enough courage to investigate it any further. Now, I want to show you a video. It might mean a great deal to you, I believe. Where are Chris and John? Can we bring them, too?" Jerome asked.

"Sure! I'll find them. Just give me a second, and wait right here!" Benedict left in a convivial mood. "Here we are!" Benedict announced as he brought Chris and John with him. "Gentlemen, please follow me. Don't worry about my guests. They know exactly what to do if I'm not here. I already asked Etienne if I could use his projection room. Okay, have a seat. I would like to show you my secret video on this big flat screen so you wouldn't miss anything. Are you ready?"

"Yes," Benedict said.

"Okay! Do you remember the first time we met? You asked me about the *Holy letter*, or the Will *of God* and I told you that this priceless piece of history is very dangerous, and can't be opened by anyone because it has written a curse on it. A few months ago, someone broke into our secret place where we kept the letter, and our camera recorded exactly what happened. Just watch and stay still."
"Where was it?" Benedict asked.

"Actually, I can't tell you that but it doesn't matter now because we changed the location. You see this dark shadow approaching the safe hidden in the wall. His face is covered by the dark mask. Someone else must have hired him but unfortunately we may never find out who he was. Look! He'd just opened the safe with the advanced decoding device. If he makes only one mistake, the alarm would automatically lock all the exits, and there is no way he could escape in one piece any time soon. Now, he is opening the double safe door and is reaching for the **Holy Letter**. Look at its simplicity. You wouldn't open it if you just found it on the street. Would you? Perhaps he was told not to open it. However, the letter looks very tempting and he simply can't resist. He reads the note on the envelope, which says do not open it. It mobilizes him even more. **Bingo!** It is too late. He breaks the seal. Just watch now very

329

carefully! He is reading the entire contents and as soon as he finished, a sort of bright radiation comes out of the letter straight into his eyes and within a second, he turns into dust. Now, look! The letter is resealing back and landing on the floor. Our guards visit this place twice a day. They were surprised that someone broke into it, and they called me immediately. I forwarded the message to the others and we met there within an hour. I took the letter and transferred it to a new location. When we glanced on the floor, we were stunned by the amount of the dust. It was so fine that you could fit it all in one hand. Do you believe it? Just look at it," Jerome concluded with accomplishment on his face.

"I must say such a curious case and quite impressive. But he scared the crap out of me! I've only seen that kind stuff in horror movies," Benedict said with a terrified look in his eyes as he glanced at Chris and John's scared faces.

"It was inevitable," Jerome added and continued.

"I just wonder why this letter is so important, and what is its purpose? The letter has been kept in many secret places, for **almost two thousand** years. They told us that God wrote it with his own *blood and gave it to Jesus* to pass it to the people. They said that *the* **blood** is still **red** and is **alive** too.

Perhaps the *DNA* analysis could be performed respectfully. But what kind of message did he give to us that is so important that so many have died for? For reasons unknown to us the *letter cannot be destroyed.* The letter has the ability for infinite **reincarnation** to itself. It is simply imperishable thus it must be very important. Perhaps people busy with wars and killing have forgotten about it. Tell me why we must wait so long to find out what is inside of it? What are we waiting for? There must be something missing in all of that mess around us, but what? Maybe you can give me a real clue," Jerome asked a bit confused.

"Do you remember our first meeting? I mentioned to you about the key and the **Holy Book Part II**. I don't know what they look like. When I found in those old scrolls that the *Holy Letter* exists, I was stunned. Now, we're talking about the *three elements*. I wish, I could tell you more," Benedict said.

"I don't see the clear picture how those **three elements** could be so important? What did God want to tell us?" Jerome added.

"We will find out soon. I thought before that the two elements must be involved in the process of discovering the *God's truth* but now I'm positively sure that the three elements are involved. There must be some kind of secret interaction between them. When we say, in the name of *God, Son and the Holy Spirit*, we're dealing with **Trinity** thus three elements. Perhaps it has to do something with that. This is my theory or let's say speculation," Benedict concluded.

"Quite an explanation but it still leaves me in the dark. I didn't recognize that the video was so scary. Sorry about that. I think Etienne would like to keep you for the rest of the evening and perhaps overnight too. Of course, if you wouldn't mind. We can have breakfast in the early morning and later we can go together to the cemetery to chase Salvatore. I have for you the tactical uniforms you will wear tomorrow," Jerome said in a lyrical tone.

"I wouldn't mind to stay, how about you Chris, John?" Benedict asked.

"It is okay with me," John said calmly.

"I like that idea. Jerome, I just thought that if you really want to know who set this man on the job of stealing your letter, we can actually find out. Can't we, Benedict?" Chris said.

"Sure, we can try if Jerome agrees," Benedict replied.

"How are you going to do that?" Jerome asked, wondering.

"I know those ancient biblical secret words which can temporarily resurrect a dead person for a few minutes only. It takes a bit of our time but it is worth it," Benedict said.

"I'm not sure I want to do that. Let me think for a moment. If I agree we must travel to that place. Am I right?" Jerome asked.

"Yes, we must be at the same location when he was killed. Chris can record all the events into his quantum computer. I think it is worth it. Perhaps some conspiracy is behind this," Benedict suggested.

"If you insist so much, let's do it then! Just follow me to my car. Chris, do you have your computer with you?" Jerome asked.

"I carry it with me all the time. It is too expensive just to abandon in any location," Chris confirmed.

They got into the car and drove away to the undisclosed location. It was an old warehouse however, fully secured. The guard opened the iron door and walked them in. Jerome took the lead. They walked through the long corridor to a small but cozy room that looked like an ancient library. Then Jerome paused for a moment in the middle of the room and said,

"It happened right here! The safe was on this wall behind the picture of the 'Knight in Black.'"

"Okay, I'll set my camera and computer on this table just a few feet from that tragic place. Just give me five minutes," Chris said.

"Okay, I'm ready. Jerome, would you sit on this chair so you can see everything clearly. Be sure to not interrupt with any questions during my session," Benedict asked politely.

"Sure, don't worry about that part. I'm good with that. Okay, boys, I'm ready," Jerome confirmed.

It was quiet and the lights were dimmed. Benedict began his session in deep concentration, speaking in an ancient tongue. Ten minutes went by and they noticed a sort of dense concentrated energy just a few inches above the floor. The image appeared which resembled the man who came to steal the letter. Benedict asked the question, "Who told you to come and steal the letter?"

"The informant," the image answered in a rusty voice.

"Can you give me his name?" Benedict asked.

"I can't but it was one of you," the image said and pointed his hand at Jerome. He was stunned but sat still. However, Jerome noticed immediately on the spirit's hand was a branded monogram, the letter Ω and **Chi-Rho** inside of it. He recalled in his memory where the person must come from.

"Who sent you here," Jerome asked.

"I can't tell you that," the spirit answered with fear in his voice.

"Why are you afraid? You're already dead and turned into very fine dust. You don't have to tell me because I know where are you coming from and who sent you here," Jerome interrupted in an angry tone. The spirits voice became weaker and his image dispersed into the air. Jerome was furious as he stood up. Chris finished his recording with the last image of the spirit frozen in the air. Jerome approached Chris and said,

"Chris show me the last two images again. I would like to show you something, perhaps you missed it. Look, do you see his hand and the monogram, *Omega* and *Chi-Rho*. I know exactly who those people are. He is coming from the **Vatican Secret Police**. He is simply a spy! I don't believe that the Vatican knows about the *Holy Letter*. We kept the secret for almost two thousand years. Our organization and the Vatican have always been two different entities. I must repeat myself that we never share our business together. We've never stepped on each other's tail until now. It would be a serious problem. The damage is already done! I wonder who told them about the letter. He mentioned the informant and pointed at me. And you know what this means!

That our secret organization of Knights has a **traitor!** I would never imagine that such a thing would ever take place in our secret society; and I just told you that I trust them with my own life. I must admit that I was mistaken. I must call for a meeting, at once. Let's go!" Jerome furiously announced as he pressed a red button on his phone. Etienne picked up the phone. Jerome said,

"Call for an emergency meeting! Every member's attendance is required! See you in half an hour."

They drove back in silence. Jerome was almost out of his mind. He talked to himself all the way until he met face to face with Etienne and then he said.

"Look, what we got! Thank you Chris, now I can show everyone that I have not fabricated anything. Would you set your computer on for the last episode? We can see again what happened. You wouldn't believe!"

Chris turned the computer on and replayed the last few moments with the ghost. Etienne looked very carefully at the image and then asked,

"What do you think? Who did it?"

"What I think! I'll tell you what I think. We have a **traitor** in our organization. I always trusted those guys but they betrayed me! Can you imagine what we are facing from now on? We're facing the Vatican' ass and likely for the rest of our life! They will do everything to get the letter even if we have to go to war. I can't control myself. Would you give me some coffee," Jerome nervously sat on the soft sofa and stared at the high-ceiling's Baroque frescoes.

"Would you like to have a Cuban cigar," Benedict asked as he offered him one.

"Sure, would you light it for me? Thank you."

"Here is your fresh coffee. Please, calm down a bit. I know it is hard but at least try," Etienne said, his hands were shaking. He sat on the chair

335

speechless. His face turned red.

"I feel bad; my cholesterol has probably gone up. I hope I won't have a heart attack tonight. It would be really bad for me! I like my life. Everyone will be here likely at eight p.m." Etienne confirmed as he was taking the heart medication under his tongue. Then he sighed with relief.

Twenty minutes later the doorman came and announced that everyone had arrived and was waiting in the conference room. It would be a challenge for Jerome to face the traitor. He was almost out of control, still smoking the cigar and drinking coffee.

"Let's go! It is time," Etienne said calmly.

"Okay, I'm ready. Please stand by me if I lose control," Jerome added with a low tone in his voice, sending a few puffs to everyone around.

"Sure, I'll be there for you. Don't worry," Etienne assured.

They walked to the conference room. Jerome asked Chris to put the computer on the table so that everyone could have easy access to see the thief.

"Thank you for coming. Please, all of you come to the table and look into these images taken by Chris just two hours ago," Jerome said in a determined voice.

All one hundred fifty members lined up to watch the holographic recording. Jerome and Etienne watched each person's expression carefully. They hoped to catch a glimpse of embarrassment in one at least. But they couldn't detect anything unusual and the members returned to their chairs one by one. Then Jerome began his angry speech,

"As you see for yourselves, we're now on the

verge of a potential war with the *Vatican*. Trust me; I never wanted to see anything like this in my life. For almost two thousand years our honorable ancestors have guarded the **Holy Letter,** living in peace and harmony with every powerful political entity on Earth. But from now on, everything will change. Or maybe some of you think that we should give the letter as a gift to the Vatican to avoid the confrontation. Not a bad idea, but tell me why? God put His trust into us because He knew we are honorable and **loyal Knights**, and can keep His secret for eternity. Perhaps, the Vatican would never find out that we're in possession of such a ***divine** piece of real **treasure.***

We have a *Traitor* in this room. He is an informant straight to the *Vatican Secret Police,* and he is one of us! Please, step forward whoever you are, and tell us why did you do this? You consciously plotted a conspiracy against the honorable organization of Knights, and the penalty is **death!** We want to know why you betrayed us. Do you have enough courage now to face us? Or are you a *coward* as well?" Jerome screamed furiously and Etienne tried to calm him down. Meantime, there was a big commotion in the audience, and someone shouted hysterically,

"Call the doctor!" Jerome and Etienne run to the scene. Jerome looked at him and said,

"We don't need any doctor. We found the *Traitor* and he took his own life! Look for yourselves! He couldn't face us! His poisonous microchip is gone from his medallion. I want all of you to look at the **traitor!** I just wonder if he betrayed us for the money or perhaps for more gold. Ashamed! What ashamed! I wonder if he acted alone. We're going to investigate this issue with much deliberation. What was his name?"

"Thibauld. He was seventy eight," Etienne added.

"Bastard! If anyone of you participated in the crime, please step forward. I always thought that I have the best Knights in this organization. You're getting the best financial treatment and respect. What more could you need?" Jerome shouted, looking at every single face. But there was no answer. Then he added,

"He is no longer one of us. Please, remove his dishonorable body from the auditorium and deliver it to his family. If he does not have a family, leave it to the dogs in the empty field on the other side of Paris. This is the punishment for traitors. There will be no funeral ceremony and no one shall participate in any.

Now, since we're facing serious consequences, we shall be ready for the potential war with the *Vatican Secret Police*.

If any of you knows anything about his activities, I want you to report it to me immediately. If you don't have anything to say to all of us then the meeting is over and you're dismissed," Jerome concluded being on the verge of an emotional explosion.

"Give me another Cuban cigar, Benedict. If you wouldn't mind! I'm going crazy! I've never been mad like this in my entire life. Do you imagine anything worse? I don't know what I must do next. We've lived peacefully for many years without destruction, and now we're facing this terrible mess or rather global catastrophe. Do you think anything could be done to correct our current position?"

"To be honest with you, there is not much at this point. The traitor ruined everything. You must find the way how to protect the **Holy Letter**. Perhaps hide it in a better place. No one shall know about its location. I'll call you when I need the Holly Letter but perhaps not so soon. You can bring it to me personally or I can come here. I am devastated myself and I can only imagine what you must feel. However, I'm an optimist and I always say the best is yet to come," Benedict said, smiling.

"I like your bold optimism, Benedict. You're a real **Knight**. I'm looking forward of doing business with you. I sincerely hope that you will remember me," Jerome said with a bit of bright light in his head.

"Sure, I'll remember you. How I can forget such an honorable Knight. We must wait a few years before my mission can be completed," Benedict added.

"A few years are nothing in comparison to *the two thousand* years we have been waiting. Hopefully this new adventure will be worth every bit of it. I'm exhausted; we shall get some rest for tomorrow. The rooms upstairs are ready," Jerome said.

"See you tomorrow," Benedict said and departed to his room.

The morning was bright and sunny. Everyone woke up in a much better mood. There was something special in the air and it made them feel good about themselves.

Jerome greeted everyone with an amicable smile on his face and they tried to cherish the moment together. As they sat down for breakfast, Jerome spoke,

"I'm in much better spirits today, though I have a headache. Yesterday was a nightmare and I would like to thank all of you for your support. Indeed, it was a moment of weakness and the truth is I'm glad that it is over. Let's enjoy coffee and the warm strawberry soup."

"Then what is our plan?" Chris asked.

"We're going to catch Salvatore at the cemetery. Hopefully, everything will go smoothly," Jerome said with optimism.

"Then what are we going to do with him when we capture him?" John asked.

"Perhaps, he must join our traitor, Thibauld in an empty field. They deserve each other," Jerome said, laughing coldly.

"Sure, perhaps you're right," John agreed with a bit of a wrinkle on his mind.

Soon the guests arrived and Etienne passed out the tactical uniforms for the undercover operation at the cemetery. It was nine thirty a.m. and they reviewed their plan quickly. There should be no mistakes at this time, they thought. Ten of the best Knights from the Special Forces were chosen for this special assignment. They were ready to leave. Within twenty minutes they reached the cemetery. They hid behind the iron heavy crosses, local trees and the vertical grave stones. They waited for over thirty minutes, and finally one of them spotted Monk Salvatore as he was coming out of the big tomb with a heavy load of treasure. He went through the pieces very fast, throwing some stuff around, and taking only

340

a few valuable ones. With his absolute ear and perfect vision, he instantly noticed that he was being watched. Then he began to run and clone his doubles to confuse everyone. The gunmen began shooting but it seemed as if the bullets always went through the Salvatore images and vanished without a trace like the Monk Salvatore himself.

The Knights came out of their hiding places and moved aggressively forward still shooting after him. Something was wrong they thought as they approached each image, standing next to the tombs. They were stunned and one of them asked,

"It must be some kind of high-tech trick. Can anyone tell us how the monk is doing all these tricks?" Then he hesitantly touched the image and his hand went through it.

"He is using the power of the holy words to reproduce his own images, like this one you just touched. Since he possesses the knowledge of a higher thing no one can take it away from him as long as he is alive. I tried to catch him many times but I can't because of that," Benedict made a comment that enlightened everyone's inner vision.

"It's hard to believe that this is a reality but I believe you Benedict," Jerome spoke in a cold voice, still pondering something intently.

"At least we can pick up a few documents he threw on the ground. Why is he still doing that? What an ass!" John exclaimed frantically.

"Well, what are we supposed to do?" someone dressed in a mask asked with an unexpected curiosity.

"We can only laugh at this point. How many

bullets did you throw in the air?" Jerome asked, laughing.

"We didn't expect a freak like that. It wasn't easy to shoot the ghost. You know, there were at least ten of them looking alike. I look like a fool!" the person evasively added with the same strange eagerness.

"Okay boys the mission is over. Let's go home," Jerome pointed out as he waved his hand to everyone. They arrived home however with great disappointment written on their faces. Perhaps they admitted in their minds that it wouldn't be so easy to deal with this particular individual after all.

"I think, Salvatore got what he wanted and now he can leave Paris to his little countryside in Europe again looking for his next quest. I shall leave Paris soon too," Benedict said sadly.

"Why don't you stay in my place and do your research in a quiet atmosphere. Don't you get tired of constantly running after Salvatore? Chris is coming back here in a few weeks to open the computer business venture with Etienne and Gautier. We will have more fun together and I wouldn't feel so lonely. John can join us too," Jerome said calmly.

"Thank you for the invitation. I'd like to do that but I must return to town to finish my latest business. Maybe on Christmas I will visit you. There are a lot of things I must figure out for myself. These few coming years are very important for me. I can't screw it up! This is what I live for," Benedict said with deep concern about his future *mission.*

"I want to thank you for all the things you have done for me. It was very crucial and certainly attentive. However, my concern from now on will be Monk Salvatore. How can we capture him? May I visit your town one day? Maybe together we can come up with some ideas. Otherwise, I must hire an army," Jerome said, laughing.

"Anytime, I'll leave you my address. I wouldn't mind having your entourage. Be sure to call me before you come. This is my cell number. I'm planning to visit my friend in Munich for a month or two. They are part of my research as well. I wouldn't worry about Salvatore at this point. He can't do much without me. He doesn't know my plans. Maybe he is smart but he can't outsmart me or ruin my mission, for sure. I just want you to be there for me when I need you. You are a very important part of this mission. I sincerely believe can't be completed without your *Holy Letter*," Benedict added with confidence.

"I'll be there for sure. You ignited a new spark inside of me which is still burning and waiting to be explored. I don't want to miss that opportunity," Jerome said as they finally reached the estate.

"I'd like to say thank you and goodbye to all of you. Hopefully, we will see each other again in a few weeks. However, it was a one of a kind adventure for me. My plane is in two hours," Chris said, smiling.

"I must leave too. My plane to London is in an hour. Thank you for your hospitality, and I'm looking forward to a new adventure with you. Hopefully, I can come with Chris next time," John said warmly.

"It was my great pleasure meeting both of you. My driver can take you to the airport. See you again soon. Chris if you still have some time before departure you can join me for lunch. Benedict, what time does your plane leave?" Jerome asked nervously.

"My plane, leaves at six so I can spend some time with both of you," Benedict happily replied. The driver was already waiting for John. Everyone went inside the Etienne estate, to enjoy conversation and plenty of different exquisite drinks. They told jokes and laughed together to cheer themselves up. Benedict and Jerome perused the maps Salvatore abandoned at the cemetery. Perhaps, the pieces were more important than they originally thought. Suddenly, the phone rang. Jerome picked up his cell phone,

"Hello! Who is it?" But there was no answer and he hung up. Then he added,

"Perhaps, Vatican spies are checking on me every time I pick up the phone. They don't know that I'm going to move the *Holy Letter* somewhere in Africa or perhaps Armenia. I don't know yet. Benedict, you must help me. I don't have a clue where I should hide it. Do you have any ideas?" Jerome lamented, still nervous.

"I can't tell you that because it wouldn't be a secret anymore. I hid my treasures in the attic in the old house but Salvatore found them and stole everything. There will always be someone who can outsmart us. I personally recommend that you hide the letter secretly and don't tell anyone. As you've seen for yourself you can't trust anybody even your own people. I just wonder how much the Vatican knows so far."

"It doesn't matter, how much! It is important that they know about it. Okay, I'll make a deal with you, as soon as I find a safe place for it, I will tell only you. I have a bad feeling," Jerome confessed.

"About what," Benedict asked wondering.

"In the worst scenario, they could kidnap me for my last confession to Pope. But I can't confess about that to anyone under any circumstances. This means that I must die. I'll poison myself before any confrontation can take place. They already know about my medallion with the poisonous microchip, perhaps they will take it away from me. But they don't know that one of my molars has another microchip with poison built in. However, I love my life, and I want to see your mission accomplished. What shall I do?"

"Jerome, you need special protection. You must increase security everywhere and now. You shall call for the meeting and form a Special Forces unit to guard the estates twenty four hours a day, seven days a week. You don't have another option. Especially, after what happened last time in your secret chamber where you kept the *Holy Letter*. I suggest, you shall start as soon as possible," Benedict suggested.

"It would be a terrible thing to be captured by the Vatican Police, and be unable to walk freely on the streets. But surely, you must be right. I will call for the meeting now. Guys, look into the security cameras. Did you invite anyone tonight? Or perhaps, we have intruders in Etienne's gardens. Get your weapons! Where are the Black-Knights special forces?" Jerome shouted and everyone got into position. Jerome called his private police. Chris and Benedict were caught by surprise.

"What shall we do?" Benedict asked.

"Nothing, just sit on the sofa and wait. My boys will control the situation. How many intruders are in the garden?" Jerome asked.

"Perhaps twenty highly trained agents or perhaps Spider-Monks. We could be in trouble, they are moving very fast. Shall we start shooting?" someone asked.

"Wait a little bit until they get closer. Don't waste your bullets. I called the police and they are on the way. They should arrive shortly," Jerome added nervously.

"It is getting dangerous. I see one guy behind the window," someone shouted.

"Then what are you waiting for? Shoot him!" Jerome exclaimed. In the meantime, the police arrived and began shooting. The Vatican Secret Police agents were highly trained monks and there was a slight chance of killing any of them. The shooting went on for a good twenty minutes. The Knights arrived for the meeting called by Jerome. They waited outside under the trees. The police wouldn't let them get any closer.

"We have a situation down there. Our fellow Knights have arrived for the meeting. Now they can see for themselves what happens if any of them becomes a traitor. It is unfortunate that this has happened in our organization. It was more than a shock for me!" Jerome nervously explained as he walked from window to window and overlooked every single man hanging outside the walls.

"They are just like Salvatore. They got that training in the same Alexandrian Academy, so it is difficult to kill anyone," Benedict pointed out.

"I don't believe that they can learn such a thing," Jerome concluded with disbelief on his face. The police run into the building looking for the monks. They run upstairs and shout,

"Jerome, are you here? Where are those guys we were chasing after?" the policeman asked.

"I don't know, did you lose them, I was watching them from the windows and they're unbelievable creatures I must say. They move just like spiders and there is no way we can get them. Now, we have a serious problem," Jerome pointed once more, completely upset.

"It is too difficult to say. Looks like they've gone," someone said calmly.

"If they've escaped today, they will probably return tomorrow. What shall we do? How can we protect our assets and our life? It seems like a hopeless situation, and I hate that!" Jerome shouted out of breath as he looked into everyone eyes. The fellow Knights entered the room fully astonished. One of them asked,

"Can you tell us what is happening here?"

"Just guess! This is what would happen if we discover a new traitor among us? We're in danger! The *Vatican Secret Police* are playing a deadly flirting game with us but they don't understand that this will end in disaster. They want to have **the Holy Letter.** But as I said they can't have it! I never believe that I will ever witness the moment of our total collapse, and thanks to one of you. I am really ashamed!

Today we must revise our loyalty and commitment to each other and to our organization. The damage is already done. It is so sad that one

347

traitor is the cause of the dissolution of our Knight society, today. We need to take a vote of pro or against my proposition. Please, meet me in ten minutes, in the conference room. The vote will be anonymous," Jerome nervously added, facing his back to his fellows. He was not only disappointed, he was mad!

"Excuse me, Jerome. I'd like to say goodbye. I must catch my plane to London. I don't think I can be of any help to you at this moment but I can stay if you want me to," Chris said in a firm voice looking straight into Jerome eyes.

"Chris, I am sorry you have to see me this mad. It is a big problem that must be solved quickly. I wish you could stay but I understand you must get back to your own life. You're coming back soon, aren't you?"

"Sure, I'll be back. Thank you for every opportunity you've given me. I believe I'll enjoy your company very soon, take care of yourself," Chris replied.

"I'll be fine! See you in a month," Jerome said with a smile on his face as he shook Chris' hand for goodbye. Chris took off to the airport. Benedict tried to console Jerome but it wasn't an easy task. Jerome's anger was blown out of proportion and only peace could save him. They stood in silence staring out of the windows for almost twenty minutes. Suddenly, Jerome interrupted,

"Let's move to the conference room. I really don't know what to say to those people but I will try. It shouldn't take more than an hour. I'm really sorry about all of that stuff. I feel embarrassed about it. It was going so well for so many years and suddenly it's blown up and it feels like sitting on a fire," Jerome said looking at Benedict.

"I understand everything, and you don't have to feel bad about it. Indeed, you face a very difficult situation at this moment. I wish, I could ease it for you but I simply can't. It is too complicated, and I don't know if I could handle it properly," Benedict replied as he followed Jerome to the conference room. Jerome was nervous and still talking.

"Thank you to all of you for coming. You already know what is happening here. We're facing a very difficult situation. Before I get to the heart of the problem, I would like to ask if any of you knew about the traitor. I'll give you a minute to think it over." It was quiet for exactly one minute as though everyone was getting ready for their last confession to God. They waited and thought; perhaps another traitor would reveal himself. Then Jerome continued his speech,

"I see no one has an answer for me. I assume that there are no more traitors between us. Maybe I'm wrong, since the damage is already done and all of us are guilty, I would like to vote for the dissolution of our secret society which is no longer secret. Please put your anonymous vote in writing on the piece of paper. Benedict will collect your vote from you within five minutes."

It was a terrible moment for each member as sadness hovered over their heads. Everyone put their vote into the basket. Benedict collected accordingly and delivered to Jerome. Jerome was horrified but despite that he continued his speech,

"Thank you for your vote. The rules are as

follow, if only one person agrees with the dissolution by saying **yes,** the secret society will be officially terminated without any further revocation. Benedict, would you keep me company. I need one of you to come forward to be my witness. I'll open each vote and pass it to Benedict and to you. What is your name Sir? Okay, to André. The first vote said, **no.** Would you confirm each one, please? We have one hundred fifty votes. It will not take long," Jerome opened each one and passed it to Benedict and André. All one hundred fifty votes said **no**. Jerome was stunned as to the unanimity of all voters. He felt good about himself and about his fellows Knights. It meant there were no more *traitors* among them. His mind was bright with optimism. He was short of breath and drank a glass of fresh water. It was a moment of happiness he was dreadfully waiting for. He stood up and said,

"I must say, I'm proud to be a **Knight** and I want to thank you for your loyalty. You're willing to sacrifice your life and save our organization. I'm one hundred percent behind all of you. We have a good reason to celebrate this great moment with our perfect aged red wine. But before we celebrate, we must find a way to protect our life and increase the private security of each Knight. We are facing a potential kidnapping by the **Vatican Secret Police**. It could happen anytime and to any of us. We must be more alert to whom we talk and what we talk about. The fact that each of you is a member of this organization must be kept confidential. Under no circumstances can any of you discuss with anyone, including your family members, our conversations or any secret meetings about when or where it is taking place. Perhaps, I missed something, let's have an open discussion," Jerome concluded.

"We should have better communication between each of us and have at least one personal security guard. I propose to make a schedule for each of us. Let's say, I have Monday off, I could be someone's security guard all day long. Perhaps you have Wednesday off; you could be my security guard. It would be better for our protection. We're well trained individuals in martial arts; we also have other skills too. We have all of the abilities to help each other and keep the secrets to ourselves," someone boldly proposed. "It is a great idea!" someone shouted from the crowd.

"It is a splendid idea, indeed. We should do it! I have this Wednesday off. I would like you to take care of this and let me know your final plan. All of us shall participate in this smart proposal. I want to know who will be my security guard," Jerome said, laughing. The red wine was served and all the members began making detailed plans.

The list of everyone's eligibility will be made soon, and each member will have a personal guard. The proposal will be in force within twelve hours.

"Smart move, at least everything ended up well. I must leave soon, Jerome. We will be in touch. Please, call me at anytime and come to see me," Benedict said.

"I will and thank you for your support. It helped to ease my pain. You have a good heart, Benedict. Thank you for that," Jerome said and they hugged goodbye.

Chapter 11. Life in the Boarding School
Rome, 4 Years Later

The time in the Boarding School went by faster than anybody would anticipate. The kids grew up fast too. Graduation was coming and there was so much excitement. The girls and boys were turning sixteen and there would be a good reason to celebrate their sweet sixteen. Peter and Patrick had already been secretly assigned to the **Omega Templars** at the Vatican Headquarters. They were the chosen ones. Thus, they would be graduating a week earlier. For the next twenty years they would continue their higher education there and guard the holy secrets of the Vatican for the rest of their life.

Charlotte and Amelie will continue their higher education at the *Alexandrian Theological Academy*. In addition, Charlotte will be taking a part-time job at the *Vatican Communication Center*, which is the closest entity to the **Omega Templars**. She was advised to take a position by the closest friends of Cardinal Benedict. She was hoping for a new method of communication with Peter and thought that this might be the best way to do it. Perhaps together, they will figure out the best way. It was the final week before Peter and Patrick departed from the Alexandrian Academy straight to the heart of the *Vatican Secret Headquarters*.

Peter called Charlotte and they arranged another secret meeting in the old St. Mark Chapel. Once again, Amelie went with Charlotte and they swam under the iron gate like they had been doing for more than four years. Patrick and Peter were already in the cave, waiting for them.

"Hi Peter! Hi Patrick! Are you excited about leaving for the Vatican?" Amelie asked.

"Sure we are! Aren't we, Patrick?" Peter said.

"I'm very excited and we're the best Spider Monks in town. Right, Peter?" Patrick announced proudly.

"Sure we are, but not only that, we're the best swimmers and martial arts fighters, skills that I'm sure will come in handy in the future. Do you want to see some of our moves? We can show you," Peter said.

"Okay guys, we'll watch you. Show us what you can really do! Perhaps it'll be your last show in this Academy," Amelie announced with a big smile on her face. The girls sat comfortably on the floor and watched the boy's masculine bodies.

"Amelie look! We learned some of the same moves with our karate coach. Maybe one day we'll be able to put them to use, you never know. We're karate girls, too, like the boys. Let's show them a few our best moves."

"Don't forget Charlotte that we're the best spider girls too."

"How long did it take you to climb the ten-story tower?" Amelie asked Patrick, laughing.

"I would say about five minutes," Patrick said.

"That's pretty good, but we were able to do it within seven minutes, not much of a difference," Amelie replied.

"Not bad girls! You are good," Patrick said, smiling. Amelie was teasing him.

"Charlotte, I'm so sorry, but it's time for me to

say goodbye. It will be tough, but I'll try to find a way to send you a message from time to time. I don't know how yet, but I'm sure I'll be able to figure something out. All I can ask is that you don't give up on me and always wait for news from me. Father Emanuel will be there to take care of you if you need some help in the future. Also, don't forget that you have friends in town. Please don't worry about me; I'll be fine, for sure. Now give me a hug," Peter said and then whispered into Charlotte's ear,

"I'll write messages to you inside of my habit, so always look very carefully for it. Once or twice a week our habits will be sent for cleaning, and you'll be in charge of that, in your *Communication Division*, where you'll be working soon. This is what I've been secretly told. So please, it's very important that you keep this information to yourself promise."

"I promise! I love you, Peter. I'll wait for your messages, and I'll wait for the date of our final mission. Father Benedict will tell me the exact time, but first you must figure out where the Key and Holy Book are located; the items Cardinal Benedict told us about a few years ago. You must write me with more details when you have a chance. God bless you!" Charlotte whispered back to his ear.

"Peter goodbye and good luck, I will love you always like my own brother," Amelie said and they exchanged a big hug.

"Good luck with your studies my sister, Amelie," Peter said, smiling.

"Goodbye Patrick, my second brother. Good luck!" Amelie said and they hugged each other.

"Goodbye Amelie."

"Goodbye Patrick, my new brother. I'll miss you," Charlotte said with tears in her eyes.

"Goodbye and good luck to both of you too, my dearest sisters," Patrick said, smiling. They looked at each other for the last time and then departed. The girls left the chapel and swam back to the other side of the iron gate.

"Let's go for a quick spa, I'm a bit tired and I've got two finals tomorrow," Amelie said.

"It couldn't be worse timing. I'm worried about Peter now and I feel bad that he and Patrick won't be able to come to our graduation party on Saturday," Charlotte sighed.

"I'm sad too. Do you think they'll be good monks? They're so young and haven't even grown up yet. I don't know what I want to do after graduation. I should stay here and do the Advanced Program, but maybe I should go back home to my small town and live with my aunt. If I do go home, I sure will miss you Charlotte," Amelie sadly confessed.

"I think you should stay here with me, we'll have more fun. I'll work part-time for the Vatican and study. In a few years I'll get my Ph.D. in philosophy and I'll be a teacher like Sister Agnes."

"Do you think I should stay? Maybe I should get my Ph.D. like you. You're right! I can't abandon my secret platonic lover, Bertrand. I would be dreadfully sad for the rest of my life, but I have noticed lately, Bertrand's been making some advances toward you. For example, last Monday, he held your arm for almost five minutes when he asked you to repeat the pronunciation of those horrible French words. I hate those words. Why doesn't he ever ask me to do that? It makes me wonder if you have some feelings for him too," Amelie asked.

"I don't! How many times do we have to go through this? I just like him as a teacher, but surely he's very handsome and charming. Believe it or not, there is something about him that I actually don't like. It's his total lack of self-confidence. It seems to me, he's always afraid of something. Who knows what might have happened to him in his past, maybe something terrifying. You would never know?"

"From one extreme to another, you're silly Charlotte. I think he's a perfect man, if only he could hear this from me. Unfortunately, it seems like he's not interested in me. There are so many nice and good-looking girls in class, but it looks like he's yours forever."

"Stop talking nonsense Amelie. You just better start thinking of what you're going to wear on graduation? I wonder if we should go shopping. What do you think?"

"I think…definitely. After my final on Wednesday we can go the dress shop. There's a nice boutique in downtown with some fantastic dresses in green, blue, pink and black. I love the green one I saw. It has a nice cut and many layers of silk under the skirt. On each shoulder it has a cute little rosette in dark green. The lady who owns the shop told me that girls from our school buy dresses from her every year for graduation. How about this coincidence? My aunt sent me some money last month as a gift for graduation. Perhaps I'll buy myself that dress. I can buy you one too if you find one you like. There's plenty of money in my account. I love my aunt, she misses me very much and I miss her too."

"You're very kind, Amelie but you don't have to buy me a dress. I'm glad that you're able to buy one and that you won't have to make one from the window curtains like you did the last time you needed a dress," Charlotte said, laughing.

"Oh, so you remember that. That was a horrible experience, not only for me, but for Sister Agnes when she saw the missing curtains. I feel like laughing every time I think of that. Let's go Charlotte. It's getting late."

"You go Amelie I'd like to stay another twenty minutes or so. It feels so good. I'll see you later; you better study hard."

"Sure, I'll do that. See you later."

The time went by fast and Charlotte left the Jacuzzi with some pleasurable thoughts. She was walking through the corridor and thinking of Father Benedict who promised to rebuild her house after it was burned down in a fire likely set by Monk Salvatore, the *false prophet*. She was left alone in this big world and it was a scary feeling, but she was ready for a new challenge. Who knows, maybe one day she would return to the countryside where she was born and live happily there for the rest of her life. As she was passing by the entry door someone whispered her name,

"Charlotte, Charlotte, come here! I have something for you." She went outside and there was Bertrand, standing and holding a big, flat box wrapped with red ribbons.

"I have a present for you for your graduation. I'm sure you'll like it. Here you go. I have to go now,"

Bertrand quickly said and left. She held the box with disbelief and didn't move. Then suddenly she ran to her room upstairs and lay on her bed speechless. Amelie was so busy studying that she didn't even notice Charlotte come in. Ten minutes later Amelie stretched her arms back at her desk and noticed Charlotte.

"You're here! I didn't see you come in. This math test is going to be tough, I'm not sure if I'm going do well. How did you do it? It's so hard for me. Please say something Charlotte. Oh what did you get, may I see it?"

"I got a present."

"Let's see what it is. Can I open it?"

"Sure, go ahead."

"Who gave it to you? You must have some secret admirer out there, don't you? And you didn't even tell me, do you know who it is?"

"If I tell you, you wouldn't believe me."

"Come on Charlotte, you've got to tell me." Amelie pulled off the bow and opened the box.

"Oh my goodness, this is the most beautiful dress I've ever seen. Now you have a dress for your graduation, and it's French too. Oh, please try it on! I want to see it on you."

"Okay, okay, I'll try it on! It's so perfect and it's exactly my size."

"Charlotte, you look like a princess, it's such a beautiful green dress. Who gave this to you?"

"It was our teacher, Bertrand. He was waiting for me in the garden when I was passing by the front door. It couldn't have been more than twenty minutes ago. He gave me this box and left so fast, I could hardly believe it. I didn't even have time to say thank you."

"You see, I told you he has a secret crush on you, a sort of platonic one. Why didn't it happen to me? You should be happy that someone cares so much about you."

"Please, don't say anything to anyone, I'll be embarrassed."

"Sure, I won't tell. Why should I? You know I'm your best friend, don't you?"

"Oh Amelie, I feel so special in this dress and the pastel green suits me so well. I'm so happy. If only my mother could see me like this, she would be so proud of me."

"You have a reason to be happy. I'm happy for you too. I wonder what Bertrand must be thinking now? His love for you deepens second after second, minute after minute, day after day. He must be going insane without you. Why do all the best parts happen to you, Charlotte?"

"Stop that, do you think that this is the best part? I'm not so sure about that. I don't know why you're so crazy about him. He's just like any other guy, he has his faults. I hope everything is finished between him and me. Amelie, I don't want anything to happen between us, despite this present he gave me. Do you understand?"

"I get your point, but love is blind, and he's not going to stop with this present, trust me. Now, I'm sure he fantasizes about you, and giving you this present is only going to make things worse because his desire for you is getting deeper and deeper. You can't stop him now."

"Amelie, when did you become an expert on love? You've never been in love yet. You just have this great imagination. On another subject, don't you have a math test tomorrow?"

"Sure I do, but studying won't make me smarter than I already am. Perhaps, I'll fail anyway. Don't worry about it. We have a more important subject to discuss. We're talking about your future life with Bertrand. Isn't it more interesting than my math test?"

"Sure, perhaps for you, Amelie, but I'm getting tired of this. I already hate Bertrand for giving me this dress. You know what, you can have the dress and you won't have to buy your own. I already have the black dress my mother bought me a long time ago. I can still fit into it."

"Are you sure Charlotte, are you sure you hate him, are you sure you don't want this dress? Oh, I love it so much! Please let me try it on!" Amelie tries the dress on.

"Oh, yes! It fits perfectly and I feel great. Thank you Charlotte, you made my day. I love you so much!"

"Alright then, I'm glad that you like it. I'll wear my old dress. Let me go try it on and see if it fits. It's been awhile and I've got bigger muscles everywhere." Charlotte tried the black dress on and said,

"Okay, it seems like it fits, but can you zip the back for me?"

"Sure, I can do that. Try not to breathe! The zipper only goes half way up, maybe your boobs have grown over the past few years. If it doesn't fit, we can go shopping on Wednesday to that boutique in downtown we talked about. That way I can buy you any dress you like. Does that sound like a deal?"

360

"Okay, we've got a deal, and anyway, you look much better in this dress than I do. I think it's a great choice for you, and to top it all off, it means more to you because it came from your dream lover. Ha! Ha!"

"Don't make fun of me, Charlotte, but you're right, it is worth more to me because Bertrand bought it. Now I'll be able to have wonderful dreams at night, knowing this dress is next to me. Thank you again. Now I've got to get back to studying."

"Sure, I won't bother you anymore. Go and concentrate. Good luck with your test tomorrow. I'll be reading a new book I just got from the library. Let me know if you need me."

The next bright day welcomed them warmly with the fresh aroma of blooming cherry trees. A new species of birds moved into the local pine trees, singing their own serenades to Mother Nature. The mere thought of more birds in the trees outside her window made Amelie angry as she glanced at them through the open window. She could only imagine having to stay here for another year or two; she again would have to eliminate those noisy beasts. The smell of fresh air brought a new optimism to her, and she was more confident about her math test.

The girls got dressed quickly in their uniforms, and ran down for breakfast. On their way, they greeted Sisters Agnes and Claudia who were standing in the hall. The Sisters were friendly and even smiled freely, waving their hands at the girls. They knew that it was the final week for all the girls, and it felt like a family gathering.

Soon enough, they will begin to miss the girls. Some of the girls will leave the Academy to continue on their own path in life. Maybe a few of them will stay here and become nuns, which is a huge commitment for a young girl to give up her personal life in exchange for an unconditional service to God. All of the girls were in a hurry to get into their classes for their final exams. Amelie was going to take her math and physics exam and Charlotte was going to take her French exam.

Bertrand was already waiting in his class. He was very happy to see Charlotte. As she walked into the classroom his eyes sparkled for a second or two.

"Chere amie, comment allez-vous? /szerami-comon-talevu/. How are you, my dear, Charlotte? It's nice to see you. How did you like the dress?" he whispered in her ear as she was passing by his desk.

"Je vais tres bien. /ze we tre-bje/. I feel very good and the dress is really beautiful. Merci bien. /mersi-bje/. Thank you very much," she whispered back to him.

"S'il vous plait. /silvu-ple/. You're welcome, my dear," he smiled and then asked the students to take their seats. Without saying another word he passed out the test booklet of one hundred fifty questions to each girl, and the test officially began. They would have two hours to answer all the questions.

Bertrand sat in his wooden chair at his desk and picked one of his favorite books to read. From time to time he would look through the open window at the beautiful chestnut trees. The sun was peeking between the green leaves, sending the warm rays everywhere. There were moments when he would close his eyes for a short time, and contemplate his life. Then occasionally, he would stare at Charlotte for a minute or two. What he thought about her while he stared, nobody knew. The exam time was about to end when Charlotte returned her booklet to the front desk.

"I'm done. Au revoir! /orewuar/. Goodbye!" she said and was about to leave.

"Au revoir! Goodbye! I'm going to miss you, Charlotte. I'll see you at the graduation party. May I reserve a dance with you?" he asked unexpectedly. Charlotte glanced at him and quickly said,

"Uh, let me think about it."

"Sure!" he replied with a masculine smile. Charlotte went out to the garden. She was happy and thought to herself that school was finally over for her, and how she would do nothing for at least a week. The following week she would begin her part-time job at the *Vatican Communication Division*. She walked in circles in the garden and finally lay on the soft grass. She stared at the blue sky and observed how the yellow sun changed into orange. It looked beautiful and friendly like a pumpkin, she thought. Then she heard a voice,

"Charlotte, where are you?" Amelie called.

"I'm over here!" Charlotte replied.

"I've been looking for you all over. How was your French test?"

"I think it went okay. I'll know in a few days. How about you, how was your math and physics tests?"

"I think they were easier than I thought. I probably passed. Did Bertrand ask you about the dress?"

"He sure did, and I told him that it was very

beautiful. He was happy."

"Did you tell him that you gave the dress to me?"

"No, I didn't. Why should I tell him? He'll find out for himself at the dance. It will be a great surprise for sure! Maybe, he'll ask you to dance, Amelie. Can you picture his face? We're definitely going to have some fun."

"It sure is going to be fun. I really want to dance with him. Hopefully, it'll happen. Are you hungry? Let's go to lunch."

"Alright, let's go. So, did you make up your mind Amelie as to what you want to do after graduation? Are you staying or leaving? You know I don't want to be alone here, right?"

"I don't know yet, it depends on a few factors."

"What kind of factors?" Charlotte asked.

"I need to talk to my aunt and make sure she doesn't need me at this point in her life, you know she's getting up there in years. I know she wants me to be a nun, but this means that sooner or later I would have to take the vows of chastity, obedience, and poverty, and I'm not sure if I want to do that! Secondly, if I do stay here, I'm going to have to eliminate those new, little bastards which just moved into the canopy of the pine trees outside our window. They sure have been noisy lately. After that, I'll stay here with you, and continue my education."

"But this time no suicidal cats, it would definitely be more fun to face Academy life together. All of these subjects have been pretty tough so far, don't you think so?" Charlotte concluded.

"You're right about that, especially the

language's classes. They were not my favorite. I'm good at the science and philosophy, but in the end, it has been fun, and most importantly, I have my platonic feeling for Bertrand, our French teacher. If I do leave, I'll take with me the very best memories."

"Amelie, you're the funniest girl I've ever met, I really like having you as my best friend."

"You're my best friend too, Charlotte."

It was Wednesday afternoon, and the girls were ready for shopping. They wouldn't know their test's results for another week.

"Charlotte, as I promised you, we're going for shopping today downtown. I think we should walk since it's so close. Are you ready?"

"Sure, I'm ready. Let's go!" They walk the couple of blocks to downtown singing a tune together.

"Look at those elegant window displays! Come here take a look at these beautiful dresses. Don't you love this red one? They must be so expensive, we should forget about this store! We're only students. Don't worry, though, the boutique where I'm taking you has much nicer dresses that are way less expensive."

"Amelie, I really don't care too much for it. We're only doing this for fun right." "Right, no stress Charlotte, we're almost there? Do you see the boutique on the corner of Via del Pergola Street, next to the Coliseum, it is named **Annabel**. It's just a couple of minutes away. Afterward, we can visit the ruins of the Coliseum since it's on our way."

"Wow, sounds good. Maybe, we'll see Julius Caesar there," Charlotte said, laughing.

"You're pretty funny Charlotte. Okay, here we

are! You're not going to believe the dresses in this place. All of the popular girls shop right here. Look at this green and pink dress. Go ahead, try on whatever you like."

"I like this pink dress. What size should I get? I think a size two should be right for me. I'm going to try it on. Amelie, follow me to the dressing room. I'll need your opinion." Charlotte tries the dress on and looks in the mirror.
She then looked at Amelie.

"Okay! What do you think?"

"What do I think? You look like a princess, but maybe a size zero will be better. Alright, it's decided, we're going to buy this pink dress for sure. Even better, it's less than the red dress we saw. I told you that the price will be right. Remember, this is a gift from me. I want to thank you for the beautiful green dress you gave me. Sure Bertrand paid a precious amount of money for it."

"Thank you, Amelie. I'm so happy and I love the color pink. Now, let's go, Julius Caesar awaits us at the Coliseum," Charlotte said erratically.

"Okay, you got yourself a deal! Let's go!"

The girls walked to the Coliseum and then sat on a stone bench, looking for comfort. Amelie performed as King Macbeth, the hero of Shakespeare's tragedy, but unfortunately she had only one spectator, but her performance made Charlotte happy again.

"I'm tired, let's take a short nap, maybe we can recall the past in our dreams. I don't feel like going back right now, and no one will be looking for us anyway," Charlotte whispered.

"Okay! I like your idea. I can dream of dancing with Bertrand right here, in the gladiator arena to the sound of Strauss' waltz. It would be a dream come true?" Amelie whispered back.

"Perhaps, it would be, Amelie. I have to be honest with you; I have a strange feeling about Bertrand. I'm afraid of him and his unpredictable behavior. Sometimes, in the way he looks at me, I feel like a devil has entered his mind. Have you ever noticed that?"

"Oh, sure I have! I've noticed. It only happens when he looks at you, Charlotte. Perhaps his desire for you grows stronger when he acknowledges that he can't have you, and that you don't care for him at all."

"Maybe you're right, Amelie. I don't care for him at all; I get so repulsed when I look at him. The worst is when I get a whiff of his masculine scent from a short distance away."

"I love that scent of his, I get so excited by it," Amelie added, laughing.

"You're such a silly goose, Amelie! I feel we waste our precious time by talking about him. I'm closing my eyes and we're not going to talk for at least fifteen minutes."

"Okay! Let's do that. We'll imagine how many gladiators and wild beasts died here for the good cause of Julius Caesar's fantasy. He was a good looking guy, too."

"Amelie stop!"

The girls fell asleep for more than forty minutes. Amelie opened her eyes, glanced at the satin blue sky, whispering, "I saw in my dream Julius playing the fife."

"A very funny dream!" a man's voice said.

"What are you doing here? Are you spying on us?" Amelie shouted at Bertrand who was standing over them like an angel. She was terrified. He laughed and said,

"I come here almost every day to relax and take a break, and for the first time I saw you two here. I wanted to surprise you when you woke up."

"Thank you, but no! You scared us for sure!" Amelie said as she sat on the bench still terrified.

"I'm sorry if you feel that way, Amelie," he continued.

"Okay, Amelie, it's time for us to go. Are you ready?" Charlotte said confidently.

"Sure, I'm ready. Let's go!"

"You wouldn't mind if I keep you company. Would you?" Bertrand asked politely.

"I wouldn't!" Amelie replied as she glanced at Charlotte.

"Okay, but let's get going," Charlotte added, feeling quite uncomfortable.

"So what brought you into town?" Bertrand asked.

"We came to go shopping and browse around a bit," Amelie replied with a smile.

"What a good idea! Your finals are over, and now you deserve a break. Everything makes sense. Are you planning any vacations?" Bertrand asked.

"No vacation for me. I have a part-time summer job at the Vatican," Charlotte replied conscientiously.

"That's quite an ambitious plan, I always admire hard working people," Bertrand added as he glanced at Charlotte, trying to catch a glimpse of her eyes. Charlotte avoided eye contact with him on purpose.

"Maybe I should get a summer job as well; otherwise I think I'll be bored. What do you think?" Amelie asked.

"You should," Bertrand replied conservatively.

"It would be quite a challenge for you, Amelie," Charlotte added.

"Are you both excited about Saturday's graduation party?" Bertrand asked again.

"Oh, yes! It's going to be a lot of fun. I love to dance!" Amelie replied.

"How about you Charlotte, why are you being so shy?" he asked.

"I like to dance more or less, it can be enjoyable at times," Charlotte coldly replied.

"This will be your sweet sixteen. Am I right?" Bertrand asked.

"Sure, we're both turning sixteen," Amelie added happily.

"We're here. Finally, we're back. Amelie, we have some work to do. Don't we? Goodbye, teacher Bertrand," Charlotte said.

"Goodbye my dear Charlotte. I'll see you soon," Bertrand replied looking at her with desire. She fully ignored him and turned her back on him. But he held her shoulder for a moment and whispered,

"Why are you running from me?" She didn't say anything and just walked forward, pulling her shoulder out of his hand. Then he backed up a bit and left. The girls run upstairs to their cozy room.

"Did you see that Amelie? I told you, he behaves very strange."

369

"I told you too that he's in love with you. Just look at yourself in the mirror at how beautiful you are: long, blond hair, green eyes and you're tall and skinny like a model. Any man could fall for you at first glance, it happens," Amelie concluded.

"Amelie, you're beautiful too. Why does it have to be me?" Charlotte said nervously.

"Don't worry about it, everything will be fine. Let's try our dresses again. We need some shoes too. I can do your hair in a new style and put some make-up on you."

"I don't need any make-up, Amelie, but I can put some on you if you like," Charlotte said.

"Let's do a rehearsal, before Saturday's party. It's a perfect time. It's not like we have a lot of things to do. Can you put some eyeliner around my eyes; you can trim my eyebrows too, maybe my hair a bit as well. Let's have some fun," Amelie proclaimed.

"Okay, I'll do that for you. How thin do you want your eyebrows to be? Maybe half of what they are now," Charlotte suggested.

"Half would be perfect. Let's do it. I'll lie down on the bed. I have all the needed instruments for the trimming. Thank you Charlotte, for doing that for me I love to be groomed like a dog," Amelie laughed.

"I like when you laugh, it makes me feel happy. Okay, I'm ready. Amelie, it could be painful. It is going pretty well. How do you like your left eyebrow now?"

"It looks fantastic but be sure the right one looks the same."

"I'll try my best. Here it looks almost the same," Charlotte enthusiastically announced.

"What do you mean almost, it better be the

same," laughed Amelie.

"It's close enough. Look for yourself!"

"Wow! You're right, close enough. Can you trim my bangs, perhaps half an inch above the eyebrows?"

"Okay, Amelie, as you wish. Just sit down! This trimmer is great and you know it would be perfect for dogs."

"We can trim a cat. I can catch one and bring it right here," Amelie said, laughing.

"Sure but you will do it."

"Don't worry about the cat. I'll trim the beast myself," she said with confidence. "Okay, Amelie, how do you like your bang? Don't you look cute?"

"Charlotte, you're such a professional. Maybe we should open a beauty salon instead. What do you think?"

"Amelie, with your bold enthusiasm we can open a Cat Salon, and I'm sure it would get business. Now, let's relax with one of your favorite teas."

"You know that a cat salon could bring us a lot of money, but yes, in the meantime, I'll make us some tea. Thank you, Charlotte for helping me."

"You're very welcome. I'm going to lie down and relax if you don't mind, and if you can bring me my tea in bed, that would be great. You don't mind, do you?" "Absolutely not it would be my pleasure, Charlotte. You deserve to relax for a while. Let's have fun and enjoy our short time on Earth. I miss my grandmother. She never told me that she was tired. We always had our evening tea together and she would reminiscence about her past. It was always a pleasure to hear what she had to say, because all her

371

stories were good and very positive. She is a real angel here on Earth, more so since my parents are gone forever." The hot water for the tea signals that it's ready.

"Okay, our tea is ready I call this one, *Memory*. Charlotte here you go."

Unfortunately, Charlotte was sleeping and didn't hear what Amelie was saying to her. Amelie put the tea on the little table next to Charlotte's bed. She then went and sat down to drink her own tea and think about what to do next. Suddenly, she ran outside the building and caught the cat, she called him Albert.

"Albert, kitty, come here. Oh good kitty. Let's go to my room and I'll give you a nice haircut." Albert cringed in her arms and they went upstairs. "Albert, you must promise me that you'll be very quiet. Promise! Okay, let's go in. Now don't meow, you'll wake up Charlotte."

Amelie opened the door, put the cat on the table and then began to trim his fur coat into the letters, CAT. Albert was standing still and closed his eyes for approval, grumbling. Amelie was delighted with her artwork. Albert was upgraded to the aristocratic provincial toy and didn't look like a street burglar anymore. She lay down on her bed with a look of accomplishment on her face. Albert positioned himself right next to her in her bed. There was absolute quiet for more than too long. Albert constantly grumbled while taking his nap.

Suddenly, Albert awoke and began to meow, non-stop, which contributed to Amelie and Charlotte waking up.

"Who's here Amelie, did you bring a cat in

here?"

"Yes and just look at him. Isn't he cute? He looks like Mr. Albert right now?" "Amelie, you're crazy. That poor cat if only he could see himself in the mirror. He would just die laughing."

"Let's see if he'll laugh and die. Albert come here; look at you in the mirror." Amelie grabbed the cat and walked to the mirror.

"What do you think, Albert? Now tell the truth. You're not laughing, so you must like it. Don't you?" Amelie proudly concluded Albert liked his new haircut as she glanced at Charlotte. "It seems like Albert isn't opposed to a new appearance, so he must like it. Don't you, Albert?"

"Amelie, that's enough. Please let the cat out. I think we should go for dinner, it's almost six p.m. I didn't get a chance to drink your tea yet, so let me give it a try before we go." Charlotte took a sip of the tea.

"It's good even when it's cold."

The dining room was full of students, some guests, and a few visitors. The Sisters were already there enjoying their meals, and very busy with conversations they were having with some visitors. The girls made their dinner brief and left quickly. There was not much to do that evening and they decided to watch some movies. They could finally relax fully and enjoy their time before the graduation party.

Over the next two days the girls spent their time helping to decorate the ballroom for the graduation ceremony. The tables and chairs were set up against the walls. The middle of the room was reserved for the dance floor. At the ceremony, Sister Agnes would make a short speech to all the students and everyone in attendance and then their diplomas would be handed to each one of them.

When Friday evening finally came, everything was quiet and everyone went to bed early. Amelie and Charlotte took the opportunity to go to the spa. It was a ritual they had been doing for the past four years. There was always something to talk about and Amelie always made their time at the spa exciting.

Saturday morning the girls woke up with a new energy, ready for their official graduation party. They skipped breakfast so they would fit into their new dresses which were both the perfect sizes for them and would cling to their body in the most beautiful way. There was no room for an extra inch or even half inch. Instead, they went for a long walk. On their way back Amelie spotted the cat, Albert, sneaking around the basement entrance. Amelie and Charlotte decided to follow him. Then Amelie said,

"I think a stranger might be hiding down in the cellar. We better check this out." Albert ran down to the basement and stopped near two big round barrels with a sweet, honey odor. Amelie smelled the cork in the top of the first barrel and it turned out it was filled with perfectly aged red wine.

"Charlotte, come here. We can try this ancient drink of youth. It smells so good. I'll pull the cork out and then you can put the rubber hose in, and then drink some of the wine."

"Okay, I can do that. I'm ready. It's so sweet, it's very good. Amelie, you should try some."

"Don't worry, I will. It's so sweet, indeed. Albert,

come here. You should try some, too. We're like a family, now," Amelie said and grabbed Albert. The cat licked some wine. The girls spent a bit of time down in the basement, enjoying the ancient drink.

"I wonder how old this wine is," Charlotte asked, having already hiccup.

"It must be a few hundred years old. Well, I've had plenty. Look! Albert's already fast asleep. Let's go Charlotte. Take out the hose and leave it next to the barrel. I'll put the cork back. Alright, everything seems to be back the way it was. We need to go. Oh, my head is spinning so fast."

"My head is spinning too. Maybe we should rest here for a moment. Albert is already drunk," Charlotte said, closing her eyes. They slept down in the basement for more than an hour. They awoke when they heard some voices coming toward them from the distance.

"Charlotte, we should hide behind that wooden barrel, someone is coming." "Okay, I'm coming. Albert please come here," Charlotte replied.

"Leave Albert alone, he probably comes down here every day. Hurry up!" Amelie shouted. They were surprised to see Sister Agnes and Sister Claudia as they approached the wine barrels and pump some of the wine into a few glass' bottles. Albert went closer to them and meowed so he could get out.

"What are you doing here, kitty? Are you hunting for mice?" Sister Claudia shouted at him.

"He looks like he's drank. Look at that poor creature. What happened to you? Who trimmed your hair like that? Claudia, do you see this poor thing?" Sister Agnes said, laughing.

"Oh holy ghost, this looks like an Amelie job. I'm going to have to ask her about this," Sister Claudia said with disbelief in her eyes, still laughing. The Sisters left and Albert followed them along the way. The girls sighed with relief.

"I was holding my hiccup in for so long, I almost choked myself. Thank you Lord for making my hiccup goes away. It took them so long to fill those few bottles."

"I'm glad you held your breath, otherwise this could have been a horrible situation. I got the hiccup too. It's probably because we haven't had any food yet. We better go to lunch, it's got to be about that time," Charlotte said as they walked out of the basement cellar. Outside the weather was beautiful and the sun was in every corner of the street and in every branch of the oaks' trees.

"Amelie, let's eat in our room. I feel a bit strange after that ancient wine," Charlotte said as she packed her lunch into a few boxes.

"That's a splendid idea! I don't feel like staying here either. Let's go, but you must admit that the wine was perfect."

Once back at the room Amelie made her daily tea and they sat at the table for lunch. Charlotte looked at Amelie and asked,

"Are you excited about the party? I don't feel like going after all. I've lost my motivation as of late."

"Yes, I'm very excited! You know me, I love to dance and have fun. You never know, we might meet some new boys from the other side of the monastery. Maybe a few of them will stay here and become monks after graduation. Don't panic, you'll be fine!"

"I want to do my hair and nails after lunch. I wonder if you could help me with that," Charlotte asked.

"Sure, I'll do your nails and you can do mine. Does that sound good?"

"Okay, you got it, Amelie! Just be sure to do the right color. I like pink and it must match my pink dress. As to my hair, I want it in a ponytail."

"Alright Charlotte, let me know when you're ready."

"I'm ready now but I want to do your nails first. I want to relax after you do mine. I picked the perfect green color for your nails and it will match your green dress. Do you like it?"

"A pastel green, it's perfect. Did you see the green shoes I have to go with the dress?" Amelie asked.

"Where did you get them? They're pretty, indeed, especially the green rosette."

"They belonged to my mother, they're quite old. They're my favorite dress pair. I inherited them with the rest of my mother's clothes. My grandmother saved everything for me after my parents were in the accident. My mom was working for Christian Dior at the time. She wore the best clothes the company made and got most of them for free. She helped to design them all. She was a pretty woman and was able to model a lot of the fancy dresses and shoes. Can you imagine life like that?"

"Wow, I never knew. She must have had a fantastic life. I love those old fashion shoes and dresses. Unfortunately, my mother didn't leave me anything, as all of her clothes and furniture was burned in the house fire. Are you ready for your manicure? I'd like to fix your hair into two ponytails, one on each side. What do you think?"

"I'm not sure if I want it done that way. I want my hair to look simple, rather naturally spread all over my shoulders. However, if you think it will look nice, we can try."

"It will take me only a few minutes to do your nails. How about you sing for me one of those French songs you like. Look! What do you think?" Charlotte asked.

"I like it! Thank you, Charlotte. Now, let's do my hair."

"You have thick hair, Amelie. I have some green ribbons for each of the ponytails, a sort of green which will perfectly match with your shoes. I think your hair looks fantastic."

"You're right, Charlotte. I love the ponytails. Give me five minutes to dry my nails, and then I'll take care of you. We have about one hour left to get ready for the party."

"That's plenty of time. I can't wait to put on my pink dress, it's stunning. Amelie, it's time. You can start my nails now."

"Okay! Did you hear the rumor that as soon as the semester starts we'll wear those ugly gray pants and shirts, similar to our nun's outfit?"

"Not only that, I heard they're going to cut our hair too. We'll look exactly like the bald monks in the temple. So tonight, we shall enjoy our graduation party as it will be the last night for us looking like normal, beautiful creatures."

"Why will they be doing that to us? That's my

concern. I don't like this idea," Amelie pointed out.

"Well, get used to it. Soon, it won't matter to any of us. Just wait and see for yourself."

"Please, do not spoil our evening with the depressing vision. Charlotte, look at your pink nails. They couldn't get pinker than this."

"Sure, they're almost too pink, but I love it! You should get dressed, Amelie. I can't wait to see you all in green."

"Sure, I'll do that in just a minute. Do you think I have a chance to dance with the French teacher tonight?"

"I don't see why not! There will be some other boys for you to dance with as well, so I wouldn't worry about filling up your dance card. We have exactly ten minutes before we have to leave. Amelie, you look like a doll. Let's go! Do you think my black shoes match this pink dress?"

"I think so! They match the black ribbon in your dress and the necklace around your neck. It looks very classic, very elegant!"

By the time they arrived, the ballroom was already full of students and faculty members. Sister Agnes was standing in the middle of the ballroom ready to give her graduation speech. Every student was already sitting at their respective spots at the dinner tables. The tables were covered with a nice, red linen, white napkins, and beautiful, colorful balloons. The aroma of fresh lilies filled the entire ballroom.

The girls took their places at a corner table. Soon after, Sister Agnes began her graduation speech. "Dear children of the Mighty God. We gather here today to celebrate this great achievement which will come only once in your lifetime. You should be so proud of yourselves to come as far as you have today. You have been able to master the knowledge of God almost to perfection. Not many young people have the courage to challenge or withstand the high pressures of the Academy's advanced program like you all have done with pride and dignity.

Some of you will leave this place soon, and we'll miss you dearly. Perhaps a few of you will stay to challenge and attain a higher knowledge of God. We'll proudly welcome you again, and try to help you in every possible way. We wish you a lot of success and all the best on whatever path you choose. Please, enjoy your dinner, and the graduation dance that will start soon after. Thank you again for your attention and God bless each and every one of you," Sister Agnes said with tears in her eyes. Sister Claudia tried to console her, but she was crying too.

The dinner service began, and the waiters began coming in and out of the kitchen serving everyone their plates. The live band played soft jazz in a dimmed corner of the ballroom. Everything was arranged to the perfection. A slight breeze of summer air could be felt coming in from the open windows. It was June twenty six, a day that Amelie and Charlotte would remember forever and never being forgotten.

Soon after dinner was served, the tables were cleaned off and soft drinks were served. As the most recent Italian pop rhythms began to play, the boys began asking the girls to dance. The girls were having a lot of fun and the ballroom began to get a bit hot. Amelie and Charlotte went out to the garden to cool

380

down a bit. They were so happy; they were making some jokes about a few of the boys, and began laughing almost to tears. A warm breeze of fresh wild flowers ascended into the air. The sky was filled with stars and was bluer than ever. The girls gazed up at the sky with amazement. The secrets of the universe were hidden between those shiny stars, they thought. Suddenly, the silence was interrupted by a soft, but masculine voice,

"Charlotte, may I dance with you?" It was Bertrand asking for his one dance, but he was disappointed to find out that the girl in the green dress wasn't Charlotte, but Amelie. His anger grew fast and he expressed it sharply,

"How did you dare to wear Charlotte's dress? It was given to her and she should be the one wearing it. I'm astonished by your behavior girls," Bertrand shouted and then quickly left. He was watching the girls from the distance but soon vanished around the corner. The girls were surprised by his reaction and began to laugh even more. Amelie said, still laughing,

"How dare you wear Charlotte's dress which I gave her? Did you hear that Charlotte? What happened to the sweet man I've adored from the beginning, and did almost to the end?"

"I heard! I heard! He must be crazy indeed."

"He only wanted to dance with you, Charlotte. He is so stupid! I hate him so much now! Maybe he wants to marry you!"

"I would say, definitely not! Let's just forget about him and go dance with the boys. It's getting late! I want to talk to one boy. I like him, his name is Jack. He's really funny and good looking too."

"I like him too, but personally, I like Francois. He's so cute! He's from Paris and he's already invited me to his house. Maybe, I'll go and visit him one day! I'm going to dance with him for the rest of the evening, since it's only ten p.m. and the party should wrap up around midnight."

"Okay! That sounds good, but Amelie, my shoes are killing me. They've shrunk for no reason. I'm going to run back to our room and change them into lower heels. Will you wait for me here? I'll be back as fast as I can."

"Take your time, Charlotte. You don't have to be hurry. This is our party, so you should be relaxed. I'll see you in a bit, don't worry. I'm going to go and dance with Francois!"

Charlotte ran through the corridor to their room upstairs, when suddenly, someone opened the office door in front of her face and grabbed her in. She was startled and asked,

"You scared me! What are you doing here?"

"I'm waiting for you, Charlotte. I have been waiting for you for more than four years or perhaps it's been all my life, but I've finally found you, and I don't want to let you go," Bertrand said in a masculine voice as he held her between his shoulders.

"You're not serious. I don't understand what you're talking about? I'm going to my room to change my shoes, and then I'm going back to the ballroom. Amelie is waiting for me. Please, let me go!"

"You don't have to go. I know you won't dance with me, but please tell me why? I don't care about Amelie, I care only for you, my darling. I want to spend some time with you, right here and right now. I love you, Charlotte. Don't you see that? Don't you see the way I look at you all the time? I want you to know that I dream of you every single night. I can't sleep and my life is pointless without you. I want to marry you and take you to my Chateau, in the South of France where we can live happily ever after. I have many businesses out there, and you can stay home and relax for the rest of your life with me. I'm serious and crazy about you, Charlotte! I must confess to you that I never wanted to be a priest. This was a mistake, a total catastrophe for me. My family pressured me my whole life to become one, but now that they're dead, I want to free myself from the bondage of my own misery. I want to be happy with you, and I want to be a normal man. I want to live with you, Charlotte, and forever!

I want to have children with you. Do you understand? You're so beautiful and you've charmed me from the first day I met you. Please, say yes, and I'll take you with me tonight. We'll run away together. I want to love you. You're my first true love. I've never felt this way about anyone before. Now that I've found you, I want to find out what love is and only with you. Please, let me make love to you," Bertrand whispered to her as he was fully overwhelmed by her.

He kneeled in front of her and held her tight, kissing every inch of her. His hands were caressing her legs and belly. He gently took off her little lingerie, kissing her and whispering over and over again,

"My love, I want to love you for the first time. I want to feel you the way only Angels can feel." He gently pulled her to the floor. She was afraid and felt strange in a way she never felt before. She whispered to him,

"Please, don't hurt me. Please, let me go. I want to go!" He held her tight as he was becoming more and more aroused. His body released the masculine scent of powerful hormones and he whispered,

"My darling, do not be afraid of me. My love for you is pure and innocent. I'm destined to take your virginity tonight." He undressed himself. He aroused her even more, kissing the delicate and sensitive places of her body over and over again. He slowly seduced her with passion, screaming his deep love for her. She too was screaming like a little fawn, she was in pain but no one heard her. She was a victim of his unconditional and blind lust which would never die. He was so emotional constantly whispering to her,

"Charlotte, my desire for you is getting deeper and stronger. I'm going crazy for your love. I want to be with you forever, and have you feel the same way about me, over and over again. You're my first true love, Charlotte. My love for you is real. You're a saint to me. I'll never abandon you. I'm a man of honor. You don't know me well yet. You only know me as a priest and teacher, but you must trust me now.

If you don't run away with me tonight, I will be forced to run away alone. But mark my words, I'll surely come back for you very soon and take you away. Please, say yes."

"I can't. Laissez-moi tranquille! Leave me alone! You're hurting me. I hate you!" she cried as she tried to fight him off, but he held her even tighter, whispering,

"I love you, Charlotte. Je voudrais./ze-vudre/. I want you. Please feel the same way I feel about you, my love."

She was ablaze with anger. She didn't fully understand what was happening to her and why? The first chapter in her life was just secretly turned over and a new chapter of her life story had begun.

"Please say something my darling, Charlotte. You are the cause of my la souffranse, /la-sufras/, suffering. I love your beautiful la poitrine,/la puatrin/, breasts. You're like le chef-d'oeuvre, /le szedowr/, a treasure for me. I know and I can assure you that my love for you is immortal and I'll die for you if I must. My love J'aime/zama/, j'aime. There is a fire inside of me burning for you, Charlotte."

He was intoxicated with his love for her. She was like a forbidden fruit for him, and he would devour it all he could. Then, in an instant, there was a moment of relief for him, and his powerful emotions came under his control. Charlotte was crying. She was afraid of him. He was on top of her, holding her tightly with his arms. She was powerless, lost between his powerful shoulders. He slowly rolled off of her and lay next to her. He then whispered in her ear,

"This is the blood of a virgin. I want you to forgive me, Charlotte. I will always love you. You have to realize that I am only twenty three years old. I will wait for you for the rest of my life if I have to, but I will pray that you will come with me to France. This is my last kiss for you as a lasting bond between us." He put his bloody lips over hers and kissed her with passion. She cried again and tried to escape, but he wouldn't let go of her. He made love to her again, loving her with all of his might and emotions.

He was like a Greek god worshipping the moment that had passed and begging for more of her love. Charlotte looked like a martyr, trying to escape. She was so frightened, like a fragile fawn in a dark forest. He held her hand and kissed it gently. He knew that he'd torn apart her secret chord, which no man had ever touched before.

Did he feel guilty? Perhaps, but the answer lies only with him; perhaps his unconditional love was the answer. He held her lingerie in his hand.

Charlotte stood up quickly and ran away.

He didn't say anything and just watched her. He then held his face between his hands and cried. Only he would know if they were tears of love or guilt.

He abandoned his frock and walked straight to his room. He was determined to leave, no matter what happened with Charlotte. He packed his suitcase then lay on his bed. The next early morning he left the Academy, without saying good-bye to anyone. He glanced up at Charlotte's window with the slight hope of seeing her there, but it was not meant to be.

After Charlotte's sprint back to her room, she was totally devastated and out of breath. She quietly opened the door, so as to not wake Amelie, who was already sleeping in her bed. She didn't even know what time it was. She quickly lay down on her bed in silence. Her dress was soaked in her blood. She looked at the bedroom wall with the fresco of the Virgin Mary on it, sobbing. She then whispered, "Saint Virgin Mary, if you've seen what I just went through, please hear me now, please make me a virgin again, please, purify my body like the holy water we bless ourselves with. Please make me the same Charlotte I was yesterday and I will always love and protect you and your honor."

Charlotte cried and sincerely believed that the Virgin Mary had heard what she asked her for. Suddenly, in the darkness of the bedroom, Charlotte saw the image of the Virgin Mary approaching her slowly and speaking in a soft voice,

"Do not worry my child. I have heard your call and I am here to heal you and restore your virginity. Please my child, do not cry and waste any more tears. You are now the same Charlotte you were yesterday. Please call on me whenever you may need me and I will be there for you. I am watching over you my child, but this man is truly in love with you. He will come back for you when the time is right. Please take care of yourself now." She touched Charlotte's belly and a bright red light appeared, at that instant, she was restored and the bleeding immediately stopped. Charlotte whispered to the vision,

"Thank you my dearest Mary. I will love you forever. Please, be my best secret friend."

She glanced back at the fresco and saw Saint Mary with a smile. It was truly a miracle, but she still couldn't believe what had just happened. She glanced around and saw Amelie, sitting on her bed and watching everything in silence.

"Charlotte, tell me what happened to you? I was looking for you everywhere, but I couldn't find you, so I decided to go to bed and must have fallen asleep." She turned on the small lamp on the nightstand and asked Charlotte with a terrified look on her face,

"Charlotte, you look like you've been hit by a truck. Where have you been? Oh, Holy Ghost! You're bleeding!"

"Bertrand raped me in his office," she whispered.

"I don't believe it! Why do all the best things happen to you?"

"Amelie, are you kidding, why are you talking crazy? You don't know what you're talking about. Do you? I don't think there was any "best" of anything. He raped me, it was awful and you can't begin to imagine how I feel right now. It's terrible. I can't even talk about it right now. Please, we must keep this a secret because I don't want anyone to find out, no scandals. Please, don't talk to Sister Agnes about any of this."

"I'm sorry, Charlotte, maybe I am a bit crazy. I just have this stupid fantasy about Bertrand. How many times did I tell you that he was in love with you, and you didn't believe me? And this is what happens, of course it was unavoidable, he's crazy in love with you. Don't worry, I'll keep a secret. I saw the vision of the Virgin Mary talking to you. What was that about? Then I saw the red light radiating from her holy hands all over your body."

"I asked her to make me a virgin again, and she did. I sincerely believe she restored my virginity."

"This is serious you know you could still be pregnant, even if you're a virgin again. If Bertrand climaxed inside of you, then his DNA is inside of you, Charlotte. What are you going to do about that?"

"I don't know yet. I forgot to ask the Virgin Mary about not being pregnant. I thought that wouldn't be possible, if she restored my virginity, but maybe I was wrong."

"Now it's too late to ask her about it, the damage has already been done, but don't worry, I'll care for the baby. I love kids and I've never had a sister or brother. It would be fun for me."

"Amelie, you're talking non-sense again. I don't want any babies with Bertrand. I'll have an abortion. He raped me, against my will. I'm too young for that. Don't you think so? I really wonder what you would do if you were in my shoes, Amelie? Honestly, just tell me the truth."

"I would keep the baby. I know it would be a big scandal, but you're Catholic and the Church is dead set against abortions. It could become a serious problem if you do. Ultimately, it will be your choice, whether or not you want to abort the precious baby that would be born looking just like Bertrand. I'm really sorry about what happened to you, Charlotte. This could become more complicated than I originally thought, but we'll find the right solution. You can count on me, Charlotte. I will not leave you alone with that baby if you're pregnant and you decide to have it."

"Amelie, you're scaring me half to death with all this pregnancy talk, but I admire your positive attitude when it comes to my misery. Let's pray that none of these things will ever happen."

"Yes, let's pray, Charlotte. We must believe that everything will be okay. Look at your bloody dress we shall dispose of it and quickly. It would be better if we don't leave any suspicious evidence of this tragic incident in our room. Please take it off and I'll wrap it in some plastic bags, and secretly dump it in the trash can."

"Okay! Let's do that. It was such a nice pink dress."

"Don't panic! Tomorrow, I'll buy you a new one, so there will be no suspicion of what happened to it."

"You're brilliant, Amelie. What would I do without you? Here you go!"

"Now, you should take a shower, Charlotte. Please, you need to relax a bit and restore yourself to pristine condition. You'll feel much better after that. In the meantime, I'll clean up all this mess and dump the dress."

Amelie wrapped the pink dress into a small bundle and ran to the back of the building to dump it onto the bottom of the trash can. She came back and sighed with relief. Charlotte had already finished her shower and was lying in her bed. Her face was as white as a ghost.

"Is there anything else in this world I can do for you, Charlotte?"

"You already have. You're my best friend and supporter. I'm very tired though, so I'd like to sleep for a bit. Thank you Amelie for everything, goodnight!"

"Goodnight Charlotte. Remember that I'm here for you."

The next morning there was a rumor at the Academy about Bertrand and his sudden disappearance, so everyone gathered in his office. The nun who does the cleaning found an abandoned frock, lying on the floor in Bertrand's office. They had no idea where he might be, and said he couldn't just leave the Academy without saying goodbye. Sister Agnes knew that something must be wrong and called

390

the police for an investigation. In addition, they found some blood on the floor next to his clothes and suspected foul play, it was possible that he was even murdered and the body dumped somewhere.

The police search team looked everywhere for any pertinent evidence. The body was not found. However, they searched all the trash cans each bag after bag for more evidence. One of the investigators with sudden enlightenment of consciousness traced Bertrand in France, after he made a long distance phone-call. The good news was that Bertrand was alive and in one piece in his estate. He said he quit his sabbatical post and for good. Thus soon the search would be called off. Everyone was stunned by the news.

Meantime, Amelie and Charlotte were standing behind the building watching the investigators and praying for a miracle. Charlotte was staring dreadfully at every single trash bag which had been worshipping one by one by the search team. The girls quivered with terrified looks in their eyes as they suspected that at any moment the tragic bundle with her bloody pink dress would be revealed to the eyes of the entire world, and then Charlotte would undergo another humiliation process in front of everyone's watchful-eyes. It was more than she could bear on her shoulders. All the people still remember her pink dress she wore last night. Thus she wouldn't take this affront and would run away somewhere, to never be found, like Bertrand. The girls were getting weaker by the minute as they watched the everlasting process which seemed to never end. Perhaps their veins suddenly stopped pumping the blood into the brain.

Amelie held Charlotte shoulder very hard to prevent her from collapsing to the ground at any moment. There were only a few bundles left to be opened. One of those bundles will be the one Amelie placed at the bottom of the same trash-can late last night.

Suddenly, one of the investigators called the total search off and they simply abandoned the last bag after Bertrand claims that the blood came from his severe nose bleed caused by the tension and stress while making his decision to abandon his vows and his priesthood....Bah!

Meantime, Charlotte recharged with the potentially deadly vision of unfathomable embarrassment collapsed to the ground unconscious.

"Charlotte, wake up! It is over! They stopped the search! The search was called off! You're okay now!" Someone asked,

"What happened to her?"

"She didn't eat yet! She is okay." Amelie answers quickly.

Charlotte opened her eyes and glanced at the stranger with a deadly expression in her eyes and said in a sulky mood, "Yes, I'm perfectly all right."

"You don't look like you're perfectly okay. But whatever you say, young lady," the stranger replied with disbelief in his eyes. Amelie glanced at the stranger with a look of a *tiger* just to scare him away. They didn't want any more scandals around as one was already enough. "Charlotte! Pull yourself together. We shall walk like distinguished ladies, now! The Sisters are looking at us with a suspicious eye. We better go and fast." "Okay, I'm almost ready just count to ten and we'll go."

"Charlotte, there is no time to count to ten because the Sisters are walking toward us. Stand up! Fast!" Amelie nervously whispered. The girls walked straight forward, and as they passed the Sisters, they waved at them. Suddenly Sister Agnes asked,

"Charlotte, are you sick? You look discontent a bit."

"I'm perfectly all right, just a bit hungry and tired after the graduation party. I'll be okay!"

The Sisters whispered something to each other and one added, "I like your pink dress, Charlotte. You should wear it more often."

"Thank you Sister, I will," Charlotte replied as she paused for a moment, her face turned pale white, and she thought they already knew about all her secrets. Then she was about to collapse again but Amelie held her shoulder tightly, as she muttered nervously to her,

"Charlotte, keep walking, keep walking. See you later Sisters," Amelie added with a big smile on her face.

"Charlotte, certainly, you don't look healthy today. Did you hear any noises last night?" Sister Agnes asked.

"Oh no we were busy, dancing with the boys until midnight," Amelie replied quickly with a horrible look in her eyes.

"All right but I didn't see your pink dress before midnight in the ballroom, Charlotte. Perhaps you left earlier," Sister added.

"Sure, she left ten minutes earlier. I remember now, she went to change her shoes" Amelie said with a defensive tone in her voice. The girls walked fast without looking back until they reached the closest bench under the pine tree where they finally rested for a few moments. There was too much emotion for two young girls. Charlotte was speechless and worried about what would happen next. They couldn't talk consciously for at least half an hour. Amelie was overwhelmed by the current events and stared at the blue sky endlessly. Suddenly Charlotte interrupted,

"Now the entire world knows about me and Bertrand. I can't escape from those peoples' eyes. They look at me as if they know all of my secrets. How can I defend myself from them? I will be obsessed with this for the rest of my life. Is there any place in this entire universe where I can run and hide? Tell me Amelie. Where is that place? "

"Stop talking nonsense. No one knows about it, only you and me so far. Perhaps God and Saint Mary know too. But they are our best friends and they witnessed exactly what happened in Bertrand's office. You can't feel guilty about it. It was not your fault. Don't think about it. Try to accept everything as is for now and wait for the result."

"What result are you talking about?" Charlotte asked.

"The result will be your cute little baby looking just like Bertrand," Amelie said innocently.

"I can't have a baby, I'll go insane. Why did this happen to me! I can't handle this issue myself and I might do something stupid. You must help me Amelie."

"Of course, I'll help you. Let's forget about it, like it never happened. Please, Charlotte, let's never talk about it again. Trust me it would help us."

"Okay, let's try that. Maybe it will help me too in such a way."

"We shall shop for your new pink dress today, and pretend that nothing ever happened to it!"

"Okay, Amelie," Charlotte agreed.

"Hopefully, tomorrow morning the cleaning service will empty the trash-cans around our facilities, and surely we'll never talk of it again."

The girls rushed to the boutique and spotted the last pink dress displayed at the window. Charlotte sighed with relief. Amelie grabbed it and asked.

"May we have that pink dress from the window display?"

"Sure, you're lucky! This is the last one, and it is fifty percent off. I almost sold it yesterday evening but the girl never came back for the dress," the sales lady announced enthusiastically.

"Then we consider ourselves very lucky today, don't we Charlotte."

"You're positive, Amelie. This will be the dress to remember for the rest of my life." She thought of it as a cursed dress for her to remember, and she would never wear it again. It would be the proverbial forbidden fruit from Adam and Eve's paradise.

"I'm glad that you like it. Madam, please, would you remove the price sticker from the dress. Thank you. It is a gift," Amelie said as she glanced angrily at Charlotte.

Indeed, it was a curious dress, not to be easily forgotten. The dress was nicely wrapped and put in the fancy bag with pink rosettes. The girls left and made the lady very happy. It was her first sale in the early morning. They walked slowly through the cobbled streets, looking at each window display just to kill time and their worries. A few young boys passed them by, waving their hands at them. But the girls didn't keep their attention to them. There was one thing on their minds at that moment: the curious pink dress.

"Finally, we're back," Amelie said as they climbed the stairs to their room. At the door was a small business card from the local flowers shop with a hand written notice about an attempted flower delivery. They will redeliver the flowers at three p.m. Charlotte almost had a heart attack. It was more than likely that the flowers were sent by Bertrand. Amelie said,

"Don't worry. I'll go to the flower shop and cancel the delivery or just refuse any further attempts. I'll take care of it; you stay here. Actually, it would be better if you go with me because the flowers are for you, and you must cancel or refuse any future deliveries. Bertrand wants to ruin your good reputation in the Academy. We don't need a new scandal right now. Let's go! Wait a second; put the dress in the room before we go."

The girls walked to the flower shop, wondering if the flowers came from Bertrand. When they arrived, they discovered, indeed, they were from Bertrand. There was a small gift card attached to it. Amelie handed it to Charlotte.

"I don't want to know what he said. But if you'd like, you can read it," Charlotte said angrily.

"Okay, I'll read it for you. He wrote, 'Dear Charlotte, my love for you is true and I'll love you forever! I'm waiting for you and if you don't come, I'll come to you soon and take you by force. I can't live without you, Love Bertrand.' Holy cow, He is really in love with you. I told you before, it is going to happen," Amelie said, excited.

"Amelie, stop that nonsense! Sir, I'd like to cancel any further delivery of any flowers to the Monastery, from this man, Bertrand."

"Madam, we're already paid for one year delivery, and it is our policy to make all deliveries to you. Otherwise we will be out of business," the man said angrily.

"I don't care if you will be out of business or not. This is your problem. I simply don't want any flowers from this man. Do you understand that?"

"I do but I can't do it! Why you don't just give them to someone else," he replied with a smile.

"Perhaps you can deliver them to the local cemetery. Can't you?"

"I can't!" he replied again.

"Stop that nonsense," Charlotte said.

"I have an idea! Stop quarrelling, both of you! Charlotte we have that little Chapel of Saint Mary next to the Monastery. He can leave the flowers there. Can you do that Sir?" Amelie said with self confidence.

"Sure, I can tell him to deliver to the Chapel of Saint Mary," he said, smiling.

"But be sure to dispose of every single personal gift card from Bertrand, before you bring the flowers. I don't want to have any trouble because of his cards. Can you remember that, Sir?" Charlotte asked politely.

"I'll tell the delivery guys to remember that! Don't worry, we got the deal! I was paid for the flowers, Saint Mary will get free flowers every week, and you will have a peace of mind." he was contented.

"Okay, we got the deal! Also you could mention to Mr. Bertrand that his flowers are not welcome here, and they will be rejected every time by Charlotte. Don't forget to tell him that!" Amelie pointed on her way out.

"I'll try to tell him that!" he shouted from the distance.

"He is a jerk! He is not going to tell him anything. Why? Because he cares only for the money from this wealthy prick," Charlotte grumbled.

"Okay, Charlotte. We have had enough for today. I'm so exhausted. Let's forget about this for now and move on. It is almost noon and time for our lunch. What a day," she murmured.

"Okay, Amelie, you're right. I'm tired too." They happily walked into the dinning room, passing Sister Agnes on their way. She noticed them and asked,

"Hello girls! This morning I saw a delivery man with a beautiful flowers arrangement. He asked for your room but you were not there."

"It was mistake! They were not for us. Someone must have sent them to the wrong address," Amelie pointed out, being scared to death. Charlotte looked at Sister, listened to every single word Amelie said and then sighed with relief.

"That is what I thought," Sister said with a smile and left.

"Oh Holy Ghost, I almost had a heart attack. Amelie, I can't go through this every single day."

"I promise you, there will be no more days like

this. We'll fix everything. No one will suspect. I feel terrible, too. I can't take it anymore all these lies. It is time to put an end to it, for good."

"Amelie I'm hungry like a wild beast."

"You better watch out what you're eating from now on. If you're really pregnant, you will gain weight fast."

"Don't say that, Amelie! It couldn't be true! I can't go through this stuff right now! I'll kill myself!"

"Be quiet, Charlotte! Someone could hear us. You don't have to kill yourself! I'll help you, I promise. We can hide the baby in a secret place. I'll find an orphanage for it! I did some research recently. As a matter of fact I found one already, at our facilities, on the campus. It is that red brick building surrounded by the rose garden, just behind the Monastery. It looks like a preschool. Then you don't have to worry about anything. I'll bring the baby there and tell them that my sister died in a car accident. How does that sound, Charlotte?"

"It sounds awfully good. You're a genius, Amelie! We'll arrange every single detail. Thank you, Amelie. Monday, my summer job will start. I want to forget all about what happened and start a new life."

"Sure, I like your determination, Charlotte. I shall apply for the same job. What do you think?"

"I think, it is a great idea and we'll be busy again. I'll miss you if you leave this place. Please, stay in the Academy for your higher education."

"I'll do that just for you, Charlotte, and for our friendship."

"Thank you, Amelie. You're my best friend, indeed. Let's enjoy our lunch as it is getting cold. After that I would like to rest in my room."

"Sure, let's do that! I'm tired myself too."

"Charlotte, before we go to our room, let's go to Saint Mary's Chapel. We should pray for you, and maybe you won't be pregnant with Bertrand's baby, even though he is so handsome."

"Amelie stop! Don't talk anymore about him. It makes everything even worse. But yes, let's go there and pray!"

"Oh! The chapel is really beautiful. I'm glad the flowers finally found the right place. Look, there is something special about this place. Some nuns talk about miracles that took place right here. Charlotte, look out there at the altar! Someone already delivered the flowers."

"Good to know! We must be sure that the gift card is removed. Let's pray but very sincerely then maybe our prayers will be answered."

"I don't see any gift card. Let's pray," Amelie replied as she glanced all over the flowers for a little gift card but couldn't find any. They prayed for more than an hour.

On Monday, Charlotte hurried to her new summer work, at the Vatican Headquarters. She found the Communication Department easily. It was in a small free standing building not so far from the North Tower where Peter currently resides. She opened the main door and entered. An older bald lady looking like a monk was sitting at the wooden desk. She glanced at Charlotte with surprise.

"Hi! My name is Charlotte and I was assigned to the summer job here."

"Okay, yes, I have your name on my special

list. I have a few openings here for a few different positions so if you have a friend, who may be looking for summer job, just bring them here. We also have a few special rules in this facility. The first one: you must wear this gray outfit, pants and tunic, like all of us. The second one: we must cut your hair. You'll be totally bald. We're a special monk division and we do service only to the North Tower. Your job is simple. You will pick the two bags with dirty laundry from the back of the North Tower, twice a week. The bags have initials, **Chi-Rho**. Then you must sort it out, whatever is inside, and deliver it to the cleaner. Do you see this blue building out there, next to the blue container? That is the cleaner. Do you understand?"

"Sure, I do. I'm ready." Then Charlotte remembers what Peter told her before he left for service to the North Tower. He will write her news on the inside of his habit. She must check each one in order to find the one belonging to Peter.

"Okay, Caroline will cut your hair and give you your uniform. Tomorrow at ten a.m. you must pick-up the same bags from the cleaner and drop them off at the same location at the back of the tower."

"Sure, it will be no problem."

"You can't be late. I think it is an easy job. In case, you can't come, you must find your own substitution for yourself and let us know who is coming. Now, go with Caroline for your haircut. Good luck!"

Charlotte followed Caroline to her office. She sat on the wooden chair. Caroline picked an electric shaver and cut her long blond hair totally off. Then she said, "You're done. Here is your new uniform. Now, go and change your clothes. It's a quarter to twelve. You have fifteen minutes only."

"Thank you. I'll do that." Charlotte rushed to the changing room, put her new clothes on, and glanced in the mirror. She was shocked by her new look but ignored it completely. She was getting ready for her new mission and it was more important than her look. She picked the two bags from the North Tower and placed them onto a small cart. She pushed the cart to the laundry facility. She found a small room where she could be alone and slowly sort all the habits. She checked twenty habits, one by one very carefully, looking for any writing. Then when she picked the last one, medium size, she found the written message inside the habit, on the back of a small pocket. Peter wrote:

'Hi Charlotte, I'm okay. I wrote you a letter and when you'll pick the bags after tomorrow at noon, I'll drop the letter from my window. This is the only way. Our habits are checked by the security for any letters or other items. Be sure you get it. Just whistle once our favorite song, like you did at home. I'll be sure that you got it. Love Peter.'

She was happy and tried to remember the size of Peter's habit. She transferred all the habits to the other room and put them on the long table to be dry cleaned. Charlotte left the cleaner and walked to the office to pick her clothes. She changed from her uniform to her casual clothes and went back to the Monastery. She was excited as her new chapter of life had just begun. She rushed to the dining room for lunch. She was late but they still served lunch until one thirty p.m. Soon afterward, she made a phone-call to Cardinal Benedict and told him that she received Peter's first message. He was excited and told her to wait outside the Monastery for Monk Emanuel to come. He will be there in five minutes and give her further instruction. Indeed, he came on time and asked for the details. He told her as soon as she gets the letter from Peter, he will meet her in the same place exactly after lunch. Charlotte was content and went to her room. Amelie greeted her with enthusiasm,

"What happened to your hair? I think, I know! Don't tell me. I remember now. Then how was your interview? Did you get the job?"

"If I didn't get the job, I wouldn't be bald. Amelie wake up! Don't you think so? Easy job, only twice a week for an hour; not a big deal, really. They have other openings. If you'd like, you can have a job too. Tomorrow you should come with me, really."

"My mind is slow today or perhaps your appearance shocked me a bit but I'm okay now. Obviously you got the job! I'll go with you tomorrow morning then both of us will look the same: bald," Amelie said, laughing.

"Stop Amelie, You're joking and I'm serious. I left my uniform out there."

"What does it look like?" "It is gray and ugly, but you'll wear it only when you work. Then you don't have to worry too much. What did you do today?"

"I was praying for half of a day just for you and the other half I was thinking what I shall do?"

"What did you come up with, Amelie?"

"Not much of anything, just some crazy fantasy of mine. You wouldn't like to hear it. I better make

403

some tea for us."

"It wouldn't hurt, indeed. I love your tea. So then, what are we drinking this evening?"

"I call this tea, **Fantasy beyond a Reason**."

"It may suit you well, Amelie," Charlotte added, laughing.

"You're back, Charlotte. You're laughing, indeed. I really tried so hard to make you laugh, and I did. You're right! This tea suits me well. Do you think I'm a bit crazy?"

"I don't think so! You've a great sense of humor, most of the time. You're indeed, a very happy person and I like that about you. Now, I know that I can count on you, too."

"Your opinion is greatly appreciated, Madam! The *Fantasy Tea* is ready and it is fully yours. Full service, this evening only!" Amelie said, laughing.

"You're funny, Amelie. Indeed your tea is a piece of art again. What did you add to it?"

"Let me think! I bought this heavy thick cherry syrup yesterday and I added a bit. I'm glad it suits you well. How do you feel, Charlotte?"

"I feel fine and optimistic so far. Everything is going well, by the book. Peter is doing well and the most important thing is that he is very happy out there."

"This is very good news. Do you remember how we swam down to the St. Mark cave, just to see Peter and Patrick on the cross? It was one of a kind experience for me. I decided to stay here, definitely. I was thinking all day long about it and there is no point in going back to France. I got that vision that my life shall be right here with you. But it could change, perhaps in the future and if it does, I will go back to Paris."

"This is good news for me. I like to be with you, too, especially after this unpleasant incident. I'll have a friendly soul to talk to. Thank you, Amelie for that."

"You're welcome, Charlotte. Let's forget about everything for a moment. I want to go to this new cafe **André.** They just opened it on the corner. I saw delicious cakes in their window display. Would you like to go with me?"

"Sure, let me change my clothes again and I shall put that green hat on my bald head. At least I will look like a girl."

"Charlotte, you look just fantastic! I wouldn't worry about that cute baldness of yours. Soon we'll be use to it, even enjoy it. Are you ready?"

"I'm ready. Amelie, do you think we'll ever grow up and be old like others?"

"Sure, it will happen faster than we think. Let's enjoy life before it happens," Amelie said with bold optimism. They reached the **André** cafe. They sat at the small table with a nice arrangement of wild flowers. Soon the waiter brought them menus.

"My name is Piero. I'll be back soon," he said on his way out. The cakes were very tempting and difficult to choose from. Amelie decided for both of them: strawberry cakes with pink jelly on the top. She said,

"Less fat is better for us. Trust me there is nothing worse than fat belly. I hate that; especially on myself. Ha!"

"You don't have any yet," Charlotte pointed out, smiling.

"I know, but you can get that stuff anytime and when you get it surely you can't get it off."

"Amelie, be more inventive for the moment. We better enjoy that cake for now. It could be my last one! I may have to go on a diet soon. I missed my period! I had a dream but Bertrand took it away from me. I thought, *my dream would never die*. Now, I have to kill that dream I dreamt; surely it will die with me soon. Who gave him the right to take it away?" Charlotte whispered with tears in her eyes.

"Oh Holy Ghost, this is really happening! You're pregnant!" Amelie whispered with excitement. But her face turned white suddenly.

"Stop Amelie, I'm terrified and feel like I'm dying from broken pride."

"You're not. You'll be fine. I know I have a dream, too. But every dream comes in different colors and shades. I dream I'll never die. Charlotte, you must keep faith in God and He will turn your pain into a positive sign. Try to be even more sophisticated than you have ever been before. It will help you to stand the abasement with dignity. I know it hurts very deep but try to think also that this man is crazy about you. I bet that he will die for you. You just don't know that! His love is pure and unconditional. There are not many loves like that in this small world. His heart talks the truth! He is blindly in love with you and this is why he couldn't wait any longer for you to grow up. His desire for you was stronger and he therefore couldn't control himself."

"Are you looking for excuses for Bertrand? Or you are giving him some credit! I don't think it is a good idea. If he was in love with me he would wait.

Just think Amelie." Charlotte was sobbing.

"A man can't control his sex drive the same way a woman does. But in this case, it wasn't only sex, it was deep pure love for you, he built over the years, for a young virgin girl, for you, his young virgin girl to be more precise. He was obsessed with you, and it was going on and on, for almost four years. He dreamt of you every night. You didn't see that because you didn't want to and perhaps you didn't care for him the same way he cares for you. But I saw every side of it. Why? Because I was like him, in love," Amelie pointed out with tears in her eyes.

"Amelie, but you don't know what love really is about. Your love for him was a platonic one. You never experienced true love. How can you be an expert on it? Now nothing is left for me in the entire universe. The worst thing is that my dream will chase, or, rather, hunt me forever!"

"Charlotte, don't say that and don't cry. It would happen faster than you think. Perhaps you'll find a new dream soon. Let's go to the chapel and pray for a new dream, together. We will return here another time when our mood improves a bit. I really relished that cake," Amelie said with a smile.

"Sure, the cake was sapid. How sad it would be to not have it anymore." "You could have more but only a smaller piece. This one was a big one, perhaps good for a hard working man!" Amelie said, laughing.

They strolled back to the St. Mary Chapel. It was quiet out there. They sat on the wooden bench. Their whispers could be heard perhaps by the Angels and the Saints only. Also it seemed like the walls were whispering back to them, perhaps their own arcane life stories. The girls were staring at the fresco of St. Mary, looking for an answer or rather a miracle to happen. The fresh roses coquettishly gazed at them from the altar and intoxicated them with the fresh-sweet aroma.

The evening was approaching fast. Accompanied by the butterflies they walked back through the park to the boarding school. One orange-brown monarch butterfly paused for a moment on Charlotte's green hat mistaking it for juicy, lush grass. The two other lovers danced in the air in a lovemaking pattern. Summer was in full bloom and created inside of them some kind of spiritual security. It would heal many wounds perhaps even those uncertain ones. With peace of mind they entered their room. Charlotte lay down on her bed, how would she handle herself in the next few months? Only God knew. Amelie sat at her desk and sang her favorite French love song. She knew that Charlotte liked that song and perhaps it would ignite a bit of buoyancy inside of her. There was not much to say or to do at that sensitive moment. Perhaps the silence was the best companion for them at that moment which was filled with a bit of melancholy.

The girls welcomed the next day, afresh with enthusiasm. After breakfast, Charlotte took Amelie to her new job's interview. It was successful and Amelie got her new job. However, it was in a different building. She will work in the pressroom building, where all the incoming and outgoing letters, newspapers, magazines and announcement are distributed to the Vatican Headquarters on a daily bases. Thus, she will be busy all day long and for five days a week.

She got her haircut and a new uniform. Charlotte congratulated Amelie on her new job and left for her daily assignment. She picked the two bags from the cleaner and delivered them to the back of the North Tower. Tomorrow at noon she'll pick-up the new bags again and the most important, she will get the letter from Peter. She returned to the office, changed her clothes and walked to the Monastery. On her way back she glanced at a few shops with the outstanding window displays. She saw a beautiful skinny red dress. She always wanted to have it but she ignored her temptation and walked straight to the campus. There was not much for her to do and it would be a long day. She went to her room and lay on the bed.

Then she thought of her new mission which will take place very soon. She's in excellent physical condition and ready for any action. What will it be like, she wondered? She'll definitely find out tomorrow. For some reason her eyelids seemed heavy and she closed them for a short nap. The time ran fast and she could hear Amelie's voice from the distance,

"Charlotte, are you there? It's time to go for dinner."

"How was your first day, Amelie?"

"I love it! It is easy. The most important thing is that I meet so many interesting people out there. Some of them are students like me, maybe five of them are interns and the rest are regulars. I met a nice guy, George, from an International Law School. He is cute and sexy! I hope he likes me too."

"I'm glad that you're happy with your new job.

Amelie, you just met a new guy, George, but please, don't rush. Give him some space to breathe before your friendship goes any further. I hope he likes bald girls," Charlotte said, laughing.

"Don't make fun of me. He has short hair too, a sort of military style. I love his dark emerald eyes and sexy lips. He is tall and very handsome. He is a totally different type than our beloved Monk Bertrand."

"I'm happy for you, Amelie. Finally you found a right subject to talk about. Likely I'll hear many stories about George, probably everyday at least he is your age."

"He is a senior thus he must be three years older than me. I always like older boys. They're mature and they know just how to treat a lady. I'm really happy about everything that happened today. Thank you Charlotte, for inspiring me to get out there and get my job, it wouldn't have happened without you."

"You're welcome and I believe this guy will be your first good friend. You're only sixteen and you haven't had any boyfriends before. Am I right?"

"Sure, you're right! However, I have those platonic ones so far. If George likes me he'll wait for me at least two years. But actually I turned seventeen last month."

"Amelie, those platonic guys don't count. Soon, you'll be busy with work and study, and there will be no place for any boyfriends. But if he really likes you, he'll wait. Okay, it's time for dinner."

"We must go to the St. Mary Chapel after dinner. I like to say 'thank you,' for everything that happened today."

"Okay, we'll go. Not many students came for dinner, today. Perhaps some went on vacation. Hopefully, they will be back in a month or two."

"Today is my favorite: fish, fries and fresh salad, I can eat this every day. I feel like I'm in the garden now. I didn't see Sister Agnes for the last few days. She didn't go for any vacation."

"I don't think so. She is somewhere around here. I like that fish too."

Fully content they rushed to the *Chapel*. Amelie opened the wooden door and they got in. However, from the distance they noticed that someone was at the altar. They hid behind the *Corinthian* column and waited. It was Sister Agnes. She was cleaning the altar and changing the water in all the flowers' vases. She picked the vase with fresh roses, the same roses which were intended for Charlotte, and rushed to fill it with fresh water. Meantime, she spread the roses loose on the altar, making a new arrangement with them and trimming each one by one. Suddenly something fell onto the floor. She bent to pick it up. She put her glasses on and began to read. It was the gift card which should have been removed by the delivery guy. The Sister sat on the front bench and didn't move for at least ten minutes.

Charlotte and Amelie were electrified, still standing behind the column. Then Charlotte whispered, "Amelie, I asked you yesterday to look for any gift card and you told me, there wasn't any. How did you look?"

"I glanced between the red heads only and I didn't see any. Perhaps, it was sitting deep inside

411

between the stems. How should I know that? Perhaps they delivered fresh roses today. You would never know," she whispered back.

"You screwed-up Amelie! What's going to happen next? Now, the entire world knows that I'm pregnant!" Charlotte whispered painfully.

"Be quiet, Charlotte! Nobody knows that yet only me. The Sister only knows that Bertrand is crazy in love with you. Now, she is thinking about her past love, Richard, who killed himself when she left him. Don't panic yet! Fortunately, for us Bertrand didn't attempt suicide yet! We must wait and see what will happen next. I'm going crazy too!" Amelie added nervously.

They waited twenty more minutes and finally Sister Agnes finished the cleaning and left. The girls sighed with relief.

"I can't believe you missed that gift card. How in all the heavens you didn't see it? I regret that I didn't check myself, this is my fault, indeed."

"Charlotte, stop! It is too late right now. Don't try to break the wall with your head. It is done! I'm sorry that it happened that way. Surely it was unintentional! We better pray."

"Okay, okay. The damage has been done anyway." Charlotte thought about how she would face Sister Agnes. Telling her the truth would be devastating for her. She closed her eyes and prayed in her mind. Amelie, overwhelmed by sorrow, prayed quietly. To her, it seemed like everything exploded out of proportion. It was supposed to be Charlotte's secret but it wasn't any longer. Suddenly she broke a long silence, asking,

"What should I say to Sister Agnes? She will ask me what happened. Should I tell her the truth or not?"

"I don't have a clue. Let me think about it for a moment."

"If I don't, she will find out sooner or later, anyway."

"You are right. It will show up sooner or later. You must tell her the truth. They found the bloody evidence at the scene. Do you remember that?" Amelie pointed out with careful deliberation.

"But I don't want to tell her the truth. I'm afraid to tell her everything. It would be like stripping me all over again in the public. I can't face the truth, never!"

"Oh, holy ghost, Charlotte. Calm down a bit and think it over. Maybe she can help you, try to be honest. I know it is extremely hard to do that but there is no other option. Think about it. Why in all the heavens did this happen to you? It could have happened to me. Perhaps I could have handled it in a better fashion."

"There is no better fashion to handle it, Amelie. It was and is the biggest embarrassment for me, and I can't help it!"

"Okay! Then what is the solution to this matter? Give me a clue, Charlotte." "There is no solution! I'm sorry, there is no solution."

"Oh heavenly Father, why did this happen to Charlotte, why couldn't he wait a year or two? We need your help. Tell us what we shall do with this matter. Please open our eyes. Let us find the right solution." Amelie prayed aloud but there was no answer.

They decided to leave but before Amelie opened the door, the voice spoke to them, **the truth.** Charlotte was surprised and paused for a moment, then quickly looked behind but there was no one standing there. Amelie said,

"Did you hear what I heard? The voice said; 'the truth.' I think God spoke to us. He heard our prayer. Now we have the answer. We shall go. I'm glad that finally we can make some sense of it."

The girls left. They rushed to their room a bit exhausted. At the door was a piece of paper written to Charlotte. It said, "Charlotte, please see me in my office." Sister Agnes. Charlotte almost passed out. Amelie held her shoulder and said,

"Okay, I'll go with you. Don't worry! At least we know the answer and this is really good. I'll handle the situation, just try to relax and don't stress yourself out! I know Sister can be unpleasant but I can take anything from her tonight. Let's go!"

"Wait! I don't feel like going. My knees are so weak. Give me a few minutes. How can I face her?"

"Be quiet! Let's go! Be brave Charlotte, Promise."

"I'll try! Oh, God! Help me, please," she cried.

They ran downstairs and paused near the office of Sister Agnes. The door was open. It seemed Sister was waiting for them. Amelie bravely walked in, pulling Charlotte behind her. Sister stood at the window looking out, like she was waiting for someone to arrive. Then she asked, still facing the window,

"I would like to hear your story, Charlotte. Tell me the truth my child. Maybe, I'll be able to help you." Charlotte was terrified but slowly confessed to Sister everything that had happened to her, detail for detail. Amelie held her hand to make her feel more secure. Sister continued to face the window and didn't show any emotions in front of the girls. When Charlotte finished, Sister said,

"Don't worry Charlotte. God will handle everything from now on. Let me think of what I can do. We'll help you. Our facility has an orphanage. We'll take care for it when the time is right. Now, come back to your everyday life and don't think of it. It is better that way. You're free to go. Goodnight!"

She didn't turn around, and the girls noticed that she was crying and gently wiping her tears with a napkin. It was shock for her to hear such an incredible story from a young girl; an obsession of a young priest who threw his habit for a young virgin girl. The desire which took the virginity of an innocent girl and left her with doubt scarred her for the rest of her life. That incident recalled the Sister's memory of her errors of her youth. She wasn't alone in her quest for an answer. She stood there for a long time and cried.

The girls left her alone and walked back to their room. Amelie interrupted the moment,

"You see, it wasn't so bad, but it seems like Sister took your case too personally. I told you, she would help you. She understood you more than you previously thought she would. Isn't it beautiful? You'll have peace of mind now."

"Thank you, Amelie for your support. I couldn't have gotten through it without you. I just want to sleep forever and never wake up."

"Life is too precious to do that. I prefer to enjoy life instead and you should do the same. I'll make us

415

tea and we shall relax. The worst part is over. Thank you God for your support."

Their evening was cut short and they went to bed tired. They thought, life is supposed to be simple but in fact it wasn't and it was only the beginning.

The glorious sun sneaked between the creases in the window's curtains and woke them up early. Amelie opened her eyes and sang her favorite French tunes. For Charlotte, the next page of her life drama was just turned. She was excited and thought of the letter she will get from Peter at noon. Amelie vigorously put her clothes on and the girls went for breakfast. Right after that, Amelie departed for work and Charlotte came back to her room to relax. She thought of writing her own memoirs. She managed to find an empty notebook and thought it would be perfect for writing her life experiences.

She began to write. The hours were passing by fast and she noticed it was time to go to work. She wrapped everything up and put the notebook in her secret drawer. She can't be late today. On her way, she stopped in the office to change her clothes. She went to pick up the laundry bags from the back of the North Tower. It was twelve noon. She stood next to the bags and glanced at the top high windows. Suddenly, the letter landed next to her feet. She picked it up gently and hid it in the small pocket under her t-shirt. She whistled her familiar tunes so that Peter would know she received the letter. She rushed back to the cleaner and entered the small room to sort out the habits. She checked the medium size but there was no additional message. She put all of them into the next room on the long table and left. She walked into the office, changed her clothes again and then finally left the facility. She rushed back to the boarding school. She wanted to be alone. In an hour, she'll meet Monk Emanuel and give him the letter from Peter. She was so excited when she opened her room. Finally, alone, she sat on her bed and secretly read the letter. Her heart almost leaped out of her chest.

'Dear Charlotte,

The moment of truth just came. Perhaps, I saw more than I should. I'm with Patrick on the same night shift. We guard the strange looking object, perhaps a key, the Cardinal mentioned in his story, for seven hours every single night. We switch the shifts with the two other monks on a weekly basis. I'll let you know soon when the time is right for our mission. So far I enjoy being here. I'm more than blessed. The secrets of the universe are unfolding in front of my eyes, day after day and week after week; I learn more each time. I wish you could be here with us.

However, I couldn't locate the book that Cardinal Benedict mentioned in his story. Perhaps, it doesn't exist! This is not a holy book he is looking for. I think it is a totally different thing which I'll tell you about, soon.

Once a week, only three of us, Patrick, Theodore and I, have a secret meeting with someone very special. You won't believe it if I tell you who is coming here. I hardly believe it myself! It is quite complicated. I don't really know where I should start my great story? The person is transparent in a new form of dense energy but you can see Him and you can talk to Him too. He is my new best friend. He can even drink water and other fluids. He laughs with us too. He can walk through the walls with ease.

He is God himself in the body of His Son, Jesus Christ. He has the same voice which had spoken to me when I was crucified for three days on the cross in the Saint Mark cave. He materialized himself into a high energy level, a sort of quantum level, and He could be visible. Probably, Benedict's friend, Chris would like to see that. Sooner or later the energy is dispersed into the air and He simply vanished. He showed us how this works too but I don't understand it. Perhaps, it is too complicated. He mentioned about a high level of the quantum energy and some kind of antimatter. But I'm not an expert on that stuff. However, it is amazing!

I fear I may shock you perhaps but this is the truth. This is a different world from the one I was living before. Once a week, He comes and greets us with a few good words and a nice friendly smile. He holds in His hands a holy object which we guard once a week, only on Wednesday. Other monks guard this object on different days. I never touch it.

It looks like a thick big book or rectangular disc-case with rounded edges. Inside the disc is a sort of dark matter suspended in the air or some kind of energy in a constant motion. He calls this book, QD or Quantum Disc. It doesn't have any pages in it. Then He puts a key, shaped like the letters Q and D which overlapped each other, on the top of the Quantum Disc.

Then He talks in an unknown language, like in the biblical times. We haven't studied that language yet. Then the miracle begins.

The covers of the disc-book open and spread apart vertically and horizontally, and then we can see so many different types of objects just hanging in the empty space, a little universe in every possible dimension, better than a real movie. The sizes of each object easily change from small to big ones and they are in constant motion, traveling in and out of the disc.

From time to time, the objects rotate around us and then come back into the disc. It looks like a micro world. I touched some of the objects. They are transparent too but have a density like pudding. I've never experienced anything like that before. I have a lot of fun. He told us that whatever we wish could materialize in front of us. Any question or desire is answered and granted.

He said that the secret of the **entire universe** is hidden within. It is a sort of *quantum memory* of the entire universe but how it works I don't know. All the missing links, we're looking for thousands of years, are stored inside of this amazing disc, you just name it. He showed us the creation of the entire universe, and it was more than we expected, it was stunning. Then I saw the creation of humans, and I wouldn't imagine anything like that. Patrick was also stunned.

He revealed to us the creation of the human's DNA, and I could touch with my finger a single gene which was magnified to the size of a small bean? It was soft and made of some kind of dense energy mass. I could see so many dimensions in it. I stuck my finger into the disk and it could read my DNA. I never saw real DNA with these many genes. It was amazing. I wondered how it really works.

Then we saw the live dinosaurs and how they died. We could walk between them. It was a bit scary. The lost civilizations stunned me the most.

Can you imagine that those people could fly to the Moon on a spacecraft we didn't build yet? We're talking about hundreds of thousands of years ago.

He showed us the future spaceship and how we can travel to the Moon and Mars or different universes within only a few days. I never thought that it could be possible. The shape of the spacecraft could be constructed in a simple but strange looking way, a sort of **tube in V** cut. But the most exciting of all was that He took us for a trip to another universe to a planet that looked like our Earth.

He told us that we have many universes and many planets like Earth. It wasn't in the ordinary way. He told us.

"It is not necessary to fly there but it would be an extraordinary if we could bring a new Earth to us." And He did. We actually could walk on the soil of a new Earth, touch the rocks, see their advanced architecture and talk to the people that looked like us. They spoke many different languages. Their civilization is very advanced. I saw many different cars perhaps running on some kind of extraordinary type of energy.

He told us that those people live in peace and harmony. They didn't experience any wars or disasters. They communicate in a better way than we do. They know the secrets of the universe from thousands of years. Who knows, perhaps they live forever. We asked Him why the people on Earth live so short and He told us His life story.

He said that we could live the same way if we could only grab the opportunity which was offered to us thousands of years ago. But we rejected that opportunity in the barbaric way. He told us that His Father sent him with a very peaceful mission to the Holy Land, Jerusalem, 2,000 years ago, in the body of a newborn baby human, little Jesus. When He grew up, God told him to reveal the secret of the entire universe to humanity and gave Jesus a **Letter**, *God's* **Will** *written with His own blood.*

But the people were busy with their own problems and didn't want to hear His story nor listen to His eternal promises. Then He gave the *Letter* to His trusted *Apostle Mark* and asked him to guard it with his life. He told the Apostle that the people are not ready to hear His truth and perhaps the *Letter* must wait a few thousand years more to be revealed one day. Indeed, the people were not ready for His revelation and rejected Him and His knowledge. He was very sad and disappointed when He told us that.

Those people valued their materialistic way of life more, the power of their own money to the point that they turned against Him. They were afraid that by accepting His truth they would lose their own power in their small and very obscure society.

They secretly plotted against Him and decided to get rid of Him for good. It was very painful when He talked about His past. He is a wonderful man. How anyone on this planet would ever be against a man like that. He trusted them almost to the end.

Thus His rejection was the cause of our misery for thousands of years. We could have lived in peace and harmony, with no wars, and with respect to each other. He said that we don't have to collect so much wealth either because we wouldn't be able to consume everything in our short life on Earth. Instead we could receive the secret of the universe and the knowledge which would enable us to travel to the other planets and to understand the real purpose of life. We could fully enjoy the life which was given to us for only short time. This secret is worth more than any money could ever buy. How sad it is that we lost this treasure, perhaps forever.

If I stay here, I will learn more and more. I remember how Cardinal Benedict was so excited about the universe. He should be here too, and join us. The scientists would go crazy when they see stuff like that. Tell the Cardinal that there must be one more element or another key to open this Quantum Disc. Jesus spoke in an ancient tongue to unlock the disk's memory, I think. Thus there must be something else to it.

He must look for that and fast. Otherwise, there will be no use for it. Or perhaps I shall ask Jesus to participate in our undercover mission. Maybe He already knows about it and wants this to happen just to give us a taste of this entire secret. Who knows? To continue my story, Jesus revealed to us special chemical elements which I don't know much about, but which are used to build a fuel for the advanced space-crafts, called antimatter. He actually pulled out of the disc the small version of the model of the real spacecraft and I could even touch and play with it, like with a real toy. He is more than **a genius**. He is the real **Creator** of this *entire universe*. I believe now that this world is real and made by the higher power. I'm lucky enough to see and experience all of that. He has the infinite power to create whatever He desires and in front of our eyes.

The most precious of it is that he likes to share his knowledge with us. Isn't it amazing? He is a real friend. Charlotte, everything is so interesting. I'd like to stay here forever. You would like to be here, too. I miss you! He told us that this Quantum Disc could be a very dangerous weapon if it gets into the wrong hands; this why we must protect it with our life. However, He mentioned that many people would be happy to see something they never imagined could even exist. It would take years to discover some of that stuff I have seen here so far.

I'll need your help. The mission will be complicated and the time will be of the essence. There must be extreme coordination between us. I can climb the walls and get from here to the ground level within five minutes. But you must be there or even meet me in half way to get the disk from me. It is large and heavy. Thus, it can be easily dropped and damaged.

The key is light and I can put it on my neck. I don't know if I should do this because the punishment for that could be death. He has trust in us though I feel a bit uncomfortable. Maybe I shall ask Him for permission. You know, in case something goes wrong, I would kill myself. Thus be sure you're fully ready for this mission. Also there is always the possibility that the security would interrupt our mission in the last minute, and then it would have to be called off. They patrol the tower once a day, at different times.

Patrick would help me. He is like a brother to me. We talk a lot about life and the future. Everything looks bright and promising. There is a lot of stuff we would learn and discover on our way to the future. I'll let you know when I'll be ready. You must write OK on my habit or whistle that favorite piece of music for me when you pick-up the laundry bags the day before the mission. Then I'll drop you an OK letter from my window before the action would take a place. I predict it would happen within a month and at the evening.

Charlotte, take care of yourself and say hi to the Cardinal Benedict and Monk Emanuel, as well as to Amelie. Love Peter. Best regards from Patrick and to all of you.'

Charlotte was excited. She glanced at the clock; it was time to meet Monk Emanuel. She hid the letter in the pocket and went out. She walked through the park and paused near the phone booth. He arrived within five minutes and she gave him the secret letter. He took the letter, hid it inside his cassock, then smiled and left quickly.

It was something to remember for the rest of that day and perhaps for both of them. Charlotte went for lunch happy. It seemed like everything was going her way. She had plenty of time and decided to go shopping or rather browsing on the cobble streets of Rome. She came home late. Amelie was already there, making good tea.

"Hello, there! Where have you been, Charlotte?"

"I walked all over downtown just to kill the time. I feel really good, now. All my doubts are gone, perhaps for good. I can start a new life now. Something has been unlocked in my mind as I was walking and thinking about my life. Can you imagine something like that? It happened fast. I'm really glad."

"Oh, Charlotte, this is great news. Finally you're back to the same Charlotte I knew weeks ago. It couldn't be better news for me.

Do you remember the cat who committed suicide, by accident of course, on the branches of a pine tree four years ago? It wasn't my fault but the Sisters blamed me for it anyway; of course later they laughed like crazy," Amelie said and laughed again. Charlotte laughed too.

"I remember it exactly and it seems just like yesterday. We laughed at that time all right but Sister Claudia and Agnes laughed even harder for another week. Perhaps we'll remember that for the rest of our life."

"Yes, Charlotte and it would be the best time of our life as well. Try my new tea, I call it, **Eternity.** It gives me more confidence about myself. Please, enjoy."

"Tea is very pleasant and I feel better, already. So how is your new boyfriend, George? You seem very quiet about him today."

"I just didn't have a chance to talk about him yet. George invited me for lunch around noon. We spent almost an hour in a small cafe located on the first floor, in the press building. I would say it was a romantic lunch. He looked into my eyes quite often and talked very politely about his life, his family and two brothers and about his hobby. I listen to him like to the best opera or a Broadway show. He was talking a lot and I enjoyed it. I learned more about him. He even told me that he had one girlfriend before, Juliet."

"He should not do that. It hurts when you hear about the other girl your boyfriend had before you. It is rather awful. I don't like it! He seems a selfish man."

"I never thought of that aspect, Charlotte. Perhaps you're right. I didn't want to hear about his past love stories. Why? Because I like him so much, it really hurts. He was my only concern. How can I fix that now? I should tell him not to talk anymore about his lost loves?"

"No! I wouldn't tell him that. I would rather wait and try to know him better. If he really cares for you, he will show his loyalty to you, sooner or later. Perhaps, he didn't mean to tell you that or just simply he's still too young, and doesn't know the proper etiquette. Just let it go this time but if he does it again, it means he is not serious about you. Perhaps he is looking for a new adventure for himself."

"Do you think at our age anyone is serious about what we do? I'm not sure myself."

"Perhaps, you're right. We're too young to be serious. He is only nineteen; it makes him too young to be serious, too."

"Then what do you propose?"

"Amelie, I don't know what to say. You should try to date him and wait to see what will come of it. People have dated like that for thousands of years. Maybe, it's the way to be. Just try to have fun and don't go for deep love. If he is in deep love with you, it would show right away. Perhaps, he will propose to you."

"Then what should I tell him?"

426

"You tell him to wait for you a bit longer. I know it would be hard but it would be a sort of rehearsal for both of you or you can call this an ordeal."

"How do you know all of that, Charlotte?"

"I just have an intuition or perhaps I read a lot of books. Amelie, I'd like to go to bed. I'm a bit tired and look what time it is."

"Oh, you're right. The clock just struck twelve. Let's go to bed and I'll tell you some stories, maybe about the King on a white horse who fell in love with a beautiful girl and chased after her for many years. Finally when he found her, he asked her to marry him."

"And what did she say?" Charlotte asked, wondering.

"She said, 'Yes!' Goodnight!"

"Goodnight, Amelie," Charlotte said as she closed her eyes, perhaps following the King's story in her dream.

The next morning after breakfast, Amelie rushed to her work and Charlotte went to *St. Mary Chapel, to* pray. She walked to the altar and glanced at the fresco of St. Mary and then at the fresh flowers perhaps delivered not too long ago. Then she noticed the gift card hidden between the red roses. She picked it and read,

'**Dear Charlotte**, I can't live without you. My unconditional love for you is killing me day after day and minute after minute. I must see you and soon! Charlotte, you're my Paradise of Love Forever.'

She put the card in her pocket and began to pray. Her eyes were filled with tears and she couldn't control it, the tears flowed like a river. She was about to leave but someone approached her and whispered to her ears,

"Charlotte you must come with us. Someone is waiting for you." She glanced at the two men standing next to her. Their faces were covered with transparent black masks. She said,

"How do you know my name? Why do you think I must go with you? I don't think so."

"We got an order to deliver you in one piece so don't try to fight us."

They grabbed her by the shoulders and walked her out of the Chapel. She glanced back at the fresco of St. Mary, whispering, help me. The gift card fell from her pocket onto the floor. A black limousine was waiting in front of the Chapel. They pushed her into the car and drove away.

The day went by fast. Amelie rushed from her work for dinner. She was hungry. She stopped in her room to change and to meet Charlotte but she wasn't there. Perhaps she went shopping again, Amelie thought. She ran to the dinning hall, picked a few pieces of fish, fries and some salad with strawberry cream, then sat at the corner table and enjoyed her meal. Within thirty minutes she returned to her room and thought of Charlotte.

Maybe she was in the Chapel, Amelie thought. She went to the Chapel but Charlotte wasn't there either. She was about to leave and noticed a gift card, lying on the floor. She picked it up and read it. Then she thought. Why was this card on the floor? Who dropped it? Maybe, Sister Agnes was here, but she already knew everything. It was likely Charlotte was in a hurry, Amelie thought.

428

She decided to go and talk to Sister Agnes. She knocked on her door. There was the welcome voice saying, "Come in!"

"Hi Sister I must talk to you."

"Sit down my child. What is happening now?"

"Charlotte disappeared! I went to the chapel, looking for her but she wasn't there. Instead I found this card on the floor. Did you go to the Chapel today, Sister?"

"No, I haven't been there yet. Show me the card. Oh, I see. It is from Bertrand again. Someone delivered a new set of flowers today. What could have happened?"

"Maybe, he kidnapped her! Oh, maybe she killed herself," Amelie cried.

"Amelie, stop that nonsense. We wait a few more hours. If she doesn't come we call the police."

"I'm just telling you that this is not Charlotte's way. If she was around, she would already come. I have a really bad feeling. We better call Bertrand and ask him if this is his doing! I'm sure he would know something. I remember what he wrote in his first gift card to Charlotte. He said that if she doesn't come to him that he is going to take her by force. I can show you this card. I believe it is still in our room somewhere. I'll go to look for it and in the meantime please call Bertrand and talk to him. It is more than important."

Amelie ran to her room in a panic. She felt like all the world was collapsing on her head at the same time. What if someone killed Charlotte, she thought, she would never forgive herself for that. She opened the door and searched through every drawer and bag.

Then she sat on the bed, tired. She whispered to herself,

"I know where the gift card is hidden. I remember, I read for Charlotte the content and I put it somewhere. Where the hell did I put it?" she shouted. Nervously she walked from corner to corner of the room, and suddenly she remembered that she dumped it in the trash bag. But where was the trash? Perhaps in the big trash can behind the building. Oh, God! What a day?" She ran outside and threw the big trash can on the ground. Then she remembered that the plastic bag was pink because they came back from the boutique that day. There it was. She grabbed the bag and tore it in half. Then she searched piece by piece and finally found it.

Immediately, she ran back to the Sister Agnes office with the last breath,

"I found it! It was in the trash can. Look! Right here! Bertrand said that he will take her by force one day! Today is that day!"

"Let me read it. You're right, my child. I called Bertrand and told him that Charlotte is missing. He said that he doesn't know anything about her disappearance and hung up the phone," Sister added with low tone in her voice. Sister Claudia was there too. Her face was pale and she was terrified.

"He's a liar!" Amelie screamed with tears in her eyes.

"Amelie, my child, calm down a bit. We'll try to solve this mystery. What shall we do?"

"Maybe, Monk Emanuel can help us. He can send some people out there," Amelie cried.

"I don't know about that but I can call him and

ask if he has some clue but I doubt he even knows what happened here, today. It will be a big scandal and could spread all over town. I don't even know the answer," Sister said embarrassed. She stood still for a moment and then picked the phone and called Emanuel. He said that he was on his way over. He showed up within five minutes.

"Hello. Now tell me what's happening here?"

"Charlotte vanished!" Sister said.

"It couldn't be. I saw her yesterday," he said.

"She disappeared today and we don't know what we should do?"Sister added. "This is very bad news! We must find her and fast," he cried.

"Bertrand likely kidnapped her!" Amelie nervously shouted.

"Why Bertrand, what does he have to do with her?" Emanuel asked.

"Oh, yes. He has a lot to do with her! Just read this gift card from him, addressed to Charlotte. She was the reason that he quit his job," Sister Agnes added and her face turned red. She was terrified again.

"Oh holy Andrew, this is a very serious issue right now and a bundle of embarrassment for all of us. We must keep this confidential as long as possible. I will take care for everything. I have some friends in Paris. They will help me to find her. Sister, do you have his address, phone numbers and other information? It would be very helpful. I must go now, and make some very important phone calls. I'll let you know what happens and very soon!" he said, trembling. Sister gave him all the important information and then he left. He was devastated. He

431

knew he must bring her back for the upcoming mission. Without her the mission would be impossible. He ran to his office and sat at the table, short of breath, pulling out all the phone numbers from his notebook. His hands were shaking. At first he called Cardinal Benedict. He was more than shocked, he was fully devastated. He was ready to fly to France, immediately. Benedict called his new friend, Jerome, and they decided to meet in his countryside estate, near Paris.

Emanuel took the first plane to Paris. He intended to meet Benedict there in a few hours. It was an emergency wake up call for everyone. Jerome called for the meeting.

Chapter 12. The Undercover Operation, Paris
Jerome Estate, July 24

Everyone arrived at the international airport in Paris that same evening. Jerome and Jacques were waiting for them. The limousine took them to Jerome's countryside estate. They didn't talk much, briefly exchanging basic information. Each of them knew exactly how dangerous this new mission would be for all of them. On top of that they were supposed to work undercover, no police or other government entities could or would be involved in this rescue operation.

Everyone sat in the conference room where most of the meetings were taken place. Only the highest ranking Knights attended the meeting. They were instructed to keep everything confidential. The security checked each member one by one. The door was closed and guarded by a special team of Knights.

Jerome stood up and described briefly a new situation everyone was facing up. It would be a dangerous operation; a recovery of the kidnapped victim. He opened a map and pointed out a few tactical moves to the Bertrand estate.

Jerome was a retired General of tactical operations in the French Navy for almost forty years. He was about to go into details of their action when suddenly he noticed a man sitting at the end of the conference room with his face covered by a hood. He interrupted and asked him,

"Sir, what do you think about my strategy? I forgot your name. Can you introduce yourself?" The man stood up and suddenly ran through the conference room straight to the half open window. He jumped out and landed on the pine tree, and then slid down to the garden and ran between bushes, trees, and finally jumped over the fence. He was fast. Someone shouted,

"Spider-Monk!" Security ran after him but he made his own doubles again, it was impossible to shoot him. Simply, he escaped and vanished outside the walls.

"It could only be the Monk Salvatore. How did he get here in the first place?" Benedict shouted.

"Gentlemen, we have an intruder! Call our special unit. We must catch him dead or alive!" Jerome said as he distributed a few guns. Then he added,

"This is a private property. How in all the heavens did he get in here? Bring me those security guards right away!"

The door opened and four security guys walked in. Jerome said, "Gentlemen, I'm paying you for your loyalty and I have bad news for you. You allowed an intruder into my secret meeting. Can you tell me how this happened? Why didn't you check his identity?"

"We checked! He showed us his chest with an engraved letter," one of them said.

"What letter did you see?" Jerome asked.

"I think it was the letter 'T.'"

"You think! Maybe it was the Omega letter. Perhaps they look alike and only to you! How long have you been working for me?"

"Two years, Sir."

"Not good enough! Be sure to look for a new job, all of you," Jerome said furiously and dismissed them quickly. Then he added,

"We're in a trouble. I mean serious trouble. This kind of error is not allowed in our organization. We're not in kindergarten! We're running a serious business here. This is about life or death. I don't believe that this man was sitting there unnoticed by any of you, Gentlemen. You know each other better than perhaps anybody else in this entire universe. Tell me then how this happened?" Jerome paused for a moment as his face turned red, ready to explode. Then he added with a fully controlled voice,

"We have been together in this organization for more than fifty years, and it seems to me that our watchfulness can easily slip. Under these circumstances, I can't talk business to you anymore. The next time you must see who is sitting next to you.

Benedict, I'd like to talk to you."

"We better go to the private room. Monk Emanuel must go with us," Benedict said.

"Oh, yes, we have been already introduced to each other. Gentlemen, please follow me. Jacques, please watch the door for us, would you? Can you imagine that? I can't trust my own people. They have been blind lately. What the hell were they thinking of? So tell me, where is this priest, Bertrand, exactly?"

"He lives in a French Chateau in South of France. I would say rather more a luxury area, than for an average citizen. This is his address," Monk Emanuel announced.

"How did he amass his wealth?" Jerome asked.

"I already checked on this. His father was a successful real estate mogul. He died two years ago in a private, two engine plane crash. He had a huge funeral ceremony, for five hundred people almost like a wedding. It left Bertrand the only child.

At first he appeared to be quite a friendly and normal monk. Then the unfortunate moment came when he met Charlotte in his French class, and slowly but intensely fell in love with her. She didn't know anything about his affection until four years later. He built up all this fantasy about the girl. After the graduation party, he simply pulled her into his office, and then seduced her. Soon after, he threw his habit onto the floor, and left the Academy for good.

I have some gift cards he has been sending her lately with the flowers arrangements. You can read it for yourself," Emanuel said in a calm voice.

"I see, and how old is she?" Jerome asked as

435

he read the gift cards.

"She is sixteen. It is more than serious! We have a problem here! How can we possibly bring her alive out of this ordeal? We must think hard before we make a mistake," Emanuel added.

"There would be no other way we can accomplish the future mission without her. She is very well trained and she is the only contact within the Vatican Headquarters, the Templars' division. Simply, Charlotte can't be substituted. We don't have another alternative right here, period," Benedict pointed out with a bit of sadness in his voice.

"I see your point. It is very sad indeed. We have our tactical team of the **Green Panthers** in our organization. However, they're killers and we must make a decision who may stay alive and who must die. I would need Charlotte's pictures and Bertrand's as well. Do you think we must kill him?" Jerome asked.

"I want to have Charlotte in one piece. I don't want to kill Bertrand unless it is necessary. I only care for Charlotte. He is just in love with her, and he doesn't have any idea who she is. I just want to bring her back; this is what I'm expecting," Benedict said precisely.

"Okay! Let's call those **Green Panthers** for a meeting. If you wouldn't mind, please, give me all the documents including Charlotte's pictures. At first, I must send a team of highly trained engineers out there to install very powerful satellite devices such as miniature speakers and cameras so we can hear them, possibly see them, too. What if she isn't there? Do you think there could be another possibility? For example she could run away, or perhaps she went for vacation," Jerome asked.

"Then we'll face an even bigger problem than this. It is ninety percent likely that she is out there at this moment. But I could be wrong, too. You never can be one hundred percent sure," Benedict added confidently. Meantime, Jerome called his high-tech engineers and asked them to come as soon as possible.

The engineers showed up within thirty minutes.

"Gentlemen, thank you for coming. This is a very sensitive matter and it shall be done without any further errors. I believe in your professional ability, I call it, *'do it right.'* You have an hour to collect needed equipment, devices, data and maps. Here is your destination! Please, be sure to call me when your job is done," Jerome said and handed them the address. They opened their high-tech computers and entered the address. The local maps appeared on the screen which showed the satellite view of Bertrand's estate, including the swimming pool and the walls surrounded it. The other maps showed more details such as the height and thickness of the wall, the type of gates, and the security systems. They showed at least ten different cameras, installed on every possible corner of his estate.

"The engineers must disable the old security system in order to install their own devices. Sure, it wouldn't be an easy task but they are the best in this field." Jerome glanced at them and asked,

"What is your estimated time for this operation?"

"We will be able to disable the system within

one to three minutes max and install at least five high-tech cameras within a minute or two. We must take at least six men on the job including the security. The surrounding area has enough green cover to make us almost invisible, at least for ten minutes. By that time our work shall be done."

"I like your attitude, Gentlemen. Do what it takes! Good luck! You're free to go. Meet me here in two hours and we can move on from there," Jerome said with self-accomplishment.

"I like their attitude as well," Benedict said.

"You haven't yet seen what my **Green Panthers** can really do. Just wait here for few more hours and you'll see for yourself. I picked only the best experts in that field. However, they're quite expensive but they worth every penny. I must admit, sometime I make mistake, too, like today, those security guys. I always checked the references but on occasion I don't, and for those security fellows I didn't. I just trusted them. But I must admit that Salvatore got the guts to come here without any invitation. I wonder how he found us here, at my home. Perhaps he followed one of us. He could be a very dangerous fellow, and could blow up any and every of our future plans. We must be very careful from now on," Jerome added with a bit of reserve.

"Sure, I trust you. I believe, with your experience, we'll succeed. I became so nervous when I found out that Charlotte was kidnapped. My heart almost stopped pumping blood for a few minutes. It was devastating news," Benedict confessed nervously.

"Sure, I believe you. I'd piss out myself! But

now everything is under control. Have some drink with me, Benedict, and perhaps your friend, Emanuel would like to join us. You should try to relax for these few days. Take your friend to Paris and show him around. I'll work during the day but at evening, I'll keep you company." Jerome replied.

"Sure, I wouldn't mind," Emanuel said with acceptance as they sat at the bar for a few cocktails.

"I want both of you to stay in my estate for at least a week. Perhaps we'll bring Charlotte back, soon. Hopefully, everything will end up well. Let's have a toast to our success, Gentlemen!"

"To our success," Benedict replied and Emanuel raised his glass with them. They relished the long afternoon together, laughing occasionally. There was much to talk about, and they tried to wash away their worries at the same time.

The hours went by fast. As the evening approached, they gathered for dinner. Jerome received a phone-call from the high-tech engineers. They were coming back soon. They would join the rest of them for dinner. It seemed everything went well. Jerome was happy and made a quick phone-call to the **Green Panthers.** He asked them to come over for the meeting. Time was of the essence, he always thought. "I have good news for you, Gentlemen. The engineers successfully installed all of the essential devices on the Bertrand's property. Jacques, I think they just arrived. Would you be so kind and bring them right here. Otherwise, they could get lost. They haven't been in this part of my estate yet."

"Sure, I wouldn't mind! Please, wait for me," Jacques replied and left.

"Hello everyone," the engineers said as they sat at the table.

"It is nice to see all of you in a one piece. Gentlemen, I would like to congratulate you on your assignment. Perhaps it wasn't an easy one."

"Everything went according to our plan. However, there were a few obstacles with their security system. After we disabled one, we found out that there was another one, perhaps the emergency one. But we were able to put it down completely within a few minutes. After dinner we'll show you how it works. The estate is quite big and they have a few security guards constantly walking in and out," one of them said.

"Gentlemen, please enjoy your dinner for now. We'll talk business in about thirty minutes. The **Green Panthers** are coming. Thus we'll have plenty of time to discuss every single detail," Jerome said with a smile.

"Jerome, you have an excellent cook here. This wild duck with pate is heaven on my palate," one of the engineers said.

"Sure, I'm lucky to have him. I love this duck, too. But you should come when the deer hunting season begins. Nothing is more tender and wild that this beast, indeed," Jerome replied, laughing.

"If you insist, I'll come," he said.

"I think all of you are invited in September. There will always be another reason to celebrate," he said, smiling.

A variety of drinks were served and everyone seemed to enjoy themselves. They exchanged a few hunting jokes as the doorkeeper announced that the *Green*

Panthers arrived. Jerome excused himself and went to meet them. He added briefly,

"I'll meet you in a conference room in a few minutes. Please, come as soon as possible, and take your drinks with you." Jerome and Jacques went to greet the Panthers. It was quite a surprise to see all of them at the same time. Jerome knew at that moment that he could count on them.

"Good evening everyone! Please, follow me to the conference room. Please, sit down and feel comfortable. The engineers are coming in a moment. Please, do have something to drink." The drinks were served by bartenders. Within five minutes the engineers showed up. Benedict and Emanuel kept them company. Everyone sat and the engineers opened their camera to show their results. One of them spoke, the others set up the computers and each picture was projected on a big flat screen with further explanation. Jerome interrupted for a moment,

"I'd like to tell you that there is no ransom to be paid. It shall be only a simply recovery of the victim without the strings attached. Her name is Charlotte and we'll show you her picture in a moment. Please, continue." One of the engineers explained the satellite position of each micro-camera and the individual microphones.

"We installed five cameras and the same amount of microphones at the following locations. The first one is at the window of a private bedroom where Bertrand and his victim would likely spend some time. The second one is at the window of the dining room. There are two cameras on each side of the entry gates, front and back. The last one is positioned on the roof which oversees the balcony of the living room.

Our proposed entry is the balcony which is close to the north side of the wall, approximately five feet away in distance, easy access. Let's play the first camera. As you see no one is in the bedroom at this moment. Now we're in the living room and we can see two people standing near the window. Let's bring them closer. They don't talk. Okay, the first one is a man, approximately six feet tall, slender, dark hair, less than thirty years old. It could be Bertrand and the second one is a woman, rather a girl. It is likely Charlotte. We can magnify her picture a bit, there she is. This is Charlotte; five and half feet, slender, no hair, bald. She is sixteen. Let's move to the kitchen area, there is nobody at this time. Now we're checking the gates. There are two security guards at each gate, walking back and forth. They will be eliminated if necessary. Now roof position, one guard is standing on the balcony looking over the gardens. So far none of them carry guns. It is unusual but perhaps good news. Thus this operation could be a peaceful one, I believe. However, they could carry shoulder guns. We can replay each position again. Also, we can change the angle and rotate each camera about 360 degrees, in case of the multiple tasks.

Each camera could be activated by voice from any distance. Any comments, Gentlemen please, feel free to ask."

"How much time do we need to recover the victim?" someone asked.

"It depends on her actual position and the security measures. Without the security, no more than ten minutes. With the security and guns, it could be an hour or more."

"Is there any possibility of a potential hostage situation?" someone asked.

"Yes, and it could complicate our operation. We want Charlotte alive."

"What about this guy, Bertrand!" someone shouted.

"We don't want to kill the priest, only if it is necessary."

"Is there any chance that the operation could possibly fail?"

"Yes, and it would be the worst scenario. They could relocate themselves to the basement or out of the estate. We must be sure that they're in. It must be a surprise for them. Tonight, we shall observe the pattern of their behavior such as where he spends most of his time. We'll strike when Charlotte is likely to be alone, if possible. Okay, Gentlemen let's get to work!" one of the engineers said.

"It looks very promising, indeed. With this advanced equipment we can do almost everything," Jerome said contently.

"Oh, yes. It is an amazing technology," Benedict confirmed and Emanuel fully agreed with him.

"Then what do you think about this operation?" Jerome asked one of the Panthers.

"I think we'll be ready for tomorrow night," he replied. The Panthers gathered to discuss the details of their action.

"This is good news! Benedict, where should she be brought, afterward?" Jerome asked.

"Perhaps here. I believe it would be the safest place for her. We stay here for a week and later she and Emanuel will travel back to Rome."

"Do you think it would be safe for her in Rome?" Jerome asked.

"She must be back to continue her summer work. This is the only way of communication with her brother at the Templars' Tower. We lose her then we lose the mission," Benedict added.

"I see! It is really very serious! It would be really sad if that ever happened. We don't want that!" Jerome said with great consideration.

"I deeply believe that the **Green Panthers** will bring her back within a day or two. I'm already nervous, what if we lose her," Benedict said.

"Think positive and everything will be okay. I hope Monk Salvatore is not going to be there. I must talk to those guys again and tell them to be on alert for any strangers. Let's talk to them now," Jerome said.

"This is a good thought. This guy could be anywhere," Benedict confirmed.

"Gentlemen, I need to interrupt your meeting for a few moments. I must tell you something that is on the top of my head. Last night, we had an intruder here who tried to get into our secret meeting. These meetings are only for the members of our secret society. We don't want him here. He is a very dangerous man, indeed. We captured him on our camera system. Henry, can you bring me the security tape from our yesterday evening meeting, please?" Jerome asked one of his engineers.

"Sure I'll do that in a second." He brought back

the tape, and then projected it onto the screen.

"Okay, everyone, please look at this guy sneaking through the open door. I would say rather legally, showing some fake tattoo on his chest, and then sneaking into this room without any consideration. His face is covered with a hood. He has guts. When I asked him for his name, he leapt through the open window, jumped onto a nearby tree and slid to the ground, only to vanish around the corner. I want you to look at each other very well, and try to memorize your own faces. If this guy comes between you, he will ruin your secret mission tomorrow. Just watch out for him," Jerome said, quite concerned.

"Tomorrow, they will be fully covered with camouflage uniforms from head to toe and it will be even easier for him to hide amongst us." Jerome asked Henry to scan with his camera if anybody was sneaking around his property as they were talking. Henry navigated all the cameras in every possible direction, around the entire estate to be sure there was no intruders. Then he said, "Jerome, it's clear!" "Thank you, Henry. I want to be sure that we're alone. Let me check if the Panthers guys already went through the details of their operation. I'll be back in a minute." In the other room, Jerome asked the Panthers,

"Gentlemen, how are you doing so far? Please, let me know when you will be done."

"Now, we're watching Bertrand and Charlotte. They just went to his bedroom. I wouldn't say that it was her wish but he forced her a bit to his bed," one of the Panthers said.

"May I watch this with you? What is really happening out there?" Jerome asked. "I don't think that we should! He confessed his unconditional love to her. You can hear him for a minute only. You see, this priest is obsessed with her. But she is still too young for him. He could face criminal charges but this is not our jurisdiction. Let's leave them alone for the best part. Our part is her recovery only and now would be the best time for that. It is exactly 10:45 p.m. I think we actually finished our search. We learned more than we wanted to. Now, we're ready to strike. Jerome, see you tomorrow perhaps around midnight or soon after. Earlier is always better."

"Thank you! Gentlemen, see you tomorrow at any time! Sure, I'll wait for you," Jerome said.

"Benedict, did you know about Charlotte and the priest's love affair?"

"I just discovered it now with you. It wasn't on my mind at all. How can he do that? She is still a kid."

"How old is he?" "I heard he is twenty three."

"How did he become a priest with this kind of attitude?" Jerome asked with a smile.

"I don't have a clue. Perhaps, he got lost."

"I don't believe this is actually happening. Let's have some drink. I know it is getting late and we shall take some rest. Where is Emanuel?" Jerome asked.

"He was very exhausted, and went to bed early. I'm tired myself. Too many things happened in this long day. It seemed like an eternity for me. However, I can have a few drinks with you. Perhaps it will help me sleep well."

"You're right! It helps, indeed!" Jerome agreed.

"Then how is your job lately, Jerome? Are you

busy?"

"Indeed, I am. I would say it is a blessing for me because I love to work. I do a few different things for military headquarters and I'm happy with that so far."

"Sure, whatever you do is great I believe. It is a wonderful thing to have a true goal in life."

"I agree with you one hundred percent. Some of those works I do just for fun but it gives me satisfaction. How do you like my drink? I try to be my own bartender from time to time."

"I would say it looks and tastes rather professional. You can be proud of yourself, Jerome."

"I'm glad you like it. I would like to keep you company but perhaps you're very tired and don't share fully my idea of staying another hour."

"I enjoy your company but indeed, I feel like a dead horse at this moment. But thank you for the entertainment and see you tomorrow. Goodnight!"

"Goodnight Benedict."

The morning brought an invigorated power to everyone and especially to Benedict and Jerome. Perhaps last night' drinks boosted them with a cosmic sort of energy. Jerome ran to the living room, greeting everyone, "Gentlemen, did you sleep well? Breakfast is waiting for us, shall we go?"

"Thank you for asking. It was a peaceful night. The aroma of fresh flowers woke me up," Benedict said content.

"Oh, yes, it was very quiet night. I haven't slept like that for long time. You've got a little paradise for yourself, here, Jerome. I'm really thrilled," Emanuel added, smiling.

"I know, perhaps you're right. This is why I'm so happy right here. We can have breakfast in the garden since you like the nature and fresh air. I'll tell my chef to serve us out there. You can go there and sit under the chestnut trees. I'll join you in a few minutes."

"We can do that! The nature could add a bit of splendor to it," Benedict replied as he walked to the garden and sat at the table. Emanuel followed him. The aroma of wild flowers was so invigorating; it brought happy memories back to each of them. They closed their eyes and relaxed.

"What do you think will happen tonight?" Benedict asked.

"I don't really know. I only hope that those Panthers bring Charlotte back, unharmed. But anything could happen out there. We don't really know this priest Bertrand. He is young and could be unpredictable, too," Emanuel said.

"Let's pray for the best," Benedict said as he closed his eyes for a moment.

Jerome walked in and interrupted, "Okay! Breakfast is on its way. It is really very pleasant under the blue sky. I received a phone-call from the **Green Panthers** and they've already positioned themselves near Bertrand's estate, monitoring his every movement. They said there is the possibility that they could strike earlier if the opportunity arises. They will update us every two hours. I think it is good enough for now. The chef is coming, let's enjoy our meal. I'm very hungry."

The aroma of fresh baked bread, sweet butter, and fried shrimps in garlic-dill sauce made them even hungrier. It was pure enjoyment and a conversation followed after. Soon Jerome asked, "Gentlemen, I know you're a bit stressed but what do you think about playing tennis with me for an hour or two? I really need the exercise. We can have some coffee at the court facility and perhaps some other drinks too."

"This is a great idea; it actually helps us to relax. I didn't play tennis for quite a long time. That is what the priesthood does!" Emanuel added with a smile.

"Sure, I wouldn't mind either. It could be fun for me," Benedict said, excited. "Okay! Then let's go. I have some polo shirts for you. Please, feel free to change. I'll wait for you. Meantime, I'll bring us some coffee."

They played hard for almost two hours. Soon after the game they went to sauna and Jacuzzi where they leisured their time with fantasy, conversation and laugh. It was early afternoon when his cell phone rang. Jerome picked it up. He received great news and was excited.

"You're the best guys I ever had. Congratulation! See you in a few hours," he spoke briefly.

"They got Charlotte!" Benedict shouted still excited.

"They did. They're coming back. Bertrand wasn't home when they captured Charlotte. She was locked in his bedroom. They went through the window. She tried to escape on her own after she fought Bertrand with her karate kicks but his five security guards disabled her. However, she is okay! They're driving her here as we speak."

"She is a very brave woman," Monk Emanuel said however, with deep concern. "She's still a kid," Benedict added.

"Sure she is!" he sadly confirmed.

"What if Bertrand runs after her again?" Jerome asked.

"It is possible and perhaps he will do that. We must watch Charlotte for the next few weeks. Emanuel will set the undercover security measure in the Vatican. We put some people on her 24/7." Benedict pointed out.

"This is a very good idea. This priest, Bertrand makes me nervous," Jerome said, smiling.

"I'm not worried about him much. My real concern is Monk Salvatore. He'll strike us in the most unexpected moment and it is difficult to predict when this really could happen. He is a monster! He could destroy our mission," Benedict pointed out with serious worries.

"I'll back you up with the **Green Panthers** in Rome. Just let me know when you need me?" Jerome said.

"It could happen within a few weeks. I hope Charlotte's mental state didn't undergo any transformation. I worry about her," Emanuel expressed his concern.

"Perhaps, we must give her some comfort after this unpleasant ordeal. Let's make a surprise party for her return. I'll bring some jazz musicians, she could relax. The dinner will be just for her. I'll ask my Chef to make something really special for her. He knows how to make those crabs, shrimps and other seafood in an outstanding manner. What do you think?"

Jerome suggested.

"A brilliant idea Jerome, I want her to feel like at home. She lost parents when she was twelve and she must be devastated right now, and giving her support would be a very wise move," Benedict said confidently.

"Okay, let's finish this Jacuzzi for now, and I shall make a few phone calls. You can stay more, if you like it," Jerome said, smiling. He put his robe on and left. He made a few calls and finally got dressed. Chef Pepe received instructions what kind of dinner he shall prepare for everyone and for Charlotte he will do something special.

Soon Benedict and Emanuel offered Jerome a hand. Benedict told him that he could play the piano, the best pieces of classical music before the jazz band arrives. Emanuel mentioned that he could play saxophone if Jerome would find one for him. Jerome replied, being surprised,

"You're very lucky fellow, Emanuel. How did you know that I have a saxophone?"

"I didn't know. I just have an intuition that perhaps you played some instrument in your youth," Emanuel replied, looking into Jerome eyes.

"You got great intuition, Emanuel! Indeed, I have one, and I played in a jazz band when I was twenty. I can still play, but definitely, if you're a saxophone virtuoso, you must entertain all of us tonight," he added, laughing.

"I'll try my best," Emanuel confirmed.

"Okay, then follow me to my music room. All my past youth, I keep in this special room. Actually, I had a few different saxophones, perhaps you want to

451

choose the best one for yourself."

"Sure, this is even better. Not all of them sound the same way. Let me blow a few. They look brand-new. You didn't use them much. Did you? If you see mine you would be surprised. It aged with me."

"You're right. I played maybe several times and lost interest later on. But I can show you, I still can play well but perhaps not like you. Let me try! It has been a long time indeed," Jerome pointed out as he picked one of his saxophones and then began to play beautifully a soft jazz.

"Not bad Jerome. I think we could play in a duet tonight. Perhaps it would be more fun. What do you think?"

"I think, we should, Emanuel. I feel that within an hour they will arrive so we have some time to practice. Maybe we'll try this piece. I'll play the beginning for you and you just follow me."

"Sure! I can do that. I'm ready," Emanuel said, excited. They played beautifully together and were ready to perform in front of their friends that evening. They laughed and rushed to the ballroom where the tables were set already to dinner. Benedict accompanied them on the piano and they made quite the team. The servers were putting red linens and wild flowers on each table. Fifty people including the band would arrive soon. The most important is Charlotte. She must feel welcome here in this huge French Chateau and maybe she can forget about her ordeal at least for the time being.

Everyone was working hard on this newly arrangement. A doorman came to announce that the Green Panthers had just arrived. The boys without saying too much set their instruments ready to entertain. They began with a soft music. It brought a great deal of optimism to everyone. Charlotte stepped into the ballroom with a big smile on her face and she was really very surprised. She was seated at the front table just next to the band. She laughed when she recognized Benedict playing the piano and Emanuel blowing the saxophone. They played a few pieces and decided to take a break. They approached Charlotte and Benedict asked with a smile,

"How did you like our performance, Charlotte?"

"It was fantastic. I love it," she said confidently.

"May we join you for dinner? My name is Jerome."

"I'm Charlotte and you perhaps already heard of me."

"It is my pleasure. Please, welcome to my castle. I hope you'll like it here."

"Certainly, I already do and especially with this kind of special welcome. Thank you! You made my day," she confirmed with laugh.

"And this is only the beginning. We have another surprise for you, Charlotte," Jerome said as a new jazz band walked in and began to play soft jazz which could melt anyone's heart. Charlotte was stunned by their professional sound. In the next few minutes the servers ran to every table with a different dish filled with exotic food. Suddenly, Chef Pepe came to Charlotte's table and personally served al-carte, his own fantastic creation of crabs, shrimps and other seafood accompanied by an exotic fire. Everything looked crispy and delicious. It was decorated with green salad.

"Charlotte, this is my Chef, Pepe. He has created something amazing especially for you," Jerome said, smiling. She complimented him with a few words,

"Pepe, it is a real fantasy and you made my entire day. It couldn't be a better one. I will remember that and I thank you so much." she smiled and glowed with happiness, indeed. She glanced at Jerome and said,

"You're a nice man and I thank you for your hospitality."

"You're very welcome and don't forget! You deserve every bit of that."

She felt like Heaven was on Earth for a moment. Everyone enjoyed this exquisite dinner with the special musical ambiance. Jerome thought of giving Charlotte something special that she would remember for the rest of her life. He remembered that his mother left him this beautiful ring with blue sapphire framed with diamonds. It would be a perfect gift for the sixteen years old girl and perhaps it would make her happy. He must find where he put it. He whispered something to Benedict's ear, and then excused himself for a few minutes.

He ran to his mother's bedroom upstairs which was locked for almost twenty years since she was gone. He looked in every drawer and finally spotted in the closet a treasure box. He put the ring there, exactly twenty years ago. He sat on the bed and recalled his past memories. The time went by fast, he thought. He took the ring, put it in a small gift box and returned to the ballroom.

The music was still on and everyone was about

to finish dinner. The waiters brought coffee and different cakes for everyone. He smiled and asked, "How was your dinner? Perhaps you would like a cup of coffee. Charlotte, I have a special gift for you from all of us. I want you to remember today and perhaps visit me one day whenever you pass by Paris. Please, let me know if you like it," he gave her a small gift box. She was surprised again and slowly opened it. Her eyes rounded even more and she was almost speechless,

"Jerome, I love it! It is extremely beautiful and looks like it is a real treasure trove too. Thank you so much to all of you. I never had any treasure like this before." She put the ring on her finger and her eyes sparked.

"You're very welcome. We thought you'd like it. It is a blue natural sapphire. It is a girl's ring and it should belong to a beautiful girl like you. Let's enjoy some cake for now. Pepe is an expert on cakes," Jerome proudly announced.

The tray full of miniature cakes was served next to each table.

"The choice is yours, Charlotte. I would suggest the fruit cake on the tiramisu base which is my favorite one. You'll like it. Just try! It is a piece of art," Jerome suggested, laughing a bit.

"Okay, I trust you! I can have one. You're definitely a cake connoisseur, Jerome. Oh yes, it is heavenly good." Benedict and Emanuel tried the same cake and were delighted, too. They glanced at Jerome face and smiled. He couldn't make a better welcome for Charlotte, they thought. Jerome glanced at them and smiled back. Within ten minutes,

Jerome's phone rang. He picked it up, and then walked away from the table. Then he whispered something to Benedict's ear and both of them went out off the ballroom.

"Benedict, we have some kind of crazy situation. The security guard, Henry, is telling me that we have some kind of intruders sneaking inside of our estate, many of them. He doesn't have a clue who those people are. I suspect they are those Spider Monks from the Vatican. You remember they were here before. Now, they are back again ready to strike. We don't want any problem right here. The **Holy Letter,** they're looking for, is not here. They must walk out empty handed.

The second option is that Bertrand followed Charlotte all the way, and maybe he wants her back. Whatever it is, it's dangerous right here and we must hide Charlotte some place. I feel the blood could be shed soon. Bring them up here; they must get into my limousine. It is waiting outside. I called the driver and he will take them to the airport and catch the first flight to Rome. I think it would be safer there. As you mentioned, Emanuel can hire body guards for Charlotte. It is the best solution so far. I really didn't expect anything like this. I don't know who those people are. Just watch, the Panthers are already on the move. I'll wait for you right here! Can you imagine that I don't have any privacy in my own house? You go fast and bring Charlotte and Emanuel."

"Okay! I'll be back in a few seconds," Benedict replied and left quickly.

"Emanuel, Charlotte, I like you to follow me, quickly. We have some intruders here. Jerome said

456

the limousine is waiting for you outside. You'll drive to the airport and take the first plane to Rome. Emanuel, you know what to do next. We have some invaders here and we don't know how many or who they are. Let's go!" he whispered.

"Jerome, we're back."

"Just follow me. I must be sure that everything is by the book. Put this black coat over you and sneak into the car. I'm really sorry about this stuff. I will miss you Charlotte. I don't have a clue what is happening right now. Trust me we will be in touch very soon. Jacques, you're taking them straight to the airport. If anyone follows you, I like you to come back. Be careful out there and be sure they're okay. I'll see you in half an hour," Jerome said and walked back. 'It could be dangerous to stand outside,' he thought.

"Those Spider Monks could be hiding anywhere and no one can ever notice them. Benedict, stay as close as you can to me. One of us could be taken as a hostage by one of those monks. Let's move to the ballroom. I must dismiss the band.

Gentlemen, thank you for your entertainment and I'll pay you for the rest of the evening. We have some changes in our plans. Thus, it would be wise if you can leave now. Thank you again and I'll call you when I need you."

As soon as the band left, Jerome sighed with relief. He communicated with the Panthers through his special phone system. They already spread themselves throughout the estate. The hunting game had just begun between the Spider- Monks and the Panthers and it could last forever.

"Benedict, do you know how to fight? I have a

457

gun and a few swords. This one is for you in case. Those individuals are very skilled creatures, I would say. They can kill you in a split of a second, and you wouldn't even think that you're already dead. Here is your gun. Take it and be ready. I don't want to lose you. I will feel guilty for the rest of my life."

"Sure, I can use both of them very well. So don't worry. What about you?"

"I'm an old champion of the old school. I'll be fine. But let's stick to each other as you never can be sure what would come next. How can I find out who those people are? Okay, I'm getting some call again. Yes, you captured one. This is good. Hopefully, he is alive. No, he is already dead. Not good! We would never find out who sent them. How did he die? He must have poisoned himself. Can you glance at his chest? Do you see any branded initials? Okay! Yes the letter Omega over X. I knew it! They are the Vatican guys for sure. But why are they here? If we could capture one monk alive then we would find out. I don't know what to say, Benedict. It is a suspicious situation. Henry said that they have such a great camouflage that no one can see them. Just be careful, look around you if any object is moving. They could stand next to you and you wouldn't even notice them. Hard to believe! They're dangerous like Monk Salvatore. I don't know what we're going to do. Looks like the Panthers will stay here for awhile."

"Perhaps, they found out about our mission, but how." Benedict wondered.

"I think the reason is Charlotte. Perhaps I'm wrong. But she vanished from the boarding school. The monks followed her to Bertrand's estate only to find out that she was kidnapped again by some new guys. Then they followed her here to find out again that she vanished. Then what will happen next? Perhaps they went to Rome to look for her, and there would be another question, why? Do you see my point?"

"I see your point. But let's hope she wasn't the real reason. This is only our speculation. However, I thought for a moment that perhaps Bertrand works for them. But now I concluded that they came after **the Holy Letter**. The Vatican gave them the order to recover the item under any circumstances. They don't have a clue where it is hidden. They think, maybe it is right here."

"No one knows where I put the letter. I wrote about it in my will and put it in the safe. When I die it will be revealed. But I thought, perhaps you should know, in case something happens to me. Or maybe those guys came after me. Who knows? I'm just thinking about their strategies. What do you think, Benedict?"

"I think anything is possible. For centuries they tried to outsmart others with more or less luck. Thus your suggestion could be right. But it is still a speculation, anyway. You should check with your Panthers."

"Come here, I like to show you how this system works. You see the flashing light on my cell phone. If you see two flashing lights, it means that they have a message for me. Then I press the green button and I can hear them. If I want to talk to them, I press the red button. It is simple. But they don't have any message for me at this time. I'm tired of being on constant alert.

Let's have some coffee. Maybe, my Chef, Pepe can make us cappuccinos."

"Okay, it's a good idea. I'm nervous myself. I almost forgot to ask you how Chris and Etienne's quantum computer business is doing."

"Great progress and they've already made a lot of money. The scientists and some corporations are buying that stuff like hot-dogs. I couldn't believe it but the system is very sophisticated, indeed. He is a genius. I'm telling you. Even some military company gave him very lucrative offers twice but I'm not sure if he took it. However, he is a typical scientist, never has any time to entertain. The worst thing is that they work at night and sleep during the day and it is difficult or rather impossible to communicate with them. But we can arrange a meeting around midnight. For them it is the beginning of their day."

"I'm glad that Chris is okay. I spoke with him a few times and he was always busy, indeed. I was planning to come over and stay for sometime but I was busy chasing my past or perhaps my future. Then I went to visit my friend, Hans, in Munich and we talked a lot about our mission. He will back me up in Rome, in case anything goes wrong."

"Benedict, you must trust those friends of yours. I hope they won't disappoint you in the end. I'll back you up, too. I know that you need my help. Besides, I want to see that miracle myself. Perhaps I sacrificed all my life to protect the God's Letter then at least at the end of my life I'd like to know why?" Jerome confessed with a smile.

"Sure, you have the right to know, why you did it. I have a letter from Charlotte's brother, Peter. As I mentioned to you, he is the key to the mission. I'd like you to read it. Perhaps, you'll really enjoy it," Benedict said.

"Sure I would love to read it. But wait for a second, my cell phone lights are on. I must take this message. Hello! The operation is called off. Why? The Spider Monks left the promises. This is good news. Where did they go? I see. I want you to stay alert all night. Tomorrow, we'll decide what we will do next. Thank you, guys. Okay! Benedict, we can talk now. Let's make some really good coffee. I'm so stressed out. Do you imagine? I don't have a peace of mind in my own house. It is terrible, isn't it?"

"Sure, it is! Let's sit and have a drink. Now you can read the letter from Peter. Here it is."

"Oh yes, finally! Thank you. Meantime, you drink coffee and relax or just read a newspaper. I didn't have a chance to read the news myself. All day long, I was very busy. Many times I'm asking myself why I must be so busy."

"This is a good question but perhaps there is no answer to it," Benedict confirmed and glanced into a newspaper, smiling.

There was ten minutes of silence. Jerome was overwhelmed by the content of Peter's letter. His eyes were opening more and more as he read further and further. Then when he finished reading he made a remark,

"It is almost an unbelievable story. But it is really fantastic news! He is talking about the same **letter** which I guarded for many years. Everything I told you was true. Peter is telling us that he could see Jesus in a sort of **quantum matter** and every week.

Do you imagine something like that? I wish to see Him too. It would be one of a kind experience for me. Inside of me is still the little boy who is dreaming. Perhaps it would be that way forever."

"Then what do you think about it?" Benedict asked.

"You told me that Peter and Charlotte are very well trained for this unusual job. Likely you can succeed. I told you, I'll back you up in Rome. I know you worry about Monk Salvatore, and now about those police type Spider-Monks. I must tell you, from my observation only that Salvatore is better than anyone else in almost everything he does.

However, I have a good feeling about Peter and Charlotte. They're very determined. Also, try to remember that we have the mysterious Letter and I feel good about this fact. You mentioned to me that you have that sure idea that those three elements must click together in order to open the secret of the entire universe. I don't imagine how it would really happen but if it happened, it would be a miracle on universal scale."

"This is what I think, but what if I am wrong in my judgment. Peter is telling us that Jesus put the **Holy Key** over the *Quantum Disc* and then spoke in an ancient tongue. Now I'm thinking maybe we need some spoken inscription. I must study this issue a little more. Or maybe we need Jesus to untangle this secret completely. I'm getting tired of this infinite search for the truth. Life can be not only so unpredictable, but so difficult, too."

"Benedict, it would take forever if you do that. We must believe in it! The ancient tongue is engraved

462

inside the **Letter,** and with the **blood of God.** You must believe in it, too!" Jerome, still excited, made his point.

"If I only knew what is written in there? Or perhaps, I shall have more faith," Benedict said with a tired voice.

"You should! You don't have to know what is written there, either. I believe that there is something extraordinary. There must be a reason why this **Holy Letter** survived for almost **2,000** years. Did you ever think of that?"

"You're right, Jerome. Maybe, I'm getting old and powerless."

"Come on, Benedict! You're still young and you already put your whole life into your mission, so you couldn't be wrong. Just believe in yourself from now on. I'm getting old and for me this mission is the only excitement left. Just think that we may see all that wonders of the entire world, more than we could ever dream of. We better check if Charlotte and Emanuel arrived in Rome. I'll call them. Just give me a second. Emanuel… Where are you? You just landed in Rome. You're okay then. Take care and let me know if you need anything. Sure! I'll be glad to see you again," Jerome said.

"I'm glad that all arrived safely. Did anyone follow them?" Benedict asked.

"He didn't mention, perhaps, everything went smoothly. I'll check back in an hour. Let's go to my office now. I must write a note to the Vatican Headquarters and ask them to take this dead man off of my property. My security guys killed him or likely he poisoned himself after he was captured. I don't know what to do with him now. Let me call Henry and ask where the monk's body is.

Henry, this is me, Jerome. I'd like to ask, where is the dead monk? In the garden, north side, okay, we'll go there. Benedict, please follow me. My garden is quite big and it may take us quite some time to find him. Okay, I see someone out there, next to the lantern. I just want to examine him for a second. Look at his chest! Will you? Do you see the initial, Omega over X? Okay! Now, look at his left hand, in the middle of it, is another initial, of the spider. We call them 'soldiers.' They send them everywhere where there is death. Thus all those guys would have the same initials. I just want to be sure with whom I'm dealing and to whom I shall write the letter. So bad! He doesn't have any ID. He doesn't have any wounds either. Look at his medallion. In the middle of it, is an empty small chamber, he removed the poison chip and swallowed. The death occurred in approximately twenty seconds. I know that stuff. I already went through it in my organization. Let's go, I must write this note to the Vatican Police. I don't want them here anymore. This is my private property and they don't have any rights or reasons to be here."

"Definitely, I agree with you one hundred percent. On the top of that, they're potential thieves. We know that they came already twice and obviously for the **Holy Letter.** I just wonder, do they really think that they're invisible? Thus why they continue to do this," Benedict pointed out. He was exasperated.

"Yes, this is why I'm writing them a letter with request to stop the game for good! If they don't, I'm going to put an electric fence around my entire estate.

And if they come again, they better learn how to fly over the fence. Do I have a second option? I don't think so!" Jerome voiced his thoughts.

"Yes! This is what you must do," Benedict said in a low voice. He closed his eyes for a moment and fell in a short nap. Meantime, Jerome composed his letter and soon after he finished it, he interrupted,

"What do you think about it? I want you to read it!"

"Oh, sure, I will. Give me that! Okay, yes, you're going straight into the bull's-eye, Jerome. I like it! Just send it as is. Someone there will be quite surprised," Benedict said fearlessly.

"I'll send it overnight by private messenger with a request for the signature. I just want to see who those people are. We shall rest for now. Look at the time! I don't believe it! It is two a.m. Goodnight Benedict! I'm going to bed. You do the same. See you tomorrow."

The night seemed longer than usual, perhaps their dreams were longer, too. Jerome woke up late and called Benedict for late breakfast. The aroma of fresh coffee spread everywhere. The Chef made the tender fish filet with steamed wild-strawberries and fried bananas. "I slept like a baby. How about you? The last night made me so tired, like never before. I'm happy and so far, all is quiet, no sign of any intruders. Let's enjoy this exquisite food. I hope you like it."

"Thank you, it tastes good. If anyone would steal me last night, I wouldn't even have noticed. This is how hard I slept. I call this stone sleep," Benedict said, being content. The telephone rang. Jerome picked it up and said, "May, I have a peaceful breakfast at least once in my life time. What are you saying? The monk's body disappeared. How in all the heavens could it happen? Maybe he flew over the fence. I didn't even send the letter to the Vatican Police yet. Did you hear, Benedict? The monk's body vanished last night and my Panthers guys were supposed to watch the property 24/7. They didn't see anybody coming in or going out. I don't believe it! Those monks are worse than rats! How did they sneak onto my estate without being seen? Maybe they went underground. Oh, holy goat! But actually, I don't care about his dead body anymore! He already escaped the mundane life and for good.

He will decompose within next few days, anyway. I just care for the way they entered my estate without being noticed. Isn't it amazing?"

"Indeed, it is unusual. How did they carry the body over the fence? Perhaps an army of monks came over last night just to steal the dead. It is like dragging the dead cat out of the mortuary," Benedict said contently.

"I don't know what should I do? Cry or perhaps pontificate on their action."

"I would rather laugh," Benedict sharpened his point.

"I like your point. Let's laugh together!"

Chapter 13. Vatican City, August 1st
Excitement in the Boarding School

Monk Emanuel hired private guards to watch

Charlotte 24/7. Amelie was happy when she saw Charlotte in a one precious piece. She said with excitement, giving her a few hugs,

"Holy Ghost; Charlotte, you're alive! I prayed for you every day. Welcome home!"

"I'm happy to be back and glad to see you too. How have you been?"

"I was so miserable without you. I chased my own ghost every night. You can't imagine how sad my life was without you. Don't worry about your job. I did all the work for you. It was easy. The bald nun was even pleasant and didn't guff about my work too much. A few times, I was late but like only five minutes, and each time she gave me that naughty look. But I'm really glad that you're back. Then tell me what did happen out there? How did they rescue you? How big is Bertrand's estate?"

"It's a long story. He has a huge and beautiful estate. You'd like it! But I don't care for that. I was rescued by some nice guys, that night. They called them the **Green Panthers.** They are better than the **Spider-Monks**, I believe. I was just lucky that Bertrand left his estate for some kind of business meeting that evening. He is a crazy man and I fought him with a few my best karate kicks. However, his guards immobilized me and locked me in the bedroom. I spent around six hours there but soon I was rescued by those nice guys. We drove from there to a big estate, near Paris where I was welcomed by Jerome who owns a huge castle. They threw a big welcome party for me. Can you imagine something like that? Monk Emanuel was there too. He played saxophone beautifully. I didn't know he was so talented. Benedict played the piano. Also Jerome played the saxophone with them. Later, I had an exquisite dinner and I received the most amazing gift from Jerome and his friends, a sapphire ring with real diamonds. Look for yourself!"

"Why doesn't anybody want to kidnap me? That is a beautiful ring indeed!" Amelie chortled.

"Amelie, your good sense of humor never left you even for a second. You couldn't live without it. Could you? But I love the ring too," Charlotte chuckled.

"Sure, I couldn't! You turned our life into a fairy-tale story and I must add a bit of spice to it from time to time to make it feel real. Now, I feel, I could dance all night. But nobody would dance with me!"

"I think it would be much better to keep it as a fairy-tale, at least for now. But surely, I love your enthusiasm, Amelie. Then how is Sister Agnes doing? Did you talk to her lately? I don't know if I can face her now. I feel so embarrassed."

"You shouldn't be! She didn't say much. I met her once in the St. Mary Chapel; she was cleaning flowers at the altar. She asked me if I had any news from you. But I didn't."

"I see, I didn't have a clue that she would take everything so personally. Now I feel guilty! Can you make our favorite tea, Amelie? I really missed it. Actually, I missed everything about this place, especially our small room and those noisy birds living in the pine trees."

"Of course, I'll make it. I was about to do it anyway. You shouldn't feel guilty. You know Sister Agnes' own love story. She still can't forgive herself

468

that she abandoned her lover, Richard. She tries to reverse the past each time but it doesn't work. Okay, tea is done. Which cup would you like?"

"With the rose flowers, please. Thank you, Amelie. I love this flavor. It must be my favorite one. I feel good now and ready to sleep. I'm exhausted. I'll talk to you tomorrow."

"Sure Charlotte. I'll read my favorite book, and within twenty minutes I'll sleep too. But your ring is so gorgeous. Look at the shiny diamonds."

"Yes, it is beautiful. You can try if you like it. Goodnight, Amelie!"

"Sure, I love to! It fits my middle finger perfectly. Can I sleep with this beautiful ring tonight?"

"Sure, you can, Amelie."

"Thank you Charlotte, goodnight!"

The next morning was just an ordinary one. The girls went for breakfast and then departed to work. Charlotte was excited to be back and was warmly greeted by her fellow workers. The pieces of the puzzle fell right into place again. She was pleased. She knew that within a week or two Peter would send her a final letter and likely it would be the last letter before their mission. She dropped the laundry bags at the cleaner and sorted out every piece. There was no message from Peter. She returned to the office, changed her clothes and walked home.

The sun was warm, the air filled with an aroma of the garden roses and the fresh soil. It felt like at home again, she thought. Someone dressed in a brown habit with a hood followed her all the way home. Perhaps, her personal Angel guard, she thought. She knew she was safe. Just before she reached the academic hall, she met Monk Emanuel, standing in front of the main door.

"Hi, Charlotte, how are you? I'm just passing by and wanted to check if you're okay."

"Sure, I'm fine and since I have the Angel guard following me, I feel very secure now."

"That is what I want to talk to you about. Actually, these two personal guards will start their work tomorrow morning. I like you to take a look at these pictures. This is Adrien, and this is Dennis. They are tall guys and one is blond, the other has brown hair. I'll call them to come over and you can meet them personally. It is better that way."

"I thought that you already hired them. I've seen one monk following me all the way here. He wore a dark habit with a hood. I haven't seen his face."

"Charlotte, it must be Monk Salvatore! I wouldn't hire monk as a private guard! As you know he could be very dangerous. I wonder what he's doing in Rome. The Vatican Police have been searching for him since he left. He knows or maybe smells something, like a hunter dog does. But what he really knows, we don't know at this point. If he learns more details, he will ruin our mission. If he could sneak into the high security Jerome estate without being seen then he could go almost everywhere now. He heard about your kidnapping by accident when he snuck into the meeting held at the Jerome estate. Jerome noticed him and tried to catch him but he escaped through the open window. It is also possible that he was in the plane with us, and we didn't notice him. He always works undercover and can change his appearance easily. I have a feeling that he already knows too much.

Let's think. He knows that you work at the Vatican facility and surely he wants to find out more about your job and why you're there. Now he knows where you live. This is not good! I'll talk to the guards to watch for Salvatore. He is easily spotted. Perhaps if they can't catch him, at least they can scare him away. I should watch him myself. I must go undercover too. I'll wear ordinary clothes and follow him. We don't have too many choices from now on. I must call Benedict and let him know what happened. I know he can't come here since he left the Vatican library secretly. The secret police are looking for him as well.

Charlotte, you're not going to your room right now. If Salvatore is watching us, we shall confuse him. We will change our plan. We're going to that small cafe **Don Philippe** just around the corner. I'll ask the guards to meet us there. We can talk about their new assignment. Let's go!" Emanuel said, excited that he was going to trick Salvatore. He picked up his cell phone and dialed the guards' number. Adrien answered the phone and agreed to meet Emanuel in the cafe. Meantime, Charlotte and Emanuel ordered some cakes and aromatic tea. He told Charlotte the story about his previous trip to Paris.

"Benedict, Chris, John and I were sitting in this nice French cafe, drinking flavorful coffee and heaving the best pastry in Paris, and suddenly we spotted Salvatore behind the window. Benedict ran after him but Salvatore vanished around the corner without a trace. We never could catch him. I don't know why? Perhaps he is too smart for us and too quick like a rabbit. My point is that he followed us almost everywhere we went. It is very strange. This is why we need some kind of security, for protection. Do you understand?"

"Sure, I do! I didn't know that he was so smart."

"Sure, he is, indeed! Oh, I see my guys are coming. Charlotte, this is Adrien and this is Dennis. Sit down, Gentlemen. I'd like to talk to you. I want you to meet Charlotte. You will watch her 24/7. We have an intruder who is following her, the monk, is five and half feet tall, skinny, wearing a habit with a hood of a different color, could be brown, gray or black. Lately, he's making his own doubles to confuse anyone who follows him.

How? He stole some powerful sacred words which allow him to make some kind of miracles. Your job is to scare him away. He is too smart to be captured so easily. But if you could do that it would be great! Good luck to you! Now, shall we have some coffee and a cake for you Gentlemen? Whatever you like it," Emanuel happily concluded.

"Nice to meet you, Charlotte," Adrien said and Dennis added, "You don't have to worry now about anything. We're here to protect you."

"Thank you, Adrien, thank you Dennis. I'm happy and perhaps can sleep better."

"Sure!" Adrien confirmed.

"I want to tell you that this monk can walk on the walls like a spider. He belongs to an ancient sect, the Omega Templars. I think we shall install iron bars

472

on Charlotte's windows and a double lock on the door. He could easily sneak through the window and you wouldn't even notice him. I think we shall do it tonight. The bars could be installed from the inside of the room. What do you think?"

"I think it is a great idea because we can't climb the walls like the spiders. I know the window's guy, Marco, and he would do it anytime if we could pay him well. I'll call him right now and ask him to come," Dennis said and dialed Marco's phone number. He spoke for a few minutes, and then said,

"Okay, let's go! Marco is on his way. We'll meet him in ten minutes. It was fast, wasn't it?"

"Sure, let's go," Emanuel said, smiling. They walked back to the boarding school. Marco arrived and they greeted each other warmly. They went upstairs to Charlotte's room. Amelie opened the door.

"Hi, guys! Hi Charlotte! What is going on here?" she asked, smiling.

"Amelie, you already met Monk Emanuel. This is Dennis and Adrien, my private guards. Marco is the window man and he is going to install iron bars, just for security purpose."

"Nice to meet you, guys. I just made some tea. Would you like to have it?" Amelie asked.

"Sure," Marco said. "Me too, I like to have some," Dennis and Adrien agreed.

Marco took the window's measurements and ran to his truck to bring the right size. He installed the bars within twenty minutes.

"Okay, it's done. Now I can join you for a cup of tea."

"Sure. Here it is!" Amelie said with a smile.

473

They were talking for awhile and soon Marco got a phone-call. He said he got another job in town and left in a hurry. Then Emanuel said in calm voice,

"Charlotte, you should not walk alone especially in the evening. Take Amelie with you even if you go for dinner or to the Chapel. This world is strange, I'm telling you girls."

Soon, Sister Agnes came and said, a bit surprised, "I'm glad that you're here Charlotte. It is nice to see all of you."

"We just installed new safety bars. The girls can sleep well tonight. This is Adrien and Dennis, Charlotte's bodyguards."

"This is good. At least, I'll have a peace of mind! My job is not so easy. Lately, I'm exhausted. These bars will solve at least half of the problems I'm facing in this boarding school. After summer, new students are coming and everything starts all over again."

"Sister, would you like to have a cup of tea?" Amelie asked.

"Why not, since I'm here, yes, let me have one. I'm so tired these days. Maybe, it would do me some good. Perhaps the stress day after day is killing me."

"Sure, all of us have the same problem. Our lives are so unpredictable that we can't control them all of the time. It is difficult to handle hundreds of tasks every single day. Perhaps we need a vacation," Emanuel said, smiling.

"Oh sure, I don't remember when I got my last one. But you're right about life. I tried to change many things in my life but it never works the way I want it to. Then I gave up! Amelie, this tea makes me feel good.

May, I have another cup."

"Yes Sister. I'm glad that you like it."

The evening went by quickly and soon the guests left. The girls went to bed early.

"Charlotte, I think, I'm in love with George," Amelie suddenly interrupted the silence, giggling.

"Does George know about it?" Charlotte asked.

"Perhaps but I'm about to tell him that."

"Amelie, I don't think it's a good idea. I would wait with that stuff. Besides, it isn't lady's etiquette to tell a man that you love him. It should be the opposite way. It is more masculine and perhaps sexy if the man tells you that he loves you. At least, I think that way."

"Oh, Charlotte, what would I do without you? I think you're right. It always has been that way at least in the European culture. He should confess his love to me, first! I'll wait! Goodnight, Charlotte."

"Sleep well and sweet dreams, Amelie."

The next few days were quiet. The guards followed Charlotte everywhere and it seemed like Salvatore wasn't to be found anywhere. Perhaps, he was hiding or decided to wait for a better opportunity. She didn't have any news from Peter either. Maybe he was sick, she thought for a moment. Emanuel contacted Benedict by phone and told him about Salvatore presence in Rome. Benedict was shocked by that terrible news. He was still in Paris, at Jerome's estate. He told Emanuel that Salvatore is likely undercover and he will go where the devil dares to go! It is inevitable that he is after Charlotte and perhaps he will change his appearance if he must to get as close as possible. Jerome decided to send a small group of **Green Panthers** to Rome. Emanuel would find quarters for them. Perhaps they could stay in the boarding school as long as it would be necessary. Most of the students left for vacation and some went home, leaving plenty of empty rooms behind. The Panthers will come within two days. He will meet them at the airport.

The next morning Charlotte and Amelie went for breakfast and later to work. It was a sunny day; the summer was in full bloom. The birds were singing beautifully that morning like they wanted to tell the girls their own love stories all over again. Charlotte went to pick the two laundry bags. She walked slowly to the cleaner and thought of Peter. Maybe this time he'll send a message. She separated the habits and checked each one. Then she reached for the last one, medium size which belonged to Peter. She turned it inside out and was looking for a message. She found one. Peter wrote, tomorrow at noon, a new letter.

She was happy that everything was okay, so far. She transferred the habits one by one to the next room and carefully set them on the long table. When she returned to pick up Peter's habit, she found that it wasn't there anymore. She looked around and thought it simply vanished. She went outside and saw a man running with the habit in his hand. The guards ran after him but he jumped over the fence like a wild jaguar and vanished. They came back empty handed. Charlotte was stunned how he came here in the first place, unnoticed by the guards. Perhaps he spent last night in the laundry room, hidden in the closets. How is she going to explain to the bald nun that one habit was stolen by a thief? It would be so embarrassing even to mention something like that. She was speechless as she stood at the same spot for a few minutes. Soon she decided to go to the office and tell her story. The nun was terrified for a minute and then asked,

"Charlotte do you know what size is missing?"

"Yes, I remember it was medium size."

"I think we have some new medium sizes in that drawer to your right. You can check. If you find one take it and tomorrow put it back with the other habits."

"Thank you and I'm sorry."

"Oh, you don't have to be sorry. It wasn't your fault, obviously. Don't worry my child, go home now. I'm glad that he didn't hurt you! It was perhaps the first robbery in twenty years. Last time, someone stole a pair of old shoes." The nun said and laughed.

The guards followed Charlotte all the way to her room. Then Adrien called Emanuel and told him the story. Emanuel came to Charlotte's room and they sat at the table and conversed.

"Charlotte, you didn't see him when you entered the cleaner's room, did you?"

"Absolutely not; the room was empty and perhaps I couldn't imagine that someone dared to hide there under the table or in the closet. It was a shock for me, indeed."

"He must have lived there like a rat, hidden for a day or two. We didn't see him on the streets for the past few days. It is a very strange situation and we didn't suspect anything like that," Dennis said, embarrassed.

"Okay, from now on you must check every

room before she even puts her foot in. She could be killed next time. Do we understand each other?" Emanuel spoke clearly but in calm voice.

"Oh, yes! We'll do that for sure. This monk, Salvatore is like a devil!" Dennis added.

"He sure is! You're free to go, Gentleman. See you later. Charlotte, are you okay now?" Emanuel wanted to be sure that she would be fully protected.

"I'll be fine. I was shocked. I didn't see him. The worst thing is that he stole Peter's habit and there was a written message from Peter."

"Oh, it is very bad then! What did he say?"

"He wrote; wait for my letter, tomorrow at noon."

"This is very good news!"

"When I'll pick up the laundry bags, hoping Peter will send me the letter. It could be a very important letter."

"It will be, indeed! I'm positively sure that Salvatore will be there tomorrow. Tonight, the **Green Panthers** are coming from Paris. Thus, tomorrow they will screen the entire area. But there is one problem; this monk is always appearing from nowhere. I don't know how to handle this awkward situation. What if Salvatore steals the letter from you? Then, he'll take over our entire operation. He already knows too much! The problem is that we can't catch him. What a devil-man!"

"Then what shall we do?"

"I shall call Benedict and soon after I'll drive to the airport to pick up the Panthers. It is only noon and you better go for lunch. I can walk you there. Don't worry for now. Just try to enjoy your meal. See you

478

later!" Emanuel said and left.

He drove straight to the international airport and waited for the plane to arrive. Meantime, he called Benedict and they discussed the details of tomorrow's operation. It must be a very sophisticated operation, he thought. There can be no room for any errors. The Panthers just arrived and Emanuel greeted them warmly. He took some of them to his big van and the others took a taxi to the Monastery. Meanwhile, Charlotte was on her bed and thought about Peter again. What if Salvatore outsmarts everyone and ruins their plan. It would be devastating for her and especially for Benedict, not to mention even Peter, Emanuel and perhaps some others who have waited for this special moment to happen. It would be a real miracle if this mission is accomplished. She got tired and lay down for a short nap. Emanuel was back and distributed all his guests throughout the empty rooms, in the entire boarding school facility. Then soon afterward, they went for lunch and discussed the details of tomorrow's short operation. Theoretically, they must assume that Salvatore would be there. Thus they made a plan how to deal with that kind of a situation. Emanuel was listening to them and finally said at the end, "Just remember that Salvatore won't wait for us. He will show up unexpectedly. You must search the entire area before the action takes place. He could be everywhere."

"Definitely, we'll search every tree, every bush and there will be no place that he can possibly hide," one of them said.

"I suggest we put a few Panthers out there

overnight. Salvatore is a very determined man, indeed. We should be equally determined or even more. Okay, gentlemen, I'm ready to go. Perhaps, you'd like to relax a bit after your trip. We have a Jacuzzi and a swimming pool in our facilities. You should take advantage of it," Emanuel added with a smile as he was about to leave. The Panther guys followed him all the way. Some went to their rooms and the others took Emanuel's offer to enjoy the hot Jacuzzi.

It was late afternoon when Amelie returned home from her work. She was happy and greeted by Charlotte, warmly, "Hello, sleeping beauty! Wake up! It is only six p.m. What are you going to do tonight? Charlotte, I have good news for you! I had lunch with George today! He is my inspiration!"

"This is great news, Amelie. Finally, someone your age could inspire you. I was so exhausted and fell asleep. I'm glad that you woke me up. I would like to relax a bit in the Jacuzzi."

"I'll join you! I have so much energy today that I could move mountains. I like my summer job. However, it will soon be over, as well as my love, too. I'll be sad. Hard to believe but a new semester starts in a few weeks."

"Just don't think too much about it for now. Try to have fun. Let's go!" she said with a smirk on her lips.

"Perhaps you're right. I shouldn't talk too much about it. We shall give rein to pleasure," Amelie said in a jocular tone. Charlotte gave her that piercing look, and they grinned. The evening went by fast. They spent an hour or more in the Jacuzzi, talking, joking and giggling. The night was peaceful and filled with dreams full of adventures.

The next morning the girls woke up a bit late, it seemed they were still dreaming. Amelie rushed to work just on time. Charlotte would go to her work around noon thus she had plenty of time. Emanuel consulted her and assured her that she will be watched by the **Green Panthers.** She shouldn't be afraid of anything. Her task was simple and there shall be no obstacles in her way, whatsoever. There was no way that Monk Salvatore could sneak anywhere near the tower. The Panthers screened the area overnight inch by inch. It should be the safest place on the planet Earth, they thought for a moment. Emanuel was excited as they were getting closer and closer to the heart of their mission. It was around noon. Charlotte was ready to go but she seemed a bit nervous. Emanuel followed her from a distance. A few 'Green Panthers' were hiding near the North Tower. They wore camouflage clothes and were almost invisible.

Charlotte walked to the office just to change her clothes. It was exactly twelve noon when she picked up the laundry bags and waited for a few seconds. The letter from Peter landed next to her feet. She picked it up and opened it. It read, **August 29 at 7:30 p.m.** She whistled her favorite song and was about to leave.
Suddenly like from the mist, Salvatore appeared and stole the letter from her, and then ran like the wind, leaving behind his doubles and dust only. The Panthers shot at him several times but he was still running. He jumped over the walls and disappeared

between the next buildings. Emanuel ran toward Charlotte, screaming, "Are you okay? I saw him as he emerged from the trash-can behind you. Those guys didn't check the trash! I don't believe it! Did you read the letter?"

"Yes, I did. **August 29 at 7:30 p.m.** Oh holy symphony! He scared me almost to death."

"Yes! Good job, Charlotte! I'll meet you for dinner later. I must leave for now." Emanuel left and the Panthers men walked quickly in different directions. Their operation failed and they were not happy about it. Within an hour they met with Emanuel in the conference room. Emanuel was unhappy and deeply stunned by the current development.

"Gentlemen, you failed to check the trash facility. How could this possibly happen?" he said with irritation in his voice.

"We looked into the trash-can last evening and it was empty at the time. He placed himself in the plastic bag, inside the trash-can perhaps later on," someone shouted nervously.

"But how did he get there without being seen? You're supposed to check every inch of the surrounding area. If you couldn't see him this time then surely you'll miss him next time, too," Emanuel threw out, nervously.

"He just outsmarted us!" someone added.

"I know. It happened already a few times. Thus it is nothing new. But we can't afford another mistake like that," Emanuel demanded, angrily.

"We can only try our best. This guy is a freak and we must study him," someone shouted again.

"Then you better study him well. Otherwise,

he'll ruin our next, very important operation. On the top of that he is a very dangerous man. If he gets what he wants, he'll destroy the entire universe. He is a sick man and must be stopped or rather killed," Emanuel added with mixed emotion. They have been debating on the monk subject for a few hours. They concluded that it wouldn't be so easy to catch him. However, they must find the way. Emanuel sat frustrated on the sofa and decided to talk to Benedict about the best and the worst part of the operation. He picked up his cell phone and called Jerome's estate where Benedict was still vacationing. The most important news was that their mission was finally set for **August 29 at 7:30 p.m.** and it made Benedict very happy. However, he was stunned by the failure of the **Green Panthers** operation and tried to understand the weirdness of the current situation. He knew it would take strength to fight Salvatore, and especially now since he's already found out about the date of their secret mission which is not a secret anymore. He'll likely hide now and emerge on the exact date of their mission. They must find him before that and eliminate him even if there is only a slight chance of success.

Charlotte came home a bit frustrated after that scary afternoon. She lay on her bed and analyzed every single move of each chessman on the chessboard in her newly opened chess game. She can't afford to make any mistakes. Her mind must be open and move fast. But how fast, certainly faster than Salvatore's mind. How many chessmen would be there? No one knows that. Peter would be one of them, perhaps Patrick and Salvatore as a king. She must be faster than all of them. But she wasn't sure if she will be able to do that. She was trained well but Salvatore had much more experience with climbing the walls than she or Peter. On the top of that he does all those tricks with his doubles. It wouldn't be a fair competition at that point. What if she failed, she thought. She wasn't feeling so secure at that point. She was tired and fell asleep. Perhaps she would find the answer to her dilemma in her dreams.

Chapter 14. Jerome's Countryside Estate Paris, August 12th.

The same evening Benedict reported all the news to Jerome. He was disappointed. The Green Panthers were recalled back to Paris the very next day after that unsuccessful operation at the Vatican North Tower. It took them quite a few days to discuss the details of their failure. Jerome was in a bad mood and poured all his anxiety on them.

"Gentlemen, we will always learn from our mistakes. Yes, I just wonder, how long time it will take us to do it right. Just remember that there will always be someone like Monk Salvatore. Why is he so fast and intelligent? We have two weeks to figure it out! Why? Because later will be too late!" Jerome walked nervously around the conference room. The drinks were served and finally he sat next to Benedict and sighed with relief. Then he sipped his wine nervously.

"What do you think is going to happen? I have mixed feelings about the mission and can sense a big failure. It looks like I can't count on the Panthers anymore. How can I protect the secret **Holy Letter**? I must take it with me to Rome. It can't walk on its own, I suppose. I don't have a clue what I shall do? Maybe you can tell me that."

"I can travel with you all the way to Rome when the time comes. I have some idea. We'll bandage the letter to your thigh. I did that myself many times and trust me this is the most secure way. No one would ever suspect anything like that," Benedict said with self-assurance as he shook his head for approval.

"That's actually not a bad idea. At least Salvatore wouldn't know. You gave me some peace of mind, Benedict. Definitely, I'll ask some of the Panthers guys to keep us company. Tell me something about that mission now. How safe will it be out there, in Rome? Where would we hide all those treasures we're about to discover?"

"I worked a very precise plan. Our secret organization in Rome will protect us and give us shelter soon after the mission is accomplished. We don't have to worry about that part. Peter and Charlotte will deliver the secret book-disc and the key to us. We have the rest. Then we'll travel to the outskirts of Rome where our organization resides, in a nice church facility, on a few acres of land. Everything out there will be under full control. You won't find a safer place on planet Earth. Thus you should not worry too much and try to relax a bit; I can see you're very tense. I want you to forget for a moment about the mission and try to live a normal life for next two weeks.

I thought, I was stressed more than anybody

485

else but perhaps I was wrong. We can do a lot of different things for the time being here. Look around your estate. It is like a lost paradise. We shall enjoy every moment of it," Benedict pointed out with happiness on his face.

"Sure, I'll try to take your advice very seriously at this time. Thank you for being my friend."

"Sure. Let's go fishing or maybe to see a movie," Benedict suggested, cheerful.

"Definitely, you're right. We should do that."

They would spend their quality time together and enjoy every moment of it. The new instructions will come from Rome and soon.

Chapter 15. The Alexandrian Theological Academy
Rome, August 14

It was a sunny Saturday morning. The girls decided to go shopping and spend some time in the fancy shops just for fun. Their main focus was a new pair of shoes and maybe a summer dress for each of them. Amelie spotted a nice red dress at the upscale window of the fancy shop as they walked by. She decided to try it on. Charlotte followed her. The sales woman handed the dress to Amelie. The girls entered the dressing-room. Amelie put the dress on and asked,

"What do you think, Charlotte?"

"You look stunning, fantastic. No words to explain the beauty of it."

"Would you like to try it?"

"Sure I can try but there is no point of buying one for me because I wouldn't wear it. You know why?"

"But anyway, put it on. I saw the red shoes with a beautiful red rosette in the middle. I'll bring them here and we can try. You just wait!" Amelie said and walked to the saleswoman and asked for the red shoes. The lady handed them to Amelie.

"Charlotte put them on. We have the same size, don't we?"

"Sure, I can try them on. Waa! I look like I jumped out of a fairy-tale book. But where is my prince? It looks awesome! Now, you shall try it. It's meant for you, Amelie. I'll borrow the dress and shoes from you when the time is right for me; perhaps in a year."

"Okay, let me try it now! It fits perfectly. I wouldn't dream of anything else at this precious moment. I must tell you that I watched this dress and shoes for almost four years. Finally, the time came as a plea, and I can buy them. I earned enough money for this little pricey dream of mine. This summer job came as a blessing to me. I can be proud of myself," Amelie said, delighted.

"You should be! These two pieces are really a priceless treasure. We shall value them for the rest of our life!"

"Indeed, we will, especially for that sweet price! Okay! Charlotte, are you ready? Now, I'd like to take you for lunch to the small cafe, **Romeo.** We have a good reason to celebrate! We've been there quite a few times."

"I love that place! We can relax with music and they have those fantastic cakes. Let's go!" The girls browsed through the streets and small shops on their way until they reached the Romeo cafe where pure pleasure and quality time awaited them. They reminisced about their funny moments and laughed a lot. The cakes never tested better. However, their enjoyment didn't last long. Suddenly, the door opened and Amelie's boyfriend, George appeared. Her heart almost leapt off her chest but was smothered by presence of another girlfriend, following behind him. George spotted Amelie as he waved his hand at her and then took his girlfriend's hand and sat at the table just next to Amelie and Charlotte. It was more than Amelie could withstand, it was slanderous for her, and then there was the shocking silence. An invisible tragic energy emanated from her. She couldn't imagine that he could have another girlfriend. Why? She deeply believed that she was that one and the only one! But life proved something different that evening. It was the biggest stunner of a day for her. It was disconcerting at first glance, mind-bending confusion. She was totally lost with her thoughts. Charlotte noticed that moment and whispered to her, "Who is he?"

"This is George, I mentioned to you many times but I didn't know that he had a girlfriend. My heart is broken and forever! How can I bear a loss like that? Let's get out of here!"

"Wait Amelie, you make me nervous, maybe they are just good friends."

"I don't think so! Look, he still holds her hand. Friends don't do that. Wake up, Charlotte!" Amelie was about to leave.

"Let's go Charlotte."

"Okay, I'm coming." Suddenly, George stood up and interrupted the moment,

"Hi Amelie, I'd like to introduce to you my girlfriend, Annette. We have been dating for almost a year."

"Sorry, we're about to leave. This is my friend, Charlotte."

"Hi Charlotte, nice to meet you," George said, smiling still holding Annette's hand.

"Nice to meet you too, guys. Sorry we're in a hurry. We're about to meet our boyfriends at the theater. But enjoy your evening. Bye now!" Charlotte replied, giving the last look at George as he was really surprised.

The girls quickly vanished behind the door. Amelie leaned against the wall and cried. She was shocked by that incredible turn. Her dreamed-love boyfriend betrayed her, she thought. Charlotte stood by her and tried to give her psychological support,

"Just let it go! There are thousands of guys like George. He didn't impress me at all. You're worth much more than he and his girlfriend together. Amelie, you're still very young and gorgeous! Just try to remember that!"

"Now, I'll become a miserable nun for sure, like Sister Agnes. At least she will have a life time of guaranteed company. Also you can have the red dress and shoes for now because I'll never wear them." she was weeping.

"Amelie, relax! It is not the end of the world! You'll be fine and one day you'll meet a fantastic guy.

I don't know what to say to make you laugh again. Just think of priest Bertrand for a moment."

"He didn't care for me either," she sadly added.

"Oh holy cow, it was a wrong example. Maybe, I must try harder. Think about the cat who committed suicide on a pine tree, four years ago," Charlotte said, laughing.

"This is much better. That bastard hung himself by an accident. If he knew that he would have died, he wouldn't have gone after that dead bird in the first place," Amelie confirmed, smiling.

"You're much better now. Can we walk home?"

"Sure! There will always be someone better than me," Amelie added with gloomy tone in her voice.

"I don't think that anyone is better than you. You must stop your destructive thinking. People are just different but this doesn't mean that they're better. You're my best friend and nothing else matters."

"Charlotte, thank you for being my best friend, I want you to wear this red dress as many times as you want otherwise it would be wasted. I didn't know that we had boyfriends waiting for us at the theater. It would be nice. Anyway, it was a brilliant move! I wouldn't have thought of anything like that," Amelie confirmed, laughing.

"You laugh. It didn't take you too long. Did it? I think, it is better to be rejected by any boyfriend than be pregnant with unwanted one. Am I right?"

"You're right, Charlotte, indeed. I'm glad that we're back at home. It was quite a hectic day after all. Let me open the door, I have the key handy. Charlotte, look on the floor! Someone had slid a bloody letter under the door. You should read it loud!" Amelie said as she reached for the letter.

"Who would write me a letter?" Charlotte said with a deep concern.

"Only Bertrand, I'm sure! Read it!" Amelie handed the letter to Charlotte.

"Okay, okay. Wait! I don't want to read any letter from a hypocrite!"

"I can do it! I love to read his letters," Amelie replied and quickly opened it. It read: 'My Love Charlotte,

I'm a lost man without your love. You didn't think for a moment that I had abandoned you. I'd never do that! You know how much I love you and my love for you is forever! Perhaps, you think that you escaped from me for awhile. I want you to know that I will never give up on you and persistently I will follow you wherever you go and whatever you do. I want to be sure that your place is next to me. Please, try to understand my position for a moment. I gave up my priesthood for you, and I wouldn't do that for any other woman. It was a humiliation for me. Perhaps, I hurt you too but I'm ready for any punishment. You're my fantasy, the morning dew, the falsetto voice singing for me the Puccini's Nessun Dorma from the Turandot for which I have been waiting all my life. I know I must wait for your love to be awakened inside of you one day and for good. I also know that I must fight for your love as this would come as a plea to me at the end. Your resistance excites me even more. I'm ready to die for your love. Simply, I can't live without you. You're addictive like heroin! I can't forget the moment of heaven, the unforgotten first touch of a virgin.

You're a Saint to me. I want you and I need you, Charlotte. I'll come for you again and take you with me to France. Please, do not try to escape from me. Loving you always… Bertrand.'

Amelie stopped reading as her eyes were filled with tears. Then she said,

"Oh, holy ravioli, Charlotte; this is a beautiful love letter! He really loves you. His love is crazy. I wish someone would write to me something like that one day. You want me to read it to you again."

"I don't think so! You can read it to yourself if you like. He is an obsessed man. Amelie, we're too young for such feelings," Charlotte said, irritated.

"Okay! I'll read it to myself. I'm a romantic soul after all," Amelie replied, smiling. She lies on her bed and quietly read the letter at least several times before she fell asleep. Indeed, it came as a shock for both of them. Charlotte didn't say much either. She lay on her bed with eyes suspended in the air. Perhaps she was looking for an answer to her puzzled life. She wrote a few pages in her journal. The wind secretly sneaked through the open window and sang the soprano lyrics for the dreaming girls all night long.

It was a glorious Sunday morning and it felt like a real day of vacation for them. The sun was high and the air was filled with a beautiful flowery aroma. Charlotte wore the red dress and shoes to make Amelie happy. Amelie put on her graduation green dress and matching shoes. They went to the Chapel for a morning prayer and later to the park. They sat on the bench under the leafy trees, and watched the day go by. Some walkers would sit next to them for a short conversation or just to finish left over coffee, and walk away. The body guards would follow the girls everywhere they went. A few young boys would stop by for a short conversation or rather flirt with them for a moment. They would laugh and joke together. Charlotte looked stunning in her fantastic red dress and brought the attention of many young boys.

They went to the near cafe **Marco** for their favorite ice-cream with two newly met students, Charles and Brian. There was much more enjoyment than originally anticipated and it caused the attention of the body guards. Soon after cafe, the boys took Charlotte and Amelie to the disco at the local university club. It was a one of a kind entertainment for the girls as they hadn't yet been in such a fancy student club. It was crowded. Many youths were dancing and singing to the sound of pop music. They sat at the small table, and the boys ordered some drinks for everyone.

The disco music was so loud that they couldn't hear each other much. Charles and Brian asked the girls to dance. They were getting intimate and felt the presence of each other. The boys were charismatic and brought much laughter to everyone. The atmosphere was getting hot, hotter than usual. Suddenly, someone approached them and asked Charlotte to dance. She said that she was dancing and it would be impossible. Charles asked the man to leave. But the stranger took out the knife from his pocket and tried to scare Charles away. The security guys quickly stepped between them. One of them said, "Okay, kids, your fun is over. Charlotte, Amelie, let's go home!"

The lights were dimmed and they couldn't see the intruder's face as he stepped aback. He was intimidated by those big masculine guys and left the club as fast as he could, perhaps he didn't want to be recognize. Then Charlotte said, "Charles, it was nice to dance with you. I truly enjoyed! Perhaps I'll see you next time."

"Sure, it would be my pleasure too. See you next Sunday, in the park," he replied.

"See you," she said, smiling.

"Brian, bye for now," Amelie said as she waved goodbye.

"See you! It was fun to be with you, Amelie. You look stunning in your green dress," he replied with a longing eye.

The girls left quickly, accompanied by the body guards, and went straight to the boarding school. It was a beautiful evening, they thought. With the pleasant memory put to rest they went to their cozy beds. It would be something to dream about all night long, for sure. Fun like that doesn't come too often.

Amelie was happy that she could replace George with Brian at that precious moment of her life. She tried to replace not only the old boyfriend but her feelings too. It happened already and faster than she thought. One of the body guards stood by the door, the other one went outside. It was a peaceful night filled with high humidity and it felt like a sauna. The guards were awake all night and there would be many nights like that. The days were passing by fast and the mission was just around the corner. The forces in France were ready to move in.

Chapter 16. Final Mission
France, Paris, August 22
A Kidnapping at the Jerome' Estate

It was very sunny Saturday morning, the final week before the mission. Everyone was excited about it, especially Benedict and Jerome. For this special weekend Jerome invited a few top members of the **Green Panthers** to discuss the details of the upcoming complicated operation. Everyone was nervous. Chris, Gautier and Etienne were there as well just to present to all the interested parties their latest version of the quantum computer.

They'd made many improvements to the appearance of the computer and its new high-resolution performance of visual objects. Benedict invited his old German friends, the scientists, Hans and Jorgen, from the Munich University for this special occasion.

They could bring their expertise on the liquid plasma, dark matter and on the latest space discoveries. There would be perhaps some unknown issues which must be solved right away. Hans and Jorgen were experts in that field. They run a big science show once a month at the Munich University, and most of the newspapers in town talk about them on a weekly basis. They are trustworthy fellows, indeed. They were warmly welcomed by Jerome and the other members of the Knight's society. Jerome expressed his gratification to all the guests and invited them to special lunch.

Meantime, he and Benedict sat at the small table to discuss some advance details in regards to the transportation of the entire operation. He revealed his burning secret, "Benedict, I must confess to you that I can't fly anymore. Thus, the plane doesn't count. I must find some reasonable accommodation for myself and perhaps I'll need your help."

"Why can't you fly?" Benedict asked.

"I get vertigo each time if I fly for more than thirty minutes. Do you believe it? I don't! I'm telling you, it is more than a disaster for me. Sometimes I don't really know if I should laugh or rather cry. It's the same story with a boat. After a short trip, the world would rock for me for at least a month. I didn't tell my friends about it yet because there was no need to do so. It seems, like I can only take the train, now.

I'm also getting a strange motion sickness on any long distance drives, as well. I checked with doctors and they said my semicircular canals of the inner ear have some problem. It's such a shame, isn't it? Perhaps, I don't need any canals. I'm getting old! Tell me then."

"No comment! But it could happen to anyone. I met a few healthy younger fellows who suffered from vertigo after a one day vacation on the cruise. They couldn't even climb the local mountains. You'd never know what could happen to all of us one day. Life is so uncertain. But I wouldn't worry too much about it. We'll take a train to Rome," Benedict said.

"This is what I thought. However, we'll be at significant risk. Not only Salvatore but all the Vatican Police will be after us. You know, they want the secret letter from us. Then I'm worried because there will be

496

no place for us to escape. Did you ever think that perhaps Salvatore is one of them? Maybe, he never escaped from the Vatican. They just let him go and asked him to bring the letter as payment for his freedom. He puzzled me from the beginning," Jerome pointed out.

"I never thought of that but there is always that possibility. But I don't think that the Vatican monks knew about the letter before. Salvatore didn't know about it until the moment he stole the ancient scrolls and my **Black Book** from me. I'll never forgive him that," Benedict replied nervously.

"I personally think that the Vatican fellows knew about the letter but they didn't know where it was. They put their spies everywhere even in my organization, and look what happened? What a mess! Can you imagine how well they organize? However, it took them a few hundred years to find it out. This is how well we protected this letter," Jerome said, laughing. His phone rang for awhile, he picked it up. He was a bit nervous, perhaps he received bad news. He stood up and walked from left to right. Then he hung up. Benedict interrupted,

"Are you okay? You look very irritated. Tell me what is happening?"

"One of our undercover Panther men called with very bad news. The Vatican Secret Police captured one of our members, Knight Clement. According to him, they already tortured him. However, Clement doesn't have a clue where the letter is. I only know!

They said, if we do not deliver the **Holy Letter** to them tonight Clement would be dead by midnight and his body would be thrown into the local river. He is one of my best friends. We grew up together. He is more than a brother to me. The situation is getting more complicated. What shall I do?"

"Why didn't he poison himself? He could have avoided torture," Benedict pointed out with concern.

"This is a good question. I deeply believe that he was captured by surprise, and didn't have the chance to do so. The medallion with the poisonous microchip was ripped from his neck. However, he has one more microchip in one of his molars but maybe they took it out, too. I suspect that those fellows knew exactly what they were after. Those guys learned some of our secrets from our trusted fellow-member who betrayed us, a few years ago. Why did he do that? No one knows! Of course he poisoned himself as you remember at our meeting but the damage was already done, and there is no way it could be fixed. I just don't know what we should do! What do you think, Benedict? You're an intelligent man."

"We must rescue him! Do you know where he's being kept?"

"The Panther's men know his location. It is somewhere in the outskirts of Rome. However, there are many abandoned old monasteries. It would be a very difficult rescue mission but perhaps we shall try. But I have some idea."

"I think we have the same idea! We'll deliver a **fake letter** to them! They never saw the original, anyway! I am an expert on forgery," Benedict said, excited, laughing.

"That is exactly what I was thinking! You just read my mind! I know exactly how the letter, stamp and inscription look like. Benedict, please follow me to my library. A long time ago, I was thinking of making a copy of the letter just in case. I even bought a similar paper, ink and other materials. But I never did it! Why? I really don't know. Perhaps, I wasn't ready. But now I'm ready! How long would it take you to make the letter?"

"Perhaps, two hours," Benedict replied.

"Okay! You must be really good in that stuff! Meantime, I'll tell the Panthers to get ready for the rescue operation. They won't be so happy but they don't have any idea what to do. Perhaps, we must send the message to the *Vatican Police Chief of Operations* that we're ready for the negotiation. Indeed, we will make them happy. We'll send a professional messenger with the **Holy Letter**. I should call the local delivery agency and arrange an express messenger. You never know what the Vatican fellows have in mind. Perhaps, they want to keep him as a hostage. I can't lose anymore of my people!"

"Brilliant! Let's do it! No time to waste!" Benedict confirmed with a new enthusiasm. They moved to the library and Jerome pulled from his storage room all of the materials he collected over the last fifty years.

"This will do it! Look at this paper. I never thought I would ever use it! It looks like the original one. I ordered it from the art store, perhaps thirty years ago. I told them to make this special paper for me. It looks a bit aged now. Here I have a few pictures of the *original* **Holy Letter**. I'd like you to glance at them. It would give you some idea. I even bought dark brown ink, perhaps is aged too. It has the

499

aroma of fresh flowers. Are you ready?" Jerome asked.

"Yes, I am!" Benedict replied.

"Meantime, I'll work on a perfect stamp. Look at this chocolate plastic bar. It must be heated until it changes into the dense liquid, the consistency of volcano lava. We'll seal the letter with it. In the middle of the stamp we must press these two letters, **Chi-Rho.** On the other side of the letter is written the sentence in old Hebrew, and it means, who ever opens this letter, I will turn into dust. It would scare them from opening it, for sure! You just copy it as is."

"Sure, I am an expert on ancient scripts. What if they open the letter, anyway," Benedict asked with wonder.

"They will turn into dust! I'm joking at this point. I can add some pyrotechnic trick to the liquid stamp. I'll put some chemical powder with low heat point. When they break the stamp, the heat will ignite the powder which releases the odorless fume. I learned this trick in high-school. It will frighten them away.

Maybe you can write inside the letter something looking like an old script taken from the first ever *written Bible*. They wouldn't know if it is real or not!" Jerome pointed out, smiling.

"Until they try to open it, I could make it very believable to them. However, we may well encounter one problem; perhaps they'll want to see if the **Holy Letter** really works. You know, they have the **Quantum Disc and the Key**. They would have all this week to think about it. Maybe we should delay delivery of the letter. I have a feeling that they already know more than you and me."

500

"Benedict, we can't do that! Don't forget the fact that the life of my best friend is at stake. We must deliver this letter as soon as possible and before midnight. Otherwise, I'll lose my best friend. Don't forget that we are giving them a fake letter. I don't think that they know much! They just discovered the Holy Letter and by pure accident. Perhaps, they didn't even know if it existed. They don't know how to use it, anyway! Don't panic! This is not good for us and makes me more nervous."

"Maybe, they've already figured it out! It has been a few years since they heard about the **Holy Letter** and from your people. I'm telling you, Jerome, don't underestimate them! Those monks are very intelligent and possess the higher theological knowledge. We can only count on our pure luck in this case. We must pray for the best luck," Benedict added, laughing.

"Okay, there is a slight possibility that you're right. But I'm certain that they didn't figure it out yet! Just think how many years it took you to figure it out!"

"I wouldn't argue with you. Perhaps, you made your point, Jerome. Let me finish this script and we can finally seal the first letter. You know what I just thought about?"

"No, I don't!" Jerome said with puzzled smile.

"Before we travel on our secret mission to Rome, next week, we should make a few more copies in case Monk Salvatore would like to have one too," Benedict said, laughing.

"That is a splendid idea! I didn't think of that! Perhaps we'll give him one. You really outsmarted me, and I'm glad that you did! Oh, Benedict what

501

would I do without you?" Jerome asked, laughing.

"If we give him one, definitely he will be suspicious. He must steal the letter from us, on his own, but we must make one available to him. I mean in a moderate way and without too much fight. Anyway, he'd run fast and likely we'd be unable to catch him. Thus, it is exactly what we want to happen," Benedict concluded and went back to his writing and to finish his perfect reproduction of the Holy Letter.

Meanwhile, Jerome arranged the details of the rescue mission with the Panthers. Then he called for the messenger to come. Benedict finished his forgery task and announced in loud voice, "Jerome, bring the liquid stamp! I am ready to seal the letter!"

"Give me a minute! I'm coming!" Jerome shouted from the small workshop room. Within seconds, he appeared with a little bucket filled with liquid.

"Show me the letter, Benedict. Wow! It looks authentic! I'm really proud of you. With those two metal pins, hold the edge of it, and I'll pour very slowly the liquid over it. Okay, it's perfect. Now, with this graver carve the letter **Chi-Rho** in the middle. Okay, a little deeper. Yes, perfect! Just like the original. Now, put the letter into the plastic bag and we'll keep it in the freezer for ten minutes. The Messenger is coming within thirty minutes. In the library, on my desk I have the black wooden box. I think it would be perfect for the transportation. The messenger shouldn't know what's inside of the box. Trust me, it is better that way."

"Okay, perhaps you're right. How many more

copies should I make? Shall three more be enough?" Benedict asked.

"It should be plenty! I'll help you later. You can start working on it. We don't have much time left. I'll overlook the **letter** and meet you in the library in ten minutes."

"Okay, see you in awhile! It looks like I have a full time job for now," Benedict added on his way out as he sent a piercing look at Jerome. Jerome glanced back at him and laughed.

"You're the best, indeed."

Benedict was back in the library. He picked a few sheets of paper and continued his task. It would be much easier for the second time, he thought. After all, it was a fun job. Soon Jerome entered the room in a hurry.

"Benedict, would you give me that black box? I want to put the letter in it. The messenger is coming within five minutes. I have a little chain in the desk's drawer. Would you pass it to me?"

"Sure, here it is. The chain comes with a small lock. Actually, it looks very serious! You'll impress them, definitely," Benedict said.

"It must look serious! Okay, it is done! Let's go out to meet the messenger. He will take a plane to Rome within thirty minutes. I hope we will have some good news from the *Vatican Police*. I would say within three hours from now. Let's hope for the best! If everything goes well, Clement should be here before 11 p.m. The **Panthers** are waiting for him near the Vatican. They're already out there. If Clement is not released on time, they will strike the Headquarters. It could be a bloody combat out there.

503

Oh, here he is! The messenger just came. Hi Sir! Here is the package which you'll deliver to this address. This is your ticket to Rome, the money and good luck! Someone will meet you at the airport in Rome. The taxi driver, Piero will take you to the designated place. Do not lose the package! It is very important. After the delivery, I'd like you to do something special for me. I want you to give the message to my friend, Clement. You tell the guards that this is very important and you must deliver it in person. You tell Clement that **his mother is dying and wants to see him right away**! Have a safe trip."

"Thank you, Sir. I'll do my best," he replied and left in a hurry. The taxi drove him to the airport. My friend's life depends on his performance, he thought to himself. Benedict glanced at Jerome and asked, "Now, what are you up to, Jerome? Tell me, you just came up with a new plan. I can sense something unusual on your behalf."

"You sense quite well. I'll tell you what I have on my mind. When I saw this delivery guy, immediately I noticed a big similarity in his appearance to Clement. They just look like twin brothers. When he delivers the message to Clement about his dying mother, Clement would know exactly what to do. This message means to him that he must escape. We're two old foxes. We played these kinds of games when we were young. You want to know how he is going to escape. He will knock out the delivery man and exchange their clothes. Clement looks just like him and wearing the dark sun glasses, no one will recognize him. The taxi driver, Piero, is our undercover agent and he will take him right away to the airport. The Panthers will be notified about his successful escape, and they'll slowly back out of the Vatican territory. It would be the best scenario."

"What if it doesn't happen?"

"Then, they must try the hard way."

"What will happen to the delivery man?"

"They will have to let him go free. They will think that he is Clement, indeed. He'll be wearing Clement's clothes, anyway. On the top of that he is innocent. He was just a victim. It would take them some time to figure it out. I believe that they'll be so excited about the *Holy Letter* that without a question they will let him go right away. But there is always that proverbial 'if.'"

"It's a splendid plan Jerome. I hope it works well. I would never have known you were such a mastermind."

"I'm glad that you like it! Let's have some coffee and we shall finish the copies of the next **Holy Letter**. You're doing so well! We have a few hours to come up with another plan. Deep in my mind, I believe that Clement will be free. We don't want a war with the Vatican. It would be a disaster for all of us. I always thought that we couldn't live with each other but we can live next to each other."

"Very well put Jerome. Could you make us some of your good coffee while I finish this third letter? Please make mine with a sweet vanilla creamer."

"Don't worry! I'll make you the best coffee. I've done it all my life," Jerome concluded with a big smile and left.

They worked hard to finish the letters with

mastery. A few hours passed and they decided to check on Clement. It was almost eleven thirty p.m. someone knocked at the door. The doorkeeper announced that a visitor just arrived. Jerome hurried to the door. He smiled as he glanced at Clement, standing at the door laughing back at him. They successfully pulled off one more trick and perhaps the last one. "Nice to see you Clement,"

"Thank you for your message. I wouldn't be here without it."

"Come and have some coffee with me and my friend Benedict."

"Good coffee! I'll consider myself a very lucky fellow tonight. When I saw the Eiffel Tower from the plane I knew I was home."

"Benedict, this is my friend, Clement. He just arrived and we shall celebrate this moment with a bottle of good red wine."

"Nice to meet you, how was your trip?" Benedict said as he shook hands with Clement.

"It was quiet and I enjoyed myself immensely. The most important thing is I am home. It couldn't be a better time for me, out there was a bit uncomfortable."

"We're glad that you're alive. Jerome is a brilliant man. I would say, rather it was a sort of miracle. Perhaps, it was a coincidence that you really look like the delivery man. You're very lucky today!"

"The wine is on its way," Jerome said as he walked into the library.

"Indeed, I'm lucky. But I'm not sure I was worth such a sacrifice. This **Holy Letter** has more value than my old body. Don't you think so?"

506

"We didn't think that way. On top of that, we came up with that ingenious idea. Didn't we?" Jerome said as he glanced at Benedict.

"What kind of idea?" Clement asked, wondering.

"Tell him Benedict what we did," Jerome said proudly.

"We forged the **Holy Letter**. We sent the Vatican Police a *fake letter*. Hopefully, they haven't figured it out yet. It would take them some time to solve the puzzle. We are counting on our luck. We need more luck for our upcoming secret mission in exactly five days," Benedict proudly said.

"It was a brilliant idea, indeed! I wouldn't know that something like that could even work. You're very brave fellows! I also didn't know that you have such a talent," he said, stunned by the news.

"It wasn't me, it was Benedict. He is the mastermind behind that. He is an expert on forgery. The copy looks identical, at least outside. We made a few more copies. Benedict, show him one."

"Sure, why not! I've already made three more. However, they are all already sealed," Benedict said and brought over a perfect copy. Clement glanced at it and commented,

"It is a real masterpiece, indeed! You have a fantastic talent, Benedict. But why would you need so many letters?"

"This is another good question, Clement. Lately there are so many strange things going on everywhere. We need those copies to protect the original letter. We've discovered that there are a few more people who would like to have the letter. So, we will let them steal the fake ones from us. Perhaps it sounds funny but we don't have a choice. Do we?" Jerome pointed out with satisfaction.

"I get your point. Very clever indeed," Clement said, still surprised.

"The Panthers are coming tonight. I believe they will arrive here within the hour. It is almost one a.m. I'll wait for them. You two go ahead and get some sleep, you must be exhausted! One more thing, did they pull the poisonous microchip from your tooth? They took your medallion for sure," Jerome asked with a smile.

"Yes they did. As a matter of fact that is why I'm still alive. *Thank you to you and to God as well.* I'm exhausted! Goodnight! See you tomorrow," Clement said on his way out. He looked tired and his face was quite swollen from the interrogation. Even though, he was happy to be alive.

"Jerome, I can keep you company. I'm not sleepy at all. I'm a bit nervous about our upcoming mission. I've been going over and over every single move and it is driving me crazy," Benedict said in a quiet tone.

"There is no reason to be nervous. You don't really know how good you are. You're a step ahead of the entire *Vatican Police.* Just think that you're already a *winner!* That is what I'm thinking. Now, I feel like I should laugh out and loud, especially after the trick I pulled with Clement. But I must tell you that I didn't have a doubt for a moment. Have more faith! You're a priest. Aren't you?"Jerome said, laughing friendly.

"Sure, you've almost convinced me. I must

508

believe in myself. I don't want to die before my mission is completed. The discovery of the **Holy Letter** will stun the world. But the discovery of the **Quantum Disc** in motion would *revolutionize* all nations. We're closer to *cracking the code* of the universe than we originally thought. Did you ever think that you would be part of that one day?"

"No, I didn't! It is happening only because of you and you should give yourself more credit for it. You probably do not recognize how ingenious you really are!" Jerome said as he glanced at Benedict.

"Thank you for believing in me," Benedict said humbly.

"I see through the window that someone has just arrived. Here is your coffee, let me go find out."

The fresh aroma of coffee spread into the air and made Benedict happy.

"Thank you, Jerome." Sipping his coffee he walked to the window and spotted an army of **Panthers** guys gathering on the compound. They talked for a moment and soon followed Jerome inside the house. They went to the dinning room. Jerome came back and asked,

"Benedict, are you hungry? Come with me. I would like to talk to them about our mission. We must make exact plans and discuss each detail. I know it is a bit late but this is very important."

"Sure, I wouldn't mind. However, I'm tired."

"It won't take long. I just want to be sure that we understand each other. They must be invisible on Vatican territory. We can't fail now. The worst thing is, I can bet, that Salvatore will be there. He will try to interrupt our operation."

"Oh, yes! I agree with you one hundred percent. It is rather urgent to discuss this." Benedict agreed with his point. They went to the dining hall to join others. The conversation lasted for almost two hours and was very fruitful.

The next morning they gathered for a quick breakfast. The **Panthers** received explicit directions as to their new mission. They would leave for Rome a day or two earlier in order to prepare the ground for their action. The mission needs some practice. Clement partially recovered from his unpleasant ordeal and decided to go back to his estate just a few miles away from Jerome. On his way out he said,

"Jerome, thank you for everything you've done for me. I wouldn't be alive without you. Now, I feel secure and can go with peace. See you soon and give my regards to Benedict."

"I will! Don't worry about anything. My driver will take you there. Take care of yourself and I will see you next week! Be sure to call your body guards. You'll need them from now on. This is your new medallion. Take care," Jerome said and walked him outside.

The black Bentley took off. Jerome went to his library, sat in the armchair, and picked the first book from the shelf. He enjoyed reading for an hour, smiling occasionally. He became tired. His eyes traveled between the bookshelves perhaps looking for some treasure book he had missed in the past. Finally, he closed his eyes for a short nap. The last few days took their toll and he fell asleep. He had a peaceful dream and he needed it more than anything else.

Meantime, Benedict relaxed in the garden reading the local newspaper. It was like sitting in a magic garden, listening to the voice of Mother Nature, he was blessed. The sun, singing birds, and aromas of fresh flowers added the perfect atmosphere to his composed mood. It was like listening to the perfect symphony. He covered his face with the newspaper and couldn't dream of anything better. That mystic moment lasted for almost two hours.

The house dog came and pulled the newspaper off of his face. He awoke from his dream quite surprised. The dog gave him a sweet look and licked his face a few times. Benedict laughed, murmuring,

"Hey, you fellow creature, go away! Let me rest a bit more." He opened his eyes and saw Jerome in the distance.

"Dragon, come here!" The dog took off and ran toward his master. Jerome threw the ball and the dog ran back and forth. Then he said, "Good job, Dragon! Bring me the ball. Oh, yes! Good boy!" Jerome paused next to Benedict and asked,

"Did you get some rest?"

"I did! Last night was exhausting, I'm happy that it is over. You have such a beautiful garden, a piece of art Mother Nature exclusively created for you. I could sleep here every day. Dragon just woke me up. You must be tired yourself."

"I took a nap in the armchair in the library reading my favorite fiction book. Now, I feel like a newborn again. Let's have something for lunch. Lately, I'm hungry more often. I think I'm getting old."

"Don't worry, Jerome, you're not alone, I'm in

the same shoes. Perhaps we're two old horses. What do you propose for lunch?"

"Let's find out what the cooks made. I'm not so picky. Whatever they cook, I like. Isn't it strange?"

"They must be good cooks otherwise you would mind."

"Perhaps, you're right, Benedict. I can smell a fried fish and some grilled shrimp. You will enjoy it too."

"I love that stuff! After lunch, we shall find out how we're going to transfer the **Holy Letter** *to* Rome. It has been on my mind for some time. We could wrap the real letter around your chest and the fake one around your ankle. The last one should have more exposure and it must be a temptation for any curious thief. We have only a few days left before our mission."

"You're right. We must practice the procedure! Tomorrow, I'll take you with me to the *secret place* not far from here, to get the *Holy Letter.* I hope the untamed Salvatore won't follow us. He could scare the crap out of anybody. He can only be fought with strength and endurance. Hopefully, we can manage every situation."

"I think we must pick the right time for our assignment. I propose four a.m. He couldn't be around at that early hour," Benedict suggested with a bit of concern.

"I have a better plan. My private jet will take us there, tomorrow after lunch. Hopefully, Salvatore can't fly can he? How about that," Jerome mockingly announced.

"Splendid! I like it better your way. But are you

sure, you can fly? You told me that you get vertigo."

"Only when I fly longer than thirty minutes, this is a fifteen minute flight. It won't do me much harm. Also, I will take some motion sickness pills before we take off. Do not worry, I'll be fine! If we must do it right, we better do it ourselves."

"Perhaps, you're right. It would save us time and aggravation." Benedict confirmed in an earnest tone.

"I'm glad that we agree on these procedures. Would you like more shrimp?"

"I love to eat that stuff but perhaps two more will not do much harm to me. I'm positively sure about it."

"Don't be too shy, we've got plenty of it. You better enjoy! Drink some red wine. The scientists said it kills cholesterol in your blood. Let me bring fresh coffee. It'll keep us awake. I'll be back in a few minutes."

"Sure, take your time." Benedict relaxed and was eager to have some wine, too. He sat on the leather sofa, giving some thought to himself. He felt good about the upcoming mission. Perhaps, his self-confidence was unexpectedly back. His dream was getting closer to materializing in front of his eyes. He gazed into the air, daydreaming or looking for a better solution to his dilemma. His silence was soon interrupted by Jerome coming in with two cups of coffee. He was singing his favorite tunes from *the Verdi* opera. It made him happy and filled his spirit with a new optimism.

"Hello, hello! I'm back! Here is your coffee, Benedict. I brought you a few cookies with almonds too. I thought you might like them."

"Thank you for thinking of me. The best of all is the fresh aroma of coffee mingled with the air. Hmm, it tastes really good, a little heaven in my mouth. I feel very relaxed now," Benedict said, sipping his coffee.

"I'm glad to hear that! Sometimes, I think we're blessed just to be alive. There are so many disasters, in the world. We should be thankful for every second of our existence. Ten minutes more and we shall go to the library and practice the wrapping of **the Holy Letter**."

"You just read my mind," Benedict confirmed, smiling.

"Also I want to show you something. It is my hunting vest. On the back of it is the interior pocket where I'll be able to put the real *letter.* It has a zipper in the front. It has been hanging in my closet for many years. Let me put it on and you will have a better idea. What do you think?" Jerome asked as he put his black vest on.

"How strong is it?" Benedict asked.

"Very strong, it already survived many battles." he laughed.

"Then we should go with it. The fake letter we will tape above your ankle, under the elastic black band. It must look like the real deal."

"I think I have something that looks quite close to that. Look! I have at least five different bands from black to white. I use them when I exercise, mostly jogging."

"It will do! Let's try and see how it will work. Are you ready?" Benedict said, excited. He picked up the fake letter.

514

"I'm ready! Okay, the band is on. Give me the letter," Jerome said and slipped it behind the band.

"Wow! It looks great and very tempting, this is exactly what we want," Benedict announced proudly.

"That's one less problem for now. Are you really sure that Salvatore will be on the same train with us? What if he tries to kill me?"

"Jerome, don't panic. The security, Panthers and I will be there. We'll pretend that we're in a deep sleep and give him the opportunity to steal the fake letter from you. You'll discretely pull one of your slacks up a bit to reveal the band and the letter. Let's practice the situation again. Ready, camera, action, go!" Benedict said, laughing.

"You're giving me a heart attack. Oh, Holy Raphael! What if I have one, on the train?" Jerome said with concern.

"You won't! This is only a rehearsal. More rehearsals are better than none. Sooner or later, it will become a simple routine, and you won't even notice it. You'll do it automatically. Did you get it?"

"Sure, sure, I got it! I wonder if there is another way of doing that."

"I don't think so! This is the only way. Jerome, concentrate. It is very important. We'll do it a few times more and soon it will be over. Just close your eyes and imagine that you're on the train."

"Okay! Let's do it!" Jerome burst out with emotion and did what he was asked. After thirty minutes of intense rehearsal they called off everything. They were stressed out and exhausted. Jerome said,

"It is pointless to simulate any particular

515

situation because we don't really know what will happen out there. Perhaps, it wouldn't happen then what are we going to do?"

"We better do it, in case. From my experience with Salvatore, I can guarantee you that the probability of it happening is ninety nine percent. He is a smart guy but we have to outsmart him. I'll bet you that there is only a one percent chance that it wouldn't happen," Benedict anxiously pointed out, a bit frustrated.

"Okay! Perhaps, you're right! Here is the letter. Let's take a break. I would like to get some rest and finish reading my book. See you later for dinner. You should get some rest as well," Jerome said on his way out.

"I'll, see you later." Benedict walked to the garden, laid on the canvas-chair and listened to the whispering of Mother Nature again. He had peace of mind and finally could relax. He knew that the upcoming ordeal wouldn't be so easy but he smiled. His faith was getting stronger each time he thought of the mission. What else could stand in his way he didn't really know yet? He closed his eyes and thought of the best nap he could get here in the womb of Mother Nature.

The next morning something special was in the air, perhaps a newly born optimism. Jerome ran to the living room quite refreshed and then greeted Benedict warmly,

"I never have this much energy perhaps, I'm getting younger! You look sparkling yourself."

"I'm doing great! I slept like an angel with no particular dream thus I feel lighter this morning. The past few nights were full of heavy and strange dreams which added an additional weight to my body. My mind is clear right now and I can think even better."

"Let's have a light breakfast and then we can play tennis for an hour. What do you think, Benedict?"

"I think it is a splendid offer and I can't refuse. Let's do it."

The breakfast was modest and quick. They were in a hurry to play tennis. Indeed, it was very relaxing and challenging at the same time. Sweating and tired, Benedict and Jerome sat on a bench.

"It is tough and I like it! Perhaps, I lost a few pounds too. But I must admit that I'm not twenty anymore."

"Me too but at least I tried my best. I'm a decade older than you. Considering that, I wasn't so bad after-all," Jerome added with a cheerful smile. They sat in canvas-chairs, drinking water, gasping and laughing together. Jerome added,

"We must get ready soon for our departure. The pilot will be here within an hour. Are you hungry? If you are, we can have a quick salad. I'm not very hungry however, we should have something."

"I think the salad would be just right for me. However, I would like to take shower," Benedict added calmly.

"Perhaps, I shall do the same," Jerome said and excused himself. They met again, twenty minutes later, at the table for the quick salad and coffee.

"After lunch, I would like to show you something that could be of interest to you. We still have some time. Doctors recommend slow-eating," Jerome pointed out with satisfaction.

517

"Sure, I always eat slowly otherwise my stomach gets easily upset. Then what is our plan?" Benedict asked, wondering.

"This is what I would like to talk to you about. I keep in my library a very special document; I'd say an old map. I've inherited it from my ancestors. You wonder what that is. It is a forgotten piece of land. Bring the coffee with you and follow me to the library. You see, I have a few secrets, however, each one I keep only to myself otherwise it wouldn't be a secret anymore. Am I right?"

"You are one hundred percent right!"

"I'm glad that you understand my point. In one of those few hundred books, I keep an old map. You see those red books in the leather covers with the gold letters on the back. I'll pull out one of them. I know exactly which one, from all the fifty books that look alike. As I've already mentioned, I inherited a huge piece of wild land where the local river meets the mountains in a sort of bay. People said that one of the kings kept his prisoners in the underwater mountain's caves. My pilot will take us there in a few minutes. Here is the map. Look, it is at least 400 years old and this is the place, a hidden cave, I'm taking you with me. Here is your diving equipment. You'll need it."

"I've never dived! I'm not sure if I'll be able to do it," Benedict pointed out with concern.

"I wouldn't worry too much if I was you. It is easier than you think. I'll teach you and perhaps assist you all the way to the cave. It only takes seven minutes," Jerome said, smiling.

"Okay, whatever you say. I trust you! Let's go

518

then," Benedict confirmed with a bit of enthusiasm, carrying his diving equipment.

"You see, my pilot, is already here," Jerome announced, taking a few pills for his motion sickness.

They got into the small jet and took off. The flight was peaceful and short, perhaps only fifteen minutes. They landed at the bottom of the valley, just walking distance to the vast bay. Jerome gave Benedict verbal instructions on how to dive. As soon as they reached their destination, Jerome said, "Okay, now I would like you to do exactly what I do. But before we do that I must turn off an electric power supply to the underwater iron gate. I installed the electric shocker at the gate in case any intruder dared to go down there. The gate protects the cave entry. I have the keys to it. Also I put a few cameras out there. The recording system is inside the cave. I think we can go now. Put this leather band with the flashlights around your head. You can see well. Here is your breathing apparatus. This part goes in your mouth. Try to be calm as much as possible and do not panic under any circumstances. I'll be there watching over you. Wear this suit as it will keep you warm. Also keep your eyes open! Everything will be fine, trust me. Okay, now follow me slowly. The water is a bit chilly but only at the beginning. Are you okay?"

"I'm freaked out a bit but I trust in every word you said. I'm ready to go," Benedict said with a skeptical eye.

They swam smoothly to the underwater foliated tracery in the Gothic gate. Jerome pulled the keys from his pocket. There were three different locks. Each key was attached to the long chain embraced around his waist. He unlocked the gate and they swam through. Jerome locked the gate behind them to be sure that no one would follow them. Finally they emerged in the middle of the dark cave. They walked through the shallow water, sat at the rocky edge and removed the breathing devices. Jerome set the lights on. He installed in the cave an electrical generator many years ago.

"What a swim," Benedict said with disbelief.

"You did very well for your first time. I don't believe how good you are. Let's rest for a few minutes. Are you okay?"

"I'm fine. You can live in this cave. Can't you? It is huge and has some unusual rock formations. Perhaps some precious metals you can find right here too," Benedict pointed out with a happy face.

"I can show you around. This cave is long and has many small sister caves spread in different directions. You can get lost here too. For many centuries no one has been here, only my father and I. For many years we'd secretly explore this cave piece after piece. Maybe, fifty years ago we found some human skeletons randomly abandoned all over the caves. He was an anthropologist and examined the bones. He said those people had died at least ten centuries ago. We gave the bones the proper burial, outside, in the mountains. Perhaps they are grateful for that."

"I'm sure they would tell you that one day. Then what else happened here?" Benedict asked, laughing.

"Not much since then but it is definitely a *perfect secret place* for hiding any treasure. There is a possibility that gold could be found between those rocks but the excavation would probably cost more than the gold itself. I wouldn't touch it. I'd rather enjoy the beauty of it. Trust me it is worth more than any money."

"Perhaps, you're right. I already feel the secrets emanating from it and see the jade formation in front of my own eyes. I wouldn't dare to destroy it for any material pleasure. It is a beauty hidden in an unspeakable form," Benedict confirmed with a smile.

"Okay, let's get the **Holy Letter** and get out of here. I would like to show you the place where I hid this priceless piece. It looks like feretory. Believe it or not, an artist, perhaps a real mastermind carved in stone, a real piece of art. He built some kind of mysterious mechanism hidden behind those rocks. Just look! When I touch this small figurine and turn it clockwise, it mobilizes that mechanism which moves the stones underneath, and then reveals a secret chamber beneath where I hid the letter. Can you believe it?" Jerome said still stunned by the wonder.

"I believe it! It is really tricky and I like it! Do you see these little fish symbols carved on every stone? I noticed some other monograms on the walls. Look, right here! Perhaps, the first Christians were living or rather hiding in this cave for a long time. It could be their first sanctuary. It must be at least two thousand years old. The Christian fugitives, perhaps hundreds of them, from Israel and Egypt found their asylum right here, in the French mountains. I can hear their whispering," Benedict said, astounded.

"I didn't think much of it but you're right. Now, I can see so many little carvings on the walls. How clever of you. Let me get the **Holy Letter** for now.

Look! I'm holding a real treasure in my hands."

"Can I touch it?" Benedict asked.

"Sure, you can," Jerome replied.

"It is indeed **the Real Letter from God. I already feel its vibration!** I wouldn't even dream of holding it. It is a priceless *treasure given to all humanity*. We don't really know its contents. However, this great gift could be a cause of war between the Vatican and us. Perhaps many would die in the name of it," Benedict said with somber thoughts.

"This is why we must do everything secretly. Not many should know about the date of our mission," Jerome underlined his point with bold enthusiasm.

"It is inevitable. It is a bit too late. Don't you think so? Too many people already know about our mission. Let's count; the **Green Panthers**, kids, us, our friends, and then Monk Salvatore plus the Vatican Police, quite a lot," Benedict pointed out with really deep concern.

"A bit too much but I wouldn't worry about all of them for now. Our concern is to reveal the truth and we hold the key to it! I'm positive. Let's go! Put your equipment on, and we should leave."

"Sure, I'm ready. I hope your pilot, Philippe, is still waiting for us."

"Don't worry; he wouldn't fly off without us. Let me look into the cameras and see if the underwater passage is clear for our return. I always do that for my own security. We must be sure that everything is okay. Follow me to my library where I built some bookshelves and put the security system. I come here once a month to check if everything is working properly. If you like you can sit on the stone bench with a real lion skin. Okay, let's check if each camera is working well. They seem okay. But here in the middle is a strange looking object. Benedict, come here. What do you think? What the hell is that?"

"Can you magnify this area? Perhaps, we have a visitor," Benedict concluded.

"It couldn't be! No one knows about this place."

"I wouldn't be so sure. Perhaps, no one knew until now."

"It looks like someone is there but the picture is not clear. Let's try from a different angle," Jerome said, typing some instructions onto the computer.

"The image looks very familiar. I see a male' Rolex on his wrist."

"Are you sure? This must be Philippe. I gave him the same Rolex on his birthday, last year. But what he is doing out there?"

"Jerome, don't you see? He doesn't have any breathing device on his face. He is dead. Perhaps, he missed us and wanted to check where we were."

"Stop joking! Likely, some bastards killed him! We have intruders at the bay. Now, we're facing a one of a kind situation. Let me think for a moment, what shall we do? We already lost the pilot and now we must find the way back to my estate alive. We must think really hard like a killer thinks. What would be his next step? Definitely, we can't go back through the gate. Wait! I want to check one more thing. Stay away from the water! Look! Someone out there switched the electric power back on. He is smart ass for sure. You put your hand into the water now and you'll be dead. I have this special device which shows that the power is on. You see the red light is on, it means the electric is on too. Definitely, whoever is out there wants us dead."

"Then what are we going to do?"

"We have another passage, approximately one hour walk from here. The exit is on the other side of the mountains. I know the way very well. I ran here many times when I was a kid. Just follow me. Let's abandon our diving equipment right here and put our regular clothes on. I have some extra clothes in my storage closet," Jerome said as he put the **Holy Letter** into his pocket.

"I thought we would get stuck here forever. Now, I feel relief. Okay, I'm ready to go."

"The good thing is that they don't know this cave. They don't have any clue that we will be out of here within an hour. Take your flashlight and try to relax for the rest of our journey. The time will fly fast."

"Then what would happen next?" Benedict asked deeply concerned.

"Benedict, do not worry! I promise you that we'll find the way. There is a footpath which takes us to a small town where I have a little cottage. We'd take rest out there and have some food. I hope the old car has some gas in it. We'll drive to my home from there, tomorrow morning."

"How far is the town?"

"Perhaps, eight miles; I'd say, total three hours walk from here."

"Not so bad. I like to walk. I hope we can make it."

"Sure, we can! We have plenty of time. I'm an old trooper. My father took me, many times, to this small town. He had some friends out there. They are probably already gone. Also I remember there was a fine girl, named Josephine. She lived in a big estate surrounded by a beautiful rose garden and cherry trees. I played with her many times. Later, I became crazy about her. At that time, I was only twelve. But it was fifty years ago or even more. However, I remember everything like it just happened yesterday. I wonder what did happen to her. How fast time flies?"

"You're right Jerome. It does speed by. I remember when I was ten how happy and carefree I was. But everything that happened is a history today at least for me."

"Did you miss anything from your past?"

"Not much happened in my life, really, no love stories just work and study. I was a monk! Just remember that. You can imagine how simple my life was. So far, I have no regrets. I love books, scripts, ancient scrolls, and research. I was never bored with that and always excited about each new discovery I made."

"I missed many things in my life. However, it is too late for any regrets. I just accepted my life the way it was. Perhaps everything that happened was my destiny. This is the way I feel about it. But the most important thing is I tried to be happy and enjoy every moment of it because each one was unique and happened only once. Look! Do you see the light out there? We're almost done. Within ten minutes we'll emerge on the other side of the cave."

"It was faster than I thought. You are a good walker," Benedict said with relief.

"When you talk, the time goes really fast. The air here is a bit heavy. I desperately need fresh air. I brought some water with me. Would you like to have a bottle?"

"Sure! I'm glad that we're almost done. You know what I'm thinking about."

"No! I have no clue," Jerome replied.

"Have you ever imagined what would happen in a cave like this if an earthquake strikes?"

"I haven't but I believe that we wouldn't feel much. The mountains are strong and solid."

"I think there is always that possibility that the cave could permanently close at the exit if the blocks of stones move vertically and horizontally."

"Perhaps, you're right at this point. It could happen at any moment. We'd better hurry," Jerome confirmed with a big smile on his face as they finally reached the exit.

"Oh, you scared me a bit. Look at the sun and feel the aroma of fresh wild flowers. I love it! I feel like we found a new paradise, perhaps lost for thousands of years. Let's sit for a moment on the green glade. I couldn't imagine anything better than this for myself." Benedict lay down on the green grass and closed his eyes for a long time. Jerome sat on the cliff, looking around or perhaps thinking of how lucky they were to be there. The good part of that was that no one knew about their new location. He too lay down, closed his eyes. Indeed, it was good nap for at least half an hour.

Jerome stood up, looked at the sky and said,

"Benedict it is time to go. The storm is coming within an hour, I believe. We better keep walking."

"I'm ready to go. Maybe if we walk fast, we can make it within two hours," Benedict replied.

"We can always try but it takes longer than that. We can run if you like," Jerome pointed out and whistled his favorite tunes.

"I'm not sure if I can run fast enough but it is not a bad idea. The nature around us is so absorbing that it would be a real pleasure to run all the way to your cottage. I'm getting a bit hungry."

"Not so far from here are tomato and cucumber fields, just next to our pathway. We can pick a few. Just wait twenty more minutes. This cave can be reached by foot only from this town. The villagers know about the cave but they don't explore it. They could be the descendants of the first Christians who found shelter in the cave, many centuries ago. The canyon around protects this place. You see, we are already near the tomato field. Let's take a few minutes break; sit down and relax. Let me try the fruits of Mother Nature. It tastes fantastically good. I feel much better now. It is tomato season thus the timing is perfect for them and for us too. Look out there is the cucumber field. How do you like the flavor?"

"I love it; it is wild! Tomatoes are very sweet and have this special spice. I feel much better now. There is nothing worse than a hungry man. Don't you agree?"

"Sure, I do. Let's take a few tomatoes home. I'll make a good salad for dinner," Jerome replied. They paused next to the cucumber field. Jerome picked a few and said,

"They have a perfect aroma but taste even better. Try one surely, you'll like it."

"I love freshly picked crispy cucumbers. Just like in my boyhood! You can eat them forever. Don't you feel that way?" Benedict made his point.

"You're right! As a kid I was crazy about freshly picked cucumbers straight from the field, and especially from the neighbor's field. For some unknown reason, they always tasted better than my own. I can eat them forever too. I'll take a few home," Jerome said, laughing.

They left the farmers fields and walked fast. They glanced at the dark heavy cumulus hanging above their heads. The air cooled down a bit. Finally they reached the streets of a small mountain's village. The rain suddenly picked up and it's pouring hard. The streets were already flooded and every single soul had vanished in that proverbial black hole.

"We look like wet horses. My cottage is one block away just around the corner. We're almost there. Try to relax and hang a little bit longer."

"Oh, Holy Anthony; I don't know if I can relax. I'm already swimming in my own shoes. Thanks for the summer otherwise I would be walking ice-cube."

"Okay, here we are! Where is my key? I almost forgot. I hid it in the flower's vase like all of us do in this town. They are very honest people. The door is open, get in Benedict. Let's get a quick shower. You take this bathroom. The towels and bathrobe are in. I will go upstairs."

"Thank you, Jerome. I'll do that," Benedict replied, squeezing a partial smile on his face.
They met in the kitchen twenty minutes later. Jerome made salad from fresh cucumbers and tomatoes, and fried mushrooms with eggs. They sat at the table and enjoyed an early dinner. Benedict served the red wine and said,

"How is the letter? Did it get wet like us?"

"No, it can't get wet or damaged. I believe, it has some kind of divine properties and is rain proof as well as any type of disaster."

"It has an amazing quality, indeed!"

"Sure, it has. Now, I would like to show you my cottage. It is a very modern piece of art inside mingled with a perfect touch of country style. I like to be here alone from time to time just to enjoy the outdoor scenery and experience the beauty of nature. Look at the mountain's view; you can die for it! From time to time I want to have this special time to myself just to contemplate my life in a solitary fashion; perhaps, only me and God."

"Sure, I fully understand that. I have those moments from time to time as well. As I got older I recognized that I want to do something special for other people. This is why my Mission is so important to me. Perhaps, they will remember me for long time."

"It sounds very altruistic but I'm glad to be part of that. I didn't recognize what was or is so important in my life, and perhaps now is the time to realize the impelling truth. I'm truly glad that I finally grew up to it!"

"Jerome, it is really nice to hear something like this from a man like you. If only more people could feel that way, this life would be more beautiful for each and every one of us. Perhaps, we would understand one another better and give each other more heart. Life would be perfect; at least we would be free of stress. What is our plan?"

"I would like to stay here overnight and tomorrow morning we will leave. I'm exhausted after

529

our adventure in the cave. I must send a few security guards and divers to pick up Philippe's body. It should never have happened. He had a gun and knew how to use it, he must have been surprised," he said in a stoic tone.

"I agree with you. It was a fatal accident. I'm fully stunned and surprised at the same time that we have the same kind of barefooted beatnik, Monk Salvatore, always following us. The worst part is we can't catch him. This renegade drives me crazy! I'm exhausted and will go to bed now. Perhaps we should feel lucky that we are still alive!" Benedict said.

"Your room is upstairs. I'll see you tomorrow. I'm going to read a book for a while," Jerome said and picked up his favorite book from the shelf. He sat in a comfortable armchair in the living room. He read a few pages trying to relax but his mind was busy putting the pieces of the puzzle together. It was more than he could handle for that evening. He struggled as his mind was in perpetual tension, wondering between contemplative inner peace and unknown tomorrow. He thought of this disturbing character, Monk Salvatore who he thought of as a martial arts demon, wandering loner, and Spider-Monk. He was a paradox to him, a sort of vague rebellious antihero. Despite his dreary thoughts, his brain sent some kind of laconic impulses to his body and finally he fell asleep. The night was peaceful and without intruders.

At early morning, Jerome served breakfast in the garden under the indigo blue sky. Soon after coffee and friendly conversation they hurried to leave. Jerome took his car and they drove away, leaving behind his peaceful cottage. Benedict glanced for the last time and said,

"I would like to come back here one day. I found a peace in this little house of yours and I'll miss it."

"I'm glad that you liked it. I must tell you that this is my favorite place too. No one ever bothers me here. I can have a peaceful breakfast at least. We'll come here more often then."

"Sure, I might move here for the summer. I've given a lot of thought about my life lately and perhaps it is time for me to settle down in one place for good. I want to write a book about my life. However, with all of the danger I've been facing, I may not live much longer."

"Don't say that Benedict. You'll live a long life. I can guarantee you. You can move here and live for as long as you like," Jerome said, smiling.

"Thank you, Jerome. I shall think seriously about your offer. Perhaps soon after the mission I will consider it. Tell me how far are we from your estate?"

"Not too far. Look at the view! Nature couldn't be more gracious to us today. Those endless fields look like a paradise. Did you ever think that perhaps we're living in one? We just don't see it. We are blind perhaps. You can smell the aroma of fresh bluebottles and poppies. I love theirs smell."

"Oh, yes! I can smell them too. It reminds me of my childhood. I would say it was the best time of my innocent life. It would never come back," Benedict pointed out with a tear in his eye.

"But you can always bring it back, in your memory," Jerome added with a smile.

Soon they reached Jerome's estate. Jerome

picked his cell phone up and dialed the number. He spoke for quite a long time. Benedict sat in the garden and sighed with relief. It was a stressful assignment for both of them, he thought. Jerome walked to the garden a bit confused.

"Philippe didn't have any family. I must take care of the funeral arrangements. I raised him like my own son. He was too young, much too young! I can't believe that he is already gone. Oh, God why did this happen?" Jerome whispered.

"We never know when God is going to call us up there. You're right, he was very young and talented man, indeed," Benedict confirmed with certainty.

"I sent already some divers, guards, and another pilot to the bay. They will fly the jet back and bring Philippe's body to the hospital for an autopsy. I would like to drive out there myself. I must see what really happened at the bay. In the meantime, come with me. I want to show you where I'll put the **Holy Letter**. Be sure you have an open eye on anyone who will try to get in. Let them wait for me outside, in the garden. I have a few Panther's guys looking around my property. You won't be alone. I'll be back in two hours. Try to relax," Jerome said on his way to the library. Benedict followed him. Using a long metal stick, Jerome pulled an ordinary book down from the highest shelf and put the **Holy Letter** in it.

"Don't worry about me. I'll be watching for strangers," Benedict replied, wandering around.

"Also try to memorize this particular book; in brown leather cover with gold letters on the back. It says in Latin, **Whoever Lives and Believes in Me**

Shall Never Die. It is easy; however, I have at least fifty of the same looking books on those upper shelves, with slightly different inscriptions. Now, I'll show you a sort of trick, I mean, it is a very sophisticated mechanism which I installed here many years ago. It will allow you to put any book back on the upper shelf without going there. Just look! You see this green book on the lower shelf, just to your right. Take it out, you'll find a black painted square inside that looks just like a mini tile. Press it with your finger. Hold the book in your hand. Do you see the metal arm emerging above you? It is made of iron and it has special sensors located at the end of each artificial finger. Now put your book between those metal fingers and wait. The sensors with a mini camera at the end of each finger will recognize this particular book and then will put it back into the exact location. Isn't it great?"

"It is splendid, definitely the work of a genius!" Benedict applauded with excitement.

"That is what I think. I asked a few of my friends to do that for me. Most of them are scientists and engineers. They work on great ideas on a daily basis. Okay, I must leave you for now. I think my driver is waiting for me. I will see you soon."

"Sure, I'll be here watching for you," Benedict replied.

Jerome left in a hurry. Benedict glanced at that special book for the last time, trying to memorize its position on the upper shelf and then left the library, locking the door behind him. He went to the garden and walked around the estate a few times to be sure that no one was hiding in the bushes. The view was very picturesque as the estate was elevated on a hill. The air was clean and scented with the aroma of acacia flowers. A few grasshoppers were jumping from green grassy juicy leaves onto the surrounding colorful flowers, perhaps playing a sort of flirting game with one another. The sun was bright and sent a stream of warm pleasurable rays to every living creature including grasshoppers and the tiny ants crawling around his feet. He paused next to the pond filled with exotic fish, lilies and the stones decorated with ancient petro-glyphs. He looked around and then thought, he was blessed, feeling a sort of pleasure beyond reason. A few wrinkles unraveled in his mind, trying to inject some originality into his imaginative thoughts. It was the place where everyone wanted to be to enjoy the quiet beauty inherent in nature. He glanced at the sun and saw the colors of red, blue, and yellow.

He heard some noises in the distance in the garden, taking nothing for granted he rushed out there to find that it was only a barking dog, playing with one of the security guards. He glanced at them and laughed.

He felt more secure and everything seemed under control. He lay on the green grass with a feeling of fulfillment and satisfaction. His mind was at peace. He lost his sense of time but the most important thing at that moment was his inner gratification. He closed his eyes and fell asleep. In his short dream he was running, trying to escape from the hunter. He stopped at the edge of a cliff. He glanced down and saw an endless deep canyon. He looked back and saw the man in black running after him. Who was that man?

He thought. Without giving it much thought, he jumped. Then he heard someone called his name, "Wake up! Benedict. Wake up!" He opened his eyes and saw Jerome standing over him laughing.

"I'm sorry! I was really exhausted. Then I had this strange dream that I jumped off the cliff and then someone called my name," he said as he lifted himself from the grassy land.

"It was me. How have you been?" Jerome asked.

"I'm okay and everything is under control. Then tell me what happened out there?"

"As I mentioned to you, some bastards cut Philippe's throat completely. It was a brutal and terrible act. I'll chase those bastards and kill them. It was good that you didn't see him. It was very scary to see my best friend in this awful condition. They took him to the hospital for an autopsy. I'll make the funeral arrangements within a day or two. I'm completely devastated and I need some rest."

"I understand and I'm startled even more than you, Jerome. We'll find the killer and justice will be done. Let's have a coffee."

"I need it! After seeing my friend in that condition, how can I be so sure that we will arrive in Rome in one piece? We still don't have enough security right here and we wouldn't have enough in the train! What are we going to do?" Jerome lamented.

"Do you know what I think now? Maybe the security is not the key."

"Then what is the key?" Jerome asked confused.

"The key is in the way we think. We must outsmart the killer by helping him. We have plan **A** for ourselves and plan **B** for the killer. These two plans must overlap at the beginning but at the end they must go in two different directions. We're not going to hide from the killer but just the opposite; we will sit next to him with our plan worked out to perfection. We're going to help the killer steal the fake letter from us and we're not going to chase him. We'll pretend that we're asleep. Try to relax for a second, would you?"

"Perhaps, you're right but I must convince myself that you're one hundred percent right and that there will be no unexpected ambush. I'm a bit superstitious, you know there will be me and the two monks," Jerome said with a doubtful eye.

"What's wrong with two monks?" Benedict asked with a cabalistic look in his eyes.

"People buzz that the two fetishists could bring bad luck," Jerome pointed out with a sly boots attitude.

"Who are those people?"

"Just some people; I don't know who they are!" Jerome said, irritated.

"Salvatore is a Monk but I'm actually a Cardinal, of course I'm still a priest but there are some significant differences according to the theory. I'm not looking for any excuses but I think your point is silly. Try to grow up Jerome," he said with amusement.

"Okay, let's not induce! Let's not get into the details either. Instead we shall have coffee. I'm getting a hiccup and my voice is becoming rusty," Jerome said with a smirk on his face as they walked inside the estate.

"Finally, you've made your point," Benedict sounded oblivious. It would be really stupid to wrangle, he thought. Jerome scanned him with a clandestine expression as they entered the living room. They sat in cozy soft chairs and relaxed, drinking fresh coffee. Jerome whistled his favorite music, showing his mirth. Benedict looked at him and said,

"Then what is your plan for tomorrow?"

"I'm just thinking that we have only two days left before our mission. I'm getting nervous. It would be wise for me to make the funeral arrangements tomorrow instead. We don't have much time. Do we?"

"I agree with you. I can help you with that if you'd like." Benedict offer sounded very realistic.

"It is very thoughtful of you and I accept your offer. I believe we will be very busy all day long. Meanwhile, I should call the hospital and the funeral parlor to arrange for the coffin. Dr. Maurice is my long time friend and certainly he wouldn't mind releasing Philippe's body tomorrow afternoon. I'll call him now if you don't mind!"

"Of course, please do that!" Benedict added with uncertainty, sipping slowly his coffee. Jerome dialed the numbers, walking nervously around the table. Surely, he was a wise man with radiating charisma. He was tall, good looking and full of energy despite his age. It didn't take him too long to move swiftly through each task. A few minutes later he clapped his hands with accomplishment and added,

"It was fast! Everything is done! Tomorrow, around noon, the coffin will be delivered to the hospital and the black limousine will take it straight to the cemetery. We'll meet Maurice around noon at the front gate."

"I wonder if anyone will come to the funeral."

"I'll go through his phone book and beginning calling his friends. Marco was his best friend, I will call him first. This is an irony of life; the best always go first!" Jerome said, frustrated.

"This is what life is about. We never know when we are going to go but if we keep our faith to the end it will be our victory."

"You must always be brave and I'm not sure I always am. Perhaps there is something wrong with my faith. I simply can't challenge the unknown," Jerome pointed out, apprehensive.

"I think you underestimate yourself. You have everything that is needed. Most of us don't see those qualities hidden inside each of us until they're discovered by someone else," Benedict pointed out courteously.

"Thank you for thinking so highly of me. You're trying to boost my self confidence and I really appreciate that!" Jerome said, expressing his gratitude.

"You're welcome. I lost my faith in the past but now I am getting it back. Let's skip that subject for a moment. I wonder if you still have that shrimp dish I enjoyed last time," Benedict pointed out with boldness.

"My Chef always makes wonderful food. I will tell him what we would like to have and he will make it for us. I'll be right back," Jerome said eagerly, calling his Chef. "He is making a seafood plate for us and it will be ready within thirty minutes," Jerome said fully content. They walked to the garden and sat on the bench under the pine trees. The evening was cool and the air was humid. It felt like sauna. They tried to relax in silence. However, their stress had built up and was heavy, hanging in the air like a tiger ready to strike. Suddenly, Chef walked over with a tray full of seafood and announced in a playful tone,

"Gentlemen, your specialty just arrived. Where shall I serve it?"

"Right here, would be great! If you wouldn't mind bringing the little table it would be even better!" Jerome pointed out.

"Sir, as you wish. Give me five minutes."

"Benedict, doesn't it look wonderful!" Jerome said with a smile.

"The aroma is so invigorating and is killing me. I must have it! Also it is calling for the neighbor's cats to join us at the same time, and we could face a serious competition," Benedict said, laughing.

Chef brought a small table set with red linen, another tray full of seafood and two glasses of red wine.

"Enjoy, please!" he said on his way out.

"Thank you! It feels like a heaven," Benedict said soberly then laughed.

"I like your sense of humor. I'm glad that you're enjoying my company. Try the crab; it is delicious, fresh from the aquarium."

"Are you serious? It tastes too good to be true."

"I'm joking! The fishermen catch the wild crabs once a week and my cooks buy them early on Friday morning. At least you laugh and I can laugh with you too."

"It is the best crab I ever had. Jerome you made my day. Thank you for that."

"You are very welcome. It is too good for me. I think I'm done with it. We shall do some exercise. I think tennis will do it. Also tonight, I like to finish my reading," Jerome added.

"Sure, if I can shed a few pounds, it would be great! I have an eating problem lately. Your Chef is simply too good."

"I will tell him you said that. I always thought that he had talent."

"What are you reading lately, Jerome?"

"I knew you'll ask me that! This fiction story is actually a translation of a few thousand years old manuscripts and the ancient scrolls found on a Crete Island, in a mountain's cave by some old philosophers and have been translated into Greek. No one knows who wrote it. It is still a mystery. However, it is said that on the Crete Island lived very intelligent and advanced society which was wiped off the planet by some kind disaster perhaps a huge earthquake or big explosion. The scientists found a few craters on the island. They said the craters are twenty thousand years old.

The civilization is teaching us how they built the first spaceship and how they traveled around the world, landing on the other planets which they named a bit different than we do today. I think Chris would like to read it. They used antimatter as a fuel and talked about quantum physics a lot.

I think we're late with our technology, thousands of years behind them. Who knows what really happened to them? I'm personally stunned by their advanced knowledge," Jerome said, astounded. Then he added, "The craters on earth were probably not made after comets hit the ground but rather after the spaceships took off the ground. The antimatter is a powerful fuel which is made after the particles collisions and this probably damaged the ground after all the spacecrafts took off at the same time. We don't know why they were in such a hurry, we can only speculate on it. Perhaps many spaceships left the Mother Earth for their permanent vacation onto the neighboring planets. They mentioned that the Earth has a few twin sisters not so far from us but in different universes. How did they know that? They found some information written on the ancient scrolls and quite a few pictures of the spaceships drawn by the masterminds. It's hard to believe that it was real or maybe it is still a science fiction. Who knows but I found this amazing?"

"Indeed, it is! The scrolls wouldn't lie. Would they? I just wonder where did all those people go and why did they abandon the Earth? They must have some particular reasons of doing that. They didn't tell us much. But for sure they were in a hurry. Maybe they ran from disaster. We will never know. There is not much written about their traveling either. Definitely, some links are missing. It is quite exciting, indeed. I'm fully involved in their mystery," Benedict pointed out with wonder and added, "I would like to read your book when you finish. Perhaps it will brighten my vision."

"Sure, I wouldn't mind! You'll enjoy it. Let's go exercise!"

"Oh, yes! I almost forgot."

They played tennis for an hour and then went for a swim.

"I've never felt better. Perhaps I lost ten pounds! I feel much lighter. Thanks to your motivation," Benedict said content.

"You're welcome! I enjoy your company as well. After the mission, I would like you to stay with me in my castle if you don't have any other plans in your life. Now you're a Knight like all of us here."

"Perhaps, I will if I survive the mission!"

"What do you mean? We're not on a suicide mission! Are we?"

"Oh no I just have too many enemies in the Vatican and I feel they might be after me right now."

"I want you to relax. The water is very soothing. I love to swim and especially after a good game. I just don't want to think about tomorrow." Jerome lamented.

That evening, Jerome went to the library to continue his reading. Benedict went to his room and watched the latest action movie.

The next morning Jerome woke up early. He didn't sleep well as he had a lot of heavy things on his mind. He went jogging around his estate and already felt the pressure of the upcoming mission. The air was cool and fresh. His heart pumped like an iron cylinder in an old well. The local birds awoke and began to sing their daily opera twits. Then a few frogs crossed his pathway, calling each other names. Jerome finally stopped and walked slowly. His head was a bit lighter and he felt good. He decided to swim to cool down a bit. Soon he emerged and lay on the canvas-chair, staring at the blue sky.

His contemplation was interrupted by Benedict walking into the garden,

"Good morning, Jerome. You're up early I thought I was the early bird."

"I couldn't sleep much. I'm glad that you can keep me company. We can have breakfast right here under the blue sky. I feel much better now. I was just looking at the sky and thought, where is that place we must all go one day?"

"Not so far I hope. You must be tense! Try to relax. We are still young fellows and should enjoy our temporal life," Benedict added.

"I just thought of Philippe. Where could he be at this time? Today is his funeral. I still can't believe he is gone. He was very young and nice fellow!"

"He could be here with us at this moment, listening to you and me and soon he will depart to the other world or perhaps just another planet like our beloved Earth."

"Do you really believe in that stuff?"

"Sure, I do! I know there is something out there for all of us perhaps something more sophisticated than our present life. This is why we must enjoy our life because it is very short, and the most important phenomenon is that we must leave our body right here in order to go there. Perhaps we will change into a new type of energy; it could be the antimatter one."

"It is interesting indeed. I'll take a quick shower. See you for breakfast." Jerome left, laughing.
They met at the table and Jerome said,

"I already know what we'll have for breakfast."

"What?" Benedict asked.

"Porridge soup; my Chef always serves me that after seafood day. He knows exactly what he is doing as the porridge will lower my cholesterol then I can live longer on our planet Earth. Isn't it a splendid gesture?"

"I like porridge soup. It tastes good. I used to have it, all the time, in my priesthood life in the monastery. Now, I'm not so picky."

"After breakfast I would like to go buy fresh flowers for Philippe's funeral in town. We can leave at ten a.m."

"We should do that. Your pilot was a really nice guy. But we still have plenty of time. Look, your favorite soup just arrived."

"Put the fresh berries on top. It will taste better."

"You're right, Jerome. Oh, yes! I like it better that way."

The coffee was served soon after and they were ready to take off. They dressed in black suits and drove to the heart of town. Jerome walked into the flower shop and Benedict followed him. They spotted in the corner beautifully arranged garlands.

"Benedict, can you pick a few of them, and I'll pay? This one with fresh tulips looks good. Perhaps, we should take one of each."

"Okay, I will take them all to the car."

"Sure, thank you. I'll be there in a few minutes," Jerome said and paid for the garlands. The car took off straight to the hospital. As soon as they arrived, Dr. Maurice greeted them at the hospital lobby. The coffin was waiting to be picked up by the hearse. The driver arrived and put the coffin into his car, and then took off to the local cemetery.

"Thank you, Maurice for everything. I will call you soon. Please feel free to visit me at any time. Every Saturday I throw a big party for my friends. Come and join me," Jerome said on his way out.

"I'll do that," Maurice said, waving goodbye to Jerome.

They arrived at the cemetery. The priest and the security guards were already there. The ceremony was brief and everyone said farewell to Philippe. His best friend Marco came with a few other fellows. He'll be remembered as a good friend and a great man. The garlands and the green marble cross were placed on the tomb. People stood for about fifteen minutes and then departed in different directions. The funeral was officially over.

"That's it! Sadly, but this is the way all of us must go!" Jerome added with disappointment.

"I wouldn't worry about it too much. Think about the benefits. We don't feel pain anymore!" Benedict added.

"You're right! Let's go then!" Jerome agreed and was about to leave. Suddenly, Benedict whispered, "Jerome, look at the cross. What do you see?"

"Oh Holy Ghost, Philippe, how did you get here? You're a real ghost! I don't believe that you are here."

"At least I didn't have to go too far. This is my place right now. Hopefully, I'll see you more often," Philippe said with a smile.

"I'm glad to see you again, at least you smile again. What a surprise! Tell me then how is it out there?" Jerome asked, wondering.

"I like it!" Philippe replied.

"Is it a safe place to be? I want to be sure in case," Jerome said.

"Sure, you can trust it. There couldn't be any better place for me than this. You'll like it too."

"Thank you but I'm not ready yet. I need more time to figure out my life, for sure," Jerome added with surprise.

"Sure! I'll wait for you."

"You'll wait long time because I'm not going there so soon! Then tell me who killed you!" Jerome asked.

"I don't really know. I didn't see his face. Someone just put a knife to my throat and I don't remember what happened next. I was probably dead."

"We'll get this bastard for sure! My life will be different without you. We'll miss you, Philippe. Wait! Don't go yet! Did you see God? Wait! Wait!" Jerome cried but Philippe was gone, whispering on his way out,

"I did! He is an extraordinary man. As a matter of fact I have another appointment with Him. See you soon."

"Do you believe it, Benedict? Maybe, it was a daydream! It looks like we have another life to go too. Isn't it fabulous?" Jerome pointed out with excitement.

"Sure, I'm glad that you finally believe it! I told you that there is something amazing awaiting us!" Benedict confirmed.

"Then tell me how this works. Our body is in the grave but the spirit is sort of flying above the ground. You're a priest and you should know more than me," Jerome asked.

"I think, we're in a form of material energy but when we die, we become a new energy, a form of light. Jesus said, '*I'm the energy of white, red, and blue light.*' He meant a quantum light of energy. He can go through walls like light does. He can squeeze through pinholes, zip around us and go through us. Chris would say that we're a combination of electromagnetic waves and photons to be exact. Thus as waves we can travel hundreds of miles and fast."

"You mean that we become a light after death and move like waves. We can jump, twist, and flip over. I like that! Benedict, you could challenge a brainpower consortium of new science, I believe."

"This is what I think it is at least at this moment! But I can only be sure of that when I die then I will let you know."

"You're funny but I believe you. I'll wait for that moment. But in case I go first, I will let you know."

"Fair enough," Benedict confirmed with a smile.

"I should have asked Philippe more questions. But now it is too late," Jerome added.

"He wouldn't know too much yet! But perhaps in his future he'll find the truth about his new identity. I don't think that he will be able to talk to us again. He'll be so busy with discovery of his present life or rather a new existence. There would be no time for any entertainment for him."

"He said he wants to see us more often. Perhaps he has a plan for us to visit his graveside again. We have a slight chance to meet him once more," Jerome happily announced.

"I think we should go. We're not going to wait for Philippe's reappearance. Everyone has already left the cemetery, an hour ago."

"You're right. It is time to go. But I must say we experienced quite a miracle up here. I have more faith now. Isn't it a good reason to live again and have a better life?" Jerome added.

"Sure, it is! You'll need it. Soon we will challenge the unknown."

"I'm ready," Jerome applauded with a newly born excitement.

They drove back to Jerome's estate feeling accomplished. It felt like a partial success at least. Tomorrow, they will face a new challenge much more complex. It was still an early afternoon and they sat down for a brief conference. Jerome spoke for a few hours to his security service. Each of them received precise instructions as to the exact time and location of the operation. There would be at least one hundred *Panthers* on the train going to Italy. Their mission is strictly confidential. The express train will leave for Rome tomorrow at eight a.m.

Finally Jerome sat with Benedict in the library alone to discuss more details.

"Benedict, we shall practice again. I'm getting nervous. Look! Here is my vest which I'm going to wear tomorrow. On the back of it is a deep pocket where I'll put the *real letter*. On the top of the vest, I'll wear my regular shirt and jacket. The fake letter I'll keep above my ankle under that elastic band and then I'll wear black socks. Tell me how I look."

"You look like a regular guy. For the training purpose be sure that one inch of the letter is sticking out of your sock. It would be more tempting for the thief. You're doing great!"

"Sure! I think I'm fully ready but still a bit nervous. Let's have some coffee. Now, I have a second thought. What are we going to do if the Vatican Secret Service runs after us? There would be no way for us to escape and there would be no choice for us; kill or to be killed. I'd prefer the first choice obviously," Jerome said, laughing.

"I wouldn't worry about that. You're a well trained **Knight,** aren't you? I'm a sort of well trained Spider-Monk too. You have trust in your security guys. Don't you? They are honorable **Knights.** They wouldn't blow it! Otherwise, it would be their execution, Samurai style. But in case the *Vatican Secret Service* gets on the same train with us I have a second plan."

"What is that?" Jerome asked.

"I'll carry another *fake letter* with me. You can be undercover. Let's say you will be dressed as a lady with a fake wig and an ugly dress. What do you think?"

"Oh Holy Ghost I never thought of that. I want to be dressed like a man. What about you? You would be in danger. This doesn't make much sense. They'll recognize you immediately. I don't think this is a good idea."

"Then what do you propose?" Benedict asked.

"Both of us should be undercover. We can wear a fake beard and mustache. You'll leave your habit right here and wear regular clothes. I would say, hiking boots, a polo shirt, and a working cargo pants."

"Not so bad! Let's do that. But we could face a

new problem. Just think for a moment Jerome. If they don't get the letter they'd be more suspicious and they would follow us to the end. We don't want this to happen. We want them out and fast. Also we want them to have the letters. Do you understand?"

"I never thought of that. You're right otherwise they would follow us all the way to Rome. We must do what is best for us and the mission."

"That's right! Let's think it over again. This would be the worst scenario. But let's assume that none of that would ever happen."

"It's hard to believe! I have a strange feeling that they're everywhere, watching us," Jerome pointed out with irritation.

"Let's be more spontaneous. You'll have *the letter* and I'll have one too, just in case there is more than one thief. I have plan B. Don't worry for now, we will find out soon and perhaps **God** will be our witness. People say what would passion be without a sinner to set it in motion?"

"Maybe, you're right! Let's leave everything to God. We shall find everything tomorrow. I'll wake you up at six a.m. if you wouldn't mind, Benedict?"

"I wouldn't mind! The next few days could be very hectic for each of us!" "Goodnight!"

The night was very peaceful. At exactly six a.m. Jerome ran upstairs to wake Benedict up. "Benedict, wake up! Breakfast is ready and we have only two hours to get to the train station."

"Okay! I heard you! I'm coming. Give me five minutes."

He got dressed and went downstairs to the dining room to meet Jerome who was already sitting

550

at the breakfast table with fresh coffee. Chef also prepared a basket full of fruits and varieties of sandwiches for their trip. Everyone was content and ready for their departure. Jerome was a little bit nervous as he ran to the library. Benedict followed him. Jerome picked the letter from the book hidden on the upper shelf and put it into his vest pocket. He ran to his room and got dressed. Then he returned to the library and said,

"Benedict, I'm ready. What about you?"

"I'm ready too. I put the *fake letter* into my sock in case. I believe that everything will go smoothly. You should do the same."

"I will. I have no fear so far! I'm perfectly all right!"

"Jerome stop, before we leave I want you to relax! You're a nervous wreck! Stop right there and take a deep breath a few times. Will you?"

"Okay! Perhaps you're right. How come you're not nervous?"

"I am but no one knows that."

"You tricked me, then. Don't laugh! Be serious! I'm ready. Let's go!"

The limousine was waiting for them in front of the house. They got in and the driver drove away. It was a beautiful morning. The air was clear and crispy filled with the aroma of summer wild flowers. The barley fields stretched endlessly, keeping them company all the way to Paris. On their way they passed the vineyards, the tulip plantation, red poppies scattered through the fields, a new construction site with a few barking dogs. It was Mother Nature bursting into tears, saying goodbye to them. A hidden voice was telling Jerome, please stay don't go! He glanced behind in a blaze. His domestic feelings were melting away. Who knows if he will return? He felt like a little boy again leaving alone for summer camp. His heart ripped open and dashed to pieces. It would be something to remember for the rest of his long trip to Rome.

Benedict meditated on the details of his mission. He glanced at Jerome and said,

"Don't stir up the fire! Leave the sentimental past behind you. I want you to concentrate on our new task on hand. You can't think of anything else at this point. Do we understand each other?"

"My heart is in despair. I haven't left my estate for a long time and I feel very weird now, like in my boyhood. It comes to me from time to time."

"Perhaps you should revisit your feelings again and implant new thoughts inside of you. We're on a very important mission from now on and there is no place for sentiments. Remember one thing; the secret knowledge is the exclusive property not to be given to everyone. You must take full advantage of that gift. Leave your mind open from now on."

"I must pull myself together again. I need a few more minutes," Jerome said, closing his eyes.

Finally, they arrived at the train station. The driver opened the door for Jerome and Benedict. They said goodbye to each other and departed in different directions. The driver glanced at them for the last time and then took off. They bought the tickets and waited for their train on the platform. Benedict looked around to be sure no one followed them. He felt secure. He wouldn't worry too much as he changed his appearance a bit and didn't look like a priest anymore. Jerome glanced at him and said,

"I feel better and my mind is on the task at hand for now. I'm back again. We're officially undercover like the rest. We should not call ourselves by our names during the entire trip."

"Stay on task, Jerome! We'd whisper to each other then. Sure we must treasure every moment spent in there because we won't know how long it will last."

"We wouldn't, indeed! Oh, I see the train is coming. We have a 'B' compartment. Most of our guys will get on at the next station. I believe we will occupy three or four compartments. Everyone is dressed casual. I have this little backpack with me."

"What is in it?" Benedict asked.

"Just the sandwiches my Chef made for us."

"Keep it! We'll need them later on, in Rome." The train stopped. "Shall we get in now? I propose we better spend the two hours in the restaurant compartment instead. I think it would be safer out there than in the regular one. We could have some drink and a light lunch. What do you think, Jerome?"

"I definitely agree with you. We would be more visible to our security guys. However, they don't know about our secret plan and maybe they wouldn't interrupt the action."

"Just leave everything to the higher power. We don't have any clue what is going to happen today. We've only speculated on the potential possibilities. Just relax for now and don't even think of it. We have better things to do. Okay, here is our compartment and next to it is the restaurant. How convenient for us.

553

Let's sit at that little table for two with the window view. We can watch the countryside and have a conversation on politics. Isn't it great?" Benedict added with excitement.

"Sure, I like your fresh idea," Jerome said with a smile.

"That's right! I see the waiter is coming with a newspaper and menu for us." "Gentlemen, here is your menu and today's newspaper. Please, enjoy and look into our special lunch menu. May I serve you a drink?"

"Sure, two glasses of red Italian wine and mineral water," Benedict said.

"Okay, I'll be back in five minutes," the waiter replied on his way out.

"Jerome, what would you like to order? Are you hungry?"

"Not much! But let's have some food just for fun. We will order the personal pizza and Romano spaghetti with shrimp and cilantro."

"It sounds good and at least our table will look busy and we will appear as though we are tourists. Let's read the newspaper. This one is for you, Jerome." "Thank you. Let's find out what is going on in the world."

The waiter returned with two glasses of red wine and said, "Gentlemen, here is your wine. Did you make your selections?"Jerome ordered for the two of them. "Great choice it would be ready in twenty five minutes. Thank you, Gentlemen," he smiled and left.

"I love to read the gossip and gibe columns first. There is always something to giggle about. What is your favorite part?" Jerome asked.

"I love politics and the stories about corrupted presidents."

"It isn't a corroborative subject at all. I'd say it is rather depressing."

"I've always tried to descry the sleazy one from the desperate one and so far I don't have a demure answer."

"Perhaps, there is no answer to this dilemma. But good luck with that. I found an interesting puzzle right here. I must solve it before we enter Rome. Let me concentrate on it," Jerome said with wonder.

Meantime, an old distinguished gentleman with a cane wearing antiquated spectacles sat at the empty table on the opposite side. He ordered coffee and chocolate cake. Then twenty minutes later the waiter came back with two pizzas and spaghetti.

"Gentlemen, here is your order. Please, enjoy! I can bring you coffee and a really nice chocolate cake if you want me too," he suggested. "Sure, it would be great," Jerome added, laughing as he was reading his favorite column.

Meanwhile, two chained convicts in orange coveralls accompanied by a convoy of three men walked into the restaurant. They sat at the corner table and ordered some food. They didn't speak. Soon the restaurant was full of new comers. The old music was tinkling from the Renaissance speakers throughout the restaurant. A few kids were jumping and hopping to its tunes. An antiquated, comely English lady came with a little white dog wearing a diamond collar. They sat at the table next to Jerome. She was kissing her little beast, chirping constantly into his ear. Her strange behavior caught Jerome's attention as he whispered into Benedict's ear,

"I think this place is too crowded. Where are all those funny fellows coming from? There are so many strange looking faces. Look at this old fellow with antiquated spectacles sitting at the middle table. He looks like an antique himself. He is staring at us. Do you think he is undercover too? Maybe this is Salvatore."

"I don't think so! He looks too old. Someone should put him into a museum, indeed," Benedict whispered back and returned to his reading.

"This pizza is so delicious. Did you try it already? If not you should," Jerome said with excitement.

"Okay, if you insist I will. Oh, yes! I like it. This spaghetti is very good as well. You're right, it is very crowded here and the room will soon be out of fresh air. Maybe we should return to our compartment."

"I think it is much safer here. No one can invade our freedom right here. We shall stay where we are," Jerome whispered to his ear fully complacent. He crossed his long legs, slightly exposing the hidden **letter**. Perhaps no one even cares. He was reading his column and laughing and had forgotten about the **letter**. Suddenly, the old gentlemen with the antiquated spectacles approached him and asked, "Pardon, Sir! If you wouldn't mind may I borrow your newspaper?"

"Not now, when I finish my columns I will let you have it. Please wait!" Jerome replied as he glanced at the antiquated man with surprise.

"Okay, I'll wait. Thank you, Sir," he replied and left. However, he didn't return to his table, he just left the restaurant in a hurry without even looking back.

"What did he ask for?" Benedict wondered.

"He wanted to borrow my newspaper. I told him, I would give it to him later."

"I see. But where is he?" Benedict replied with wonder.

"I don't have a clue. Why do you want to know? Is this important?" Jerome grumbled, still reading and laughing.

"Can you check if your letter is still in the sock?" Benedict whispered to him.

"Of course, it is. No one has attacked us yet."

"I wouldn't expect any attack but rather an intelligent approach. You better check it!" Benedict said pushing Jerome a bit.

"Okay, okay! Let me look! Which leg was it?"

"Jerome, you're funny. You don't even remember where you put it?"

"I don't see, perhaps I lost it!" Jerome said in a panic attack.

"You didn't! The old antiquated fellow stole it from you when he asked you for the newspaper. How clever he is. Only *Salvatore* could pull a trick like that on us, and without a fight. He was sitting there watching us for more than an hour and thinking of an intelligent strategy," Benedict said, laughing.

"How brilliant he is! But this is exactly what you wanted! Isn't it?" Jerome replied with disbelief in his eyes.

"Oh, yes, exactly! I wouldn't be surprised if he stole you too. You probably wouldn't even notice that! Would you?" Benedict said, laughing heavily.

"Perhaps, you're right. Then what would

happen?" Jerome asked still in shock after what happened.

"I have bad feelings that some of this crowd is undercover *Vatican Secret Service.* I have a plan. Listen carefully. You go to the bathroom and lock the door behind you. Do not open it under any circumstances. Within twenty five minutes we will be in Rome. You must go now," Benedict whispered in his ear.

"What about you?" Jerome asked sincerely.

"Do not worry. I'll open the window, climb on the roof to play the game with them. They will try to steal the **letter** from me. But before I let them do that they must fight for it. I see two fellows are permanently staring at me," Benedict whispered back.

"Benedict, this is very dangerous game. What if they kill you?"

"Don't forget that I'm one of them too. I was trained to be a **Spider-Monk**. I've already told you that. It would take me exactly twenty five minutes before I let them steal the **letter**. I'll meet you at the next stop on the platform," Benedict whispered to Jerome.

Then he waited exactly five minutes before he got up and left. Suddenly Benedict stood up and slowly opened the window. He glanced through and noticed the two men approaching him. Then without waiting he swiftly slid through the window onto the roof of the train and began to run.

The train was moving at least sixty five miles per hour. He was trained how to run on trains and the task was simply a pleasure to him. The two fellows ran after him. He jumped to the next wagon and continued running. The fellows were trained very well too and they were young. Within a moment he noticed the two other fellows in the orange jumpsuits, running from the opposite direction toward him.

They were for sure not real convicts as he previously thought. Benedict didn't have a choice and slid under the moving wagon. Then he carefully made his way from one to the next wagon. Finally he emerged on the other side of the train. The fellows speedily followed him. They were really good, he thought. He must do some tricks before they get him. He was good in prevision.

He opened the window and slid inside and then escaped through the opposite window on the other side of the train. The perspiration swept down his forehead but he was pertinacious. Six new guys followed him aggressively. He knew they didn't have much of a chance with him but they were still dangerous. He played with time. He glanced at his watch and noticed that fifteen minutes had already passed. He still had ten more minutes left in his game. He climbed onto the roof and began to run again in slow motion letting the guys get a bit closer. Then there was another dangerous slide under the train's belly. If he made one wrong move, it would be fatal, he thought. He moved with symphonic intervals, swaddling underneath. His hands and feet were constantly in synchronous motion. *It was rather an **art** than a game.* Others would need hundreds of hours of training in order to perform such a task. It was quite a spectacle which not only enraged his enemy but set them on fire.

The train slowed down a bit, a sign for

Benedict to let the **letter** go and fast. He climbed slowly onto the roof, leaving behind his foot with the **letter** hidden in his sock. Surely it was easy to spot and was grabbed by one of the fellows in the orange jumpsuits. With the raving eye the man swiftly put the letter inside his chest pocket and vanished into the train almost without a trace.

Benedict still laying flat on the roof was breathing heavily but he was happy. His heart was pumping fast and loud like a local oil drill. He closed his eyes and the train finally stopped. The passengers were walking out of the train without even noticing that anything unusual had taken place over the past twenty odd minutes. It was a brilliant move. The **Panthers** perhaps appeared to be sleeping well, Benedict thought.

Everything was going exactly the way he had planned for it to happen. The most important fact was that not even a drop of blood was shed. Benedict opened his eyes and slid to the platform. He saw a variety of colors in his eyes which dispersed within a few minutes and then he spotted Jerome standing next to the pillar. He was glad to see him alive. *The Panthers* emerged from the train and followed them.

"I don't believe that you made it in one piece. I was terrified when I heard hundreds of footsteps running on the roof. I never prayed so hard in my life. But I'm glad that I did," Jerome said, complimenting Benedict on his bravery.

"I don't believe myself that I actually did what I did, at my age! Perhaps it was a miracle," Benedict said with a smile and then spotted a pensive looking Monk Emanuel just fifty feet away. They approached him but he seemed very distracted. "Hi Emanuel, it is me, Benedict."

"Oh Saint Peter, what have you done to yourself? I didn't recognize you."

"It was the necessary thing for this particular trip. We tricked them. There was the possibility that we could lose the **real letter**," he whispered into Emanuel's ear and then caressed his long beard and mustache.

"Oh, Saint Magdalena, I'm glad that you didn't!" he whispered back.

"Jerome is undercover as well. Perhaps you didn't recognize him either. All those men are our special security force. We'll need them tomorrow. Do you have accommodations for all of us?"

"Yes, I've rented three tourist's busses. I'll take all of you to the pension at the St. Clair Monastery, fifty miles from Rome. The pension is huge and it serves as a boarding house during the academic year. In summer it is almost empty and only a few tourists occasionally stop by. The facility has five hundred rooms and the best cooks in town. I've already placed an order for our dinner. Hurry up! Maybe we can catch afternoon tea. I hired an extra fifty cooks for this coming week."

"Thank you, Emanuel. You've really thought of everything." Benedict cheerfully announced.

"Indeed, I did! And who wouldn't for a mission like this!" he added with a smile.

"Gentlemen, please identify yourselves before you enter the bus!" Jerome shouted as he checked everyone's identification. The buses took off for their destination. The landscape was very picturesque. The chestnut-trees stretched on both sides of the street for miles. Within half an hour they arrived to a real architectural treasure, the XVII century monastery surrounded by cypress bushes sculptured in every possible way, some resembling animals, some of famous scholars. The carved marble heads of angels and demons were curiously staring at everyone from each and every wall, exhaling centuries of history or perhaps confessing their own sins. The sculptures of lions seemed to roar the echoes of the past at every new comer or perhaps tried to challenge or provoke them.

Emanuel gave a short tour throughout the church facilities and then invited everyone to dinner. The waiters served three different courses. They seemed to enjoy quite an exquisite meal and a great service at the same time. After dinner, Jerome conducted a meeting with the *Panthers in* a huge conference room. He gave advice to each of them. He pointed out once more, saying,

"**Tomorrow, at 7:30 p.m.** each of you must be at the Vatican facility fully equipped, undercover and ready for action. You must know exactly what to do as there will be no time for any additional instructions. We'll get two very important Holy artifacts which you'll protect with your life.

They're priceless! Neither of them can be lost! You must bring them right here and better be sure that no one is following you. After the action, you must disperse immediately. There is the possibility that some of you may be captured by **the Vatican Police.** We don't want this to happen. Thus you must watch each other's backs. Now, I want you to review the

Vatican map very carefully and study your positions and especially the potential positions of your enemy. Be sure you're on time because the enemy could be awaiting you! In an hour, I'll meet you at the training facilities, behind the monastery, for an additional exercise conducted by your Commanders. See you shortly."

Emanuel distributed the keys to everyone. Soon after, he rushed to meet Benedict. They sat at the table for coffee again and discussed a few more details. Benedict asked,

What are we going to do with Peter and Charlotte? They could be in danger. Do they know about the time of the action?"

"They're ready. They must come with us soon after the operation. They'll wear masks during the entire action and no one will find out their identities. We must protect them with our own lives. They're fast and you would not believe how good they've turned out to be.

There is the possibility that Peter's friend Patrick and Charlotte's friend Amelie will back them up on the tower's walls. They were trained together.

Monk Salvatore could be the major problem. He can ruin the entire operation. He is very fast and the best spider monk I've ever known. He is the size of Peter and he could complicate everything. Instead of Salvatore, Peter could become a main target. We must talk to Jerome about it! It is very urgent! He must inform each of the Panthers about it. I don't really know how this will work. Peter and Charlotte are young, ambitious, and full of energy. They've gotten the best training; however, they don't know how dangerous their mission is.

They will be proud of themselves one day for sure," Emanuel said with deep concern.

"I hope they survive this mission. It is so sad even to think they wouldn't. My entire life will be in ruin. I promised them a better and brighter future and I like to keep my promises! I'll call Jerome to come over for a short conference with us," Benedict confirmed and dialed his number. Jerome showed up shortly and joined them for coffee.

"What is the problem?" he asked.

"We're facing a new possibility that Monk Salvatore could show up on the same wall where Peter would be. Thus Peter would become an immediate target. They have a similar posture, the same height and weight. They look too much alike. From the distance no one would recognize who is who? What are we going to do about that?" Benedict pointed out seriously.

"I've just learned something new. They'd cease fire. I will talk to them shortly. You should come with me just to give me some new input," Jerome said.

"If Peter gets **the Holy Disc** and the **Key,** he was told to pass them to Charlotte. If he doesn't this means that Salvatore got the pieces," Emanuel said.

"We don't want this to happen. He will likely run away and maybe no one will ever find him. However, he **stole the fake letter** which is useless but he doesn't know that! It is really bad news for him. He will be unable *to unlock the secrets of the universe* by himself but he can destroy the **Key** or even the **Holy Book,**" Benedict pointed out seriously.

"It should never happen. It would delay the

entire mission," Emanuel added with a spark of optimism.

"Gentlemen, there is one more thing on my mind. What if the Vatican Police discover some strange activities at the tower and decide to check them out. It could be devastating for all of us!"

"So far they don't know about our operation. But we better be ready for the worst. They are cooking something out there after they *stole another fake letter* from us. They don't know it is fake." Benedict pointed out again, smiling.

"It could be very complicated if they show up near there. We must discuss these new options with my guys. It looks like my hit men could be very busy tomorrow," Jerome said with concern.

"We don't want blood to be shed out there because it could be Peter or Charlotte's blood. Everything must be done in as safe manner as possible," Benedict added.

"Okay, let's talk! The Commanders will bring to the training high-tech computers and we can look into the details of the entire operation if you like. For some reason I have a good feeling about tomorrow mission," Jerome announced, smiling.

"I share your feelings. We'll keep everything in perspective and not think negatively," Emanuel confirmed with positive attitude.

They walked onto the training field and spotted a few *Commanders*. A higher ranking *Commander* was pointing something out on the map with his finger. "These red marks are our forces, and the blue marks are enemy forces. If we have a confrontation there is at least fifty-fifty chance of winning.

Our top hit men's positions are marked in green color. It shouldn't take more than ten minutes to complete the entire operation and another five minutes for all of them to completely disperse into the crowd. Everyone should arrive back here within twenty few minutes."

"It sounds terrific but we must make some changes to our plan. We could have two potential intruders on the tower's walls. One of them is Monk Salvatore, a very dangerous man, and the second one is the Vatican Police.

We should have no more than two to four men on the tower's walls at the same time. Anyone else would be our enemy. The problem is that it will be difficult for your hit men to tell who is who from a distance. There are young people who may sacrifice their life for the cause of our mission. We've trained them too long for this special task and we don't want to lose them," Benedict pointed out.

"Sure! Voltaire once said '*we owe respect to the living; to the dead we owe only the truth*.' I understand your point perfectly then we must make some adjustments. The hit men have just arrived, let's talk to them about this," the Commander pointed out. He filled the hit men in on the changes to the plan and then turned back to Jerome, "Jerome, I'll see you later. You are welcome to stay and watch our training."

"I think, we are done for now. I'll leave everything else to your best judgment. Thank you and see you later," Jerome replied with satisfaction on his way out. Benedict and Emanuel were fully content as they followed Jerome to the boarding facility. They paused at the front door and looked around. Benedict said,

"I like this place. It is very peaceful. I wouldn't mind staying here forever?"

"I like it too but I thought you preferred my countryside place," Jerome pointed out.

"I could live here for a season and then stay at your place near Paris another season," Benedict said, laughing.

"It would be fun for you," Jerome added with a smile.

"Let's have something to drink and go to bed early. I'm exhausted and I really need some rest," Benedict added as he glanced at them with a sleepy look.

"Tomorrow could prove to be one of the most difficult days in our lives," Emanuel stated strongly.

"Yes. I will see you tomorrow morning for breakfast. I'll check on my guys at the training facility again, and then I'll go to sleep soon after," Jerome said and left.

"Goodnight!" Emanuel said on his way out.

"Sure, sleep well!" Benedict added.

That night seemed to last forever at least for Benedict who woke up very late the next day and missed his breakfast. Emanuel knocked on his door at ten a.m., saying,

"Benedict, I brought you breakfast. Perhaps you're hungry."

"I'm coming. Thank you for thinking of me. I slept so well! You can't imagine how good I feel now. I haven't slept like that for a century. What did you bring me?"

"A chicken sandwich," replied Emanuel.

"Wonderful, I'm hungry like a wolf."

"Okay, then enjoy! I also brought hot coffee for you. Last night was so quiet that I could finally dream. Usually I don't dream. I think, I'm ready for the mission and the most important thing is that I don't have any fear!" Emanuel whispered.

"This is good news! I feel great and believe everything will go fine today. Did you see Jerome?"

"We had breakfast together. He asked about you. I told him that you were still asleep. He laughed. He sounded very optimistic and said that the *Panthers* are ready for action. However, they made a few adjustments and some minor changes. I was glad to hear it. Jerome said that we'll have more guests coming for lunch. Guess who is coming?"

"Chris and John are coming."

"Yes, you're right! He'll pick them up from the airport before lunch and he asked me if we would like to go with him? I said, yes!" Emanuel confirmed, excited.

"It is the right time for them to come. Hopefully Hans and Jorgen will come too. We'll need their expertise tonight. They have extensive knowledge about the entire universe. Chris could record all the events tonight. There have been so many changes, I must say, since the last time I saw Chris. I heard from Jerome that he is very successful with his quantum computer business venture with his friends, Etienne and Gautier. I'm very happy for him. Okay, I think, I'm done with the sandwich and coffee as well. Just give me five minutes," Benedict said enthusiastically and went to change his morning clothes.

568

They hurried to meet Jerome. He was already outside, in the garden, waiting for the driver to take him to the airport.

"Hello, guys! I'm glad you decided to go with me. The driver just arrived. Get in and let's go! The two big Vans will follow us. Chris mentioned to me that some additional experts are coming from France, Germany and a few of the best known fellow professors from other countries. Perhaps twenty of them in all," Jerome added, laughing.

"It is good news! We will need more specialists. Let's find out who they are," Benedict said, wondering.

"Sure, we'll be there within half an hour," Jerome confirmed.

"I feel like I'm already set on fire," Emanuel pointed out.

They arrived to the international airport. From the distance, they saw Chris with a large group of people, waiting outside looking around. Soon he spotted Benedict and waved at him. The Vans parked in front of them.

"I'm happy to see all of you. I'd like to introduce you to some great scientists, friends of Etienne and Hans. The group to my right came from the Paris Institute of *'Nuclear Fusion of DNA'* and the other group is working on pioneer research on the *'Quantum State of DNA,'* at the Microbiology Institute in Munich. Also we have a few international Professors working on a challenging project on the 'Interaction between Inorganic Compounds and Antimatter,' at the Warsaw Institute of Advanced Technology. Gentlemen, please, introduce yourselves," Chris announced full of energy.

"Nice to meet all of you and please, get into the Vans; the drivers will take us to the boarding facilities at the countryside. Sure, we'll talk soon about your interesting research and listen to your scientific expertise," Benedict said as he greeted everyone. John, Gautier, and Jorgen arrived there too.

The two big Vans left the airport and drove straight to the heart of the monastery. Everyone was impressed by the beauty of the enchanting gardens and the unique architecture of the ancient buildings. Emanuel entertained each and everyone with the historical details of the monastery. Two hours later a special lunch was served to all of them. They took pleasure in the palatable food. After lunch, they walked into the garden and sat at the tables set under the acacia trees where they relished fresh coffee and held a precise conversation on the current discoveries of the universe.

The discussion was turbulent and full of polemics. Chris was impressed by their new research study and tried to find some connection to his own research as well. He pointed out with excitement,

"I and my two friends, Gautier and Etienne, *cracked the code of the mysterious **new element Q,*** the main element of my new quantum computer's memory. We examined it in the physics lab and found that this particular element is a compound of two different components; antimatter which forms spherical bonds like a bridge and a coded brain of its own DNA. Now we know that the *element Q* can think. We were able to replicate it successfully. Tonight I'll record all the events and you'll be able to see a fully animated picture which will be permanently stored in the computer memory. You haven't seen anything like this before."

"Very impressive, indeed I'd be glad to look into your mysterious *element Q*. My name is Dr. Bruno. I must admit that you're a bit more advanced with your research than we are at this point. However, we're always trying to do something new in our Microbiology Institute in Munich. On a daily basis, we train the Messenger RNA to deliver different messages to the DNA at the quantum level. We want to find out how trainable the messenger is, how much information could be transported each time and how the DNA is able to translate all the information which was received.

We sincerely believe that it could be used in the future by other scientists and engineers to build special inject-able microchips with an army of trained Messengers RNA. We want them to deliver or trade the healthy information to or with the deformed genes of human DNA.

They will carry a piece of a healthy gene or enzyme to replace the sick part of the genes in the entire structure of the DNA. With this, we would be able to cure cancer, diabetes, tumors, and other deadly diseases without surgery. The treatment will be quick and effective."

"Quite a promising approach, perhaps soon we can see it in action," Chris pointed out and others confronted the news with admiration. It has a great potential they thought. Then one of the scientists said,

"My Institute of Advanced Technology in Warsaw is doing something different but perhaps there could be some kind of connection to your research. My name is Harry. A few of us and a group of international scientists are looking into a phenomenon of the interaction between a specific inorganic compound and antimatter. We're trying to extend the life span of susceptible antimatter by combining it with specific inorganic compounds. We've already found a few of them which have bound to the antimatter through high energy level bonds and behave like little independent vibrating entities. We're able to convert the antimatter to matter and reverse the process by using the chemical bonds as a buffer in a subatomic level.

Our space engineers use this new approach to build a spacecraft that runs on an antimatter-fuel engine.

The prototype should be finished at the end of this year. Perhaps at the end of this year all of us could travel to Mars. Be sure to pack your backpacks. It would take us only a few days to get there."

"I've already packed mine," Jerome said, laughing.

"Me too," Emanuel shouted. Everyone was so excited about the great scientific news. Then one of them said,

"Hans told us that we would witness some kind of miracle tonight. This is why all of us came here?"

"Perhaps we will learn something new," someone added.

"He was right and tonight you will indeed witness something spectacular. You will find all the answers to your dilemma. Just be ready for what you wish because whatever you see tonight will be very real," Benedict said with an enigmatic smile. Everyone looked at him with disbelief.

"What are we going to see tonight?" one man asked.

"I don't know but you'll find out very soon," Emanuel answered with self confidence. Then Jerome interrupted,

"Gentlemen, you are probably tired from your trip. I will show you to your rooms now so you can get some rest. Dinner will be served at six p.m. I'll see you this evening at the training facility behind the monastery where we will gather for this special miracle evening. Get your cameras ready."

They went to the conference room and called the Panthers and their Commanders to come over. They must get ready soon for their departure to the Vatican City. They went for an early dinner and discussed details of the entire operation once more at the table. Everyone was in a good mood and excited. One of the Commanders said,

"I've already sent my guys out there. They're getting the best positions for themselves. We should leave in twenty minutes."

"John, Chris, Etienne, Gautier, Hans and Jorgen, you will stay here and wait for us. I want you to take care of your guests. Benedict and Emanuel will go with me. It is better that way. I want you to keep this letter for me. I'll need it as soon as I arrive. Be sure you keep your eye on it," Jerome said and handed the **Holy Letter** to Chris.

Chris glanced at him and said, "You can count on me. I'll put it into my chest pocket."

"See you later guys," Jerome said and left

quickly. He was calm but seemed a bit nervous inside.

Chapter 17. The End Game
Mission Accomplished

The Vatican City was getting crowded with undercover agents and the guards. It was **7:25 p.m**. Peter was instructed to be on the **North Tower's** walls with the miracle **Key** and the **Holy Book** exactly at 7:30 p.m. Benedict glanced nervously around. It was a quiet evening and no one suspected anything yet. He was looking for Charlotte and Amelie but they were hiding somewhere. He whispered,

"Jerome, I want you to stay right here. I'll go with Emanuel a bit closer to the tower to check on Charlotte. You wait for us."

As he walked toward the North Tower, he spotted Peter on the wall and perhaps Patrick next to him. One of them threw the backpack to Charlotte as she climbed closer to Peter and then she grabbed the package with the **Holy Book** and threw it to Amelie who was standing by. They moved so fast. Benedict approached Amelie and said,

"God bless you Amelie. I'm Benedict, the Messenger of God. Please give me the book." Amelie handed him the *book* and quickly climbed back to stand by Charlotte. Emanuel took the **Holy Book** from Benedict and ran fast to Jerome, saying,

"Jerome, get into the car with a few of the **Panthers** and drive to the monastery. Be sure no one follows you. Now, we must get the key."

"Okay, I'll do that!" Jerome took the **Holy**

Book. It was heavy, he thought. Then he ran to his car, grabbing a few guards along his way. They left immediately and drove fast. Another car with a few *Panthers* in it kept them company to be sure no one was following them. Everything seemed to work well and on time.

Suddenly from nowhere, another person dressed in a frock showed up on the tower's wall. It must be Monk Salvatore, Benedict thought. He became nervous. Charlotte climbed the walls fast and Amelie followed her. Charlotte was close to Peter as he was passing the **Holy Key** to her. Patrick was above him. She grabbed it firmly but was approached by the fully masked spider monk. She thought it must be Salvatore. She began to climb the wall fast, from left to right and up and down. There was no time to look where Peter or Amelie were at that moment. She wanted to drop **the Key** to them but couldn't find them. Suddenly, the monk grabbed the **Key** from Charlotte and ran away. Benedict was stunned while he watched it. He must get the **Key** back, he thought. Emanuel followed him. The monk was fast and he was already on the ground and looking to escape. He spotted an opened window and went through it to the tower's basement. He knew this place well and thought it would be difficult to find him out there.

Peter, Charlotte, Amelie, and Patrick followed him. The basement was dark. Benedict lit the match and saw plenty of sarcophagi arranged in rows. Perhaps all the Roman Popes were resting there. He spotted the monk moving on the ceiling like a cat. Peter and Charlotte ran after him. It would be an impossible task, Benedict thought. Then a few

Panthers stepped in with laser guns. They began shooting. It was noisy and dangerous. Benedict tried to locate Charlotte and Peter but it was impossible to distinguish in the darkness who was who. He decided to run after the monk himself. He lit another match and looked around. Then there he was, still glued onto the wall.

Benedict jumped on him. They began to struggle for a moment. The masked monk kicked Benedict straight into his stomach and escaped through the same window he came in. Benedict collapsed onto the floor. He lit another match and soon followed the monk through the open window. As he stood in front of the tower he spotted the **Vatican Police** getting into their cars. Perhaps they heard the shooting, he thought. He hid behind the trees and waited. He saw Emanuel standing at the corner of the street looking around. He walked toward him. "Where are all the guys? Where did they go?" Benedict asked.

"Right there, let's go! Where have you been? I was looking for you. I thought they shot you," Emanuel whispered surprised to see Benedict in one piece.

"Not so easy! I'm okay! I must tell you that we have the Vatican Police on our neck. We better hurry. Did you see Peter and Charlotte? Remember, we must protect them."

"They're out there. Hurry up, those guys are moving fast! We don't want to lose them. The *Panthers* are finally doing their job but they make a lot of noise. They moved to St. Peter's Basilica."

"I was fighting the monk but he was able to

defeat me. Can you imagine that? He is good. Perhaps I'm getting old! Watch out! The Vatican Police are driving in our direction. Let's hide! Hurry up!" Benedict shouted as they ran into the green bushes. The police cars passed them by. One of the policemen was looking around. As soon as the street was clear they began to run. It was getting dark and their visibility diminished. Accidentally, they ran into the masked monk. Benedict grabbed him by the neck and then shouted,

"Get **the Key** from his neck! Hurry up! Finally I got you."

Emanuel grabbed the **Key** from the monk's neck and put it behind his own shirt to be sure it was safe. They struggled for a moment. The monk was small but very powerful like an *iron man* and he was fast. He punched Benedict in the stomach and escaped. Benedict held his stomach and muttered. Emanuel caught the monk by the frock but received from him a big kick in his face. He was in pain and let Salvatore go as he fell onto the ground in excruciating pain. The **Panthers** ran after the monk.

One of the **Commanders** ran into Benedict and asked, "Are you okay?" as he lifted him up a bit.

"Stop all the guys! We got the **Holy Key**! We must hurry as the **Vatican Police** are after us and will be here in a minute. Let's go! Let's go! Where are Charlotte and Peter?"

"They are coming," the Commander replied and then shouted through his phone,

"Abort the operation at once and get into your cars! Go! Go! Go!"

Peter, Charlotte, Patrick and Amelie showed up.

Emanuel shouted at them,

"Let's run to the black Van parked on the street, just follow me. Hurry up! The **Vatican Police** are after us. Let's go! Let's go!"

"I'll take my car," the Commander said and ran in a different direction. The police were just around the corner. Benedict knew that there was not enough time to escape. As soon as they got into the Van, the police were sitting on their tail.

"Don't panic! Charlotte, Peter, all of you, get down! I'll try to lose them," Benedict said. He was very nervous. He glanced into the mirror and spotted the Commander's car driving behind six police cars. Suddenly, the Commander's car sped up in front of Benedict's black Van, dragging the two police cars behind. Benedict slowed down a bit and let them go. The situation didn't look promising, Benedict thought. It would be difficult to get rid of them. His phone rang, he picked it up.

"Don't follow me Benedict. I'll try to get rid of them as soon as possible. I'm a trained Panther man, don't worry about me. I sent for three black Jeeps with the best trained Panthers. They will be here in five minutes to give you support. They will take care of those four police cars driving behind you. However, try to escape on your own as soon as we pass downtown. The best place to lose them is the cemetery. Try to drag them out there. It is already dark and it should be easy. You know that place better than me. Don't you?" the Commander said as he pushed the gas pedal to the limit and vanished around the next corner.

Benedict remembered when he was a kid living

in the boarding school, he loved to play at the cemetery with his two best friends and he knew the place well. There was an old park near the cemetery where he often hid between five hundred years old trees. His mind focused on the task as he entered downtown. In five minutes he must make a sharp left turn into the vast cemetery area. He sped up rapidly. The police followed him. At the corner he made a sharp left turn and then drove fast. He spotted three black jeeps following him. They were fast, he thought. His phone was ringing again and he nervously picked it up.

"This is Commander Bob; turn off your headlights now! Push the gas pedal a bit harder and when you see the forest, drive straight in. We'll take care for those guys behind you. Good luck!"

Benedict turned the headlights off. It was dark but he remembered exactly where he must turn to hide. There was another right turn and then a left turn and then small wild paths going straight between the dense trees. He pulled over and turned the engine off. The Panthers and police cars sped passed them. Everyone sighed with relief. They were saved. Then he asked,

"Are you alive, boys and girls? You should be proud of yourself."

"Yes we are! But it was scary! We're lucky tonight," Patrick replied.

"I've never been chased before," Amelie said, frightened.

"Me either!" Charlotte shouted equally frightened.

"I'm okay. It was a one of a kind chase," Peter

added, laughing.

"I'm glad that we're alive. They would kill us if they caught us," Emanuel said with a pale face, shaking a bit.

"Within forty minutes we will arrive at the monastery. Try to relax all of you," Benedict said in a calm voice and then laughed, trying to loosen the stiff atmosphere. In the distance he saw a big explosion. What car is that, he thought. The *Panthers* are good, he repeated in his mind, they must come back unharmed; we don't want the **Vatican Police** at the monastery.

"Benedict it is time to go," Emanuel interrupted his thoughts.

"I want you to drive, Emanuel. A lot of stuff is on my mind. I can't drive."

"Okay! I can do that. No problem! I'm much younger than you. Relax a bit then," Emanuel admitted as he glanced at Benedict. He was stressed out and depressed. It seemed like all his enthusiasm was gone.

They drove back to the main street. It was quiet and no one followed them. Emanuel was happy as he touched the **Holy Key** hanging on his neck. He was scared to look at it and afraid maybe someone would see him. He must hurry and deliver it safely. Without the **Key**, they would not accomplish their **mission**. The kids were so excited about their operation and talked constantly about how dangerous it was. Benedict was assuring everyone about how brave they were. Then he picked up his cell phone and dialed the number.

"Jerome is speaking."

"We're on our way. We will be at the monastery in twenty minutes. Call for a short meeting with Hans, Chris, and the other scientists in the conference room," he said with a smirk.

"Are you okay?"Jerome asked concerned.

"I'm just totally exhausted but still alive. We almost got caught. See you soon."

"See you!" Jerome replied happily and ran to announce the good news to Chris and the others.

In the meantime, the Commander was struggling to get rid of two more Vatican Police cars. It seemed like they were driving endlessly trying to lose or rather destroy each other. Emanuel arrived at the monastery. Chris and Jerome ran to greet them. Benedict said,

"Put double security around the monastery to be sure not even a mouse will get in. I need cold coffee and fast. My blood pressure went down so much and I feel bad. The monk kicked me in the stomach twice and I believe I have some internal bleeding."

"We have a doctor here. Let's get you to him," Jerome said with deep concern. "We don't have time for a doctor now," Benedict said.

"It will take us only a few minutes," Jerome said and called the doctor.

He came quickly and examined Benedict. Then he said,

"I have some herbal fluid which will stop the internal bleeding for a time but you will need surgery, just a few stitches to stop the bleeding. If we have a laser machine here I could do it. Meantime, drink this remedy. Your stomach is full of blood. Within five minutes you must throw up the clogged blood from your stomach. Come with me to my temporary small lab upstairs. It will take us exactly fifteen minutes," doctor said and gave him a bottle of medicine.

"It is bad news," Benedict said, opening the bottle and drinking the strange fluid. It tasted terrible like freshly excavated tar pit.

"Don't worry. He is the best doctor I've ever had. I'll go with you," Jerome said.

They ran to the Monastery. Benedict went straight to the bathroom to throw everything up. Jerome held his shoulders as he became weak. Doctor gave him another medication to drink to help healing. It was sweet and tasted like berries. Benedict sat on the chair and relaxed.

"It was quick! I feel much better now and lighter," he said.

"Sure, you just threw up a gallon of the heavily clogged blood from your stomach. Now relax and have a frozen coffee drink. It will help you to recuperate. Do not lift any heavy objects. Just remember no food for at least six hours. I'll do the laser surgery on you in the hospital. Be sure you come back soon after your show is over," the doctor said.

Jerome walked with Benedict back to the conference room where everybody was waiting for them. Emanuel asked,

"What did the doctor say?" "I'll be fine," Benedict replied.

"In six hours he will undergo laser surgery. His stomach is cracked into pieces after the monk kicked him," Jerome added.

"Saint Anthony; this is bad news! I hope the doctor will fix you up! But why wait so long? Why not now? Time is of the essence," Emanuel added with sadness in his voice.

"He said, I'll be fine for a few hours and I don't feel any pain now," Benedict summarized with a smile.

"But you're in danger! You should do it now!" Emanuel insisted.

"I think we better go. Don't panic, I'm fine. Everyone is waiting for us," Benedict firmly added. Indeed many people were sitting in the conference room and they were quite excited. The security guards stood by the door. No outsiders are allowed into the meeting. Then Emanuel took **the Holy Key** off of his neck and put it on the table. It was a beautiful object indeed. Everyone came over to look at it. It wasn't just any *key*, it was carved into the letter **Omega** in precious gold metal and a metal chain was permanently attached to it. The biblical ornaments were carved in black, covering the edges and the center of the key. On the back of the *key* were two deep incisions.

Then Jerome put the **Holy Book** next to **the Holy Key**. He was proud to hold it for a moment. It wasn't just a regular book. Its black colored metallic front cover was deeply carved with the **Omega letter** in the middle. There were many curves with secret symbols at the edges. The book was thick and heavy. Everyone was staring at the objects, wondering without much of an idea what to do next. The pieces were beautiful but no one dared to touch them. Perhaps they were afraid or didn't have enough courage to do so. Benedict suggested, giving a short speech,

"Let's open the **Holy Book**. Tonight we'll witness the biggest secrets of the universe hidden for millions years in this mystery book or rather the **Quantum Disc**. I think the time came like a plea and to all of us; and this is only the beginning."

"I can do that," Jerome said and turned the first cover page with much satisfaction and adoration. He had waited for that precious moment all his life. To witness this miracle was a dream come true. And there it was, white upon white silky metallic page with a gold inscription on it written in the unknown text.

"I don't know what is written right here but it is stunning? I've never seen anything as beautiful as this," Jerome added.

"Perhaps we've discovered the lost ancient language. But it is a stunning edition," someone said and others agreed.

"Let me look at this closely. I know most of the biblical dialects but this one is unknown to me. I've never worked with that language. Chris maybe your computer can help us," Benedict said disappointed, perhaps not feeling so well.

"Sure, my quantum computer can **crack the code** and translate the unknown text to the desired language. Let's translate it into the *Aramaic tongue*," Chris replied, excited.

"Let's do that! Anybody here have a better idea? Let us know now," Jerome said as he glanced around but there were no volunteers.

Chris set his quantum computer on and scanned the holy page into the memory modem. He was an expert on the computer's languages. Benedict asked Peter and Patrick,

"How does this magic book work? You wrote in the letter to Charlotte about the miracle Jesus performed in front of your eyes, bringing the blue heaven to you, in the North Tower. Do you remember how he did it?"

"Yes! But something is missing here. Jesus spoke an ancient tongue as He touched the book. We're unable to repeat it. But at least you got the *Book and the Key*," Peter replied and Patrick shook his head in approval. Benedict glanced at Jerome's hands, holding the **Holy Letter** and waiting for this special moment to happen.

"Benedict, you told me we only needed these three elements for it to work. What is missing here?" Jerome asked with disbelief and put the *letter* back into his shirt pocket.

"Let's wait for Chris to crack the code. I have a feeling it must be something very simple. We just haven't thought of it yet. Hans by any chance did you bring the original **Holy Box** we found in the **Egyptian Monastery**, in the cave, which I gave to you to examine many years ago? Maybe the secret is hidden in there," Benedict said firmly.

"I believe we did. Jorgen, did you pack the **Holy Box**?" Hans asked.

"Of course, it's in my room. Let me bring it," Jorgen said as he went to his room upstairs. Three security guards followed him. Meanwhile, Chris and Etienne were working hard on the code. Chris was writing a new program each time, sending different commands to the computer in order to untangle the secret text. A few scientists joined them with a few suggestions. Benedict moved closer to the computer to be part of the search for the unknown. His head was spinning around like a boomerang from constantly analyzing what was missing. Now, the computer was searching for the right answer.

Suddenly, something popped up on the screen. Chris shouted, "Bingo! We got the answer!" Benedict got excited as he glanced at the computer screen. It was an ancient Christian tongue.

"Benedict, you must know this language. Look very carefully! Is it anything familiar to you?" Chris shouted, still excited.

"It is familiar to me. I must concentrate and recall it from my memory. Five years ago I found an **old scroll** written in the same language. This symbol means, *find,* this one is for the *key.* The next one is about the number *three* or three-cornered," Benedict said in a calm voice, feeling satisfied.

"I've seen these mysterious symbols before in one of those old bibles I've been working with lately! I'm sure this is the symbol of *Trinity* for **Father, Son and Holy Spirit**! It looks like a triangle with a circle around it. It is different than the latest version of it in the modern bible," John proudly announced. Sure he studied all his life thousands of ancient Christian manuscripts.

"Let me solve the puzzle. **Find the Key of Trinity**," Chris said, excited.

"It makes sense. We need another key," Benedict said, still puzzled.

"You've indicated that the **Omega Key** is not enough," Jerome asked.

"It is not enough. It would be a different **key,** rather an additional one," Benedict added. Meantime, Jorgen came and said,

"Here is the **Holy box**! Let's solve the puzzle."

"Perhaps the answer we're looking for is here, inside the box itself," Benedict pointed out as he examined the box carefully. He noticed a slight mark underneath the box. Hans spotted it and said, opening a small computer bag.

"We need to do an X-ray of the box. I have here the portable X-ray equipment I brought with me. It has the ability to analyze each picture taken within a few minutes. It is simple and time saving."

"I thought, that you already did all the analysis many years ago," Benedict pointed out angry and disappointed.

"I only examined it visually. It was my mistake. Sorry about that. The box looked like any ordinary box and had no indications of any hidden treasures. Look, I already set up the X-ray computer and this is the computer's pad which is screening and analyzing each object at the same time. Now, I'm moving the pad all over the box and onto this strange mark you just discovered underneath of the box. There is something there, look! The computer screen is showing exactly what the object looks like. And it looks like a triangle. It shows its depth and dimensions. Let's move inside the box for now. Oh, right here! It is some kind of mechanism or rather strange looking *lock hidden inside of the bottom.* It looks like a **scarab**," Hans pointed out with disbelief.

"It is strange. Will we be able to extract it?" Benedict asked.

"That is a very good question. I don't really know. However, the object is not so deep inside. The structure seemed very delicate and fragile. It would be impossible to take it out without breaking it," Hans concluded.

"Guys, maybe if we put the **Holy Book**, the **Key** and everything that was originally inside the box for centuries, it will click by itself," Jorgen suggested. He was always good in solving mysteries.

"I think it is a good idea. Let's do it!" Hans pointed out.

"Wait a minute! Before we put this in, I would like to examine this **Holy Book** a bit further. It is a piece of art and it is very unusual. You are giving up so fast. I like to know what is inside. Don't you want to know? It is sealed perfectly with a pure gold. But on the back of it I see a deeply *engraved triangle* the same we just saw on Hans X-ray computer. Isn't it amazing? These two elements will fit perfectly like a pair of leather gloves. Perhaps, Jorgen is right, we should put it in the same box the way it was originally. Everything has a purpose in life," Benedict pointed out with curiosity.

Emanuel gently put the **Holy Book** inside **the box** and the **Omega Key** on top of it.

"What shall we do next?" Jerome asked.

"Don't get nervous! Just relax. We must simply wait a few minutes," Benedict said calmly. It was silent and everyone was scared to breathe. A few minutes passed and suddenly they heard a **click.**

"Did you hear it? It is working!" Benedict shouted.

"Yes! Let's move out off the conference room.

What if this suddenly explodes? All of us will die!"
Etienne pointed out nervously. Gautier, Jerome and
some others agreed.

"That is very thoughtful of you. Let's move
outside," Benedict said.

They took the **Holy Box** outside and delicately put it
on the green grass at the back of the **Monastery**.
Everyone stared silently at the *box*. Some moved
back in fear of an explosion. Others waited for the
miracle.

Suddenly, a ***vapor came*** out of **the Holy Box**.
It formed into a **white dense light and flattened then
turned into horizontal platform just a few feet
above the box. The Holy Letter** *left* **Jerome's** pocket
and **flew** by itself straight onto the top of the platform
and *lined up parallel to it*. The **Letter** slowly opened
by itself and **heavy fumes** *came* out of it and then
turned into bright light of blue, red and yellow.

People were surprised and asked, "What is
happening? This is like magic in a fairly tale story."

"This **is God's Last Will and Testament**, the
**letter written by Him in his own blood to all
humans**. After **two thousand years** of waiting in the
underground chambers **this Holy Letter** finally
surfaced to unravel **the truth** about the **universe** and
our *existence*. To answer where we came from and
where we are going. It would be more than fascination
to know **the truth**.

The **Holy Letter** was secretly kept by the
descendants of real **Templars**, the **honorable men**
who called themselves the true **Knights**, without any
knowledge of the purpose of it until tonight. They
guarded the **Holy Letter** with their own life. I would

like to thank to all of them and especially to **Cardinal Benedict**, an ambitious man, who has worked so hard for many years toward his **great mission of cracking the secret code of the universe**, which is going to be finally completed tonight. I have waited all of my life for a moment like this. I'm ready to see this miracle with my own eyes," Jerome announced proudly with tears in his eyes.

His heart was ready to leap out of his chest as he saw the **letter simultaneously** *merging with the white vapor and vanish beneath the platform.* The **blue, red, and yellow rays radiated with great intensity** in every possible direction. Everyone looked with disbelief into that extreme phenomena unfolding before their own eyes. They were stunned as some of them repeatedly shouted from excitement and perhaps happiness, "Miracle; miracle!"

What a moment to remember for the rest of their life. Suddenly the **Holy Book** split open and spread apart vertically and horizontally. A huge noise followed after. Then the top cover was lifted a few hundred feet above them. Meanwhile the transparent **plasma a sort of glazed vapor** filled the entire interior of the **Holy Book**, spreading hundreds of feet in each direction. It looked like a perfect ecliptic sphere filled **with blue air**, the **quantum world**. It felt like being in a different world with a heavenly blue sky. The **glazed vapor overlapped** everyone around and incorporated them into a new oxygenated atmosphere. The air was clean and fresh and felt a bit flowery.

Above them was **a firmament** filled with all of the **planets** and **stars** they could only imagine.

It was like watching many **different universes**, being close to one another. It was beautiful and everyone seemed very happy. Charlotte, Peter, Patrick, and Amelie were holding hands afraid they'd get lost. Benedict approached them and asked,

"How do you feel?"

"It feels wonderful. A sort of paradise! I love it!" Charlotte replied, excited.

"All of you should be proud of yourselves. It would never have happened without you. Do you remember when you asked me what **your mission** was? The answer is, this is your **mission**, my dear Charlotte," Benedict said, smiling.

"How long will it last?" Patrick asked.

"Perhaps a day or two, I wish it could last forever. I'm very happy here. Just look around. You'll discover soon that this is better than any science lab. Here everything is very advanced. Whatever you **wish for can happen**. Just be careful what you wish. I want you to explore and ask any questions as all of them have an answer right here," Benedict said, smiling. It was the biggest achievement of his life so far. He went to join Chris and the others, leaving the kids alone with their own fantasy world.

Peter spotted some strange looking transparent equipment, a sort of computer but without any plastic covers or buttons or even any keys. It was hanging in empty airspace, a few feet above the ground. There was no wire attached to it either. He said, wondering.

"Guys, let's explore that stuff. How does it really work? Okay, we can ask any question and it should be answered, this is what Benedict told us.

591

Let's try."

"I want to see my own DNA," Charlotte asked, very excited as she jumped up and down a few times. Suddenly the blue small button formed and popped out upward from the computer area in front of her eyes. It wasn't just any button. It was made of dense plasma like material in bluish color, and the plasma was circulating clockwise inside of the button.

"Put your finger into it," Peter said without thinking.

"Okay, I did it!" Charlotte replied as she dipped her finger into the gel like substance.

"Look! Your DNA is coming out from nowhere and rotating in the air just above our heads. It is very colorful as each chemical element has a different color by nature. It is very interesting. Look at those colorful genes! We can even touch them one by one. It is soft and very, very long. How long can it be? Isn't it cool? Look! Another DNA strand is coming beneath the first one. You've got two different DNA's! How is this possible?" Peter asked, wondering.

"Charlotte is pregnant. Thus one DNA belongs to her and the other one to the baby. Let's find out if this is a boy or a girl. If this is a boy we will name him Jean-Pierre. But if this is a girl we will call her Beatrice," Amelie announced, giggling.

"Who is the father?" Peter asked, stunned.

"The priest Bertrand, our French teacher, but he has already quit and returned to Paris. He wants Charlotte and the baby back in his million dollar French Chateau," Amelie said, chuckling.

"Oh, holy Francis; how did this happen? I don't believe it! What are you going to do, Charlotte?" Peter asked.

"It is too late for any tears. Everything is taken care of. The baby will go to the orphanage at the monastery's facilities. It has been there for centuries. This is what Sister Agnes told us. Don't worry Peter. She will be fine, now let's get to the point. I'll ask if the baby is a girl or boy. Wait! The answer is coming. It is a boy and his DNA is flashing with the chromosome 'Y' in red. That's fantastic that the answer came so quickly. Hello! Is this the real world or are we imagining everything?" Amelie shouted, as she happily turned around a few times.

"We are in a quantum world and it is unbelievable. I didn't know that anything like that could even exist!" Patrick said in a loud voice.

"I have a second question. What is the color of the baby's eyes?" Amelie asked.

"Amelie, you're going crazy! Drop the baby subject. You're making me nervous," Charlotte said with disbelief on her face.

"But this is important. You wouldn't have any regrets. We want to know the color of his eyes. Oh, here is the answer. The gene is flashing in a green color thus he has green eyes. Isn't it wonderful? And I have last question. I like to see the baby boy!" Amelie said. Suddenly, the baby appeared in the air looking at everyone with beautiful green eyes.

"He looks just like Bertrand!" Amelie said with a sigh.

"Wow! He is beautiful." Charlotte opened her eyes wide with disbelief.

"I wonder if we can send this image to a different location. Charlotte can you stand over there

593

a bit farther, I'll give a new command to the computer, 'Please send the baby image to Charlotte.' Look guys! The computer is sending the image. It has an amazing ability! Where are we? Everything here is so perfect! What are we going to do next?" Patrick shouted loudly.

"Look guys, the baby is smiling. Do you think he can hear us?" Charlotte asked.

"Perhaps he does but he doesn't know what we are talking about?" Patrick said.

"I think he understand us. Let's teach him something new. I will wave my hand at him. Look! He does the same thing. It means that he understands. Let's teach him a few words. Let's say, mama. Oh, he is talking," Amelie says, "Oh, this cute little beast can talk. Okay, now say, Charlotte. I already love you little Jean-Pierre. Say, love. Wow! He did! Maybe we can teach him math and calculus. Look guys, one finger and another finger are two fingers. He is really doing that. You're smart! Can you imagine if we can teach him math right now before he is born then he will be a genius soon after his birth? Perhaps we can send him straight to the university. Isn't it a splendid idea?" Amelie said with disbelief.

"Everything is possible in this **Quantum World**. Okay, now we can ask something else. The baby image vanished. Bye little Jean-Pierre," Patrick said with a smile.

"What is that white vapor built of? I wonder," Peter asked.

"It could be built of antimatter," Patrick added.

"I want to know if I have any diseases," Amelie said as she put her forefinger into the blue button. Her

DNA popped out around them and a few different flashing points appeared on her strand of DNA. Under the red colored gene was written; potential heart attack at the age of fifty five; under the other violet gene was written; potential brain cancer, size one and half inch x one point one inch, location: left front part of the brain, at the age of sixty eight; under the yellow gene was written; car accident at the age of sixty nine.

"How can the computer tell you such a thing, I want to change the course of my genetic history and my destiny perhaps too by erasing the bad genes from my DNA. Let's try! Make me healthy, fix all the bad genes!" Amelie requested as she put her finger back into the blue button. Everyone wondered what was going to happen? The computer made some calculations. Suddenly, they saw a few activities on her DNA. Some kind of vapor flowed over and throughout Amelie's body and then vanished within a few seconds. Her new DNA popped out in the air free of any bad genes. She was cured but knew she must drive safe in the future to avoid a potential car accident. Amelie shouted with happiness,

"Did you see what happened? I'm free of any diseases now! I'll die of natural causes at the age of 100 if I drive safe of course at the age of 69. Isn't it great? You should do the same guys just in case. Peter let's see what the computer says about you. You don't want to die early from an unknown disease. Do you?"

"I'm fine but if you insist I can do it," Peter said and put his finger into the blue button. The DNA strand popped into the air with one flashing gene colored in orange with a written message underneath; short life span, colon cancer at the age of thirty three. Peter was stunned and said, "Cure me!" The vapor appeared around him and vanished within a few seconds. His new DNA popped out free of diseases.

"Your turn Patrick and Charlotte, You must do it and now," Amelie said nervously. Charlotte agreed. Her DNA showed a dark green gene which read; Parkinson's at the age of forty five. She was surprised and said,

"Cure me, please." The transformation of the damaged gene to a brand new one went successfully. Next there appeared the DNA of her baby with two flashing bad genes. One read; heart attack at the age of forty three, potential Alzheimer at the age of sixty three. It was scary and she said, "Cure my baby." The computer repeated the same operation twice and showed two perfect DNA strands hers and the baby boy. She sighed with relief.

Then Patrick's DNA was almost perfect except one little mark under the white gene. It read tooth is missing; the fifth molar, lower right jaw.

"Re-grow my missing tooth," Patrick gave the command in a firm voice, smiling. Suddenly the white vapor entered Patrick's mouth and within thirty seconds a new fifth molar appeared. They were stunned and Patrick said, smiling, "I would never think of that. It is amazing! I would like to stay here forever. Perhaps my life would be very easy right here as I hate all my dentists." They laughed and then relaxed for a few moments.

"I'm thirsty. Do you have any water guys?" Amelie asked.

"I have one for you," Peter said and handed her a bottle of water. She opened it and drank a few sips and then said, "It tastes terrible. I have an idea. We should ask the computer to analyze the water then we'll see exactly what we drink every day."

"Good idea. It is time to face the truth," Peter said.

"I'll give the computer a new command, 'Water analysis,'" Amelie said with great confidence.

The computer screen appeared with the message which read; pour an ounce of water into the designated cylinder. Amelie filled the cylinder with water. Then a white vapor was poured into it and within 10 seconds the computer screen said; high level of heavy metals, acute toxicity of mercury, methyl mercury, arsenic, cadmium and lead. Side effect: damage to nervous system, paralyses, short life span, death.

"Oh Holy Ghost, I'd be dead soon," Amelie said as she threw the bottle away. The water spilled but it was absorbed immediately by the quantum medium. The same happened to the bottle. It simply evaporated into a single chemical element and vanished within.

"A trash free environment, I like it! No pollution and no damage. This is exactly what we need," Patrick stated firmly, laughing with disbelief.

"Let's explore an ancient world. I want to know where the Lost Atlantis everybody has been looking for centuries is," Amelie said, wondering.

"We can find out quickly. Show us the Lost Atlantis," Patrick asked.

The geological map appeared in front of their

eyes which spread several feet in every direction. The satellite is showing live pictures of the Mediterranean Sea from every possible angle. Now the underwater cameras penetrate the bottom of the sea almost inch by inch, pointing the exact location of the sunken Atlantis; twenty miles to the north of Crete. Then the same camera is dragging the image of Atlantis out from the bottom of the sea to the surface and placing it straight on the ground perhaps as it was almost four thousand five hundred years ago. The people are walking on the streets wearing colorful dresses and suits similar to the twentieth century fashion industry. They are laughing and talking. Suddenly Amelie interrupted,

"Look, she is wearing the same pink dress you wore on our graduation. Maybe, this is you in a previous life. It is just several inches longer."

"You have a good sense of humor, Amelie. But you better look at the architecture. Look at those colorful manmade mosaics. I like this one. It looks like a statue of Poseidon driving six winged horses. It is made of bright colored stone and pure gold. It is really beautiful. The palaces are astonishingly beautiful," Charlotte said enchanted.

"Girls, you better look at their cars. This one looks like a Ferrari to me and this one is almost like a convertible BMW. Look! That man is getting into his car. I wonder what kind of fuel they use. He didn't use a key so it must be a different mechanism. Let's enlarge this part next to the speedometer or perhaps we shall ask the computer a specific question. What kind of fuel is his car using?" Patrick asked.

The computer enlarged a small square device located

at the front of the car. Underneath was written; rechargeable antimatter fuel device.

"Wow! It looks like a small battery. Can you imagine that Peter? They already use antimatter. Hard do believe how they developed that kind of advanced technology? I'm really impressed. What happened to Atlantis?" Patrick asked.

The screen read; it was destroyed by a massive volcanic explosion in 3500 BC.

"Can we go to Atlantis now? But bring us back here before the volcanic eruption," Peter asked but confirmed his request at the same time. The computer opened the plasma matter and invited the boys in. At the top of the computer's screen was written a small note in green color which read; Ejection within the three days of a quantum time. One day could be the equivalent to a week or more or maybe only to a few hours. Who knows? The boys were unsure of the two different time zones. The quantum medium pulled them in. Charlotte and Amelie watched them on the screen. They were a part of Atlantis' everyday life.

The first thing they asked a man was if they could drive his car. The computer screen was on audio thus the girls could hear every single word of their conversation. It was a live show. The man introduced himself,

"My name is Mikos. I'm specialist on antimatter devices and this car is my own design. This is what I do for a living. Yes, please be my guests. I can give you a ride."

"I'm Peter and this is my friend Patrick. We would like to know what kind of fuel your car uses? Also can you show us Atlantis?"

"We use antimatter as a main power for our cars, spaceships and entire cooling systems. It would be my pleasure to give you a tour through Atlantis. This is truly paradise on planet Earth. We have the best and the most advanced technology we've inherited from our ancestors. We travel around the universe mostly to our closest friendly planets like Earth. People like you and me live out there. Their technology is much more advanced than ours but they are glad to share their knowledge with us. My next flight to their planet is tomorrow. I've already postponed my visit few times and they were a bit unhappy with that. I promised them I'll be there tomorrow for sure. If you like I can take you with me."

"Sure, we would love to go with you," Patrick shouted with excitement.

"Yes! I would like to go there. It would be one of a kind adventure for me," Peter agreed with much enthusiasm.

"Okay! You've got yourself a deal. Perhaps you want to ask your father permission. Where do you live? I can take you there," Mikos said with a smile.

"We don't need permission. Actually we came from the 20th century, through the quantum medium. This is a sort of vacation for us," Patrick admitted bravely.

"What is the name of the city you live in?" Mikos asked.

"We live in Rome right now," Peter said.

"Let me check on my map. Okay, we must wait a few minutes as my remote computer is locating the exact location of your city. We've got the answer which reads; Rome does not exist at this moment yet.

It will be established on 21 of April 753 BC by Romulus and Remus. Okay boys the answer is very precise. I don't know what to say to you but I believe you that you're from the future. Hmm…it is very interesting; hardly to believe. Nice to meet you, boys. Tell me something about your technology. You must be much more advanced than we are at this moment."

"We are actually behind your technology more than 3,500 years," Patrick said, laughing.

"You must be joking. How did this happen?" Mikos said with disbelief.

"Within two or three days your Atlantis will be wiped off the map forever by a huge volcanic explosion. You'd better send your people to another friendly planet or evacuate them to the other part of the continent at least a few thousands miles away from Atlantis. Get the maps, all the technology you have, and other valuable things like books and travel fast to a safe place before it is too late," Patrick said.

"Are you serious? Let me call my friends, to the Headquarters, with a request of an immediate evacuation. It's hard to believe but perhaps you're right," Mikos said as he pressed the button on the front board of his car and talked to his friends.

"Hard to believe," he repeated.

"We're serious you are sitting on top of an explosive volcano. You better get out of here and fast," Patrick confirmed with alarming request.

"I have some visitors from the future here and we're coming to you with a friendly visit. It is very important! Please wait for us," Mikos said and drove up to an ancient palace, where the Headquarters of the local powerful governmental entity was located.

The place was full of colorful mosaics. Mikos opened the door and said,

"Hello gentlemen! How are you? We have an emergency situation. This is Peter and Patrick. They've come from the future through the quantum medium. They're saying our technology is much more advanced than theirs because our civilization will die within two or three days by the enormous explosion of a powerful volcano we're currently sitting on. We will be exterminated together with our great technology. This is what they meant exactly. Thus the evacuation is necessary, we must take all the ships, people, and animals right now and travel at least a few thousands miles away from Atlantis.

Some of us could travel to our friendly planet. However, we don't have enough spacecrafts to accommodate all the people that live here in Atlantis but at least we can take one tenth of our population to the Zeus Planet."

"You're speaking as if you are standing on a fire. How can we be sure that the boys are telling us the truth?" President Amatos asked.

"Call our best geologists and ask them to take a quick geological survey. They have been flirting with their girls lately instead of doing their job. I call this negligence and it should be punishable," Mikos said angrily.

"Mikos perhaps you're right. I always trust you. I'll call them now," Amatos said as he pressed the button and talked to the geologists at the local institute. He asked them to conduct a survey at once and come up with the answer within ten minutes. Then he added with a sarcastic tone in his voice,

"They have all the advance technology and equipment to do exactly that and on an everyday basis but instead they're busy playing with the girls," Amatos confirmed.

"Okay, I'm glad that at least we agreed to this point and will be able to evacuate the majority of our people. Perhaps we can't save all of Atlantis but we can save most of our advanced technology, valuable maps and priceless books. I will take most of my precious stuff with me on a trip to Zeus. I'm also taking my new friends with me. They must return to their 20th century civilization within two quantum days. Hopefully, we will be back from our trip before the explosion. Okay, gentlemen, I must say goodbye to you and perhaps see you soon," Mikos replied with a friendly smile on his face.

"Gentlemen, it was a great pleasure of knowing you. Sorry about the unfortunate circumstances we met under. Good luck on your trip to Zeus. Mikos, I'll talk to you later. Wait! I just received the information from the geological institute. You are right, indeed! They say it will be the biggest volcanic blast known in human's history," Amatos said stunned and with a big surprise in his eyes.

"You see! The boys are telling us the truth! Please conduct evacuation and at once. See you soon Amatos," Mikos said with full satisfaction, feeling like a hero.

"Good luck to all of you!" Peter said on his way out.

"Boys thank you for saving our people. I'm grateful for that. Have a safe trip." Amotos said with deep concern.

They left the building in a hurry. Mikos drove his car straight to his charming estate. Then he said,

"Boys, you must help me to pack most of my valuable things. Let's start from my personal gold, precious stones, and then all the priceless maps, books, and a few clothes. Obviously we need something to drink and a bit of food. Those packages are compacted food supplies; we'll need them soon in space. Just put everything into those big backpacks. My spacecraft is waiting for us in my backyard." Patrick packed the last big bag. They transferred everything one by one to the spacecraft. The boys paused for a moment in front of it.

"It is a beautiful piece of art. Peter look at its modern shape. It looks like an underwater diving bird. How does it run?" Patrick asked. They had never seen anything like this.

"It has five batteries that run on antimatter. I'll show you the most simple and most efficient engine ever made. Look at this small box made of strong almost unbreakable material. It is stronger than any chemical ever known. It is a composition of a new inorganic element bonded together with very strong compacted double bonds on a quantum level. It is heavier than any regular element because of huge contraction of the atoms. It has a very high energy level. It holds the antimatter so it can not escape. The body of the spacecraft is built of a similar material but a bit lighter. The material is so strong that it can withstand the impact of flying comets. Most importantly, it has the ability to rebuild any exterior damage within tenth of a second. Each element has its own memory and the ability of instant recovery like

604

T-cells in the human body. I've worked almost all of my life on this special project. I forgot to tell you that each battery lasts up to one year and it can be fully recharged with a new injection of antimatter.

We can travel to a few different universes with this amount of antimatter. We use the same source of energy to fuel our cars, airplanes, and air-conditioning systems as I already mentioned to you shortly. It is very convenient and energy efficient. But the most important thing is that it is pollution free. Now you have fifteen minutes to compose yourselves and we can leave Earth. Meanwhile, I'll make some food for us," Mikos happily announced. The boys checked everything to make sure it was packed properly. "Mikos, we're ready to go," Patrick said with excitement.

"Let's go then! I can't believe that I must say goodbye to my beautiful estate forever. I built this place with the best architects on Earth. I'm telling you I feel so bad."

"It is very sad but hopefully you can rebuild the same house on planet Zeus or somewhere else on Earth when we come back," Peter said.

"I have one out there but I'm especially attached to this one. Let's go! There is no time for sentiments."

They boarded the spacecraft. As soon as they stepped in, the doors closed automatically. Then Mikos comforted them,

"Boys, this will be the best adventure of your entire life. Fasten your belts and we can fly like birds. Look at this busy board. It looks very complicated but actually everything right here is quite simple. The navigation system is automatic and we don't have to worry about anything. It'll tell us exactly our position, and what we're going to see around our spacecraft. Thus you can see the best space movie ever made. It will be a live show. Are you ready?"

"Sure, we are!" Peter confirmed. Patrick glanced at him and said, "I'm ready!"

"At first we'll experience a bit of gravitational motion for a short period of time but it would go away soon after we pass the atmosphere zone. Stay calm and don't panic."

"We'll try our best," Patrick added with a smile.

They took off rapidly. Soon the computer screens announced a strong meteor shower expected within next fifteen minutes. Mikos said with a calm voice,

"Don't worry boys it is normal. It will be a spectacular show that should last twenty minutes. The meteors are different shapes and very colorful objects. They're no bigger than a small bean and will not harm the ship. Just enjoy the show!" The show was spectacular and did last twenty minutes, exactly as Mikos said. Soon Patrick spotted a strange object on the screen and asked,

"What is that?"

"Oh, this is the suicidal planet on its death path to its destruction. It happens from time to time in the universe and it is like dancing with disaster. It is no danger to our Earth as it is almost 295 light-years away from our planet. A light-year is about 5.8 trillion miles. Scientists already calculated everything. There are many planets like that but we don't see them often."

"How about the stuff to our left," Peter spotted another blast.

"This is likely a really huge, gamma-ray blast. You don't see such a blast often. Scientists say that gamma-ray bursts are the universe's most luminous explosions and occur when massive stars run out of nuclear fuel and collapse. Long bursts last more than two seconds and occur in massive stars that are undergoing a total collapse and form a black hole into which the rest of the stars would fall into one day. Which is a mere blink of the eye on the cosmic time scale, the computer will tell us how far it is. It is around 9 billion light-years from Earth. It is very far and not harmful to us either. Just imagine our Sun is only 8 light minutes from Earth and Pluto for example 12 light hours away. This is what scientists have calculated so far. I wouldn't worry too much even though it looks scary," Mikos said, laughing.

"Peter, look over here!" Patrick shouted. Peter was stunned by the spectacular view.

"Boys, you're so excited. I've seen this stuff so many times. This we call a galactic collision or galaxies in gridlock. It is so beautiful and colorful. As you see small galaxies collide and merge into one larger galaxy. When they smash into each other they emit long lasting rainbows of X-ray supernova. This is why you see so many different colors almost like fireworks," Mikos explained.

"Look at those stars, millions of them out there," Peter said.

"Oh, yes. Those stars are moving really fast. I would say at stunning speeds, perhaps greater than one million mph, scientists revealed. I would say at about twice the speed of our Sun through the Milky Way. Isn't it amazing? They belong to the other galaxy, far away from us and maybe over 10 billion years old. I learned in school that our galaxy is just over 3 billion years old. But I must tell you that we have old stars and new ones too. The new star will shine for billions of years until all its hydrogen gas changes to helium, a sort of thermonuclear fusion. Then later all the atoms are being compacted together and the dying start is getting smaller and heavier each time. The enormous energy is created in the form of light and heat. Our Sun is a star that emits the same type of energy. But stars die when all of the hydrogen turns into helium. The star becomes smaller because matter gets packed so tightly that the force of gravity pulls the stars into itself. There is no space left between the atoms. Electrons and protons inside the atoms are pushed together and become neutrons instead. The star will get small but its mass is huge and heavy. Can you imagine how much a teaspoon of this star would weigh?" Mikos pointed out, looking at the stars.

"Perhaps a few tons," Patrick said.

"A bit more, It would weigh half a trillion kilograms," Mikos said and laughed.

"Oh, Holy Francis, it couldn't be!" Peter shouted with surprise.

"Hard to believe, but perhaps the scientists are right," Patrick said fully stunned.

"If you can picture a long train loaded with bricks. That's as much as a teaspoonful will weigh! When the old dying star is collapsing, particles called neutrinos are forced out of atoms and the star shines even more brightly. Also the gravity is huge and nothing can escape it, not even light which moves faster than anything else in the entire universe. The star becomes a black hole. There are many black holes at the center of most galaxies. It is very interesting to find where they are as they're very dangerous planets," Mikos added with an enigmatic smile.

"I see another planet out there," Peter said.

"Yes, it is our beloved Mars. We are alike but the Zeus scientists have recently discovered that perhaps we inhabited Mars once and then we moved to the planet Earth when a disaster struck."

"How could that be?" Patrick asked.

"They measured the Sun's distance and found out that it shrank a bit with time and Mars' orbit moved back from the Sun causing the climate change. The Mars atmosphere diluted with time and exposed life to the harmful ultraviolet rays. The plants died and the people were dying too. The ocean, lakes, and rivers evaporated slowly and left naked rocks. Red dust covered Mars. The temperature dropped below zero. However, before the disaster occurred, people found the advanced technology which allowed them to travel to the closest planet Earth. They built spacecraft's and small groups of scientists and their families were able to escape to the planet Earth.

Another speculation circulates between scientists that the people themselves destroyed the planet Mars with their deadly nuclear experiments and high pollution to the point that the atmosphere depleted, leaving the bare planet Mars without any protection from deadly ultraviolet rays. There are many similarities between Mars and Earth. Mars seems to have four seasons, as Earth does. It has also north and south poles with ice caps as well as many active volcanoes and canyons. This is what I was told. History has a tendency to repeat itself. My research team has found that Earth is slightly moving away from the Sun and our ozone layer is greatly depleted. Perhaps Earth will become just like Mars in the near future. As I mentioned to you, Atlantis has advanced technology and our people are able to travel to the planets farther than Mars. We can go to different universes too. But now you are telling me that Atlantis is going to be destroyed and our great advanced technology will vanish for more than a few thousand years or maybe even forever! I just don't want to believe it! It is very scary to know Atlantis will be destroyed! It is unfair! I wish I could change the course of history. How weak we people are that we are unable to do that. This is more than upsetting!" Mikos said angrily with a tear in his eye.

"I think it is unfair. But I know the facts from history that this explosion was so powerful it was heard at the North Pole. If you can imagine the magnitude of it then you would recognize how serious it was and how dangerous the volcano is. Why did you build Atlantis on top of the deadly volcano?" Patrick asked with wonder.

"It wasn't me for sure. Perhaps my ancestors landed there temporarily on their way somewhere else and didn't think to check. I feel so guilty for their mistakes. But it is too late for any changes," Mikos sadly said.

"It is too late, indeed. The whole world is

looking for the lost Atlantis today. But at least we found it. Right Peter! They'll find it one day for sure! Let's forget for a moment about Earth and focus on our trip to Zeus. I just wonder how this navigation system works. How fast are we going to reach our destination forth and back within two days?" Patrick asked, still excited.

"The spacecraft is flying through the empty orbits abandoned by the very old stars which died billion of years ago and dispersed into space. Those empty orbits are connected like freeways and function as vacuum tubes which suck into one direction only. Those empty tubes look like a pressed letter 8 or sinusoids connected at the ends. There are so many of those huge in size tubes in the shape of letters 8 which are connected in few median points and run into so many different dimensions in the space making enormous nets of universes. Just image a constantly growing cube with different universes around connected one to another.

In those vacuum tubes the traveling spacecraft doesn't have any friction thus it can travel with the speed of light plus the speed of suction within," Mikos said.

"It is amazing! But how will we be able to come back to Earth? I would get lost between all those universes going to meet my friends somewhere. Too many temptations on our way," Peter said, smiling.

"Indeed, there are so many places you want to be at the same time. Just image you are driving from one big city to another and on the way you want to stop in a small little town because it is cute and different. This is why this spacecraft has a navigation system and is told to go from Earth to the Zeus planet without stopping anywhere else. The computer screen shows you the time and distance left to reach the final destination. Thus on our way back the spacecraft will follow the reversed sinusoid within the same force in the vacuum tube. We must reprogram this spacecraft before we leave *Zeus*. We don't want to land in Atlantis because there will be no Atlantis anymore according to you," Mikos sadly said.

"It is true! I wonder what the planet *Zeus* looks like. What kind of life is out there?" Patrick asked still very excited.

"It has the same atmosphere, the same green trees and beautiful gardens. The air is clean, the water is blue like our sky and there are no diseases and no pollution. People live in peace and harmony. Small populations live on the planet *Zeus*. Most of them travel and have established their lives on a few other planets not so far from *Zeus*. They love to go to Andromeda and Icarius. Just two days away from *Zeus*.

They have only two seasons there. The summer is warm but never hot and the spring is long, a bit rainy and they have those beautiful gardens all over and warm lakes. Their technology is very advanced. There are no cables, no fumes, and no traffic. The cars are small, light, and fast and run on antimatter.

They have automatic navigational systems. You don't have to drive them personally; they'll take you to the location indicated by you. You don't own them but you can drive them as a sort of public properties. The cars are serviced by a group of technicians on a weekly basis. However, the scientists are looking for a new type of energy. They have discovered a new element with super electromagnetic quality. Perhaps someone will come out with a new type of car's engine. The *Zeus* people love music, theatre, and opera like we do. They have built everything by themselves and for themselves.

Their houses look like something you have seen in Atlantis or even better with very high standards of living. And most importantly, they don't have to buy those houses because they build them for themselves. Thus the rent is free. The food is free too. They have beautiful shopping centers where they shop for free too. It is difficult to explain but Zeus' people are not greedy. They take only what they need when they need it. Their houses are very neat, clean, and they don't put out much trash or storage areas. Simply they don't need too much. They eat everyday of course in beautiful, upscale restaurants. The restaurants have the best cooks you can imagine and the food is heavenly good, I would say. The farmers have huge plantations around each town and deliver fresh veggies and fruits daily. Their services are great.

People shop and wear the best designed clothes and they travel to different towns when they have the particular need. Everyone works and is busy most of the time. People have businesses; they fix the roads, write books, and more. They use the quantum computers in schools and homes. The kids study calculus in the first grade and go through the relativity theory in fifth grade, and then study quantum physics in eighth grade.

The society works together and this is why they are so successful. Their contribution to every project and their involvement in it is so great. Believe it or not they are very creative. It is something similar to what we had in Atlantis so far.

I was always busy out there. The houses are built with great taste by talented and the best architects. Artists would make mosaics, water fountains, beautiful marble columns, and spectacular gardens. I must say that their life is beautiful and with no stress," Mikos said.

"I like your stories, Mikos. We came from a different world with many more problems and worries than anybody could ever imagine. Perhaps our people should move to the planet *Zeus only to learn from them different way of living and better values.* Actually they wouldn't believe us that something like this could even exist. We don't have the advanced spacecraft technology yet. Perhaps it was lost with Atlantis forever. Who knows what happened in the past," Peter said.

"Perhaps you're right. It would be difficult to convince anyone about that. Don't worry about it right now. Time goes fast and soon we will arrive. Look to your right boys. We're passing Jupiter right now. This 'halo' around it is made of vapor and clouds. It has a very cold atmosphere but hot inside and no life so far has been detected. On your left you see *Saturn*. It is ten times bigger than Earth and it takes *Saturn* thirty years to go around the Sun. It is made mostly of hydrogen and helium. One of its twenty two moons has an atmosphere similar to Venus and some form of life could be there. Okay boys we are twenty minutes away from *Zeus*. Get ready for landing."

"It was fantastic trip. I didn't feel much pressure in my body. How about you Peter?" Patrick asked.

"I feel great. I never thought that I could fly to a different universe in my entire life and within a day. Thank you Mikos for taking us on this amazing adventure," Peter said.

"You are very welcome. I hope you'll have more fun soon. After landing we will go to dinner and then we'll stop in my place for a few minutes. After that I'll show you my town. Tomorrow morning we'll be on our way back to Earth," Mikos said, smiling.
"This is a great plan and I like it!" Peter agreed.

Meanwhile, in Rome, Charlotte and Amelie were searching for more answers in the quantum world. So many new people came and some students enjoyed the quantum phenomena. Amelie spotted one girl standing next to the huge computer, several feet away from them.

"Charlotte, look at that girl. She looks like Alice from Wonderland. Isn't it strange? I like her braids with the red bows on the ends. I wonder which school she is from. Let's ask her name. I bet you she'll say she is Alice."

"Leave her alone, Amelie. Your good humor never left you. We better check what Benedict and the others are doing. Hopefully, Peter and Patrick will be back soon. I wonder what they have found out on their trip to the other universe. This guy named, Mikos promised to take them there for the best adventure of their life."

"They will be back soon. Don't worry. I see a group of people out there. I wonder what they're talking about." Amelie said as they paused near a group of scientists and listened to their theories about monkey's genetic life. Someone said that the monkey is thinking for centuries how to become a Human and which gene to mutate to become one. Another scientist pointed out at the monkey picture displayed on the computer screen and said,

"I personally believe or perhaps I'm convinced that the monkey, ape man, and human evolved parallel to each other. The cave man died without a trace. Many species grew up next to each other without being related one to another. *Darwin* was right about evolution for most of the species and their adaptation. I don't dare to contradict his genius. Having almost the same *DNA* and behaving alike doesn't indicate that we came from each other. We can't find the link because there never was one. Each species was given their own very specific *DNA* and the genes come with it which make us look like we do today. If monkey genes haven't mutated for billions of years it would indicate that they were meant to be just monkeys. Their genes wouldn't mutate because there was and is no reason for any type of mutation within. But if we can mutate the right genes in their DNA perhaps monkey becomes a human just overnight. But there is no need for that either.

Sure we can replace more genes in other species *DNA* in order to make them humans. But there is no need for that because humans are almost perfect and the highest in rank of intelligence on the planet Earth. We are the Homo Sapiens Recens and it will likely stay that way for centuries to come. We are a perfect creation of the real mastermind Creator perhaps God himself. We have the ability to create advanced technologies which allow us to travel to the moon and soon to other planets or different universes.

All species have those special bonds which make us like each other, tolerate or live with each other. We're in a biological harmony and can't live without each other. Now look at those two different *DNAs* and tell me why they are different and if we really want to make monkey a Human." Everyone looked at the two different rotating strands of *DNA* in the air just above their heads. The genes indicated many differences between the *DNAs* of the two different species. Amelie looked at the strands and said,

"Charlotte what do you think? Did we really come from monkeys?"

"I sincerely believe that we didn't. There must be a better explanation for that. But perhaps it is an individual point of view. I think, we, mean our genes and *DNA,* are a creation of a higher creator, God Himself."

The scientists began to argue about human evolution and one of them shouted,

"Darwin was right! Let's ask the computer. Show me the missing link in human evolution." The computer made a few calculations and popped out a picture of real ape-man with the written text underneath the picture; the latest image of ape-man, extinct 150 million years ago, and no core evidence was found. The ape man's *DNA* appeared in the air with a few flashing genes in green.

"Show me the human *DNA'* strands," another scholar asked the computer. The *DNA* popped out.

The bystanders looked carefully at two almost alike *DNA* strands but they were pondering about the green genes.

"What do the green genes stand for? Show me the differences," someone shouted. More and more people were gathering around. The green gene configuration appeared and it was totally different from the similar human gene configuration at the same location on the *DNA*. The first one from the ape man was Alfa-helix with a left spin configuration and the human one was Beta-helix with a right spin configuration. It would indicate they belong to two different species.

"You see, we are different indeed. I'm glad," someone said, laughing.

"Then where did we come from?" someone else asked. Several of *DNA* strands appeared in the air. Suddenly each strand of *DNA* spun around into a different species. One spun into the human body, the other into the monkey body, the next into the lion, tiger, dinosaur, thousands of different animals appeared. We were created from a single strand of *DNA*. We were encoded from day one. This is why we are who we are. Someone shouted,

"Mix the two different strands of *DNA* and give us a new species."

The computer calculated several equations and many other possibilities and finally gave a written answer on the screen which read; **cannot combine any strand of any DNA of two different species**. Material highly decoded. Everyone looked at each other and someone asked,

"How did the dinosaurs die?" someone

shouted. The computer showed the live dinosaurs at North Pole inside of a dense jungle forest with many rivers around, living in peace and harmony. Suddenly a flying asteroid hit the center of the jungle on a sunny day and then darkness occurred which lasted for years. The consequences of the impact included a change of the magnetic pole and the movement of the axis angle. The climate began to change year after year and the jungle turned into ice. The dinosaurs died from cold and starvation.

"Show me the creation of the entire universe," another person said.

The computer screen threw into space sparkling comets, little stars and the wind spun them around into a few different planets and the Sun appeared in a gold hot color. Then more stars were thrown into space and they combined one with another and grew bigger and bigger. Then the process repeated itself constantly. The stars travelled fast and collided with other objects only to form new planets. The universe was growing infinitely in every possible direction. The planet Earth appeared on the screen with new sisters like Earth spread in several different dimensions which belonged to different universes and the process repeated itself constantly. Everyone looked at the creation and one fellow said,

"It looks like someone is throwing those stars into space for a purpose perhaps God does it himself. Where are those new Earth like planets?" The computer screen released layers of nets going into different directions with flashing red points spread evenly on 8 different axis. Under each point was written; Alfa-Earth, Beta-Earth, Gamma-Earth, Delta-

Earth, Omega-Earth, Kappa-Earth, Lambda-Earth, Pi-Earth. Each was a twin sister to the planet Earth but located in a different universe. People were wondering how it was possible that we have so many Earth like planets. Someone said,

"It looks like we have millions of different universes'. The nets are growing infinitely in every possible dimension. Isn't it fantastic! Thus we can travel from one universe to another one for the rest of our lives. We just need the perfect spacecraft to take us there. Show us the spacecraft!"

The screen showed the model of the advanced spacecraft that runs on antimatter. People were stunned by its beauty and simplicity. There were hundreds of new questions and hundreds of them were answered.

"How can we travel so far if we have such short life spans? We will never make it," someone shouted.

"Oh, yes! If we can be young forever we can travel to many universes. Show us the way to become young again," the next person standing by requested.

The computer released into the air the human *DNA* with many genes flashing in yellow. It was written below; enzyme replacement therapy. Then the screen showed a microchip filled with yellow fluid with a written description: inject-able enzyme. Press to your skin in a desirable place and wait a few minutes. Someone said,

"My name is Marco. I'm 65 years old and I'm a scientist, working on rejuvenation research. I can try this microchip on my aged skin. Please give me the microchip." The microchip popped out of the screen. He looked at it then picked it up with his fingers and gently pressed it onto his forehead between his eyebrows. Everyone looked at him and waited a few minutes. Suddenly his aged face became at least 40 years younger. He looked twenty five again. People were stunned and asked for the microchip.

"It is a miracle. I can make a fortune with this microchip. If I only knew how to get the same enzyme for mass production," he said.

"Hey you fellow, you're too greedy. You should be thankful for being young again. Money can't buy you happiness," one man shouted and others agreed.

"No one will live forever. This is impossible," one lady said.

"I would disagree. If we only knew which genes are responsible for the death process we can fix the problem for good. I shall ask and perhaps it would be delivered. Show me the genes of death in the human's DNA," one scientist asked.

The DNA appeared with three flashing genes in blue, red, and green in designated positions; C-2, C-5, and C-8. Below was written; the blue gene indicated oxygen; the red gene was for the heart and the green for the brain. If you remove or damage any of the genes death occurs. They have a tendency to shorten the life span by their slow deterioration in time; environmental impact; C-2, C-5, and C-8 genes are fully replaceable.

"I can be the master of life and death if I can only have the knowledge of it," someone said.

"Leave that part to God! Smart ass!" an old man shouted and asked,

"Show me the immortal life." The computer showed a small creature looking like a jellyfish called by the scientists, '**The Turritopsis Nutricula**.' It was written under it; the only animal in the world, discovered so far, to have a truly fountain of youth. It never dies and can reverse its aging process! It can regenerate its entire body over and over again and is able to bypass death.

"It is fantastic discovery. Maybe we can learn from the creature its secrets of life," someone said with disbelief.

The people were searching for every possible answer to their own life dilemmas.

In the meantime, Chris was recording every single event with his quantum computer. A few scientists approached him and one of them asked,

"How is this quantum world working? It is like a dream. We can get answer for every question right here. What is behind all this stuff?"

"Definitely, it must be the work of God! But it means that life has existed in the universe for billions of years and we're just discovering it right now. We couldn't just appear here on Mother Earth over night. Perhaps we lost the access to some very important information in the past which we inherited from our ancestors but it was destroyed by natural disasters like fires, wars, volcanic eruptions, and earthquakes. I mean, millions of valuable and priceless maps, books, secrets, treasures, perhaps many advanced technologies given to us millions of years ago have vanished forever. I try to understand the quantum world around us. I think that every single element right here has its own memory hidden in its quantum state. I'd say, each element has an individual matrix inherited with its birth and it is for them like *DNA* is for us. Since the element has memory it can be trainable. Thus we can teach every element a different task. But in order to do that we must get into the quantum world of each element. It would be quite a challenge but it could be done! As a matter of fact, we are right now in a quantum world. I'm trying to understand how it really works. But I know for sure that it exists," Chris concluded, giving serious consideration to the matter.

"You've got your point. It is just too perfect and too complicated for a regular fellow like me," the man said and smiled.

Jerome, John, Etienne and Gautier ran to Chris with an urgent message.

"Benedict collapsed out there near the quantum computer. I'm looking for a doctor. He was supposed to have surgery after six hours. I don't have a clue where is the doctor and his laser equipment? We can't lose him like that!" Jerome shouted in panic.

"I'll take my computer out there. Where is he?" Chris asked.

"Twenty feet away near that huge computer; Charlotte and Amelie are there trying to help him."

"Benedict, what is happening?" Jerome asked.

"My stomach is in pain. I think I'm having a second infection, perhaps I'm dying."

"Wait, not yet! Where is the doctor? I must help you. Where the hell is he? Benedict, I want to thank you for your mission. Do not go yet. We love you. You've opened the people's eyes to the universal truth. Maybe they'll become a better people now."

"Thank you, Jerome. You know, this mission will be impossible without you! You're an exceptional man and I'll miss you. But I am happy too that my dream is fulfilled. Where is my Peter? Peter! Thank you, my child. Charlotte thank you and I love you," Benedict whispered.

"Peter and Patrick went inside *the quantum computer* to save Atlantis from the volcanic eruption. They're supposed to be back soon," Amelie said as she was surprised to see Benedict in this terrible condition.

"Kids, always will be the kids! They can't do that. The volcano is too powerful and nothing can stop its eruption," Benedict whispered, smiling.

Everyone gathered at the quantum computer and looked at the huge screen. The Atlantis was still there. The people were walking without knowing that soon their Atlantis will disappear from the map and forever.

"I don't see Peter and Patrick out there. They must be in a trouble." Chris concluded. Charlotte became nervous and said, "We must help them, now!"

"We can't do this! We do not know how to find them," Chris said nervously, walking back and forth.

Suddenly, someone approached them and said,

"Do not worry my child. I'll find them. I'm looking for them too. They are my best friends. Okay let's look into the computer's quantum world to find what is happening out there. I don't see them anywhere around. So many people have already left Atlantis and the volcano fumes are very intense right now. It is likely that within an hour it will erupt," **God** in Jesus said with concern as he blew the fumes away from a small group of people, trying to escape.

Everyone looked at Him with disbelief. It must

be another miracle, they thought.

"We heard their conversation with a local man named Mikos. He took them for a tour drive around Atlantis and promised to take them for a day or two to the planet Zeus, in another universe. He has his own spacecraft that runs on antimatter and perhaps they are on their way back to Earth," Charlotte said.

"I see my child. They are very brave kids. I admire their interest in our universe. Okay, let's look into the map of the entire universe. Where could they be? Unfortunately, they got lost. Accidentally, their spacecraft was sucked into the wrong tube and they landed in another universe, not so far from here. They should be back in an hour however, they're in danger. Trust me; I'll will bring them back right here," He said, smiling.

Suddenly, everyone's attention was interrupted by the voice of a man. No one could tell where it was coming from. No one could see him. Everyone looked at the next quantum computer where the girl looking like Alice was standing and talking with a masculine voice,

"They will **never come back**! I'll **destroy them**. I'll **destroy the whole universe** within five minutes."

The bystanders were surprised to hear such a threat from an innocent looking girl. But Alice wasn't a girl. Benedict was sure that it was none other than **Monk Salvatore** himself undercover. He used one of his old tricks again in order to get here. He couldn't get here because of high security measure then he changed his appearance to sixteen year old Alice and got here with a group of school kids. He was a lucky fellow. Without warning the comets and stars were pouring from the sky into the quantum world. Then Jesus asked him,

"Why are you so angry, my child? I can help you."

"I'm nobody's child. I grew up in the orphanage with no parents. They were killed when I was only four by the **Holy Confiscators** sent by the **Vatican**. They took everything from me including my pride. Now it is time to pay them back for everything they have done to me. Leave me alone. It is too late anyway! I've changed the orbits of the entire universe. We will have a big explosion soon and much worse than the one that destroyed **Atlantis.** Earth will collide with another planet as I speak. I hate everything and everyone! Benedict, surely you wouldn't need your **Black Book** anymore. All the secrets you put there will die with me and you too," **Salvatore s**houted, laughing so loud and waving the **Black Book** above his head. The quantum world was shaking quite a bit and the meteors were dropping from the blue sky into them. It was dangerous and everyone began to pray. God in Jesus looked at him and said,

"You underestimate my power **Salvatore**."

"You can't save the world! It is too late! In one minute we will die, all of us and you too. Now the entire universe belongs to me. I am the master of your destiny! Ha!! The **Earth is** finally mine too and it is about to collide with another planet in just thirty few seconds," Salvatore said and laughed even louder, shouting at the same time,

"I hate everyone! I hate everything! Now, **I am the master of the entire universe. I will tell you when you must die! And I'm telling you right now**

that you will die in twenty five seconds!"

"Do you really think that you can do that? I'm telling you that you are wrong!" God said and changed **Salvatore** into a **cute green frog**, *wearing Alice's dress* and two braids with *red bows*. Everyone laughed.

God approached the computer and tried to fix the **mess Salvatore** made. He reversed the orbit's positions and put back every single star where it belonged to. It took Him almost an hour. The light was restored in the quantum world and everyone sighed with relief. Charlotte began to panic and said,

"We must bring back Peter and Patrick. Where are they? Look! Atlantis is almost gone. The explosion is so powerful; it destroyed the entire island completely. I don't believe it!"

Everyone looked at the vanishing **Atlantis** with disbelief. Jesus approached them and said,

"Don't worry. I'll bring them back in one precious piece. Look! They are right here, a few hundred miles away. To avoid the collision with **Atlantis** I'll change the course of their journey a bit. They're approaching us and will land right here in a few minutes. Please make space available for them."

Everyone backed up at least fifty feet in each direction. Jesus smiled and said,

"Here they are!"

The **spacecraft** landed just a few inches from His feet. Obviously they didn't have a clue what was happening. The doors opened and Mikos came out with Patrick and Peter. Then Patrick said to Mikos,

"Welcome Captain Mikos to the *future*. This is our world. What a surprise! I didn't have a clue that we would ever be back here with all of you, guys! Mikos, I would like to introduce you to someone very special. We didn't have much time to discuss the details either but this is my best friend, **God in Jesus.**"

"Nice to meet you Mikos, I'm glad to have you here and your spacecraft in one piece. Everyone here is wondering how it really works? You can show them around and teach them about this technology which has been lost for quite a bit. Perhaps they can fly with you," Jesus said, smiling.

"It would be my great pleasure. But how did we land here? I don't really understand that. My navigation system was set up for landing **near Atlantis.**"

"Trust me you wouldn't like to land near there right now. You have landed in a different time dimension without knowing that. I brought you here. But if you would like to glance at **Atlantis** then look at the computer's screen for the prerecorded volcanic explosion which occurred just a few minutes ago. You must be thankful to be here and alive," Jesus said, smiling. Mikos glanced at the volcanic eruption with disbelief. Atlantis vanished in front of his eyes. It couldn't be, he thought.

"Peter and Patrick, you were right. Thank you for saving most of my people. They will be grateful to you one day. I'm so pleased to be here with all of you. When you told me that we must evacuate all the people from the island I didn't believe you. But soon after the scientists confirmed that you were right they told everyone to evacuate and fast. They did leave the island within the last two days before the volcano

explosion. We've lost that beautiful island forever."
Mikos said with tears in his eyes. Jesus put His hand
on his shoulder and said,

"You are saved. It happened thousands of
years ago. You're alive. Isn't it something great to
celebrate?

Because you're in a **quantum world** where the
impossible is possible, I was able to bring you here.
You can bring the past in front of your own eyes just
in a second. You can ask here any question and here
you'll get the answer. Every wish is granted. Isn't it a
beautiful world? This is the secret of the universe
which unfolds in front of us. **Two thousand years
ago I came to Earth to reveal the same secret to
you**. It was given to me by my **Father God himself**,
the **secret written with his own blood**.

But you were not ready to listen to me. Instead,
you rejected me! I have come again today to ask you
if you're ready. If I didn't come today, one of you
would've destroyed the life which was given to all of
you as a **precious gift from God.**

Tell me when you will be ready then I'll come
again. Remember, we have choices in life. Make the
right choices for yourselves. Now, look out there! You
see the *blue ocean and the green trees* next to it.
You can find *inner peace* out there. Go and see for
yourselves!" God in Jesus said as He blessed
everyone who went there.

The old couple walked to the ocean and
washed their faces in pure clean water. They became
young again. Everyone looked at them with disbelief.
Many went there to join them. They laughed and were
happy together. Perhaps they found **new values in**

629

life.

Meantime, the other people were constantly asking for more miracles as they occupied many **quantum computers**. One fellow said,

"Give me all the diamonds, the pink ones too, and pure gold. Make my hand of gold. Build for me five castles to my right and ten to my left. Make me the richest man in this kingdom on Earth. Make my teeth in diamonds." All his wishes were granted. The other fellow confessed to the computer his secret desires,

"Make me free of debt. Make me find a true love. Make me rich too."

"Fill my pockets with precious stones," the third man asked. Many of them asked for the impossible to happen and they received it.

In the meantime, God in Jesus said,

"Peter, Patrick, I'm waiting for you. Come with me! Let's discover more secrets of the universe together and enjoy life. We should have more fun." Then He looked at Charlotte and said, "You follow your heart my child. Someone there really loves you and is waiting for you. Make the right choice for yourself and your baby boy. Sometimes we must forgive others even though it is hard. My heart is with you." Then He walked to Benedict and asked,

"If you don't mind I'd like to have my **Lost Memoirs** back. My private life is written there by me and I would like to keep it for myself."

"Sure, I wouldn't mind, it belongs to you. I just never thought I would be in possession of this precious book. But it happened by pure accident. Trust me!" Benedict said a bit embarrassed.

"Sure, I understand and I trust you. Don't worry! By the way, this is your **Black Book** perhaps you want to have it back. I want to thank you for your great mission, for *cracking the secret code of the Universe.* You're a very brave man indeed. You gave the people hope and you **open their eyes perhaps to something new** and I believe they will **become a better people.** If you need me in the future just call my name and I'll be there for you," Jesus said and smiled. He walked a few feet away, opened his hands and said,

"**God I fulfilled your secret wish**. Now I'm ready to go but I'll be back soon and only to complete your deepest desire. I came to claim back the **Holy Letter** and the **Holy Book** with a **Key** you in-trusted in me almost **2,000 years ago**. At this time I must take the holy objects with me. I can only promise you that one day I'll give it back to the people if they will be **truly ready** to receive it." Then He opened His hands and the **Holy Quantum Book** folded back and landed in his hands with the **Holy Letter**. Then He said,

"Peter will you hold the **Holy Book** for me? Patrick will you guard the **Key?** I will take care of the **Holy Letter**. Thank you, Jerome for guarding the **Letter** for so many years. You're a man of honor. I will value you favor for favor and I will give you **Eternal Life.** God bless all of you. Peter, Patrick, let's go!" He said, smiling.

Thus the **quantum world vanished** with God in Jesus as He walked away; leaving behind some *whose dreams finally came true.* Everyone was fulfilled one way or another. Some of them became young and happy, some of them rich and some cured of dangerous diseases. It couldn't be a better world on Earth, they thought. Chris recorded everything in his quantum computer. Benedict, Jerome, Etienne, Gautier, and Emanuel witnessed the incredible miracles they would remember for the rest of their lives. Mikos was given his life back and he would teach the scientists how to build the antimatter' spacecraft.

Monk Salvatore became a little **frog** and perhaps he could contribute to the environment in the future with a bit of good luck. Or in the worst scenario he could end up on a French menu in a local French restaurant.

The little girl ran around and paused next to **Alice the frog**. She picked the frog up and put it in her pocket. She thought it would be a great addition to her toy's collection.

Jerome ran to dying Benedict slapping his forehead very, very hard. Did you see the miracle? I was taken by the miraculous appearance of God. Forgive me Benedict, I didn't ask Jesus to heal you and now He is gone. My tears will never be enough for you are dying."

"It's okay my friend Jerome. I can die a happy man for I **cracked the secret code of the entire universe** and I stopped that *bastard Salvatore*. What more could I want than that. God thanks me for that. I am a happy man now. One more thing, I want you to take my ***Black Book*** and drop in my mail box this is the number. I want Charlotte to have it as a sort of inheritance from me." Benedict whispered and then looked towards the heavens closing slowly his eyes for final time. He was dead. There was a holy smile on his lips. Jerome screamed, "Wait! Wait! Don't leave yet! My life will be empty without you. Travel safe my brother and may God be with you forever."

Everyone cried. Charlotte, Amelie, John, Chris, Jerome and others were standing next to Benedict body for long time. There was no hope of bringing him back. It was too late as he vanished with the quantum world forever. The doctor came but it was too late. Cardinal Benedict will be remembered as a great man, fantastic friend and a holy father.

Charlotte and Amelie returned to the boarding school to continue their education. She would cry many times. Benedict was like a father and the best friend to her. She will miss him very much. Chris, John and Emanuel fulfilled their secret dreams and would live long happy lives. They will visit Charlotte from time to time.

One evening, Jerome sat for coffee and thought to himself,

'I feel good about myself that I could fulfill some people's dreams and give others hope. It feels really good. My life has meaning now. Thank you, Benedict. I already missed you! My life will be miserable without you. No more fun!'

During last night, Benedict appeared in Jerome dreams and told him,

"I agree with you. *It is not important how much you can get from others it is priceless how much you* can give to others. I feel my life had more value since that miraculous night. I am grateful for that. One more thing; you must assume my responsibilities to the children especially Charlotte. She will need you very soon. I miss you too my dearest friend. As I said before, I'll wait for you. Try to enjoy life to the fullest."

Chapter 18. Bertrand's Choice
The Boarding School, One year later

Charlotte gave birth to a healthy baby boy. Sister Agnes arrived to the hospital just in time. She was told that Charlotte was a virgin. She thought, perhaps it was a miracle. She walked to Charlotte's room and asked,

"What is the baby's name?"

"Jean-Pierre," Amelie interrupted, holding the baby in her hands.

"Hello Amelie. I must take him to the orphanage today. I made all the arrangements with the Sisters. Don't worry! You come back to school next week like nothing happened. Take care of yourself and I will see you later," Sister said.

"Isn't he a precious little darling? He looks just like daddy," Amelie said in a soft voice.

"He is precious indeed but I must take him now. Give me the baby," Sister said in a cold voice. She looked at him and said, "Indeed he looks like Father Bertrand. We will have a problem if he sees the baby. Perhaps he will want to take him. Maybe we should give the baby to him. At least he is wealthy and can bring up the baby in a proper manner," Sister said with a smile.

"I'll miss the baby. I told Charlotte that I'll take care of Jean-Pierre every day after school. What do you think, Sister Agnes?" Amelie asked with concern.

"Okay, we will keep the baby for now. Whatever happened to Charlotte must be kept strictly confidential. No other girls should ever know about this scandal. The Alexandrian Boarding School has a great reputation in Europe and I would like to keep it that way. These kinds of scandals are not acceptable in the Christian school," Sister added, leaving the room with the baby in her arms.

"How do you feel, Charlotte? When can I take you home?"

"I feel okay. Maybe this afternoon, I see doctor Jack is coming. I'll ask him. Doctor, I would like to go home today," Charlotte said.

"Let me look at you. Show me your tongue. It looks good. I'll check your heart now. It is perfect. I think you should rest at least six hours. You can go home at eight p.m.," he said on his way out.

"Thank you doctor Jack," Charlotte replied.

"Perfect! I'll come around eight and we will go to this French restaurant on the corner. It is my treat. Meantime, I want you to rest. You look a bit exhausted. I have a surprise for you but I'll tell you later. Just wait for me," Amelie said and left in a hurry. She went straight to shop in downtown. In a small Italian boutique she found beautiful baby clothes. She bought a few pieces in blue for little Jean-Pierre and asked the lady to wrap it in a nice gift box with blue silky ribbon.

Amelie walked back to the boarding school. So many things have happened lately that she had too

635

much on her mind. At her door someone left flowers with a little envelope addressed to Charlotte. Amelie took the flowers in. She knew that the letter must be from Bertrand. Indeed, it was. The envelope was opened. She wondered if she should read it. It looked so tempting. She couldn't wait until eight p.m. and decided to open it. It read,

'My Dear Charlotte,

You think that I have forgotten you but I didn't. One of my good friends informed me today that our son was born. I can't hold my feelings to tell the world that I'm the happiest man on Earth. I want you to be with me. Your rejection makes my love even stronger. I promise I'll be there soon and take you and my son with me. Perhaps he is the best looking little fellow. I already miss you when I put the last dot over the letter i. Please accept this little gift from me. I want you to buy my son everything that he needs to grow up fast and become a man. I'm sending my love to both of you.

Loving you forever, Bertrand.'

Amelie sealed the letter back. She was almost breathless. Her eyes were filled with tears for the lost love of a man who never even noticed her. Bertrand was indeed a very generous man. He included a check for **$100,000** as a little gift for his baby boy. Amelie's heart was torn apart. She lay on her bed and thought of the past. Everything seemed like only yesterday.

Now Charlotte was a mother, she would never have thought of that either. She closed her eyes for a moment and tried to get in touch with her inner self in the deepest part of her mind. It was hard. The moment lasted longer than she suspected. When she opened her eyes it was already seven p.m. She rushed to change her clothes. Before she left she took a rose from Bertrand's lovely bouquet. The evening was beautiful and she seemed attached to every brick on the street, every shop in town and every little restaurant she visited in the past. She knew every sheltering tree by name. The academic year will be over in just two weeks and she would have the same summer job at the Vatican Headquarters that she had previously. She entered the hospital, ran upstairs to Charlotte's room and said,

"Here I am! This rose is for you. Let's go!"

"Okay, I'm ready and very happy to leave this depressing place. Thank you for this charming rose. It smells beautiful."

The girls walked outside and stopped at the French restaurant on the corner. Amelie said,

"You can order whatever you like. This is your day Charlotte."

"Thank you and perhaps I already know what I want. Salmon filet with spinach and lime on the side. What about you?"

"Me! I want French fries, white fish filet with green dill and cucumber salad with lemon dressing. I always eat the same stuff and it never bothers me. I'm really happy for you that you got back on your feet again, Charlotte. I just can't imagine what you went through. Perhaps I will never understand it. You're a very brave girl. Let's think only about good stuff from now on. Just remember that I'm your friend forever," Amelie said.

"I know we're friends forever and no one is

going to change that. Not even little Jean-Pierre. I would like to see him at least once a week," Charlotte added with a smile.

"Sister said that we can see him every day but we must be sure to keep it a secret. If anyone asks you who the little boy is you must tell them that your cousin died in a car accident and left the little boy in the orphanage. You're his closest relative. But perhaps no one will ever ask that question. Finally our dinner is coming. Let's forget about everything and celebrate this special evening. My famous French fries I can't live without them. They are not healthy the doctors said."

"Don't worry we're young and can manage it. I can eat salmon every day. Thank you for taking me to dinner. I feel much better now."

"Sure, no problem you know me I like to share. I have a surprise for you at home actually two of them. Let's go home I can't wait."

"Okay, I'm almost done. It was delicious. I would like to take the cakes home. We can have them with your favorite tea."

The girls left the cafe and walked home. It was cool and really nice evening. The stars were twinkling as if they wanted to tell their night stories. They passed glamorous window displays, little shops, and the opera house and finally they entered their room. Amelie said,

"Close your eyes. Which surprise do you want to see first?"

"You make the decision for me. I'm already excited and can't think clearly."

"Okay, perhaps this one is the best," Amelie

said and gave her the gift box with a blue ribbon. Charlotte opened her eyes and said,

"This must be something exclusive. It is so beautifully wrapped. This is very cute; Jean-Pierre will love it. Tomorrow we'll visit him and put this handsome outfit on him. Thank you, Amelie. You're a very precious friend, indeed."

"I'm really glad that you like it. It was the best piece in the entire boutique. Now look at the flowers there is a special letter for you. This is the second surprise," Amelie added with a smile.

"Okay, but can you read it for me?"

"Okay! Let me open it first. Wow! Look at this check. This is a special gift for **$100,000**. Can you imagine something like that? Everything is for Jean-Pierre."

"I don't know if I can accept this gift."

"Charlotte, look at me. You must accept this gift because this is for your precious baby. Tomorrow, we're going to open a checking account in the bank across the street. Now I can read you the letter. But promise you won't get mad."

"Okay, I will read it myself. I already know who wrote it. Give me the letter."

Charlotte sat at the table and read the love letter from Bertrand. She didn't say much. "Are you okay, Charlotte? Promise tomorrow we will open a new bank account for you," Amelie asked to be sure.

"Okay, you got yourself a deal. You're right! This is for Jean-Pierre not for me. He needs security for his better future. Thank you, Amelie for thinking of him so seriously. I must calm down a bit with my emotions. Perhaps being so stubborn I do more damage to myself than good. I've already learned a bad lesson."

"You're fine. You did the right things in the past and you had the right to do it. You were angry and you had reasons to be angry. It is normal. Now, I want you to be smart, Charlotte," Amelie said with encouragement.

"Let's have some tea with the cake we brought. I would like to rest a bit. Thank you for everything you have done for me. It was more than enough."

"You relax for now and I'll make the perfect tea for us. Tonight we will drink **Sonata,** a special flavor made from the summer flowers mixed with a bit of black tea. Just think in a positive way from now on."

Charlotte lay down on her bed and closed her eyes. She was out of power. Amelie made a quick tea for her and served her in bed.

"Here is your tea. Have a sip."

"Thank you, Amelie. It is fantastic. I'm very tired. I must sleep for now. Goodnight!"

"Goodnight Charlotte!"

Amelie went to bed within the hour. The night was peaceful and smelled of summer. The next morning Charlotte woke up early and finished her evening tea. Amelie was a bit tired. She was carrying too many problems on her shoulders. They went to the cafeteria. Soon after breakfast Charlotte picked up the baby clothes and put them into a small bag. They went to the orphanage. Sister Penelope opened the door for them. Amelie said in a firm tone,

"We would like to see small baby Jean-Pierre. We have a gift for him."

"Okay, girls follow me. Sister Agnes told me

640

that the two of you will visit the baby from time to time. He is in this little room. Let me check if he is awake. Wait right here. Okay, you can come in. Oh, this is a very precious blue jumpsuit. He will love it. I'll help you to dress him. It is not so easy when the baby is so soft and flexible. Yes, he looks great in this outfit. Okay now you can go. See you next time."

"Thank you Sister. We'll be back soon," Amelie said on their way out. The girls were happy and went for a short walk around the orphanage. Charlotte said,

"I'm so grateful for Sister Agnes that she was able to arrange everything so perfect. I don't have to worry about anything. She is better than mother which I don't have. I want to donate some of my money to the orphanage. Let's open the bank account now. I brought the check with me."

They went straight to the local bank and Charlotte deposited her money in her new bank account. Then she asked for a check in amount of ten thousand dollars as a gift for the orphanage. As soon as she received the check she said, "Let's visit the orphanage and give the check to Sister Penelope. I'll feel guilty if I don't do it today."

"Okay, let's deliver the check. She will be very pleased to receive such a gift," Amelie agreed. The girls walked to the orphanage. From the distance they spotted Sister Agnes as she was about to leave the facility.

"Hello girls. How do you do?"

"Hello Sister! I have a gift check and want to donate it to the orphanage," Charlotte said.

"It is very generous of you. I'll help you with that. Let's go inside. I just spoke to Sister Penelope.

She has worked here all her life. She loves kids. She would be more than happy to receive a gift like that. Show me the check. Oh, Holy Ghost! This is a lot of money. Thank you Charlotte and God bless you. Just follow me. Oh, there she is. Sister Penelope, we would like to talk to you," Sister Agnes said as she was so excited.

"I'm coming. What is so urgent?" she asked.

"The girls want to donate a check in amount of ten thousand dollars. Here it is!" Sister Agnes said happily. Sister Penelope held her heart as if she was about to lose it at any moment and then said,

"Thank you so much! It is quite a big amount of money! I'm speechless. It will last for many months. The kids will have better food and other nutrition. Oh, God thank you for sending to us these beautiful and good hearted girls. We don't get checks like this that often. You've made me so happy today."

"Okay Sister, we shall go now. See you later," Sister Agnes said, giving her a big hug.

"Thank you Sister Penelope, for taking care of little Jean-Pierre, I will see you soon," Charlotte said with a smile.

"Bye for now and come see me more often," Sister Penelope added, still very emotional.

"Girls, you did a good thing and God will bless you for it. I don't want to ask you where the money came from. It is not important at this time. God will judge us only on the good things we do. Enjoy your day," Sister Agnes pointed out with an enigmatic smile. Perhaps she knew that the money came from Father Bertrand but she didn't want to say it. She became more discreet or rather diplomatic lately.

Six months passed and Jean-Pierre grew bigger. The letters and flowers from Bertrand came every week. Then another check came one afternoon with a long letter for Charlotte. Bertrand was waiting for her to make a decision but she never wrote him back. Amelie was getting nervous and tried to convince Charlotte that she should at least write him back once a month about the boy. Charlotte was stubborn and played a waiting game that made Bertrand almost insane. He needed her so desperately and his baby too. Perhaps he couldn't wait any longer.

A few months later in late June, Charlotte and Amelie took Jean-Pierre for a long walk to the local park. He was a year old and could already walk. He was a charming cute little boy and made everyone so happy especially the Sisters as they loved him so dearly. The morning was beautiful; the wild flowers had just opened and spread their invigorating aroma all over. Amelie was running after the sweet little boy.

Charlotte spread the blanket over the grassy ground then opened the picnic basket with breakfast prepared by Sister Penelope for Jean-Pierre and for her and Amelie too. How sweet of her, she thought. Sister even made fresh orange juice for them. Charlotte put the sandwiches on freshly starched red linen napkins and then called Amelie and the baby to join her,

"Jean-Pierre, your breakfast is ready. Amelie I have a sandwich for you too. Come here!"

"We're coming! Wait! Come here Jean-Pierre. Yes, my little darling," Amelie said with a sweet tone in her voice. She really adored the little boy. They enjoyed breakfast and Amelie said,

"Give me the bottle. I'll feed him. Here is your food Jean-Pierre. You can hold the bottle yourself, how nice."

"I think he can have a piece of sandwich with us. Look he is eating bread with ham. I can't wait until he grows up. It seems like time has stopped for us. Don't you feel that?"

"Yes, I feel like everything is so slow and will last forever. I can take Jean-Pierre with me for a vacation next year to Paris. I would like to visit my aunt. She loves children and when she sees him she will go crazy," Amelie said, excited.

"We will think about this. It is so peaceful right here. I've never felt better. Come with me Jean-Pierre for a little walk again. Amelie, you relax for a few minutes. I'll play with the baby. Come here my sweet heart. You can run but be careful. Jean-Pierre, say Amelie."

"Amelie loves Jean-Pierre," the baby said.

"Charlotte, did you hear what he said? It is true! Amelie loves Jean-Pierre and Jean-Pierre loves Amelie. I always tell him that."

"Jean-Pierre loves Amelie too!" the baby said and pointed out with his little finger at her and then jumped.

"How sweet; now say, Charlotte loves Jean-Pierre."

"Jean-Pierre loves Charlotte too," baby said and laughed. It was so sweet and brought a tear to the girls' eyes. The baby ran around and Charlotte chased him constantly.

"Don't go so far, Charlotte!" Amelie shouted

and waved her hands at them. Then she lay on the green grass, looked at the blue sky and whispered,

"Thank you God for a beautiful sky." Then she sighed with relief. Perhaps ten minutes later she heard Charlotte from the distance.

"Amelie, help me!" Charlotte shouted loud. Amelie glanced at them and saw a black Ferrari and two tall guys standing by the doors pushing Charlotte and Jean-Pierre in. The doors were closed and the car took off. Amelie ran after them but couldn't catch up. It was pointless anyway to run after the speeding car. One of the car windows opened and someone dropped a piece of paper which landed in front of Amelie's feet. She picked it up. The letter read,
Dear Amelie,

'This is Bertrand. Please, do not call the Police. This is not kidnapping even though it looks like it. This is a very private matter and I would like to keep it private. You know how much I love Charlotte and my baby boy. I want them to be with me for the rest of my life. Give this letter to Sister Agnes perhaps she will understand me more. I'll send a donation to her orphanage from time to time as appreciation for the great work she does with all of the kids out there. I'm so sad that it was the only way to proceed.

My love for Charlotte grows greater day after day and I can't live without her. When I found out about baby boy my heart was torn apart. I want to fix the error of my past. It would perhaps never happen if she wasn't so resistant and told me that she would wait for me. Please try to understand my pain. I wish we can be friends again and you can visit us one day in my French Chateau. Give my deepest regards to all

the Sisters.
Sincerely,
Bertrand.'

Amelie froze for a moment from shock in the middle of the street. She just couldn't believe that this great adventure finally came to an end. She lost her best friend and her dream ran away too at the same time. She took the picnic basket and walked slowly back to the boarding school. She knocked at Sister Agnes' door.

"Come in," Sister said as she greeted her warmly in.

"What is happening now, Amelie? Your face is almost white, did you get food poisoning?"

Amelie gave her the letter and then collapsed onto the chair dropping the basket on the floor. Sister brought a cold drink and slowly poured it into Amelie's mouth.

"Wake up! Wake up! Amelie," she repeated until Amelie opened her eyes. Then she took the letter and read it. She sat on the chair and whispered to herself,

"Bastard couldn't wait! I hate that man! Amelie don't worry. I think perhaps it is the best solution for now. At least we would avoid the biggest scandal in Rome. What would the Church say about it? We already went through a nightmare right here. I think we should let it go and wait for Charlotte's letter. I'm sure she will write soon.

Oh, my child you look terrible. I'll make you a powerful drink. It will put you on your feet again. Please sit right here and relax. Can you imagine what we're going through? Here is your drink. It is fermented cherry with its own flowery flavor. I like it myself. We must think positive from now on my child.

Let's listen to classical music and talk. I know what you're going through and I feel sorry for you but I'll talk to Monk Emanuel about it. He will know what to do next," Sister Agnes said sipping her drink.

Two weeks had passed and finally Amelie received a letter from Charlotte. She waited too long for the news. Excited she sat on the bench under the pine tree and began to read it.

Dear Amelie,

I miss you so much and can't imagine a day without you and your funny jokes. *Jean-Pierre* is telling me how much he loves you at least five times a day. I try to find a reason for everything that happened but so far I have no answer. Perhaps I haven't fully grown up yet. Bertrand is crazy about *Jean-Pierre* and is always preoccupied with him. I'm glad and think that he is the best baby-sitter *Jean-Pierre* could ever have.

I'm still afraid of him and I plan to escape again. You must call *Monk Emanuel* and tell him everything what happened. I believe he and Jerome will help me.

Every day he brings me fresh flowers and drags me to the best places around town. At least five body guards follow us everywhere we go. I asked him if you can visit me and he said okay.

I'll send you a ticket within the next two days. Since you still have vacation perhaps you wouldn't mind visiting me. Please, give my regards to Sister Agnes and Sister Penelope. Please, write me very soon.

I'm going crazy in this enormous *Chateau* with

fifty six rooms.
Missing you always,
Charlotte and Jean-Pierre
P.S.
Don't worry about Bertrand he wants to be your friend again.

Amelie's heart almost leaped out of her chest. She picked up a pen and paper and began to write,
Dear Charlotte,
I felt like the entire big world collapsed on me that awful afternoon. Now, I feel relief that you and our beloved Jean-Pierre are okay.

My heart almost cracked in half when I witnessed your kidnapping. I ran to Sister Agnes with the letter someone threw from the car's window. I was stunned and she was too. She told me do not panic and wait for your letter. She said we shall keep this a secret otherwise it could be another scandal in the Vatican City and the boarding school. But she promised to talk to Monk Emanuel about your kidnapping.

We talked for a long time. We even shed a few tears together. I've already packed my bag and I'm waiting for the ticket from you. I'm coming to rescue you. I already talked to Monk Emanuel. Perhaps he will contact Jerome and the **Green Panthers**. Wait for us! Miss you and see you soon.
Your best friend forever,
Amelie'

The ticket arrived the next day. Jerome called Amelie from Paris. He will wait for her at the airport.

Amelie took the taxi to the airport. The plane arrived in Paris a few hours later. Jerome was waiting for her in the black Van. The **Green Panthers** stood by ready for a rescue mission.

"How are you Amelie? Nice to see you, again."

"I'm terrified!"

"Don't worry. We came with a special rescue plan and I want you to stay as close to me as possible," Jerome said with deep concern.

"Sure! It would be no problem! I can wait forever only to see Charlotte again," Amelie replied. Jerome looked at her and laughed.

"I promised my dear friend Cardinal Benedict before he left us that I would watch after Charlotte for the rest of my life. I missed him so badly!" Jerome said with tear in his eye.

Soon a black limousine pulled up in front of them. The Green Panther's Commander came out and said,

"Where is the letter?"

"Here it is. Be sure Bertrand reads it and gives you an answer before your departure," Jerome said.

"Sure! It will be done!" Commander said and drove away. Within fifteen minutes he arrived to Bertrand's estate.

The estate's iron gate was already opened. The black limousine drove through it.

In the distance Bertrand was already waiting. He received phone call from Jerome that a messenger is coming with a special letter.

Commander handed the letter to Bertrand and waited near the pine tree for his answer.

Bertrand opened the letter and it read:

"Bertrand you are charged with the following:

1. Assault and Rape

2. Kidnapping and imprisoning Charlotte in your chateau in France
3. Second kidnapping and imprisoning both Charlotte and her baby boy

The above charges carry a penalty of 75 years. If you're guilty of these charges you will spend the rest of your life in prison. Your second option is; you let them go free and right now!" Bertrand paused for a moment.

"And why should I do that?" Bertrand replied.

"I will tell you why? You are an arrogant bastard! Did you for a moment think that the Church would willingly become your co-conspirator aiding and abetting your vile debauchery to steal the pure innocent from an unsuspecting child?

Now we come to your choice! You can go to prison where you spend the rest of your life in a solitary confinement or you let Charlotte and the baby boy go free! You do not have a third option!" Commander spit the words out of his mouth as though they each were deadly ASPS.

"Let me think about it." Bertrand said nervously and left.

"You have exactly five minutes to think about it. I brought with me Special Forces of **the Green Panthers** in case if you say 'no.'" Commander added and looked at his watch.

Within exactly five minutes the chateau mahogany door has been opened and Charlotte with the baby boy walked out.

She ran with a big smile on her face. Commander opened the limousine door and they got in. The limousine drove back to the previous destination. Jerome and Amelie were nervous when the limousine arrived.

"Hi, Amelie! I'm so happy to see you again."

Amelie gave her a big hug and said,

"I thought I will never see you again."

"Thank you Jerome for saving my life once more. You are my best friend and forever," Charlotte replied with tear in her eye.

"Girls, let's go for good lunch in my estate. My Chef Pepe made something special for you," Jerome said with a big smile on his face.

He glanced at the blue sky and thought for a moment, "Benedict you can rest in peace now. Do not worry; I'll take care of Charlotte and her baby boy."

Just a week before Cardinal Benedict died he sent a small package to Peter in the Vatican City. Inside was the key to the secret box. He wrote,

'**Dear Peter**,

I just finished my final chapter in the **Black Book**. This is a gift for you and Charlotte and perhaps one day one of you would publish my secret stories. It can't be forgotten. Give the key to Charlotte and ask her to go to the same box she did many years ago. The **Black Book** is there, waiting for you. I'm getting old and perhaps this is the last chapter of my life. For you it is just the beginning.

Yours Friend,

Cardinal Benedict or if you prefer Father Benedict.